"Larry Brown has slapped his own fresh tattoo on the big right arm of Southern Lit." —*Washington Post Book World*

PRAISE FOR **FACING THE MUSIC**

"A stunning debut short story collection."
—*The Atlanta Journal-Constitution*

"If his first book . . . were itself a fire, it would require five alarms. The stories are that strong." —*The Orlando Sentinel*

"Larry Brown . . . is a choir of Southern voices, all by himself."
—*The Dallas Morning News*

"Ten raw and strictly 100-proof stories make up one of the more exciting debuts of recent memory—fiction that's gritty and genuine, and funny in a hard-luck way." —*Kirkus Reviews*

"Like his profession, Larry Brown's stories are not for the delicate or the fainthearted. His characters are limited people who are under siege. . . . Their stories manage to touch us in surprisingly potent ways." —*The Cleveland Plain Dealer*

PRAISE FOR **DIRTY WORK**

"There has been no anti-war novel . . . quite like *Dirty Work*."
—*The New York Times*

"A novel of the first order. . . . A gem." —*The Washington Post*

"Explodes like a land mine. . . . A marvelous book."
—*The Kansas City Star*

"A real knockout." —*New York Newsday*

"An unforgettable, unshakable novel."
—*The New York Times Book Review*

A MIRACLE OF CATFISH

Also by Larry Brown

LARRY BROWN

A MIRACLE OF CATFISH

A novel in progress

A SHANNON RAVENEL BOOK

ALGONQUIN BOOKS OF CHAPEL HILL 2007

ℝ

A SHANNON RAVENEL BOOK

Published by
ALGONQUIN BOOKS OF CHAPEL HILL
Post Office Box 2225
Chapel Hill, North Carolina 27515-2225

a division of
WORKMAN PUBLISHING
225 Varick Street
New York, New York 10014

LIBRARY OF CONGRESS CATALOGING-IN-PUBLICATION DATA
Brown, Larry, 1951 July 9–2004 November 24
    A miracle of catfish : a novel in progress / by Larry Brown.—1st ed.
        p. cm.
    "A Shannon Ravenel Book."
    ISBN-13: 978-1-56512-536-0; ISBN-10: 1-56512-536-3
    1. Fatherhood—Fiction.   2. Mississippi—Fiction.   3. Domestic
fiction.   I. Title.
PS3552.R6927M57 2007
813'.54—dc22   2006043056

10 9 8 7 6 5 4 3 2 1

FIRST EDITION

For Lauren of New York: You my shining pride, girl

LARRY BROWN:

PASSION TO BRILLIANCE

BY BARRY HANNAH

> When death comes for
> him
> it should be
> ashamed
>
> —Charles Bukowski

—We both loved Bukowski, the everlasting redundant universal grouch. Fail again, fail better.

—I can't remember him ever out of cowboy boots.

—When he got famous and went on tour we discussed his wardrobe. He'd just shopped and bought some Dockers.

—In Seattle together at a book thing we sat and ate a plate of small, sweet to larger oysters similar to our Gulf ones. He'd found this restaurant. Tucked his bib in, face lit up like a baby's, happy as a clam.

—I think we were both drunk at the Wells' house. In front of my publisher Sam Lawrence, Brown hooted and hunched my leg like a dog. The next day Lawrence offered him a large book contract. There is no story line here. Algonquin, home of Shannon Ravenel, who had helped shape Brown hugely, upped the ante and he stayed. I suppose there is a story line here.

—I never heard him give a negative blast to another writer. I did hear him repeat a truly wretched sentence from a writer, and giggle. Very wryly. Happy in the eyes like a child. Maybe somebody had actually scored somewhere beneath Brown's early badness.

—When *Father and Son* came out I got an ecstatic call from Kaye Gibbons, the beautiful Carolina writer, telling me what an act of genius it was. I agreed. I was flat out envious. But he had worked so hard and wrought so much from his beginnings it was impossible not to be happy for Larry, always.

—He visited my class and told them of a negative review he'd received from another writer. He was amazed, again like an incredulous boy, very hurt over what was, he felt, a personal betrayal by a fellow worker. I paid little attention to reviews, and I was refreshed, really, by his direct honest humanity.

—He told me and the class that he was disheartened by teaching at the colleges and summer workshops he was invited to (including our own Ole Miss). He loved talking about stories well enough, but he could not stand working with those who were not given over totally to writing, as he was.

—More happy face of a boy: He told me he had introduced bigger, faster-growing Florida bass minnows into the pond where he let me fish. I fished like God's expert in the following years and caught exactly one Florida bass one happy afternoon alone. (Rubber bream minnow with spinner.) For that fish I at last say thanks to my gone pal. He is buried beside his infant daughter at this pond on family land. You can imagine the bittersweet emotion from your feet up when I visit this pond and steal from his hospitality again. (White Rooster Tail, yellow or green beetle spin.) Twilight on the writing cabin, solar powered, he never quite finished.

—Not once did a bad word pass between us. There was no time for that. You always felt this with Larry, who considered himself a late bloomer, a late guest at the table.

—You understand the beauty of the town and county libraries and the exponential reach of a fine bookstore where, as far as I know, almost all of Brown's literary education came from. Lucky creatures here in Oxford. Josephine Haxton (the most excellent broad, nom de plumed Ellen Douglas) gave him multitudes in the single college course he had. Richard Howorth was a kind hand early on. Larry found Conrad, Faulkner, O'Connor, Hemingway, and Carver. Brown knew the biographies of writers much better than anyone I know. The marines, the firehouse, and life gave him the rest. He was an early, avid reader, encouraged by his mother, I believe.

—He was not a saint and we should remember that to their wives all men are garbagemen trying to make a comeback. True also is that in eulogies the worst people try to stand on the shoulders of the dead in order to levitate their own dear egos. God knows, I'm trying not to do this.

—I haven't been the same since he and my good publisher, Sam Lawrence, passed away. I don't write as well and I write more slowly. Such is his absence, but Brown would want us to crawl past this mood. He did, hundreds of times. No excuses. Ask his pals Tom Rankin and Jonny Miles, fierce artists themselves. Ask Mark Richard, likewise.

—His Mississippi hill country brogue was so thick I had to translate Brown to our French publisher at Gallimard who spoke perfect English. The man shed tears of exasperation over Brown's refusal to travel to France, where Brown's books were big. He begged me to intercede, but it was rough because I wasn't his mother. I still miss the trip to Paris he and I might have made together.

—In the early eighties he showed me stories that were so bad, I'd duck out the back of the bar when I saw him coming down the walk with the inevitable manila envelope. I couldn't stand hurting his feelings. I loved his sincerity. I didn't give him a cold prayer in hell as to a future in literature. When he published in Harley Davidson's *Easy Rider,* a story about a galoot, a sheriff, and a marijuana patch, as I recall, I cheered but secretly believed he'd then peaked out.

—Brown was an example of an *élan vital,* the creative life force about which the philosopher Bergson wrote. Animals get better because they want to, not just to survive. Passion begat brilliance in Larry Brown. I love it. My throat is raw from teaching the life of Brown to students. Work, work. The pleasure deeper than fun. It gets good when you turn pro.

—In Texas last year when Larry Wells called about Larry's passing, I was having a physical spell and could not fly to his funeral. I've never forgiven myself although my wife, Susan, represented us. His absence in Oxford is intolerable to me still. His wife, Mary Annie, actually took time to write me back during the first stunned period of mourning. Her letter and she are dear to me, even though I see her rarely.

— Two nights after his death a great band in San Marcos dedicated the night's performance to him. Such was the reaction of musicians, an untold amount of whom were his fans.

—At his house I found out his record collection about matched mine. Crazed love going on here.

—He never asked me for a blurb. A small mountain of creeps have never known this courtesy which came naturally to him. The publisher or the agent asks, always with the intro that the author is an almost rabid fan of mine. That is correct form, this is what God says.

—Once, when he was judging NEA fellowship fiction with George Plimpton, he came across a strangely familiar piece. Some arrant dufus had plagiarized a Larry Brown story. Where is this fool? Where is the hooting jail for this pissant? No doubt a rabid fan of Larry's, but please. Brown enjoyed it. Grinning like a kid.

EDITOR'S NOTE

In November 2004 Larry Brown sent the manuscupt of his all but completed sixth novel, *A Miracle of Catfish*, to his agent, Liz Darhansoff, of Darhansoff, Verrill, Feldman, in New York. He had made notes for the two or three chapters to end the novel and would start work on them after the Thanksgiving holiday. To the shock and sorrow of his immediate family and the wider family of his readers, Larry Brown died of a massive heart attack on November 24, the day before Thanksgiving, at home in Lafayette County, Mississippi. He was fifty-three years old.

Algonquin Books of Chapel Hill, publisher of all but one of Larry Brown's nine previous books, is proud to be the publisher of the novel he was writing when he died. And I am personally honored by the request of his wife, Mary Annie Brown, and her advisers, Tom Rankin and Jonny Miles, that I edit the unfinished manuscript *A Miracle of Catfish* for publication.

Once Larry Brown had mastered his laconic style, the first-draft manuscripts of his books were nearly always so polished stylistically that my job as editor mostly involved showing him the places I felt the novels would benefit from trimming. He was, as a novelist, likely to write more than he needed. Having honed his skills on the short-story form, he reveled in the wide spaces that novels offer. I rarely found reason to suggest expansion. But I did find places I thought would gain by careful snipping and shaving.

Ever the professional, he almost never argued, though many years after the publication of his first novel, *Dirty Work*, he liked to remind me that I had asked him to cut the first two hundred pages of the first-draft manuscript—and, he was always careful to add, that he'd done it without any dispute. This was only slight exaggeration on both counts.

Never having edited a manuscript for posthumous publication, I consulted other novelists and critics about the kind of editing I might do and should do under such circumstances. Our conversations led to a consensus that making *any* changes—substantive or minor—to the plot, the structure, the characterizations, would be inappropriate. No word changes, no syntax changes, and certainly no effort at "ending" the novel should be made. (The author's notes of his plans for the final chapters, typed in at the end of a rough table of contents, were found among his papers. They follow the last page of the novel as written.)

But what about cuts? The towering 710-page manuscript on my desk reminded me of the first draft manuscripts of two of Larry Brown's earlier books, *Joe* and *Fay,* and I felt strongly that some cutting—to streamline the narrative and lighten some sections that went on past the point—was in order. But I also felt that cuts to the manuscript would be permissible only if the printed book were designed so that the reader would know where these had been made; by the same token, scholars could easily compare the book with the original archived manuscript.

So the unfinished novel you have in your hands is Larry Brown's first-draft manuscript with editorial cuts (including drafted chapter titles I believe he meant to revise if not omit) that I hope improve the flow and that I believe he would have accepted pretty readily. *A Miracle of Catfish* is still a very long novel, albeit an unfinished one. If you do have the opportunity to compare it with the manuscript now available to students of Brown's work in the Department of Archives and Special Collections of the J. D. Williams Library at the University of Mississippi in Oxford and you take issue with the cuts, I am certainly willing to share my reasons for them. I would, in fact, be happy to explain myself, as I would have had to explain myself to Larry Brown had he lived to finish the work.

The experience of working with Larry Brown over the course of his all too short writing career was a high point of my own career in publishing. He was a writer who started from scratch and taught himself not only how to write about what he knew but how to write literature in the process. As he expressed it so clearly in a speech delivered to the

Fellowship of Southern Writers in 1989, a year after publication of his first book:

> It took a long time for me to understand what literature was, and why it was so hard to write, and what it could do to you once you understood it. For me, very simply it meant that I could meet people on the page who were as real as the people I met in my own life . . . Even though they were only words on paper, they were as real to me as my wife and my children. And when I saw that, it was like a curtain fell away from my eyes. I saw that the greatest rewards that could be had from the printed page came from literature and that to be able to write it was the highest form of the art of writing . . . I don't think it was meant to be easy. I think that from the first it was meant to be hard for the few people who came along and wanted to write it, because the standards are so high and the rewards so great.[*]

Larry Brown's determination, his relentless hard work, his unswerving respect for his art, and his honesty in exposing the depth of human emotion paid off. His characters—those real people—live on, just as he intended.

For me, and I hope for you, it doesn't really matter that *A Miracle of Catfish* wasn't quite completed. What he meant it to say is as clear as can be.

—Shannon Ravenel
January 2007

---

[*] "A Late Start," a talk given at the Fifth Biennial Conference on Southern Literature, April 8, 1989, Chattanooga, Tennessee.

The author was especially grateful to Paula Klepzig Brown for sharing her knowledge of the specifics of Tourettes syndrome.

A MIRACLE OF CATFISH

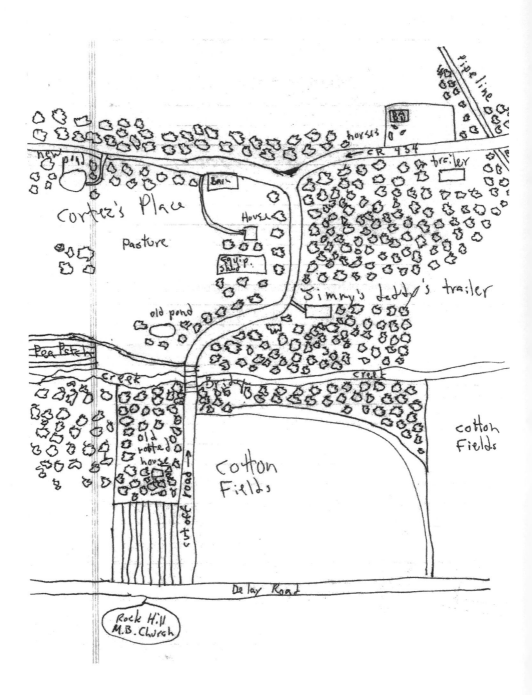

THE NOVEL'S SETTING, HAND DRAWN BY THE AUTHOR.

1

The blessed shade lived on the ridge. The white oaks stood with their green tops hanging thick under the sun, and a big old man in faded blue overalls walked in the June heat beneath them. He crunched lightly, ankles deep in dry brown leaves, feet wary for copperheads the same color. He was mopping at the sweat on his brow with his forearm, and he was holding his hand out to bash at the webs of spiders that hung in his path. There was a glade carpeted with lush beds of poison ivy, quiet gardens, no place for a nap. A fox squirrel went up a tree and flowed his tail like water over a limb and then lay down on top of it, his legs hanging, his head low to the limb. An unseen little buddy. An old white-faced boar squirrel with a nut sac that laid out behind him like two pecans in a bag. A breeze lifted and blew a cool wind that for a moment stirred his eyelashes. He twitched his parti-colored nose. He probably appreciated the breeze in some squirrel way.

The old man looked around. There were two sloping walls of trees, a natural place to build a pond. Cortez Sharp could see it plain as day. He'd been seeing it for a while. He wondered if Lucinda would want to take that retard fishing after he got the pond built. And some catfish in it. Course it'd take a while to get them up to eating size. Not a year probably. He didn't think it took them that long to get them up to eating size at the catfish farms down in the Delta. He'd go buy some catfish feed at the Co-op. He'd seen it before, in the stifling heat of the tin-roofed warehouse, stacked in fifty-pound bags on pallets beside fertilizer and seed. Each bag had a picture of a catfish on it. He saw one of those boys who worked in the Co-op's warehouse kill a big woodchuck in there with a shovel one day and then he stretched it out bloody on a pallet with its stained yellow buck teeth showing and Cortez didn't think woodchucks even lived in Mississippi. Was a woodchuck a groundhog? What was that thing about if a woodchuck could chuck wood? Probably came in on a load of feed from somewhere up north. Maybe late in the evenings when it was cooling off he could do it. Throw it out there on the water like raindrops. He'd have a special bucket just for that. Or maybe a steel garbage can. Have a lid for it. Keep the fire ants out of it. He wondered if that retard of hers even knew how to fish. He wondered how big the fish would get if he just kept on feeding them instead of catching and eating them. He could catch and eat a few of them. Just not all of them. Leave a few in there to see how big they'd get. What if they got to weighing ten pounds? If he kept feeding them and they kept growing they would. What if they got to weighing twenty? What if they got up to thirty? What would that feel like on a rod and reel? He might have to go get a new one. They might break his old one. Shitfire. They might break a *new* one. Wouldn't that be something? What if they got so big they were uncatchable? How fun would that be?

Standing there in the baking woods he looked around again. Why did she want him? What good was he? Cortez just didn't understand it. He knew they slept together. Hell, lived together. He was tired of worrying over it. There wasn't anything he could do about it anyway. She evidently saw something in him. He guessed he could show the dumb son of a bitch how to catch a fish. Maybe that wouldn't be too complicated for him. But that retard sure had him a dirty mouth.

He stood there for a while, [. . .]* and then the old man turned and went away [. . .]. The squirrel lay on his limb and listened to him go, then jumped to another tree, and another, and another, and soon he was just a faint trembling high in the leafy treetops as he gamboled his way into the woods to be unseen again for a while. Maybe. There were hawks in the woods, and when their shadows came sailing by he sought the undersides of branches where perhaps he wouldn't be taloned to death, then fed in bloody pieces to thinly feathered hawklets with hooked beaks that lived in high nests made from big sticks in trees like these. Meat-eaters that grew and finally flew. On gloomy and rainy winter days they gripped with their talons their high and swaying limbs, as the wind riffled the tiny spotted feathers on the backs of their necks, as they coldly surveyed the naked gray oaks of their range and then spread their wings to cruise the pine-covered ridges that lay before them to the ends of the world.

*Throughout, "[. . .]" indicates that a passage has been cut by the editor.

2

Soon a yellow D9 Cat, wrenched and welded together by beer-drinking, polka-dancing union members up north, arrived, and then there was no more silence in the simple woods. This American juggernaut crawled with steel treads churning over a hill jetting black smoke, and its progress could be gauged by the shaking treetops with their rafts of dark green leaves waving and then bending before it, like masts in a wild sea, and then slamming to the ground. In this way, tearing and shoving, the machine made its way into the glade of poison ivy and began to push down white oaks and bulldoze them into a pile. The soft earth that had lain hidden beneath rotted leaf mold for millenniums was torn up and printed with dozer tracks and shown to the unflinching sun, where it lay curled and cracked and began to dry and flake and be clambered upon by red fire ants. The sun was hot and the day went on. Things formerly in the shade now got some light. A box turtle moved away dryly rustling, scaly clawed reptilian feet digging for purchase in the dead leaves, bright fingers of yellow stippling its round brown shell. A clan of local crows flew in and lit and walked around on some limbs and started saying in their crow language, *What the hell's up? Anything to eat?*

The dozer dude ate his lunch. Fried chicken, cold biscuits, some olives in a plastic bag. A nicely folded paper towel. A homemade fried apple pie crimped around the delicately crusted edges with a fork as evenly as teeth on a gear. Then a good nap beneath the shade of a giant bur oak with a black Cat cap with the yellow letters over his face. The crows sat and jeered and watched him from their limbs.

You think we ought to sneak in on the ground for them scraps? He ain't got no gun. Least I don't see one.

Naw, man, he may be just playing possum. They do that sometimes. That's how my uncle got killed. My mama told me. Fell for one of them owl decoys and a good mouth caller. Let's just watch him for a while.

I think he done eat it all anyway. What was it? Fried chicken?

Yeah. Fried chicken. Wing and a leg and a thigh.

That's another bird, too. I mean if you think about it. Seems kinda cannibalistic if you know what I mean.

I ain't related to no chicken, but I can see that other biscuit from here.

Well, if you so badass, why don't you just fly your black ass on in there and get it?

I could if I wanted to. I'm swuft.

In your dreams maybe.

I caught a rat other day. Beat a hawk to it.

A hawk would whip your young ass.

I can dive-bomb like a freight train.

Well, do it, punk. Fly on in there and get that biscuit.

I think I'll just wait till the time's right.

That's what I figured. Set up here in a tree and talk shit like a juvenile.

Later on in the afternoon diesel smoke drifted again through the woods, and deer at their grazing in sun-dappled and beech-shaded hollows stopped and smelled it, and their little spotted ones stopped and smelled it, too. It seemed to alarm them a bit. They were used to smelling honeysuckle, cedar, tender shoots of grass, acorns, somebody's nice patch of purple hull peas if they could find it. For which they'd often get the hell shot out of them with oo buckshot. Maybe Brenneke rifled slugs. Depending upon whose place they were on, maybe even machine-gun slugs. They trotted off toward a trail that led into the forest, single file, tails down, not scared, just moving away to somewhere else, picking up a few more ticks. The bucks' horns were just bulbous branches full of blood at this time of year. They lived there and they weren't about to move just because somebody was building a pond. A regular drinking hole in the woods was actually a pretty good idea.

3

Jimmy's daddy was lying in the hot gravel in front of his trailer with his head beneath a 1955 Chevy two-door sedan with a wrench in his hand, studying the rusty undersides of it. Saturday. Everybody gone. Shopping in Tupelo with the kids. Nice and quiet. The radio was going through the window of the trailer. Mainstream country. Lots of commercials for car lots and mobile homes. The Shania Twain they were still playing was six months old. Like maybe the station couldn't afford any more records. But he knew better than that. On a busy street where clouds floated across the face of a glass-paneled tower in Nashville, there was some guy sitting in an office drinking good Kentucky bourbon with a pile of demo tapes on his desk, and he was the one who decided who got on the radio and who didn't. This one was in, that one was out. Rusty had told him all about it. If you wanted to get into country music, the deck was already stacked against you. Unless maybe you were Garth Brooks. Hell. Even if you *were* Garth Brooks.

This car was special. It was unique as far as cubic inches. Most of the V8-equipped '55s came out with 283s in them, but this was one of the rare ones with a 265-horsepower 265. You didn't see a lot of them. You could still get parts for it. Water pumps. Rebuilt generators. Tie-rod ends. He reached his finger out and touched a black spot of oil. He pulled his finger back and looked at it. On it was a black spot of oil.

He wiped it on his jeans and reached up with the wrench for one of the rust-frozen nuts that held what was left of the manifold gasket between the rust-flaked exhaust manifold and the rusted exhaust pipe, a gasket that was ruined with heat, crumbling apart, leaking exhaust, and making a lot of noise but probably increasing his horsepower half a horse or a horse or a horse and a half since putting headers on one everybody said would give it about five. He knew it would come off a lot easier if he had some WD-40 to put on it, painted blue-and-white spray can, take the little red plastic straw off the side where it was taped to the can, stick it in the nozzle where you could pinpoint your spray and spray the threads, watch it foam whitely, inhale that high giddy petroleum aroma and know it would help, let the thin greasy liquid soak deeply into the threads and penetrate the rust and help his wrench to free it. But Johnette had used up his last can trying to get some charcoal going in the grill—stoned again—and he hadn't thought to run by AutoZone yesterday to see Rusty and get some more. He needed some better tools, too, by God, just for this car. Not this piece of shit off brand stuff from years ago at Otasco he was still using. Something that wouldn't slip on a nut and bust your knuckles. Johnette was still on his ass over paying eighty-five hundred dollars for the car, just about draining the savings, but most of what had been in savings had been off his settlement on his and Rusty's wreck from when they ran into all those chicken coops in the road and wrecked his Bronco, so it was his money anyway. What he needed to do was just tell Johnette that he needed the shit, and go on up there and get it. Stick it on a credit card just like she did whenever she went to Tupelo and wanted a new lamp. Pay for it later. But have the use of it now. She didn't wait for what she wanted. Why should he? This car was like a free car. It didn't really count. It was like a gift. But it wasn't going to pass inspection being so loud. Unless maybe Rusty knew some-body who'd slip it through and give him a sticker. They wouldn't slip it through at Gateway, that was for sure. They checked everything on one out there. Exhaust system, headlights, windshield glass, taillights, brake lights, ball joints, turn signals, horn, tire tread. He didn't know what the big deal was. He thought it sounded good loud. But they wouldn't pass it loud. And they had all the power when you went out there. When you slipped yourself into their domain. And you had to deal with it. On the other hand they were bonded. They could get in a lot of trouble doing strangers favors.

This wrench wasn't going to get it. He should have known he'd need a socket. That nut was kind of up in a little hole there with that flange sticking down around it. Dumbass. Now he'd have to roll over. Crawl back out. Crawl over to the toolbox. Move it closer. Then get back under. Shit took forever. And what if he couldn't break it loose then? Break it off, that wouldn't be good. Unless he could break both of them off and put new ones on. But he didn't have any new ones. He'd have to go to town for that. He didn't have time for that. Not today. He had to go drink some beer with Rusty after a while. In about another hour, when he got off. That Old Milwaukee was sitting over there in the Igloo chest right now. Packed in ice. Little rock salt sprinkled over the top of it. So damn cold it would make your teeth ache. Yep. And it was almost time for one. How sweet it was gonna be. All right, now. The bottom was a half inch. He didn't know what the top was. Probably a half inch.

He rooted around in his tray and found a half-inch socket and an extension and snapped them together and snapped them to the ratchet handle. He ratcheted it to see which way it was going. Wrong way. He flipped the lever. Now it was going right. He knew it was going to back off counterclockwise. He found a box-end half-inch wrench to hold the top of the bolt in case it turned on him and crawled back up under there. He put the box end on the bolt head and held it. He put the socket on the nut and pulled. He needed to grow some grass. Damn gravel was rough on your back working on a car. Trailer had been sitting here over a year and he still didn't have any grass back there by the pine tree. He'd been meaning to go out to Wal-Mart and get some grass seed and sow some. But there wasn't time to do everything. He hoped Johnette wasn't wanting to go over to Seafood Junction at Algoma tonight and eat again just because it was Saturday. It was good, yeah, but it was expensive as hell. Bunch of assholes you didn't even know always eating over there. Damn dry county, too. He pulled on it harder. If they took Jimmy and them it was really expensive. It was a lot cheaper to just drop them off down at Mama Carol's and let her feed them some hot dogs. And since they didn't serve any beer over there, they wouldn't let you bring any in either. He pulled on it harder. So he had to just keep it in the cooler, down in the floorboard by her feet, and drink a few on the way over there, and then drink another one in the parking lot, while she sat there and told him to come on and hurry up, that people were looking at him, and that it was a dry county, until he turned it up and finished it, and they got out, and went on in. He knew people could probably smell beer on his breath if they got close to him. Fuck em. If they didn't like it they could kiss his white ass. It might be a dry county but it was a free country. Long as the cops didn't catch you. He pulled on it harder. And half the time they saw the Baptist preacher over there, and he knew that son of a bitch had already smelled beer on his breath three or four times, and one time they'd had to sit down and *eat* with the bastard just because of the way it happened, it hadn't been his suggestion, it had been the preacher's, and Johnette didn't have the guts to say No, and went ahead and said Yes, and Jimmy's daddy hadn't gone back out to the Bronco for another beer after his first plate from the seafood buffet line like he usually did because he was *so* pissed off. He pulled on it harder. And then when she got up to fix her another plate after she'd finished her first one, which had been totally loaded with fried catfish fillets and fried shrimp and fried green tomatoes, he'd had to sit there and talk to the preacher all by himself, which hadn't been just real comfortable, and he didn't have anything *against* the fucking preacher, but she'd stayed gone and stayed gone filling up her damn plate again and the preacher started talking about his mother's dog they'd had to put to sleep because it was so old—it was like twenty-three years old, maybe, he couldn't remember exactly how old now—and how terrible all that had been, and how close everybody in his family had been to the dog, because the dog had almost saved his little brother's life by dragging him out of a pond one time, only not in time, about thirty minutes too late, actually, and the preacher just stopped eating and started letting his food get cold and went into this long very detailed spiel complete with tangents that went nowhere about how everybody in the family which included their kinfolks up in Akron felt like the dog was the last connection they had with his little brother, which made it a lot worse when the dog finally died, because it had been on life support for a while, just because everybody in the family already knew how bad it was going to be when the dog died, and they were trying to put it off as long as they could, and had even chipped in money to the vet hospital to try and keep the dog going, and he'd nodded and agreed and said it was awful and a shame and that he didn't know why stuff like that had to happen and had kept shoving catfish fillets and french fries and fried shrimp and hush puppies and bites of fried frog legs into his mouth, and wishing he had a cold beer to go along with it instead of this iced tea, and he could see Johnette just taking all the time in the world refilling her plate at the buffet line, talking to people she didn't even know, laughing, wearing those tight shorts with her fat ass, never even looking back at him to see how he was doing by himself with the preacher. That was the kind of shit she did. Drove him batty. Talking on the telephone. To who? Who knew? Why'd he want to marry a woman with two kids already? From two different marriages? What had he been thinking? She wasn't fat when they were going together, hell no, she wanted him to marry her and support her kids. Now look at her. Fat as a fucking hog. And love to fuck when they were going together? Oh my God. She'd damn near break a nail on your zipper trying to get to it. Now it was too much damn trouble. Who wanted to fuck her fat ass anyway? He was feeding both hers, though, wasn't he? And he was buying Jimmy that go-kart, he didn't care what she said. [. . .]

The wrench slipped off while he was pulling really hard and he busted his knuckle on the rusty exhaust pipe something horrible. Oh God. It hurt so terrible bad he thought he was going to throw up. Oh *shit!* It hurt like a son of a bitch. It hurt so bad it made his stomach hurt. He didn't even want to look and see how much hide he'd torn off this time. He just gritted his teeth and laid his head back on the gravel and put his hand between his knees and squeezed it hard with his knees and didn't look at it and looked at the side of his transmission instead. Something was wrong with third gear in it. It made a bad noise in third gear but Rusty said he knew a guy down at Bruce who could fix it. But it would run the way it was. You just had to get some RPMs built up in second before you dropped it into fourth. It would grind a little bit. He needed to get some insurance on this thing, too, before something happened to it. Some asshole might slam on the brakes in front of him with no warning.

He looked at his black knuckle. Some skin was torn off it and some blood was leaking out of the black grease. It still hurt like a son of a bitch. He needed some WD-40 after all. It might be worth going to town just for the sake of his knuckles. He wondered if this son of a bitch would crank. He thought that battery had a weak cell. Or maybe that re-built voltage regulator wasn't regulating the voltage just exactly right.

He pulled his head out from under the car. Somebody was coming up the road that led past his trailer, and it was just gravel, and it hadn't rained in a long time, and a big cloud of dust rolled up and in and drifted over him when the car went on up the road, and got all in his hair, and settled over the pores of the skin on his face, and he lay there on his back and cussed whoever it was for driving up the road he lived on. He raised up and looked over the fender to see who it was. It was a white Jeep. Mail girl. [. . .] In a way that he couldn't have explained to anybody, he thought of the road as his. He wondered if that old man up the road was building a catfish pond with that dozer he kept hearing. He sure hoped so. The old man would have to stock it sometime if he wanted some fish in it. And a mess of catfish would be nice. Especially if it was free. Be better than fucking Seafood Junction. [. . .]

4

A Tommy's Big Red Fish Truck had compartments. For gloves, dip nets, clear polyethylene fish-hauling bags, for little cardboard boxes of thick rubber bands to tie tightly around the necks of the bags after the little fish were in there, in ice cold water, with plenty of oxygen shot in there through a hose to get them safely to your pond, scales to weigh fish, fish fertilizer to make the fish grow, turtle traps to catch turtles that robbed fishermen of their catch by eating them off the stringer where it was tethered to the side of a boat or a dock or a bank, bream traps to keep bream from overcrowding in ponds, spare canisters of oxygen, fish feed, sales slips, promotional brochures, order forms, and other fish-selling paraphernalia [. . .]. It had compressors and generators and refrigeration units built in. There were pens and pencils, black Magic Markers, sure. One always stayed parked in Tommy's driveway when he wasn't in Vegas so that he could make deliveries to privately owned fish ponds and lakes across the mid-South and Midwest in order to secure capital. Tommy's hair had turned white from trying to secure so much capital.

Mostly a Tommy's Big Red Fish Truck had tanks of live fish. It had channel catfish anywhere from four to eleven inches long. It had black crappie one to three. It had largemouth bass two to four. It had hybrid bluegill one to six. It had straight bluegill one to three. It had one- to three-inch redear bream. It had fathead minnows. They were small. It had white amur grass carp. And they were about a foot long. You didn't need them unless you had lily pad problems and you wouldn't think to eat them unless you were Chinese.

It was built on a Ford chassis and it had banks of compartments down two sides with the tanks inside them, so that there was a walkway up the middle of the back of the truck, and it was a very heavy truck because a truck like that had to be built very heavy because of all the water on it that weighed so much, about eight pounds per gallon, which adds up pretty fast, hundred gallons, eight hundred pounds, so it had a big axle and dual wheels on the back for that same reason as well, and it was red like a new wagon at Christmas. Or a fire truck. It was probably the closest thing there was to a fire truck.

[. . .]

It also had counters that were made of wood, and unfortunately it was some kind of wood that splintered easily, and some of Tommy's boys and even Tommy himself sometimes got a splinter in his hand and that was the only thing that wasn't cool about the truck, because if it went in deep enough, then you had to get a straight pin and dip it in a bottle of alcohol that was in another compartment of the truck or strike a cigarette lighter and hold the pin over the flame for a few seconds in order to sterilize it and then stick it in the hole in whoever's finger and make it come out by poking it around in the hole and it was enough to make the boys on the fish truck dance around beside the compartments whenever it happened. They'd be talking while it was happening but they wouldn't be talking normally. They'd have their eyes closed while Tommy dug around in there with a straight pin and a bunch of people who were lined up to buy some fish off the truck watched. There was a lot of pain to be had in just a finger. Which was usually where they got finned, too. By those eleven-inch catfish. That were just aching to get into somebody's pond. And eat. And grow. And be free. Unlike Ursula.

5

She lay undulant in her dark Arkansas barn, in the cool and highly oxygenated water of her round and almost musically bubbling tank, her dorsal and tail fins trembling slightly, waving gently. Her whiskers stuck out about a foot in front of her massive maw. A long time ago when she was a virtual baby she had lived in a river and there were different things to eat that washed in from rainwater, things like grubs and red worms and night crawlers and lightning bugs and praying mantises and fire ants and army ants and carpenter ants and ground puppies or newts and stink bugs and skinks and aphids and caterpillars and weevils and carpet beetles and those little bitty bright green tree frogs you see sometimes, the ones with suction pads on their toes. Climb right up a window. Sit there watching you eat supper with big round eyes. Holler like hell in the summertime. *Mbeeeeeeeeeeeee!*

Now all she got was floating chunks of fish feed, and all it was was dog food anyway, except that it was made in smaller pellets, like BBs, and they put it in a different bag, one with a picture of a catfish on it, but not a catfish as big as she was since she was bigger than the bag.

She was not a behemoth. She was a beauty. She was the nightmare fish of small boys and she came from the depths of sweaty dreams to suck them and their feeble cane poles from the bank or the boat dock to a soggy grave.

There was nothing for her to do but swim endlessly, be a fish factory. A maw-jawed mamaw. Endlessly turning in her tank like a soul sentenced to purgatory forever. She'd stopped bumping the walls long since.

The last time Tommy had put her on the table she'd about flopped her big ass off it onto the bloody and slick concrete floor, it being bloody and slick from him dressing a mess of small ones for a fish fry later that night, back when things had been going really good, for him anyway, not for her, since she was still just swimming around in the same place she'd been in for so long, the mother lode of his fish factory, but now she was almost too big for him to handle by himself. She could still turn around in the tank. Barely. She was a fish factory that kept working, eating and swimming, laying her eggs, having those eggs collected, laying some more, having them collected, over and over, all done in a dimly lit barn that smelled of straw and horses except where she lay in the cool black water, where machines with dim red lights hissed and kept her alive, and eating and laying her eggs, and once in a while a handful of feed sprinkled across the top of her dark tank like midnight raindrops.

[. . .]

6

After the dozer dude had been working for a couple of days in the woods, Cortez called the Co-op in town, wanting to talk to Toby Tubby, an old fellow who worked there and who Cortez had known since first grade in Potlockney. They'd done some things they probably shouldn't have. Buried a boy alive one time, for about an hour, when they were kids. Just for the fun of it. Just to scare the shit out of him. Went and ate lunch and then came back. When they dug him back up he was almost dead. Cortez had done some other things after he got grown. A long time ago. Back during the early sixties. Things that involved wearing long white robes. And carrying guns. And keeping your head covered up with a hood. And listening to speeches at rallies where crosses were burning. And throwing bricks at U.S. marshals on the campus of the University of Mississippi in 1962 when they admitted Meredith. He had quit all that shit when he saw that it was useless and might get him in jail. After Robert Kennedy stuck his nose into it. Little squirrel-headed bastard.

But whoever answered the phone, some kid, sounded like, said that Toby wasn't there, that he was off since it was Wednesday afternoon. And Cortez knew that. He knew Toby was off on Wednesdays. He knew that as well as he knew Lucinda was screwing a damn retard in Atlanta. An artist. Artist, my ass. How could he be an artist if he wasn't smart enough to get through the third grade? It was probably on Lucinda to pay most of the bills. Buy their groceries. Pay the light bill. Phone bill, garbage bill, water bill. But she seemed to make pretty good money modeling that large ladies' underwear. He didn't know why he hadn't just called Toby at home. He'd know just as much about the fish at home as he would at work. And Cortez didn't really want to talk to anybody else about the fish. He wanted to talk to somebody he knew who wouldn't go blab it to everybody he knew. He wondered if Gunsmoke was there.

"Is Gunsmoke there?" he said.

"No sir, he ain't here," the person who sounded like a kid said.

"Is this Gunsmoke's boy?" Cortez said.

"No sir, this is Jeff."

"Is Gunsmoke's boy's name not Jeff?" Cortez said.

"No sir, that's Jim, people gets us confused, happens all the time, it ain't just you, God knows I wished it was. Maybe I could be happier."

"Is Jim there?" Cortez said, ignoring whatever bullshit the kid was talking about about being happier.

"No sir, he ain't here neither. And not likely to be here no time soon since he's in St. Louis, Missouri, watching a ballgame. I believe it's a doubleheader, but he said it wasn't on TV. Now is they something I could help you with? Hi, I'm Jeff."

Cortez thought about it over the phone. He didn't want to talk to just anybody about these fish. He didn't want the whole world to know he was building a pond and was going to stock it with catfish. He didn't want to talk to somebody who might go blab it. He might as well go put it in the newspaper if he was going to do that. Hell, take out an ad. Shit, rent a billboard. But he wanted to find out something about it as soon as he could just because he was so excited about it. Like how big they were now, how much they cost at what size, when you fed them, how often you fed them, how much weight they'd gain, how long it would take, all that stuff. Did you have to get some stuff to pour in your pond? He knew some people poured stuff in their ponds. But one guy he knew of, he poured some stuff in his pond and it turned the water kind of a sickly-looking green. Like a Jell-O fruit pond. He didn't guess you just *had* to pour stuff in your pond. Maybe he needed some brochures. They probably had some from the big red fish truck. He'd seen it down there in the parking lot before, people lined up, getting fish. They always put an ad in the paper before they came. He needed to look for that ad because he'd be standing in that line one day before long. He'd get there early. Before the crowd rushed in and bought up all the fish. He wondered if they delivered. That might be something else he needed to ask Toby about.

"I'll just call back when Toby's there," he said, and hung up abruptly, as he always did, with anybody. [. . .]

7

My name is Newell Naramore and I live over close to Schooner Bottom. I used to live over close to Muckaloon Bottom but I moved. Used to be Muckaloon was all growed up, but I've took my dozer to a good bit of it. It ain't near as rough as it used to be. But you can't cat hunt in there like you used to could no more neither. I used to have some cat dogs. I had one named Venus of Byhalia one time was a hellacious cat dog.

I like fried chicken for my lunch. My wife knows that and she gets up ever morning five days a week and fixes it for me. I mean lessen it's a holiday. That's the first thing I smell ever morning when I get up: chicken frying. My wife's good to cook me fried quail that I've shot for breakfast, too, with some cat-head biscuits and milk gravy and a couple of brown eggs over easy. We don't have chickens no more but she knows I like them brown eggs and gets em at Kroger. I think a man does a better day's work when he's had him a good breakfast. And I think he sleeps a lot better if he'll take him just one straight shot of whisky right fore he lays his head down on the pillow.

This here pond, now, what I'm gonna do, I'm gonna—well, you can see what I'm doing—I'm pushing all these trees out a here and I don't know why that old man didn't let somebody cut them good white oaks for him and get the money, shit, I know for a fact them big ones right there is worth eight hundred dollars apiece for cabinet-grade plywood in Memphis, but it's his wood and ever body says he don't like nobody on his place.

It ain't nothing to me what he does. I told him over the phone it's fifty bucks a hour to unload this dozer and he never blinked. But what I'm gonna do—I might ask him if he cares for me coming back over here and cutting them white oaks up for firewood—I could sell it and make me some money—I got my eye on a new rifle I been thinking about buying—Remington Model 700 bolt action—I seen one in Pontotoc for three hundred dollars—them's some damn nice trees I got piled up there. It's a shame for em to just rot. Long as it took to grow em. If he'd let me have em, I could spread em out on the ground with this dozer right here and saw em up to where I could get my brother-in-law's truck up next to em. He's got a side loader on it. He could drive right up in here long as it ain't wet.

And when I get all this cleaned out then I'm gonna build me some lanes and I'm gonna start pushing dirt down yonder to the end of them two ridges and start building up a levee. You got to know what you're doing to do it. See, you got to level your levee. You'd think ever body would know that—level, levee—but they don't. Some of these buttholes'll build a levee that ain't level. But I've done shot this one here with a transit. I know how much dirt I got to move. I got to move approximately 267 cubic yards. That's a shitload of dirt, mister. I'll have a borrow pit right there in front of where the levee's gonna be, and that'll be the deepest part of the pond. It'll be almost as deep as the back side of the levee. I'd say it's gonna be about eighteen or nineteen feet. It'll be plenty deep enough to drown in if you don't know how to swim. If I had kids after this thing fills up with water I wouldn't let em down here at all unless they could swim. Course I ain't got none yet. You can see I ain't that old.

8

Sometimes Cortez in the summertime afternoons had dreams that weren't really dreams but things his mind made up by itself. Not real. But they looked real to the inside part of his brain that made them up in the first place. They had color and light and texture and dialogue. And mood. Lots of mood. Sometimes it was blue lights and a smoky bar. Sometimes it was wood smoke and a campfire.

Another thing they had was sex. Sometimes in the afternoons, just before a nap took hold, somewhere between sleep and REM, before it officially became a nap, especially if he was on his old army cot on his back porch, screened in with a few flowers that needed watering in pots and a water-blistered coffee table, damp enough with mildew so that spiders were not a concern, some rags of raw cotton stuffed in a few holes in the screens, a slight breeze working its way through the leaves of the big pecans out back, he'd somehow wind up in a place that was about six feet above his body, on his back, and he would hover in the air there and would lift right through the roof and then roll over and start flying around. He could go way high, super fast. He could get to going so fast that he knew in some part of his brain that wasn't totally awake that he was breaking some kind of speed barriers. Sometimes he was wrapped in sadness. Sometimes he was enveloped in elation. One time he saw that blue-and-white clouds were hurtling toward him, and they began to part and peel off to the side and swallow him, and he traveled through splotches of vivid orange blinking colors for what looked to be millions of miles at supersonic speeds to the center of a place where naked dancing-girl angels waited panting and ready on the mossy banks of a clean river, where the shade beneath the trees was deep and strong, and the lips of the young women who were pulling at his clothes sweet as the juice of a freshly picked peach.

But those were just half dreams. They didn't have anything to do with his real life, which didn't have any sex in it at all. None. Zero. Not even a hand job. Mostly his life was taking care of his wife and his cows and raising a garden in the summertime and shooting the deer when they came to get his peas and working on his tractor when it broke and mowing his grass with his little John Deere mower that he'd been using for nineteen years without any trouble except a new battery four times and two tires on the back, a cable, a carburetor, and watching each season pass and wondering which one would finally get him. He didn't want to go in the spring because the fish were biting and the weather was too pretty. He didn't want to go in the summer because of homegrown tomato sandwiches every day. He didn't want to go in the fall because the leaves were turning and wood smoke was in the air and you could kill some squirrels. And in the winter, somebody had to feed these damn cows or they'd starve. As far as he could see, there wasn't going to be any really convenient time to go. So he was hoping just to keep going.

But he wasn't having a dream today. Today he wasn't even going to sleep. He was lying on his cot and he could hear her TV programs going in there like always. They had more shit on TV than you could believe now. They had one of those satellite dishes on the roof now. They'd try to sell you anything. You could send off for videotapes of college girls pulling their shirts up and showing their bosoms, and he wanted one of those, but they didn't have a VCR and he would have been scared to order it anyway because of his wife. She was in a wheelchair and was up all night, and the TV hardly ever went off, and he just kept his hearing aid turned down, and if she wanted something she just rapped on the floor with her cane that she never used anymore since she couldn't get up anymore, and when he felt the vibration of the cane on the floor, he turned his hearing aid up and asked her what the hell she wanted now.

She was a lot of trouble. A lot of trouble. She was a lot more trouble now than what she used to be, before she'd had the stroke. About the only way for him to get away out of her reach was to go outside and do something, and not look back toward the house, because if he was outside doing something and she decided she wanted something, she could pick up this police bullhorn she'd ordered from somewhere, probably the damn TV, and call him with that, and about the only way not to hear that was to be on the tractor with its loud muffler, and it helped to be some distance away from the house, too, like down by the creek where the pea patch was, where he had hell keeping the deer out of there, and had shot as many as six or seven a night. Probably have to do it again this summer, too. Always did. Every year. Never failed. Good thing the ammo was still easy to get.

Cortez Sharp lay there a while longer and tried to go to sleep, but he kept wondering how the dozer guy was going on the pond. He'd already been out there this morning to see how it was going and it looked like it was going pretty good, but he didn't want to stop the dozer guy to ask him how it was going since he was getting fifty dollars an hour. Cortez preferred to go over during the dozer guy's lunch break and ask him how it was going then. That way he figured it didn't cost him anything. It was going to be a pretty big pond. The dozer guy had told him two days ago that he was moving over two hundred cubic yards of dirt, which didn't mean anything to Cortez since he wasn't a dirt man or a construction man. The dozer man had said that it was a shitload of dirt, but then, after he finished eating his fried chicken and what looked like a really well-made fried apple pie, he told Cortez that he usually took a nap after lunch, so Cortez left.

He raised his wrist and looked at his watch. It was almost three o'clock. The dozer guy was probably back at work now. If the damn TV hadn't been so loud in the living room, he could have turned his hearing aid up and would have probably been able to hear the diesel engine on the dozer running over there on the hill. Cortez could hardly stand to sit in the house while he knew the dozer guy was on the dozer moving dirt for the pond, kind of like the way people who are having a house built will come over every afternoon when the carpenters leave, for months, but, too, some people were funny about you watching them work, even if you were paying them, so Cortez didn't want to just drive up and sit there in his pickup and watch the man work. But he could hardly stand not to.

So he sat up. He laced on his boots. Maybe he could walk over and sit down behind a tree and peek out from behind it once in a while.

He went into the living room where his wife was sitting in her wheelchair watching the television. The volume was way up as usual. And it always seemed like it got louder during the commercials. His wife turned her head for a moment but she didn't say anything. After another moment she turned it back. He wondered how long it was going to take her to die. She wasn't able to cook anything. She wasn't able to clean house either, but he had a woman come in a few days a week for that. She fixed things that could be kept in the refrigerator for a few days, or frozen, and taken out and thawed out, or microwaved. They had one of them now. Lucinda gave it to them two years ago. It would heat up day-old biscuits pretty good.

"What you doing?" he said. He thought he might cut the grass later.

"I ain't doing nothing," she said. "Watching TV."

"Hmh," he said. He didn't know how she could watch so much TV. There didn't seem like there was ever anything on it but bad news. Or some kind of sex stuff on those talk shows. Some woman almost as old as his wife had a show where folks called in and asked questions about sex problems they were having and she'd tell them about digital stimulation, and she talked about using jelly sometimes. One night he saw her tell the audience how to give somebody a blow job, using a rubber dick as a teaching aid. Rubbing her fingers all up and down it. He got pretty excited. His wife was asleep when he watched that one. He thought.

"I'm gonna go over and see how he's doing," he said.

"I don't see why you don't just let him alone and let him work."

It wasn't the first time she'd said that. It was about the seventh or maybe eighth or ninth or tenth time she'd said that. He was getting about tired of her saying that. She wasn't excited about the pond the way he was. She never had liked to fish anyway. Never had wanted Lucinda around any water very much. Always afraid she'd fall in and drown. In a foot of water. Even after she was over five years old. Even after she was ten years old. Like she wouldn't be able to put her hands down on the bottom and push her head out of the water. She always stayed on her. She was the one who ran her off. Always telling her, Don't do this, don't do that. *Don't wade in up past your knees! Sit up straight! Keep your legs crossed, them boys'll look up your dress! Stop picking your nose. Why don't you go to the bathroom? Mash that zit!* And now look where she was. Didn't know how to swim and lived in Atlanta with a retard. Sleeping in the same bed with one. Acted like she just hated to have to come home for Christmas. Like coming home for Christmas was just too much shit to have to put up with. Cortez couldn't understand why Lucinda didn't have a regular boyfriend. Somebody who could do something besides make art. *Oh, he paints,* Lucinda said. Right. He'd seen some pictures of it, what he painted. Looked like what a chimpanzee could do with a brush and his own shit if he could shit in different colors. It didn't seem right that she didn't have somebody smart enough to make it through grammar school.

"I just want to go see how much he's got done," he said.

"I'm getting hungry," his wife said.

"Eat them biscuits," he said, and went out the door.

His truck was parked in back near a big chinaberry where his PTO post-hole digger hung on a rusty log chain. It was a hell of a lot easier to get it back on the tractor if he left it hanging on the chain, and he'd been doing it for years. It was getting to be just about too much for him now, since he was finally after all this time older and a little bit weaker, to take it off and put it back on, since it weighed over three hundred pounds, and was one dangerous son-of-a-bitching piece of machinery, almost as dangerous as a Bush Hog, and he was afraid he'd drop the damn thing on himself one day, and then where would he be with her in there watching those trashy people taking their clothes off and talking about how many people they'd screwed while they were married to some other damn fool who was sitting there in a chair listening to it in front of an audience? She'd never hear him yelling. It might take days for somebody to find him. It had been hanging there for seven months, ever since he'd finished putting that new two-hundred-foot section of fence in on the east side by the road. Close to where those people had that trailer and kept all those little bitty dogs. He wondered if those little dogs would tree squirrels. But he was going to have to put it on sometime. Almost that whole section down there by the creek was rotted and he'd need to dig some new holes for some of that. It was the oldest part and he knew some of those posts had been in there for forty years. He didn't want to even think about what he'd been doing forty years ago. Damn sure not this. Living with an old woman you couldn't stand to even talk to. Listening to her snoring at night. Putting up with all her shit. All her bitching. Getting her medicine from town. Fixing her something to eat. Having to help her get dressed. Damn, he got tired of it. He'd thought about hiring somebody to help around the house just with her. He didn't know how much longer he could handle her by himself. She was four years older than him and he didn't know why in hell he'd married her. It must have seemed like a good idea at the time. But sometimes things didn't work out over time. Sometimes over time you found out that you'd messed up pretty bad. That's how he felt most of the time. Most of the time he just wanted to be left alone. He couldn't believe his only daughter was living with a retard in Atlanta. And didn't even know how to swim.

9

The first thing Jimmy's daddy did after he gave Jimmy a red go-kart was to get on the go-kart himself, just to make sure everything was working. He filled it up with some gas from the shed, then took it speeding down the dirt road, over the wooden bridge and past the rotted old house and the cotton fields, while the children screamed and waved their arms in the gravel. They and the herd of tiny yelping dogs ran after him, following his thin cloud of dust down toward the paved county road. Jimmy was running harder than his two half sisters, his little knees pumping, his hands balled into fists, his tennis shoes untied, yelling through rotten front teeth.

Jimmy's daddy looked both ways before he pulled out. He'd always wanted one of these little sons of bitches. His parents had stayed so broke from drinking beer all the time [. . .] that they never could have bought him one, no need to ask. Same way with a car. He'd had to buy his own after working in a sawmill for Halter Wellums, some old guy his daddy knew, for thirteen weeks in the summertime, off-bearing pine slabs. Talk about splinters, shit. Get one of them bastards about a half inch long buried up in your finger and have to take a straight pin and dig around in there with it. Make you want to shit in your britches. And that was just the down payment. And then the son of a bitch dropped a rod. And broke a crankshaft. And needed a new chunk for the rear end. And had a bad rattle in the dash. Drive you nuts going down a dirt road.

He had to say one thing: the little son of a bitch felt like it would run. Hell fire it ought to, five horse. He looked back at the kids running down the road behind him and he waved them back and they stopped, because Jimmy's daddy's kids were nothing if not well trained. They knew how to say Yes sir and No sir and to not interrupt adults. Jimmy's daddy's kids knew better than that shit. They better. Get the shit slapped out of them if they didn't. He got the shit slapped out of him plenty when he was a kid and it didn't hurt him none except that he didn't much like his daddy.

He looked back over his shoulder at them. The three of them were standing in a group under a sweet gum tree, yelling some things he couldn't hear for the motor on the go-kart. The sink needed fixing, but a workingman deserved to fish and ride around on the weekends drinking beer, too. The tiny dogs had their mouths up in the air barking. Jimmy's daddy spurted a rooster tail of gravel from a back tire and shot onto the county road and was almost run down by a tall black Kenworth tractor blaring its air horn and hurtling toward him at sixty with a load of forty-foot sweet gum logs, limber and bouncing, red flags tied to their ends, scraps of bark whirling in a cloud following it. *Oh shit!* Jimmy's daddy whipped the wheel to the left, which let him with a severe jolt into the ditch and the Kenworth past, but he heard the wail of its angry air horn for a long way down the road. One mad son of a bitch. And who could blame him?

He sat in the bottom of the ditch heaving for a few seconds, his chin down on his chest. Damn. He'd nearly gotten mashed flat as a fucking bug. He lifted his head. Right in front of the kids, too. He was glad Johnette wasn't home yet. She would have had plenty to say about that. She had plenty to say about everything. And hell, the kids would go ahead and tell her he'd nearly gotten run over. The little shits told her everything. Somebody was cutting the grass across the road at the Rock Hill Missionary Baptist Church. Some black guy on a riding mower. Looked like a Cub Cadet. How come they had church all day? Didn't they get hungry?

Jimmy's daddy had to get off the go-kart to push it out of the ditch, and he was sweating and needing a beer. He made sure nothing was coming before he got it back up on the pavement. He saw somebody with a garbage bag in a ditch picking up cans but it didn't look like his daddy.

Once Jimmy's daddy got the go-kart out on the actual blacktop, he found out that it was almost impossible to turn it over. He found out by steadily increasing his speed and then cutting the wheel sharply, and no matter how hard he turned it or how fast he was going, he couldn't turn it over. It only took about three minutes to find that out. By then the children were standing down at the end of the dirt road, and Jimmy was jumping up and down, and the tiny dogs were moiling around thick as maggots on a dead mouse.

He's wanting his go-kart, Jimmy's daddy thought, and he was going to let him have it pretty soon, but first he started weaving in between the broken yellow stripes in the middle of the road, weaving, speeding up, cutting the wheel, working it into a rhythm, getting it going back and forth, making it slide, making it slide, working to a glide, making a slide, having a ride, enjoying the glide, and then a wheel caught on a rough place where the road guys had patched the asphalt and it flipped. Jimmy's daddy felt the blacktop scraping very painfully across the top of his head and knew the go-kart was on top of him and then it flipped again and slammed Jimmy's daddy upright in the middle of the highway, and a car was coming. He stomped the gas and shot back into the dirt road. The children and the [. . .] dogs covered him and the go-kart like ants. In the midst of all the excitement, Jimmy burned his hand pretty badly on the hot muffler. He cried hard, he cried fast.

A few hours later Jimmy's daddy was lying on the king-sized bed in his trailer's master bedroom. He hated its frilly purple curtains, made him want to fucking puke, propped up against a real comfortable pile of pillows, sipping a cold one and watching his deer-hunting tapes. He had some he'd gotten for Christmas last year where they slowed the action when the arrow hit the deer and you could actually see the arrow going all the way through the deer, appearing out the other side as a shiny red blip, and even though the deer took off running, you knew that son of a bitch was dead. He might run a little ways. He wouldn't run far. He might get dizzy and run in circles. He'd lie down. Bleed out. If you left him alone and waited. Didn't start trying to track him right away. There was plenty of time. No big hurry. You could have a smoke or two. Take a piss. Take a shit if you had some toilet paper with you. Son of a bitch wasn't going to just resume his peaceful browsing life after having almost three feet of tubular aluminum shot all the way through him at however many feet per second.

With a razor-sharp broadhead.

With razor blade inserts.

With spring-loaded tips that would actually insert the razor blade inserts into the deer's aorta if you hit the aorta. Son of a bitch didn't have a snowball's chance in hell.

The top of Jimmy's daddy's head was bandaged up. Johnette had done it, poured some alcohol on it, which hurt like crazy, stung [. . .]. Then she put some Neosporin on it and a couple of Band-Aids. Wasn't any trouble with the hair interfering because he was so bald. Thirty-two years old and hardly anything left up there at all. He wore it long, with a cap, at work and on the weekends. He rarely took the cap off. Only at home or at a funeral or some other function where he had to be in a church, which wasn't often, thank God. [. . .]

So he was just having some cold beers and watching people with compound bows up in trees on tree stands waiting for deer, and whispering to each other, and turning to whisper things to the cameraman, who was up in the tree with them, their breath fogging in the cold. He wondered how they kept from fogging up the camera lens. It had gotten completely dark before Johnette had gotten Jimmy off his go-kart. Jimmy had asked his mama to get him up an hour early in the morning so that he could get in an extra hour of driving his go-kart tomorrow. There was also a small problem. There was probably less than a pint of gas left in the shed, which wouldn't run him all day, not if he drove it the way Jimmy's daddy knew Jimmy was going to drive it. He'd already told Jimmy that, and Jimmy had begged him to go to the store down the highway, just a few miles, wouldn't take long, before they closed tonight, please please *please,* Daddy, and get him a fresh gallon of gas, and Jimmy's daddy knew he should have, but he'd also been bleeding at the time and needed prompt medical attention, and a few cold beers, and then he didn't want to drive down to the store on the other side of Yocona after he caught a buzz. It was a regular Texaco gas station / country store, and they had a bulletin board in there next to the ice-cream box, and there were sometimes things on it. Once he'd seen a computer-printed note that said:

LOST: Small beagle dog, white with brown spots called Bobby. He is a house dog, not a hunting dog. He will not hunt cause he is scared of guns. Please do not shoot a gun around him. Please be careful if you find him cause he has a broke tail.

Next to it was a picture of an alligator snapping turtle the size of a picnic table hanging from a tree limb. Somebody had probably caught it out of the river. They made sandwiches at the store and they also cooked pizzas at the store and there were always a lot of people standing around waiting for the pizzas to cook, or for the sandwiches to get made, and they also had some tanning beds, so people were in and out for that, sometimes slightly chubby country young ladies in two-piece swimming suits and short terry-cloth robes, and house shoes, and all the old retired country geezers, who'd farmed all their lives and fixed fences and messed with cows and pulled cows out of mud holes or worked for the state highway maintenance department their whole lives, and didn't have anything better to do than sit around the store all day and sip coffee and eat sausage-and-biscuits and play dominoes at a big table in the back, liked to sit around some more and wait for some of the young ladies to maybe show up, and the people who owned the store must not have wanted to pay for very much help, because there was usually only one very nervous and upset young girl to work the counter and the register and the tanning beds and the gas machine and get crickets for people and fix flats and make sandwiches and still keep churning out the pizzas, which included sausage, pepperoni, and combos, taking her plastic gloves off and then putting them back on, probably went through about twenty or thirty pair a day, and usually there was a screaming baby in a playpen behind the counter, because it seemed that each of the young girls who worked at the store had a baby they had to bring to work, and sometimes Jimmy's daddy saw a toddler standing in dirty underpants on the gravel out by the gas pumps eating cigarette butts, and then there were people who pulled up for gas, and kept coming in to pay, and others who pulled in behind them and waited for the ones in front to move so that they could get up to the pumps, and the gravel parking lot wasn't very big, so it, too, was often crowded with delivery vehicles that included gas trucks, milk trucks, bread trucks, drink trucks, and even Cockrell Banana Company trucks, so it had gotten to where sometimes it was so crowded inside with people standing around waiting on one thing or another that you had to stand around and wait for them to get through with their waiting and step on up to the counter and pay for whatever it was that they'd been waiting for for ten minutes even if you were only buying a five-cent piece of gum. Sometimes it wasn't worth the trip. So Jimmy's daddy hadn't gone for the gas. [. . .] But he knew he'd have to talk to Jimmy before Jimmy went to sleep.

And pretty soon he did. Jimmy came running into the bedroom in his pajama bottoms with a big Band-Aid on his badly burned hand and climbed up on the bed next to his daddy and put his hands on his daddy's chest. He'd had a bath but his fingernails still showed crescents of black.

"Daddy," Jimmy said.

"Yeah," Jimmy's daddy said, and leaned his head around him in order to see a guy make a shot he'd already seen him make about forty-three times.

"What am I gonna do about my *gas*?"

"I don't know," Jimmy's daddy said, and took a sip from his beer. "Get some tomorrow. Get on to bed now."

And since Jimmy's daddy's kids always minded him, that was the end of that. You dang tootin', Fig Newton.

The next day at work at the stove factory, Jimmy's daddy didn't tell anybody about his near-fatal accident with the go-kart. He'd told some people about seeing a matching pair of pale yellow oblong UFOs one time about fifteen years ago when he was parked with some old girl on a dirt road and had almost gotten laughed out of the break room, even though there was no doubt that those two guys in Pascagoula had been picked up by aliens back in '73, because they'd both passed lie detector tests and told the exact same story over and over, to different police officers in different offices and under hypnosis. He wished he could talk to those guys. See if their experience had any connection to his. He kept his cap on even when he had to crawl up under a Towmotor and fix it.

At lunch he lifted his cap briefly to check his head in the mirror in the bathroom and it looked okay. Damn, that new girl down on the line had some big titties. Whew. He hadn't seen any like that in a while. He didn't see any blood leaking through the Band-Aids. It was sore as a rising, though. He touched it gently with his fingertips. It sure had been fun sliding the go-kart until it tipped over. He bet he could have slid it forever if he'd had it on some smooth concrete, like maybe a slab for a house before they put the house on it. You'd have to watch out for those plumbing pipes stubbed up, though.

* * *

That afternoon, when Jimmy's daddy got home with the gas, they'd already been out of gas for over twenty minutes and were almost frantic. Since the motor had cooled down, Jimmy's daddy let Jimmy fill the tank himself, cautioning him sharply about sloshing it and wasting it. Told him to slow down, be careful. Jimmy slowed down, was careful. Then he cranked it, got into the seat, and roared away. Jimmy's daddy walked up the steps into the trailer and got a cold one and sat down on the couch. Damn, he was tired. Crawling around on that hard concrete all day. They were going to have to take that big press apart. What a pain in the ass that was going to be. Take two weeks probably. Slow down production in the Press Department. Front office would raise hell. Well, fuck *them*. He could hear the go-kart going around and around the trailer, and then he didn't. He sat there and listened. He could hear the kids talking. He took another sip of beer. Then the go-kart fired up and took off again. Had they flipped it already?

Jimmy's daddy got up and went to the back door where he'd been meaning to build a back porch. There wasn't any porch, just a drop of about four feet to the ground. Another thing Johnette stayed on his ass about all the time. He opened the door and looked out just in time to see all three of them on the go-kart, the tiny dogs yelping and running alongside, all of them going up the dirt road toward the woods and pastures that belonged to that old man who was building that pond. Jimmy's daddy had already walked over there and looked at it. He wondered again if he was going to put some catfish in it whenever it got filled up with water. That'd be nice. Just walk over there at night and catch a few. He listened. He could hear the motor noise getting smaller and smaller. He knew they'd probably get it stuck in a mud hole. And would want him to stop what he was doing and come get it out. Fat chance of that.

He took a drink and shut the door. If they got it stuck they could just get it out.

Little shits.

Little heathens.

That was what his daddy always used to call him: little heathen. And of course that was where he got all the ass-whipping philosophy, too. You could see it didn't hurt him any. Hell, he turned out fine.

[. . .]

10

Jimmy and his two half sisters and the herd of tiny dogs stopped on top of the hill in the shady green woods and looked down into the pool of sunshine below them. The go-kart sat there running, the new muffler keeping it not too loud. Yet. Later it would get louder. Later the chain would get loose. Then it would come off. He'd put it on. It would come back off. He'd put it back on. It would come back off. Back on, back off. It would get to where it would come off all the time. It would get to where it would stay off more than it stayed on. Jimmy would try to fix it. Jimmy wouldn't know how because the go-kart had not been built with any kind of a chain-tightening system to account for normal chain stretching. It would turn out that Jimmy's daddy had bought a cheap go-kart, an off-brand piece-of-shit go-kart probably made by some fly-by-night operation that had already landed somewhere else by now. Jimmy would get desperate. Jimmy would do something he wasn't supposed to do, which was get into his daddy's tools in the shed. He'd take a good whacking for that one. His little pale butt naked that night getting into the tub would wear five or six deep red stripes from that little escapade. But all this was before all the trouble with the pond. Right now the pond wasn't even finished. But there was an enormous hole where the great trees had once stood and it was laddered with tracks and that was what had almost taken the children's breath, sitting in the go-kart, watching the dozer dude work in the clearing he had made in the middle of the woods, a small yellow machine in a large bowl of brown sun-warmed earth. Worms popping up all over. All kinds of birds flying down and getting them with their beaks, stretching them out of their holes until they popped in two, hungry little buddies gobbling those hermaphroditic babies down in the July heat.

The dozer was running backward hard with black smoke pouring from the pipe and the man on the seat was looking over his shoulder. If he saw the children watching him, he didn't let on. He stopped and lowered the blade and pushed it into the earth, making the dirt pile up on the blade until it almost ran over the back side, and then he pushed the dirt up an incline he was building, digging it out below him, pushing it up, coming back for more, slowly hollowing and hollowing the earth, and the green remaining trees all around held him in partial shade that he kept running in and out of steadily like a shuttle on a loom. Far down the hill sat a redbrick house.

"What's he doing?" Evelyn, the older half sister, said. She was thirteen. Wore a purple evening gown most of the time. Black patent leather shoes with silver buckles and light blue argyle socks. Freckles and red hair and granny glasses. Wanted to be an architect in Ecuador.

"I don't know," Jimmy said. "Looks like a racetrack, don't it."

"It's a drive-in movie theater," his other half sister, Velma, said. She was eleven, only a year and a half older than Jimmy, had black hair, a different daddy from Evelyn's. She wore jeans and tops. Knew how to roller skate. Didn't get to go much. Crazy about Tim McGraw and mayonnaise sandwiches. Would wind up pregnant in Chicago by Navajo progressive country singers by the time she was seventeen.

"Aw shit, it ain't no drive-in movie theater," Jimmy said.

"It's a parking lot," Evelyn said. She reached down and picked up one of the little dogs. It sniffed Jimmy's elbow.

"It's a new hamburger joint," Jimmy said.

"Now, would they put a hamburger joint out in the woods like this?" Evelyn said, and put down the dog. They sat there watching. The dozer man saw them sitting there and waved briefly, then turned his machine and went the other way with it, scraping and moving more dirt. He was down in the bottom of the big hole, with one side going out at a gradual slant into the remaining trees and the other ending abruptly where all the dirt was being pushed up in a sloping wall almost like a small piece of the Great Wall of China.

"Oh shit!" Jimmy said. "It's a fucking catfish pond!"

"Don't say fucking," Evelyn said. "You don't even know what it is, you little rotten-tooth fucker."

"I do, too," Jimmy said.

"Shit. You wouldn't know which arm to look under for it. Would you?"

"I would, too," Jimmy said.

"Okay, which one, then, if you know so damn much?" Evelyn said.

"Well. I know what a motherfucker is," Jimmy said uncertainly.

"I'm gonna tell," Velma said.

"Tell what?" Evelyn said.

"Way y'all talking."

"How we talking?" Evelyn said.

"Dirty," Velma said.

"Oh you shut up, you little whore," Evelyn said, and slapped her.

"I'm gonna tell Mama," Velma said, and cried. Evelyn kicked her off the go-kart where she rolled in the dirt and cried some more.

"I bet he puts some catfish in there," Jimmy said. Then he hit the gas and the shiny red go-kart spun in a tight circle in the loose dirt, the chain clattering, the herd of tiny dogs cavorting and somersaulting in the dust, they and the little girl chasing the go-kart bouncing back through the brown leaves on the old log road and the green leaves in the shady woods toward the grassless mobile home that was no longer mobile, merely home.

11

It looked mighty fine when the dozer dude was done. Great big dry brown hole. A big brown bowl. Not a speck of grass in it. And nary a torn tree root sticking up through the huge levee where it might cause a leak. Nineteen and a half feet deep. Newell knew a nice spillway worked, too. It cost Cortez Sharp six thousand for three weeks of dirt pushing but he felt like it was plenty worth it. Cortez had gobs of money stashed in the First National Bank in Oxford. Last time he'd checked he had about seven hundred thousand. Inherited a lot of it from his daddy. Land. Cows. Timber. Cotton. He didn't really give a shit about the money. It wouldn't do him any good after he was dead. It might do Lucinda some good. Maybe she could build her a house somewhere. Stop paying rent. Throwing money away. But it wasn't any of his business if she wanted to throw her money away. He just wished she'd get rid of *him*.

He paid the dozer dude in cash, counting the remaining hundreds into his muddy hands under one of the last monster white oaks. The dozer dude had left it for shade and he said that he always tried to leave a place better than he'd found it. It looked like he had.

He asked Cortez about coming back and getting the wood one weekend, but got a crisp No with no explanation. Then the dozer dude left. To be seen there only one more time. And years down the road.

Cortez Sharp stood there looking out over the vast expanse of his new but empty pond. It had turned out so much better than he'd dared to hope for that it was like a big bubble of happiness in his heart and it was wide open, open to the sky that would bring the rain to fall. And slowly fill up the pond. Once the rain, then the fish on the fish truck. So he set in to wait. For all of it.

He waited the first day on his front porch in a rocker, watching the sky for any signs of darkness from his old and slightly chipped redbrick house. He had a pretty big yard out there but no flowers this year.

The sun shone bright and the TV droned on in the living room, coming through the wall. All the fools hollering and selling.

He kept going over there to look at it. He'd stand there and look at it and wonder how many rains it would take to fill it up. And how it would look once it was done. He'd have to pick a spot to feed them. Maybe underneath the big white oak that was left. Shady there. Once the pond filled up, the tree would be close to the water.

One day he walked down and stood in the bottom of it, marveling over how deep it was, and how high over his head it was, and looked up at the lip of the levee. A little boy in baggy shorts was standing on top of it watching him. A little boy who grinned through rotten teeth and waved.

"Get the hell off my place!" Cortez yelled, and the little boy dropped from sight like a puppet snatched from a puppeteer's stage.

He'd be back, of course.

12

It was a bad stretch of road between Oklahoma and home, but Tommy didn't stop to rest. He was way behind, pushing hard, trying to get back before daylight. So much work to do. So little time to do it. Shouldn't have lost all that money. Shouldn't have done it again. Not again. Now he was going to have to work even harder, maybe get mad over nothing at the barn and fire a few people. He could sell the new pickup. He'd have to. And what the hell was Audrey going to say? She'd probably leave him for sure now. After all his promises. And all her begging and crying for him not to let them go under. Now that they'd come so far. And had done so good. All the work he'd done would be shot in the ass. All the work she'd done, too. She'd been out there in the brood ponds with him day after day back in the old days, gathering the little fish in chest waders, holding her end of the seine, when they were still hopeful for things to get better. And they had. He still remembered the day she'd come up with the idea of painting all the trucks a shiny bright red, like a fire truck, and getting them fixed with gold letters like a fire truck, only all theirs said TOMMY'S BIG RED FISH TRUCK. And it had worked. His big red fish trucks were rolling everywhere, hauling catfish and bass and crappie as far as Iowa City and Minneapolis. There were lakes all over the place and they always needed more fish. And he'd taken it to them for years, in little towns all over the Midwest and the south, dipping out fish for long lines of customers who had arrived early to meet him and his truck, all day long, different towns, more highways, more stops, until he'd sold everything he had on the truck. The fact that they were all happy to see him and eager to buy his fish and talk to him had always made his job a lot more pleasant, so that it was easy to get up and go to work in the mornings, and it made him feel like he was doing a good thing for his fellow man. He saw a lot of old guys, and lots of times they told him they were stocking ponds for their grandchildren, little girls and boys who would hold rods and reels or cane poles in their hands and sit on the shady bank of some farm pond with the old guy, close to him, watching their bobbers, talking quietly as they waited for the fish to bite. He envied them spending time with children. That had to be precious. Sometimes they even brought the kids to see his truck.

He pulled in for burnt coffee at Stillwater, a college town. He had to take the big truck by a service station and gas it up anyway, and he stood out there in the new concrete parking lot under a bright overhead light at a BP just like all the others around the country and watched laughing kids lounging around their cars and playing their music loud. Kids these days, they were troubled. They were lost. That was why so many of them ended up in prison. All because nobody cared about them. Or they didn't have a daddy around. Or got mistreated when they were little. Some people didn't even need to have kids. He didn't know how people could do the stuff they did. But look at him. Standing on the concrete in Stillwater, needing sleep, putting more gas on a card that was already almost overdrawn. He should have walked out when he was up eighty-seven thousand dollars. Three months ago. He could have walked out the door with the money and paid almost everything off. Instead of being how he was now. One hundred fifty-three thousand dollars down. It was scary. He was going to have to make that payment to the bank. And it was nineteen thousand dollars. Where was it going to come from? Hell. If he sold the fish farm he might as well just go ahead and die. He didn't want to go back to working for somebody else's fish farm.

You could have held it together, he told himself. *But no. Not you.* [. . .]

He finished and went inside and paid for the gas and the coffee and some gum. He climbed back up into the seat and started it and pulled out. He could feel the water sloshing in the tanks. He knew that all the fish back there were already dead, black crappie, redear bream, channel catfish, bass. The aerators had been off too long while he was in the Indian casino. He'd have to dump them somewhere before long or he'd have a rotted clotted mess to clean up back there when he got home. Oklahoma's roads were lonely and black and strung with rusted barbed wire. The radio played songs by homeboys. Toby Keith. Vince Gill. Garth Brooks. The radio sang their songs and the tires sang theirs through the night toward Crowley's Ridge, the geological phenomenon where he lived. Lots of hawks there, too. Almost one for every fence post. Redtails mostly. They were there because of all the updrafts around Crowley's

Ridge that made it easy to sail and lift without having to flap their wings very much. It was the same reason fish liked water. It was easy for them to live in.

And what would he do about Ursula?

Oh shit. What *would* he do about Ursula?

13

They were men and women, boys and girls, some small ones not big enough to drive one yet since they were still in Pampers strapped on their mothers' backs like papooses in knapsacks with holes cut for their chubby legs. The grown people wore caps and T-shirts and blue jeans and dungarees and pants suits and overalls and some of the women who were older had their hair in pink curlers. They were on ATVs, Kawasakis, Yamahas, Suzukis, Polarises, Hondas, Arctic Cats, green and red and blue and black and tan, all slowly churning dust, all headed somewhere in a solid line, like covered wagons crossing a prairie, up the gravel into that slanting evening sun on the road that climbed the hill past Jimmy's daddy's trailer's yard that had no grass.

He stood there transfixed and watched them with a new exhaust manifold gasket for the '55 in his hand. They came from somewhere out of the river bottom, he supposed, and they were always strung out in a line that proceeded with dignity and purpose, their hands firmly locked on the handlebars, their cold beers between their legs, riding in foam-rubber Koozies, riding along with them. Sometimes they lifted one hand and took a drink. Whenever they came by they all waved, even the children. Even the little children. Some of them were holding their own bottles and waved with them. Their coolers were in racks behind them, strapped snugly down with black rubber cargo cords like NAPA sells. A few outriders had nylon-stocked .22 rifles slung across the handlebars as if looking for trouble. Or free meat. What with twenty-pound loggerheads crossing the roads in dry spells looking for water sometimes. The chance feral suckling piglet, trapped squealing in rusted roadside hog wire. The succulent vealish steaks of the apparently orphaned spotted fawn. Jake turkeys too stupid to run from a gun. Sometimes they displayed their captured roadkill, dead bunnies or stiffened squirrels strapped to coolers like coup feathers that danced on a war lance.

They were strung out behind each other in a long line and they raised a thin stream of dust like horses on a trail and they swept uphill in a caravan of four-wheelers, the fat black rubber tires churning, the little papooses asleep or bawling, the old darkly tanned guys in their retirement years with their John Deere caps sipping beer as they rode, the children bringing up the trail end. Into the wooded hills. Into the sunset. Drinking cold beer. In a caravan. Where did they go? What did they see? The sight of them always put a longing in Jimmy's daddy's heart to go with them, down the road, into the woods, wherever they were going, wherever that was. Maybe one day he would. Maybe one day he could.

14

It didn't rain. It didn't rain and it didn't rain and it didn't rain. It didn't rain a drop. It would not rain. It refused to rain. It didn't rain in the morning, didn't rain at lunch, and it sure as hell didn't rain in the afternoon or in the evenings or at night. It didn't rain at all. And that was just the first week.

Cortez Sharp sat around on the porch and waited for it to rain. He studied the sky, but the sky didn't need to be studied. The sky was clear. It didn't have any rain clouds in it. There was no thunder in the distance to hear. No crackling lightning walked blasting down from the line of the dim watershed in the distance to stab the nights jagged in white electric fire.

He watched the weather report. This was not something new. Being a farmer, he'd always watched the weather report, ever since they'd invented TVs and started selling them. The first one he'd owned, back when he was still farming with mules, was a large wood cabinet model, an RCA Victor with a round screen. Had that little label with that dog listening to a gramophone. Back before Victor got out of the picture. That must have been back in the late forties. And it wouldn't pick up much. There wasn't much to pick up. Just the big stations and their few small affiliates around Memphis and Tupelo and Columbus. Later on, on up in the sixties, on Saturday afternoons, you could get *The Porter Wagoner Show* out of Nashville with Dolly Parton before she got famous. But even before he'd gotten a TV, he'd always listened to the weather on the radio. That was back when he used to pick up the Grand Ole Opry live out of Nashville. He'd listened to Hank Williams himself for a couple of years in the very early fifties. He used to listen to him duet with Kitty Wells. That was fifty years ago. Then he died in the backseat of a Cadillac. Where did the time get off to that quick? And why did it go so much faster when you got older? How come you didn't think about it when you were young?

[. . .]

One day about two o'clock it pissed down a few measly raindrops.

Big deal. [. . .] There was a cloud up there about as big as a box of dog biscuits. A few drops hit the tin roof and splattered off into the dust and soaked away and that was it. Cortez leaned out from the porch and held his hand out. When he pulled it back it was dry. [. . .]

And it didn't rain. Not there. It rained in other places. [. . .] It rained in Texas plenty. It rained in the rain forests all the time. But it didn't rain there. It wouldn't rain there at all, while he was waiting for it. So he decided to stop waiting for it. He just ignored it. He just tried to forget about it. But that didn't do any good because it still didn't rain. One day when it didn't rain fed into another day when it didn't rain like locomotives hooked together on a train and it didn't rain again and it didn't rain again [. . .]. Which actually got to be good. Because that meant that the time had to be drawing nearer when it would actually rain. Because he knew it wouldn't just go forever without raining. Because everything would dry up and die if that happened. The rivers would all run dry. All the crops would fail. All the animals would die of thirst. There'd be a big famine like in the Bible. But that wouldn't happen. Not in Mississippi. It would have to rain sometime. He didn't know for sure what the longest amount of time was that he'd gone through without seeing it rain, but it couldn't be over a couple of months. He'd lost a few corn crops from lack of rain, years and years ago, but never cotton. Cotton could make it without rain if it had to, if you had a good stand up, if it was clean and wasn't full of weevils and cockleburs, and it might not be the biggest cotton in the world, it might not be over knee high, but it would make a crop and a check. [. . .] But watermelons? Which were mostly water? With no rain? Forget about it. Let the coyotes have them. Which reminded him that he needed to shoot a few of them sons of bitches, too. He was getting tired of hearing them at night. They got all those little bitty dogs down the road stirred up. He thought he'd seen a doghouse up under the trailer before. He wondered if those little bitty dogs lived up under there. He wondered where they'd gotten those little bitty dogs. He didn't think he'd ever seen any that small. Lucinda when she was a girl had one of them little Chihuahua dogs and it was a lot bigger than these little dogs down the road. Hell, they weren't much bigger than baby rabbits. Where the hell'd they get them damn dogs at?

[. . .]

It just stayed dry and hot and the stalks of Clemson okra in Cortez's garden grew tall and clustered their fruit together in curvy green fingers and he walked among them carrying a yellow Tupperware bowl from the kitchen and cut the pods off with a paring knife. His tomatoes ripened slowly, hanging heavily from their vines under the shade of the rough leaves, growing from a solid shiny green at the top to a red that began halfway up, and he set them on the old wooden table in the shade of the chinaberry tree and they were firm and delicious when he made a tomato sandwich for lunch. Sometimes he made his wife one. She didn't have any teeth. He didn't have enough to write home about. She could gum hers enough to swallow it if she had some cold milk to go along with it. He hardly ever talked to her. If he did it was about the pond. She hadn't even seen it. She hadn't said anything about wanting to see it. If she did want to see it, he would have to pick her up out of her wheelchair and carry her out to the truck and then set her down somewhere for a second while he opened the door and put her in. Then he'd have to go back in the house and get her wheelchair and load it into the back end. Then drive her over there. Then get the wheelchair out. Then put her in it. Then try to push her wheelchair down that rough old log road.

But that would be a lot of trouble. He didn't figure she cared anything about seeing the pond. Only thing she cared about seeing was *Oprah Winfrey*. Lucinda liked her, too. So did that dirty-mouthed retard who lived with Lucinda. Whenever they were here, which was usually only at Christmas, all three of them watched *Oprah Winfrey* in the afternoons. Those were good times to try and have a nap in his bedroom where hopefully he'd wind up back on the clean river's mossy banks with the naked angel girls. He'd been trying to have that dream again but it hadn't happened yet. He sure wanted it to.

Meanwhile it didn't rain. He wondered, once his pond got full, if it would get low if it didn't rain for a while. He knew how ponds were. In hot weather they went down when it didn't rain. Evaporated some of that water. Which came back down somewhere as rain. It didn't come back down over the pond, though, he knew that. It might come back down in Finland. Or Argentina. There was no telling where the rain that fell on his place had originally come from. Maybe Mexico. Maybe Massachusetts.

But it didn't rain, so he drove back out to the pond through the old log road and walked down in it again. What he saw were tire tracks. Small ones. Donuts cut in the new dry dirt. And a bunch of little tiny tracks like a horse trail, only they were paw prints. They looked like dog tracks. And there were footprints. One set that was barefooted, another one that had shoes. Not tennis shoes. A plain flat track like maybe a patent leather shoe would leave.

Damn kids at that trailer. Had to be. He'd seen that go-kart come flying by, throwing gravel everywhere. They were down here messing around and they didn't have any business messing around down here. He'd get some POSTED signs is what he'd do. Stick them up around the pond. They had some at Sneed's. They were coming in on this old road is where they were coming in. He could get some wire and put up a barrier. Maybe barbed wire. No, not barbed wire. That might hurt one of them. They might come flying along in that go-kart and not see it and it might put one of them's eye out. Or he could just go down to that trailer and tell their daddy to keep them off his place. That might work better than putting up signs and a wire barrier. But he didn't look like he was home very much. He saw him going up and down the road in that junky-ass old car. Looked like a '56.

In a way he guessed he didn't blame them. They were kids. They got excited easily. He knew they'd get excited about a big new hole in the ground and would probably wonder what it was. He knew that little boy he'd seen on the levee was one of them. He didn't know much about the family. He'd seen the man's wife out in the yard a few times hanging clothes on a line she'd strung between a pine tree and a stick somebody had propped up in the ground. He'd noticed that she had a nice big butt. Cortez had always liked a nice big butt. His wife had always had kind of a flat, skinny butt, not really much of a butt, kind of like a partly deflated balloon. He didn't know why in the hell he'd married her. He'd noticed that the back of the trailer didn't have any steps on it. And the back door looked like it was about four feet off the ground. Long way to step down. You'd have to *jump* down. It looked like the guy would have built a back porch by now. A man needed a back porch. He was sure glad he had one. He knew that trailer had been there for over a year. What he'd heard was that they'd bought that piece of land off old Harvey Miller's boy after Harvey died. And then Harvey's boy had come up there and bulldozed them a piece of a driveway in and put a culvert in and put some gravel down, even around the back, and it looked like they'd want some grass around that trailer instead of just gravel, but it wasn't any of his business how they wanted to live. Just as long as those kids stayed off his land. That was one thing he wasn't going to put up with: somebody coming on his land.

Cortez got to going down the road some afternoons in his pickup to see if he could see some places where it had rained. He thought maybe it might have rained down near Serepta, so he rode down there to see. But it was dry down there, didn't look like it had rained. He rode over toward Bruce to see if it had rained down there, but it hadn't, so he turned and rode through Water Valley to see if it had rained there. It hadn't. It hadn't rained in Banner. Or Pine Flat. Or DeLay. Or Paris. Or Potlockney. Or Spring Hill. Or Toccopola. Or Dogtown. All the roads and trees and grasses and yards and pastures were dry. There weren't any mud puddles out in the cotton fields. He stopped his truck on the bridge over Yocona River to see how low the water was and it was low. Bad low. The banks were about fifty or sixty feet high. He didn't see any people fishing. A long time ago the river was full of people fishing. A long time ago people would regularly burn the brush along the banks so they could get down there and put out set hooks. There weren't as many ticks in the woods then, either. A long time ago the river was so full of bass that people drove down into Halter Wellums's pasture on Sunday afternoons and he charged them fifty cents a car to park, just at the bluffs. He could remember seeing people climbing up some steep trails that went down the bluffs back then, coming up with stringers of bass long as your leg. And it went on like that for years. Then two businessmen who lived up in Oxford, one of them a drugstore owner, came down to get some fish quick and poured some Red Panther cotton poison in the river, just intending to kill a few fish, enough for a fish fry, maybe, with some cold beer and cards, but what they didn't know, being a couple of businessmen from town who didn't know anything about Red Panther cotton poison, was that the stuff was very concentrated, kind of like frozen orange juice, and once they poured a couple of gallons of it in the river, it washed on down and diluted and diluted and diluted some more and then it started killing fish for miles and miles downstream, truckloads of fish, tractor trailers of fish, down through the whole length of the Yocona River, all the way to the mouth of Enid Reservoir, and even killed some down there in the actual lake. Which was a federal impoundment. Paid for and built by U.S. taxpayer dollars. Anybody could fish in it who had a valid fishing license. It didn't matter where you were from. You could be from Zanzibar and if you had a valid fishing license, you could fish down there. You just couldn't pour cotton poison in it. But somebody had. And those guys down there didn't think it was too funny. They didn't crack too many dead-fish jokes about it. They took it pretty damn seriously. The U.S. Army Corps of Engineers was in tight control of everything down there, and some members of their units went out in their boats and stood around in them after they got them stopped and started counting dead fish floated up all over the place, bream, crappie, buffalo, carp, flathead catfish, blue catfish, White River catfish, channel catfish, willow catfish, largemouth bass, white bass, paddlefish, alligator gar, too, and got up to a couple of thousand and lost count, got really pissed, even outraged, started counting again and then said to hell with it, did an investigation instead and sent investigators around asking questions to neighbors who lived near the river around Yocona and then owing to their deductions and snooping around and asking more questions and even *paying* some people to talk, leaned hard on Halter Wellums, with the full backing of the U.S. government, and he had to give the businessmen from Oxford up and the corps of engineers put those two guys' asses in a sling. They hung their heads before a judge is what they did, and said they were sorry and that they wouldn't ever do it again, and paid a huge fine. He seemed to remember it was about twenty thousand dollars, and that was a long time ago, when twenty thousand dollars was a lot of money. But Cortez remembered easily what it looked like. It was a terrible thing to see, all those rotting fish on the surface of the river, [. . .] large and small, some flathead catfish that were sixty- and seventy-pounders, their pale rounded bellies turned up, too, flies walking on their bellies, maggots working them over in the water. He saw buzzards walk from one side of the river to the other across the backs of dead ones where there was a fishjam up against a logjam. That ruined the fishing in the river for a long time. Just because a couple of assholes wanted some fish without fishing.

It didn't rain for so long that Cortez Sharp got sick of waiting. But there was nothing to do but just wait some more. So that's what he did. [. . .]

15

The two-man press was the largest one in northern Mississippi at that time, imported from Germany, a green monolithic monster that rose twenty-two feet above the grime-encrusted, fourteen-inch-thick concrete floor of the loudly slamming, wheel-whirring stove factory: *wham! bang! pow! blang!* all day long. All night long when they were running the third shift. It was the kind of press some company like GM could use to make car fenders. Or say if GE needed a bunch of washing-machine panels, or cooktops, it could make them as well. With the proper dies. The press was driven down and back up by a pair of big round gears on top. They were eight feet in diameter and a foot thick with teeth the size of steam irons. Beneath the press was a concrete pit six feet deep and fourteen feet wide and ten feet long where the slugs of round or rectangular or oblong or oval metal that were punched out by the various dies used in the press fell and stuck together with white lithium grease, which dripped down like melting candle wax from the machine. Somebody had to go down in there with a snow shovel and some five-gallon buckets once in a while and clean all that shit out, but Jimmy's daddy's job was to take the left gear off the press and fix a bad crack in it before it killed somebody. He didn't really know what the hell he was doing, had just transferred to Maintenance from Spot-Welding a few months ago, was just doing what they told him to do: take a big gear off. John Wayne Payne, the guy he accidentally crushed, had evolved over the years into a nonpareil forklift driver who still lived with his mother in Water Valley and was smooth and efficient and deadly quiet, his Towmotor muffler noise muffled way down by good mufflers that were put on at the Towmotor factory. He was so good that he could drive his lift up to a railroad car full of dishwashers, stacked in their soft cardboard cartons four high, cross the dockboard without looking down, and squinch his eyes up behind his glasses and peer through the greasy yellow mast and insert the hand-grinder-sharpened tips of his forks between the first and second dishwasher and lift out three without tearing a carton.

He could take that same quiet propane-swigging machine and go down the dim and lonely aisles between the tall, rusted steel die racks, next to the Press Department, where hundreds of dies that sometimes weighed thousands of pounds were stacked on dark oily shelves, and pluck one from its resting place thirty-three feet high as nimbly as an osprey grabs a mullet from a marsh. [. . .] One day they'd staged an in-plant forklift-driving contest, no contest. If anybody in the plant had a flat tire by lunchtime, he'd drive his lift out on the parking lot while he ate his sandwich with one hand and raise the car with it to keep anybody from having to jack it up. He'd eaten unfried baloney on white with mayonnaise and two or three drops of Louisiana Red Hot Sauce every single work day on his lunch break for the last nineteen years. Only two sick days, and was actually sick both times, the flu once, and then the heartbreak of salmonella poisoning from some bad chicken his mother fried one Sunday. Didn't make her sick. Didn't like chicken.

But in order to get this gear down off this crucial machine, which was dangerous as hell, since they were way up there in the air messing around with very heavy stuff, which could kill or amputate somebody or maybe even several somebodies real easy if something happened, say something gave, or broke, or slipped, as something sometimes does, what they'd done through an outside contractor in Dallas was set up near the big monster press a huge yellow Mitsubishi bridge-building crane they'd brought in through the tall back doors of the factory and amid all the workers and the other presses and the moving forklifts like the one John Wayne Payne drove and the slamming and the whirring, and Jimmy's daddy had gone up on a wooden pallet on another forklift, one they called Big Mama, to attach a chain on the crane to the gear and knock out the retaining pin and catch it before it fell and then force the gear off its spline with a hydraulic press so that they could lower it to the floor and fix the crack, weld the crack, and that was taking a while, a couple of days, and slowing down everything in the Press Department, because people who were supposed to be working in the middle of all the bedlam were always standing around rubbernecking and watching them take the big press apart, because it was pretty amazing, what they were doing, up in the air like that, and now Jimmy's daddy was pausing for a smoke break twenty feet off the floor, standing on the pallet, looking out over everything, the Spot-Welding Department and the Tool-and-Die Department and the Porcelain Department and even down to the edge of the line where they were putting the stoves together, and he could just barely catch a glimpse of that new girl with the God-awful titties who worked down there, unbelievable, like half-grown watermelons, the same woman everybody in the break room snuck looks at while they were eating their baloney sandwiches. Everybody was chickenshit to say anything to her. Jimmy's daddy wanted to say something to her, something like *Hey, baby, you want to come over here and sit on my face?* Who knew? Hell, she might say yes. Fuck her damn brains out maybe. In the parking lot? At lunch? Was that too much to hope for? Reckon what she ate for lunch? Probably not baloney.

[. . .]

"You gonna stand there all day with your thumb up your ass or you gonna get that gear off that spline?"

Jimmy's daddy looked down. Collums's face was still looking up. Collums. Chief of the Maintenance Department. Hardly ever said anything. Big guy, gray haired. No teeth on top. Kept his hands on his hips a lot. Mysterious background. Maybe from up north. Had kind of a nasal voice. Always wore neat blue coveralls and a neat blue cap. You never saw any grease on him. It was almost like grease wouldn't stick to him, and he practically lived in grease. Had the habit of staring at something he was going to fix for a very long time before fixing it. Like he was thinking about how he was going to fix it. Could fix anything mechanical. Could fix any machine in the entire plant, didn't matter what it was: sheet metal brake, computer, forklift, cherry picker, spot-weld machine, glue gun, press, Mr. Coffee, time clock, Towmotor. Could fix any machine on the entire parking lot: Ford, Chevy, GMC, Dodge, Mitsubishi, Honda, Toyota, Buick. Could weld anything. Could weld aluminum. Most people couldn't even think about welding aluminum. Drank a half pint of whisky every afternoon. Stopped at C&M liquor store down on South Lamar every afternoon and got one. Jimmy's daddy didn't know how many he drank on the weekends because he didn't see him on the weekends. He didn't *want* to see him on the weekends. He saw enough of him five days a week. Jimmy's daddy dropped his cigarette on the pallet and was going to step on it, but it fell through a crack and landed on top of somebody's head down on the floor and the somebody looked up and said something. Fuck him if he didn't like it.

"Yeah, just had a smoke, Collums, I'm about to get it," he said.

"Don't let that pin jump out," Collums said.

"You done already told me twice."

Then he picked up his hammer and started hitting on the retaining pin again. It was about four inches in diameter, about twenty-four inches long, and it was hard to drive out, even with the locking collar off, but he was making progress, hitting it with some steady long swings, only thing, the small sledgehammer gave your arms and shoulders out after a while, and you had to stop and rest, you couldn't just keep swinging it forever. But he was making progress. It was moving out a little, not much. It was a very tight fit. He guessed it was supposed to be that way.

Jimmy's daddy kept hitting it. Where in hell could those people be going on those four-wheelers? How'd they keep from getting caught by the cops since four-wheelers weren't legal on roads, just off-roads? He'd seen some deputies loading some four-wheelers up on a car hauler one night on the road down below his trailer, where he'd almost wrecked the go-kart. He kept hitting it. He needed to get an inspection sticker on the '55 before he ran through a roadblock one afternoon. He kept hitting it. Suddenly it jumped out and before he could grab it or try to it fell and bounced off the edge of the press and turned in midair, a flying cylindrical metal projectile, and catapulted into the gray block wall of the Grinding Department and knocked a big chunk out of it about a foot above some guy grinding something with sparks showering his face and dark goggles. Cement dust rained down on the guy's head and he looked up. It bounced off that wall without killing him, but then bounced across the floor tumbling like a runaway bowling pin. It hit a good-looking secretary from the front office wearing safety glasses who was walking back to the front office through the Press Department in the leg and, since it weighed nearly eighty pounds, broke it. She screamed and fell and kept screaming. A shard of bloody bone was sticking out of her leg and there was grease on her red dress and Jimmy's daddy could see that she was wearing black bikini panties. John Wayne Payne quietly passed beneath Jimmy's daddy on his lift at almost the same moment. That was when the crack in the gear, which must have been much worse than they'd thought, gave way close to the chain, and the enormous gear broke into two halves, one to crash thunderously straight down to the floor twenty-two feet beneath, shattering concrete, knocking workers off their feet, raising a big cloud of dust, narrowly missing two running workers, the other to fall directly on the yellow steel cage over John Wayne Payne's Towmotor, which was not built to adequately protect the driver from something that weighed as much as half the big gear. It made a horrible sound. Like a bomb. Dust flew out.

It looked pretty awful down there from what Jimmy's daddy could see. There was a lot of sickening blood. People were gathered around. More were coming. The word was spreading through the plant and from his high perch he could see people walking and running up from the line and the Porcelain Department. Shipping Department. Stockroom. Maintenance. Spot-Welding. Paint. He wondered if the new girl with the big titties was going to run up from the line. Guys in ties were running from the front office. Some of them, when they got there, kept going and ran off behind sheet metal brakes and other presses to hurl. The secretary kept screaming. People were gathered around her, too, making kind of a human wall around her. He thought her name was Ethel. He wondered if she wore black panties all the time. He guessed they'd fire his ass now. Even though it wasn't really his fault.

It was so bad that the ambulance people who came to get what was left of John Wayne Payne vomited on the fourteen-inch-thick floor in front of everybody. These were hardened people. And Jimmy's daddy had to stand up there and watch all that. It made him think about just going ahead and changing jobs and made him so nervous he had to have another cigarette before somebody got on Big Mama and brought him on down. That's when he got a real good look at what he'd accidentally done to John Wayne Payne. [. . .]

16

Same day all that happened, while Cortez Sharp was still waiting for rain, Jimmy made a headlight for his go-kart. He found an old flashlight and went into some of his mama's drawers in the kitchen while she was taking a nap on her bed with the door open and her hands between her legs and moaning and found some loose D batteries and stuck them inside the barrel of the flashlight and screwed the top back on and wondered if it would work and when he pushed the button sure enough it did.

He went out and looked at his go-kart, parked under the big pine tree in back. He bent down and touched the chain. It was really loose. It would hardly stay on unless he drove kind of slow. He didn't want to ask his daddy to fix it any more since his daddy had gotten so mad about it the last time he'd asked him to fix it, which was last week. He'd asked his mama to find out if they made new chains for his go-kart, but she'd told him to ask his daddy, so Jimmy kept his own counsel on that. He wasn't asking Daddy shit.

He found a piece of a roll of his daddy's black friction tape among the old camp stoves and boxes of hunting magazines and broken fishing rods and tackle boxes full of worthless rusted crap in the shed and taped the flashlight to the front of the go-kart, out there between where his feet sat when he was driving it. Then he sat down in the seat and looked at his once-clean machine. It had become battered. Dusty. Greasy and gravel specked, the red paint rock pecked here and there. A sad machine now where once was shiny and bright. He turned the steering wheel in his hands. He wished it was still new. He remembered how good it ran when it was new. How quiet and fast. Back then he could go up in the woods with it, or up and down the dirt road in front of the trailer as swiftly as he wanted, and it wouldn't matter. The wind would fly in his hair and he'd know a feeling of freedom such as he'd never felt or known was possible. Now the chain was so loose that he couldn't take it up in the woods, because the rough ground would make the chain come back off, and now also if he went too fast on the dirt road, it would come off. It wasn't nearly as much fun to drive around as it once had been. Now you had to kind of nurse it along like a bad leg.

He didn't know where the girls were. Maybe walking up and down the road. The girls didn't want to have anything to do with him now, since his go-kart had become crippled. They just stayed in their room and listened to Tim McGraw or walked up and down the road. Sometimes they went wading down in the creek, but his daddy had told him not to, because of the snakes, so he didn't. It didn't seem quite fair, though, for them to get to go down there and wade around in the clear running water on hot days while he had to just sit on the bridge and watch them. But Jimmy already knew that a lot of stuff in the world wasn't fair. Like having to go to school? That wasn't fair. How about having to do homework? Was that fair? How about not being able to afford Kenny Chesney tickets for a concert in Tupelo? Was that fair? Shoot, naw it wasn't fair.

He sat out there in the heat for a while and thought about walking over to the empty catfish pond to look at it again. He wished it would rain, in a way, so the pond would get filled up, and in another way he hoped it wouldn't rain, because when it rained the road he lived on got so muddy that you couldn't get out and do anything and just had to sit in the trailer with your half sisters and listen to them talk about Britney Spears. Or go sit out in the shed with the lizards that changed colors, brown to green, green to brown, over and over, like real slow traffic lights.

Jimmy looked up the road. That old man was mean. Jimmy hadn't seen him up close since that time he'd yelled at him, but he'd seen him come down the road in his truck since then. The old man had stuck up some signs in the woods that said POSTED, and he'd strung some hog wire across the road in the woods that ran down to the empty pond, but Jimmy could always walk through the woods if he wanted to go over there bad enough. He wondered what it was going to look like when it got filled up. It looked like it was going to be pretty big. It was going to be plenty big enough to swim in. Jimmy didn't know how to swim. Not yet. But his daddy had told him he was going to teach him how. Jimmy could hardly wait for that.

One of the dogs came out from under the trailer where they lived in a tiny doghouse and crawled up in Jimmy's lap and went to sleep. Jimmy sat there, waiting for him to wake up. And then he thought about his daddy's tools in the shed. Big mistake.

That night, after Jimmy's daddy had whipped him really hard and left those stripes on his butt for messing with his tools, Jimmy's butt was still stinging and he'd cried until it felt like his whole head was stopped up. Like a wet sponge was filling up his brain. His mama'd had to make his daddy finally stop whipping him, because it felt for a while there like he was never going to stop, and his mama and his daddy had yelled some pretty nasty things at each other. She was a fat lazy stupid Hamburger Helping bitch, and he was a limp-dick white-trash red-neck drunk. They'd hurled these insults at each other with Evelyn sitting on the living-room Naugahyde couch in her evening gown, smoking a cabbage cigarette and having a glass of cooking sherry, chewing on her black fingernails while she studied a library book about Frank Lloyd Wright. His mama had gone into the girls' room crying and slammed the door. Then the girls had gone back there, too. They were all piled up in the bed back there together watching a movie. He hated Evelyn's guts. She thought she was better than him. Said her daddy was in the oil business in Texas. Said one day her daddy was going to come back and get her and buy her a Corvette. Jimmy knew that was bullshit. Jimmy's daddy had told him it was bullshit because Evelyn's daddy was a Corvette thief and was doing time for that in Huntsville, wherever that was. But right now Jimmy's daddy wasn't telling him anything. Right now Jimmy's daddy was back there in his bedroom with the door closed drinking beer and watching his hog-hunting videos. Jimmy was sitting by himself in the living room. Jimmy had watched a few of those videos a few times. In one, guys out in the woods had a bunch of dogs, about twelve or thirteen of them, some of them pit bulls, some of them Airedales, and the dogs chased these huge hairy wild hogs down, and held them by the ears with their teeth until the hunters could get there and stab the hogs to death with big Bowie knives and some spears they'd evidently made. It looked kind of scary to Jimmy. There was a lot of barking and squealing and blood. He didn't know if he wanted to hunt or not.

His daddy always went deer hunting in the winter but he never killed anything. Not even a squirrel. Not even a rabbit. And when he didn't kill anything, it put him in a bad mood. So, since he never killed anything, he always came back from hunting in a bad mood. He'd come in before lunch on a cold Saturday in his hunting clothes and he'd already be drinking. He'd come in with a beer in his hand and sit down with his muddy boots on and yell at the girls, *Turn that goddamn TV down! Jesus Christ! Why don't y'all clean this fucking pigpen up? Johnette? Where's my goddamn binoculars?* Then he'd start in telling Jimmy's mama what a lousy morning he'd had, that he only saw some does, started to shoot one of them nanny sons of bitches, could have, easy, twenty times, they'd eat just as good, but Rusty and them would have cut his shirttail off and the fine was high as hell if you got caught with one, damn near froze his ass off and wished he'd eaten some breakfast before he took off, how about cooking him up some French toast and sausage? Couple of fried eggs maybe?

Jimmy thought about telling his daddy he was sorry about getting into his tools. He wondered if that would make his daddy feel any better toward him. Jimmy loved his daddy so much that he couldn't *stand* for his daddy to be mad at him, although he often seemed to be mad at him. Well, not mad at him. Not all the time. There were plenty of times when he was mad at him, sure, but a lot of times he was just grouchy in general. Jimmy thought his daddy probably had to work too hard to support them was why he stayed in a bad mood so much of the time. He rarely even spoke to the girls unless it was to tell them to stop doing something or other. Jimmy knew his daddy had been through a bad day. Jimmy's mama had told him that something happened at the plant. She didn't say a word about what it was, but she said it in a way that let Jimmy know that it was something very bad and that his daddy was connected to it and that was why he'd whipped him so hard for getting into his tools and then gone back to his room with some beer. Jimmy wished he'd known that something bad had happened at the plant and that his daddy would be coming home early because of it, because then he wouldn't have gotten the tools out, thinking he could fix the go-kart and have the tools put away again before his daddy came home, but there he was when his daddy rolled up at two thirty, an hour and a half early, sitting there with the left back wheel of the go-kart propped off the ground on a brick, and all his daddy's tools scattered out in the gravel in a pile. Caught red-handed on a red go-kart.

Jimmy eased painfully off the couch. It was dark outside but too early for bed. He eased down the hall past some piled-up clothes toward his mama and daddy's bedroom. He didn't make any noise. He stopped on the linoleum outside the bedroom door and listened. He put his head up against the door and could hear a video going, but he couldn't tell which one it was. He listened to see if he could hear any wild hogs squealing. It might be those guys up in trees with bows and arrows again and if so were whispering so the deer they were trying to shoot wouldn't hear them. He reached for the doorknob. He didn't touch it. He just held his hand near it. It wasn't the first time he'd done that, held his hand near it. He knew he wasn't supposed to open that door if it was closed. Ever. Never. It was forbidden. Some things were forbidden. You didn't drink the last Coke in the refrigerator. You didn't eat all the Oreos and ice cream. You didn't bother your daddy at night or if he was in a real bad mood. But he was sure thinking about going in and telling his daddy he was sorry about the tools. He didn't want his daddy to stay mad at him. And maybe he wasn't still mad. Maybe he was almost over it. But what if his daddy was in the middle of his favorite part of the video and Jimmy interrupted him and he got mad again and started whipping him again? He didn't think he could take another whipping tonight. The lick that knocked him up against the tub made him hit his head on the basin, but he didn't say anything about it because he'd been afraid that might make his daddy just whip him worse. There was a knot there now. He rubbed it. A lump. Tender. Why'd his daddy want to hit him so hard? Didn't his daddy love him? If he loved him, why'd he want to hit him so hard? Knock him up against the bathtub? Call him a little shit?

Those were questions he couldn't answer. So he didn't open the door, or even knock. He just went back up to the living room and on back to his room and put on his tennis shoes and went outside. The go-kart was sitting in the dark out there, and he stood in the darkness with it and listened to the crickets screaming in the trees and the tree frogs calling and the bugs up in the woods calling to each other in the hot electric black that had settled over everything. He saw a falling star that shot flaming white and died.

He knew his go-kart well enough that he could crank it in the dark, and he did. It sat there running, the chain rattling, bad loose, loose as a goose. Jimmy knelt down and felt it. It might not even run much more at all. But maybe if he went very slowly, crept maybe, he could creep up the road and back. He looked toward the trailer to see if anybody was going to come out and tell him not to go anywhere, but nobody did. He sat down in the seat, wincing a little, and reached forward and turned his flashlight headlight on. It shone out there pretty good. A lot better than he would have thought. It was almost like a real headlight. Jimmy pushed on the gas pedal gently and the flashlight lit his way out of the driveway and onto the dusty tan gravel of the road.

It was pretty fun. It was more fun that he would have thought it would be. He wished he'd thought of this a long time ago, when the go-kart was still running good. He could have run up and down the road all night. Nah. They would have made him go to bed eventually, even though he got to stay up pretty late in the summer. When he was on vacation. Like now. He didn't even want to think about going back to school, so he didn't. He just went slowly on down the road, seeing what was on the road out there in the night. And every moment he was waiting for the chain to come off.

But for some reason it didn't. It stayed on past the curve down the hill and Jimmy kept taking it easy, letting it just roll along, bumping gently in the gravel, on down the road toward the wooden bridge. It was kind of a good place to hang out in the summer. It had some big trees for shade nearby, growing on the banks of the creek, and people sometimes came down there and shot .22 rifles at cans and things. Sometimes they sat down there in the shade in lawn chairs and drank beer, and he'd seen his daddy and Mister Rusty take a leak there one time when they were riding around drinking beer.

Suddenly Jimmy passed through a cold place, near an old house that was overgrown and almost hidden, just off the road. The only thing that could be seen of it was a rusted piece of tin on the roof. It was surrounded by tall weeds and vines and trees that had grown almost completely over it, maybe even through it. He had felt this cold spot before, walking down to the bridge. Then he was on the other side of it and it was normal again. Hot summer night breeze, crickets calling, stars shining high above.

He stopped on the bridge and sat there for a few minutes, trying to see what was down in there. Somebody had shot a big gray crane and thrown it off in there one time. Somebody else had shot a road sign and thrown it off in there, too. The creek wasn't deep enough to fish in unless it had been raining lately, and Jimmy had seen some snakes down in there, too. A copperhead and a water moccasin. Jimmy knew his snakes.

He pushed on the gas lightly and rolled to the end of the bridge and then down into the gravel again. If he kept going straight he'd wind up on the paved road, but he knew better than to go down there. And he didn't want to get too far away from home in case the chain came off. It might be better to turn around. His butt was hurting anyway. Maybe he needed to just go home and go to bed and try for a better day tomorrow. Maybe he could get a paper route and save enough money to buy a new chain. Or his own tools. Or a '55 Chevy like his daddy had.

So he turned it around at the edge of the cotton field where he'd found the spear point, where a long culvert had been installed in the middle of the ditch and pit run gravel graded over it to make a road in and out for the tractors and spray rigs and pickers that moved through the field. It was a big one, about ninety acres, and Jimmy had watched them from the bridge at night in the fall, the round yellow lights of the pickers moving through the darkness as they rolled the length of the long rows and plucked the cotton from its stalks. And when he turned around and got back on the road and headed back toward home, he saw her standing on the bridge.

He stopped. She was standing there, looking at him and crying. She was big and beautiful, and she was wearing a long, old-timey dress. A black lady. Jimmy knew she was not real. She was more like a silhouette. She was standing right in the middle of that cold place. And that cold place was right in front of that old house that you couldn't see for all the stuff that had grown up around it. And then she was gone.

Scared the living shit out of him, and the chain didn't come off even though he spurted all the way up the road with gravel flying out behind him, rattling off into the woods like something that was chasing him. Something was.

17

Johnette was lying behind closed curtains, almost fully clothed, on a bed in a dim room in the Downtown Inn, just off the square in Oxford, already stoned. She had removed her panty hose, balled them up, and put them under her pillow for later retrieval. Or maybe she'd just throw them away. She had to make sure Jimmy's daddy didn't see the charge for the room on the Visa card statement, not that he ever looked at it anyway. He didn't like to mess with paying for things on a credit card. She took care of all that stuff, bills and statements and things like that. She hadn't fucked anybody besides Jimmy's daddy for the last ten years except for the guy she was about to fuck again, on her lunch hour this time, since he was off from work today. She kept in touch with him through her cell phone, another thing that Jimmy's daddy didn't have any interest in. She couldn't think of much he was interested in besides hunting videos and fishing and riding around and drinking beer. She had some addictions herself and knew how they were. She loved going to Margaritaville, but she rarely got the chance unless she got out with some of the girls from the bank on one of their business trips to places scattered throughout North Mississippi. It was harder to take a trip now. She had to think about the kids. It wasn't like it used to be when they'd first married. She'd been on pills and cough syrup back then. She was off all that shit now. Some of the girls at the bank had given her some kind of herb and she'd been enjoying that for a change. Only thing wrong with it was that it made you hungry. She knew she needed to lose some weight. She was a little overweight, sure. She tried to watch what she ate, but Lord she got hungry sometimes. Didn't everybody? Sure they did. Hell yes they did. There was nothing better than a big plate of whole fried catfish, all crisp and hot and brown, with some lemon wedges on the side, and some sliced white onions on top. Unless it was those good cold shrimp on ice. Or fried green tomatoes. And all the desserts they had at the Seafood Junction at Algoma were good. They made their own biscuit pudding. Strawberry pie with all that whipped cream on top of it.

Any flavor ice cream you wanted. But she'd gotten to where she hated to go over there with him. He acted like such an asshole. Always had to sit in the parking lot and drink a whole beer before he could go in. This was always after he'd had four on the way over there. He had to drink them fast because it wasn't far once you got past Toccopola. And he acted so ugly all the way home that time he had to talk to the preacher for three minutes by himself. She knew she was fat. She just wished he'd stop calling her fat. Fat hog. Fat bitch. Dumb fat bitch. Stupid fat bitch. She didn't know you weren't supposed to spray WD-40 on charcoal to try and get it started, it didn't say not to on the can. Laid out in the gravel and messed with that junky old car he'd blown all that insurance money on when the kids needed things, lots of things, and they needed some new furniture, and a new stove, cheap son of a bitch that came with the trailer only had two burners working now. That made it take twice as long to cook supper if you were cooking a meal that took all four burners. She knew they sold new burners for stoves somewhere. But she didn't know how to get them. Or where to get them. And he wouldn't do it. Didn't have time to. Bitched all the time about it only being two burners, though. Why didn't he build a back porch? And Jimmy's teeth needed fixing. They needed fixing bad. She didn't know what they were going to do about that. She guessed maybe she could see if there was some place around town where she could wait tables on the weekends. Maybe Friday and Saturday nights. Make a little extra money and try to get his teeth fixed. But who would watch the kids? Not him. He was always out on Friday and Saturday nights. Every weekend. So how was she going to get the money for Jimmy's teeth? *Steal it from the bank?* No. Too risky. She'd get caught.

She was lying on her back on top of the bedspread with her thick legs slightly spread, and she was just looking at the ceiling. It was quiet in the room. Nice and cool and dark. She heard something kick on and run for a while, maybe an ice machine outside, and then it kicked back off. She heard something come rolling by her door, something that sounded like a cart, and the sounds of two women talking. Maids.

She was listening for the approaching footsteps that would sort of announce the soon-to-follow knock on the door. She was bracing herself for that, for the knock on the door. Would it be soft, would it be sharp, would there be one, two, three raps? Would her heart leap when she heard it? It was broad daylight outside. Anybody could come by and see her car parked out there, even though she'd tried to kind of hide it by the swimming pool.

Johnette hadn't been satisfied in a long time. She hadn't been satisfied with her name her whole life. Used to argue with her mother and daddy about it. *Why didn't you just drop the* h? she'd say. And she didn't know why she'd gotten married again, because she'd already tried it two times before this and that should have told her something. But you never learned. You wanted love. You wanted love and good sex and you put up with a couple of not apparently sorry sons of bitches who gave you love and good sex for a while, and a couple of kids, but then when they both turned out bad you figured that was all you deserved to get in your life, two of the assholes, and then the third one made it three in a row. If that was a football game three in a row and you were the quarterback throwing the football and each marriage was an interception, you'd be headed for the bench to cool down pretty quick. Or the showers. Or the parking lot. Or a bus out of town.

But it was hard for a woman to make it on her own. And raise two children. Three now. Put clothes on their backs and food on the table and try to keep the cuss words out of their mouths. It was awful how Evelyn talked to Velma. Picked on her. Called her names and slapped her. Wouldn't share her stuff with her. But it was impossible to watch them every minute. There was too much to do when she was home. Cook. Clean. Wash their clothes. Pick up after them. Worry about having enough money to make the payments on a trailer and still have enough left for everything else you had to take care of every month. Pay the light bill and the phone bill. Son of a bitch couldn't even build a back porch. Which made them not have a back door they could use. The back door was there, and it opened and closed just fine, but it was also four feet off the ground. It would be embarrassing if anybody came over and saw it, but that was one thing they didn't have to worry much about, since nobody ever came over except for Rusty, and Rusty knew how he was. Hell yeah. Asshole buddies. He'd rather go ride around and drink beer with Rusty than just about anything. Never gave her a look much anymore. Except once in a while when he was drunk and came in wanting it and didn't even want to kiss or hold her or anything, just wanted to fuck her. [. . .] Selfish son of a bitch always thinking of himself first every time, even when it came to the kids. And Jimmy. She let him whip him too hard. She shouldn't have let him whip him that hard. She should have knocked him in the head with something the way Ellen Barkin did Robert De Niro when he was beating up Leonardo DiCaprio in *This Boy's Life*. Got into his tools, big deal. Like that pile of shit in that rusty old box was worth whipping his own kid like that.

She kept lying there on the bed, with not even the TV on. She knew there were people sitting in new cars out on the hot street in front of the hotel, waiting for the red lights to turn green, listening to their stereos and running their air conditioners. Watching the people at the gas station across the corner work on cars and change flats. People walking up and down the streets shopping or going into cafes and restaurants for lunch with friends.

And here she was. Waiting for some guy to come in and get naked and kiss her a few times and suck her nipples for a while and finger her some, enough to get her wet, then get on his knees on top of the bedspread between her legs, panting like a hot dog and leaning in toward her, holding himself, ready to push it in. That's what she was waiting for. Gladly.

Then there came the footsteps.

Oh boy. Here we go.

Yep. He was knocking and she'd left the toe of one of her shoes just between the jamb and the door.

"Come on in, baby," she said.

So he did. And he damn sure wasn't Jimmy's daddy.

She didn't think.

But hell, who knew?

18

Down below the barn, in the partial shade of a line of river birches along the creek, where an unborn baby was buried inside his mother without a name, Cortez Sharp's peas were wanting a drink of water. The dirt they grew in was nothing but dust, and the only moisture they got was the faint mist of dew that gathered on their veined leaves each night, a thin sheen that was gone almost as soon as the climbing sun's rays touched the pea patch from across the Cutoff road. He had planted them way too late, but they'd still make.

Just back of the pea patch, behind a skimpy brake of tall green cane, good for fishing poles or bean stakes, the bank sloped down through sandy ground and patches of velvety green moss to the rocky bed of the creek, which was only a trickle now. There were holes here and there, where catfish and bream lived and bass lay low and waited for more water to come, but the beavers had all said to hell with it and left and gone on down the tributary to the river bottom, overland, eating bark as they went, looking for some water to dam. And thence to build houses where they could raise their junior beavs. Now their abandoned slides were impotent dusty troughs down the banks where frogs sat and sang under the stars. Coons grabbed them sometimes. Fat juicies. Brief little struggles. Snakes, too, big scaly cottonmouths, fanged them between their back legs. Then the frog would be hopping, trying to jump, the venom slowly working on him. Not a pretty sight. Slid whole feet first down a snake's throat. Maybe one last croak in the dark of the sandy cane brake: *Cr-oak!*

Behind the house, down the hill, his corn stood browning day by day under the sun. Cortez had pulled some shucks open to see barely anything inside there kernel-wise. No Silver Queen this year, dadgumit. Would have to get it at the store if he got any. If they had any. He might be able to go over to the Amish community close to Pontotoc and get some if they'd had any rain over there. You could get it over there for a dime an ear and it was good stuff. His wife couldn't eat it anymore, of course, without teeth. She could try. She could mush the shit out of a cob with her gums, but no teeth made it pretty hard to do anything much but just kind of maul it without actually getting any down your throat, which was all that mattered, he guessed.

Each evening he stood on the porch and studied the sky. On the prettiest evenings the gray patches of clouds reddened in the wake of the sinking orange ball and were backlit in some kind of old beauty that fell behind the curve of the world and turned the sky into a painting he never tired of watching. The days had been hot and long. All things dry. The grass in the yard had slowed its growing and grown brown patches instead. And the bottom of the future pond was cracked open in places, so dry it was.

His wife wanted the air conditioner on all the time now. She wouldn't sit out on the porch and try to catch the breeze. There wasn't a TV out here. She wasn't going to sit somewhere there wasn't a TV. Hell no. Shit no. She might miss some jackoff selling make-your-peter-hard or make-your-peter-longer medicine. He didn't know if she even knew what she was watching or not. She'd watch just about anything. She watched *Bonanza* religiously, every morning Monday through Friday. She watched *The Andy Griffith Show* and *I Dream of Jeannie*. She never missed a single episode of *Leave It to Beaver,* and she always was up for watching *Forensic Files* as well as Lifetime's movies for women. She was a big fan of *The Big Valley*.

Most days the flies were pretty bad on the front porch. He kept a flyswatter on the front porch and sometimes went into fits of flyswatting that went on for ten or fifteen minutes, and he'd keep count of how many he killed on the porch posts and the rocking metal chairs they'd had for so long, 27, 35, 52. And it didn't seem to matter how many he killed one day, because there'd always be more back the next day. Even if he killed 100. Or 150. The most he'd ever killed at one session was 236 but that had taken a long time. About two hours. Missed no telling how many. Got the posts all bloody with mashed fly guts because some of them had probably been biting his cows. Damn TV blaring in there ninety to nothing. Made him want to shoot the son of a bitch sometimes. Shoot her, too. Just go ahead and kill her. Put her out of her damn misery. For damn sure put him out of his. She was going to die anyway. One of these days. She needed a hearing aid, too. Had done about drove them both deaf with the damn TV.

It was hard not to go over and look at the pond, but on the other hand he knew that nothing had changed and that there wasn't any need of going over there and looking at it. But sometimes he went anyway because he liked to stand there in the bottom of it and look at the high walls of dirt around him, still bearing lots of dozer tracks, and visualize what it was going to look like when it got filled up with all that water. Maybe ducks would come in. He'd be fishing. He could get a boat and paddle around. A boat dock to tie the boat to maybe. He wondered how muddy it would be when it first filled up. Probably pretty muddy. It probably took a while for all those dirt particles to settle down. He just wished it would rain. Hell, it had to rain sometime. It couldn't just keep on going like this. This wasn't the Sahara Desert.

[. . .]

He couldn't get any fish until the pond filled up. He couldn't feed any fish until he got some fish. It was taking too long and it was getting worse than waiting for Christmas when you were a kid. Not that he ever got much for Christmas when he was a kid. An orange, if he was lucky. Maybe a sucker. Times were hard back then. Back in the thirties. He never would have thought he'd have made it this far. He'd figured something would get him before now, a bull, somebody's husband. But nothing had, and he was still going. He didn't know how much longer his wife could keep going. He wouldn't be surprised if he woke up one morning and found her cold beside him. He'd been looking for that, in fact. Another stroke could take her out. He'd seen it. Damn pills didn't do no good if you didn't take them. And she said she didn't care if she lived or died anyway. She'd been that way ever since Raif died. He didn't feel that way. He never had felt that way. No matter how bad he'd felt in other ways. He wanted to keep on going and everybody else could do whatever they wanted to, long as they just left him the hell alone.

He'd been looking around for fresh sign of the trailer kid in the bottom of the pond, in the undisturbed dirt, but there was nothing new, just the old circle of tracks he'd found just before he'd seen the kid. He didn't really feel bad about yelling at the kid to get the hell off his place, but in another way he kind of wished he hadn't done it. Hell, he was just a kid. He remembered how he was when he was a kid. Into everything. Mean as a yard dog. But it wasn't any wonder, the way he was raised. It was hard coming up back then. They didn't have any of this shit they had now. All this crap on the damn TV. They didn't have time to watch TV. They didn't have no damn TV. And besides that they had to work. You couldn't just sit around on your ass all day and half the night and watch a bunch of jerkoffs in a box. You had to have some food and you had to raise it. Pigs and goats and cows and chickens and peas and corn and beets and sweet potatoes and tomatoes and beans and okra and squash and watermelons and peppers and you had to milk a cow, too, had to churn your butter, kill your hog on a cold morning, scald him in a barrel of hot water, scrape all the hair off with a dull knife, cut him up and cook out the fat, cure the hams and bacon in the smokehouse. Keep your milk cold in the springhouse. These kids now didn't know shit. What they did know they got off the damn TV. Looked like all they cared about was getting almost naked and shaking their ass.

He sat around on the front porch and swatted flies, and picked his to-matoes, and cut his okra every few days, and picked some squash, didn't really need any more, just had it for the hell of it, was really in a routine of growing it whether they needed it not, and they didn't, because she couldn't cook and he wasn't that crazy about squash anyway unless it was fried and he didn't know how to do that. He wound up just throw-ing it over the fence, then cutting down the rest of the plants. They were drying up from lack of rain anyway.

And then one evening, when he was out in the barn, looking at some old issues of a magazine called *Hustler* that he'd found down the road in a Dumpster, staying away from his wife, he heard it thunder, far off. He went outside and looked south, and dark rain clouds were grouped down there. It had been sunny all day but now within the last thirty minutes while he'd been looking at pictures of naked women simulating sex acts with vegetables, this bad weather had come up good.

He stood there and felt the wind stirring in his thick hair. The leaves on the big pecans were starting to waft up and show their paler under-sides, and he saw a bolt of pure white light up the inside of a gray cloud far off. Deep thunder rolled booming out of the sky echoing again and again and the wind picked up as the ceiling blackened and moved his way. Birds fled before it, scattering in the wind, wavering, dodging in its path. The sky rumbled and Cortez saw the beauty of the world God made.

He looked toward the house. She was scared to death of a storm. Always had been, ever since she was fourteen and a tornado blew her whole house away with two of her sisters in it. They found both of them down in the river bottom, one of them with all her clothes torn off, sitting as if she were only asleep against a giant cypress. The other one was up in the tree, green leaves and splinters of blue painted wood caught all in her golden hair like a garland. And because of all that his wife never got over being scared of a storm. All the time when Raif was growing up, whenever the least little cloud came up, he had to stop what he was doing and go get in the storm house with them. And sit there. Among the canned beets and candles and oil lamps. Old lumpy magazines. Sit there while it rained and listen to the wind blow and the rain hit things. Listen to that sizzling sound when it came down hard, without stopping, straight down, pouring, raining like a cow pissing on a flat rock. He'd gotten plenty from Queen on days like that, in the rain, not out in it but inside the old house that smelled like her. She smelled like dirt, like the ground, but not in a bad way. A good way. No need thinking about that now either. He'd almost lost his head that time. And no telling what would have happened if he had. The world had certainly changed. You couldn't do stuff like that anymore. Just bury somebody out in the woods. You wouldn't be able to get away with it. You'd have to pay. And most days he didn't want to have to pay.

Cortez Sharp walked across his backyard and waited for the first drops to hit him, but when he got to the back porch he was still dry. He went inside and sat down on his mildewed cot and leaned his back against the beadboard wall and watched the wind have its way with the leaves of the chinaberry tree, and then he saw rain as dust swirled up from the first fat drops of water falling at the edge of the yard. The birds were flying across, weaving in the wind, cardinals and bluebirds that hung around and ate from the bird feeders she made him fill up once a week in the summertime.

He heard one of his cows bawl down in the pasture and knew it was calling its calf to its side. Animals knew things. They knew when a storm was coming. They'd start moving for shelter, get up under a bunch of trees, and wait it out. But sometimes they got struck by lightning that way, too. Worst damn smell you ever smelled. He'd had ten killed under a tree one night. A bull and nine cows. Almost wiped him out. His whole herd at that time. Had Queen gone? For good maybe? He hadn't heard her in a long time. He hoped she'd gone. Went back to wherever dead people went to. He didn't want to hear her anymore. He didn't need any reminding. He couldn't have done anything besides what he had done. Not in the world they had lived in. Mississippi almost forty years ago.

And then it started raining hard. He watched it come down and thicken in intensity and the outline of the barn began to fade behind the wall of rain, and it poured down in the yard and started running off the eaves and puddling next to the house and splashing up against the old red bricks. The sky closed up and became a solid color like steel and more water came down. It thundered and the wind blew and the storm rolled up to his place and then it came down as hard as he'd ever seen it.

He sat there and listened to it and watched it and wondered how much of it was going into the pond. He wondered if it would fill up any, or if it would all soak into the ground the first time. He knew that had to happen. He knew enough water had to come down at once so that it all couldn't soak away, but could pool and start making a pond.

He could imagine what the pea patch looked like, water already beginning to stand in the rows and flood the young plants, and now in a few days the grass would spring up, probably, but that was okay, he could take the tractor down and run the scratchers through the stalks again. He needed to clean his gun, get ready for the deer. They'd be coming. Bastards. They were lying up now, under bushes, waiting for the rain to be over, or maybe not even caring that it was raining. Maybe it didn't bother them. Maybe they liked it.

He knew what was happening on his place. The creek was filling with water that was running down off the banks, and his fine fat cows were standing under trees in the pasture with water smeared on their sleek black hides. The woods were whispering in raindrops and water was rolling fast downhill toward the empty hole where his new pond sat, and Cortez saw it in his mind's eye, the muddy ground in the bottom pinging up little geysers of mud as the drops plinked down, and the water pooling in the bottom, slowly rising up the sides, gradually filling, becoming what it was intended to be, now with the rain at long last, and the thunder, and the wind blowing and stirring the tops of the trees.

Out at the far edge of the rain he counted seven crows slowly flapping, making their way into the big red oaks down by the creek. He'd seen the crows before. He thought they must have a roost around here somewhere. It would be hard to find. A man had to have good eyes to spot a crow's nest and his were old. But Cortez knew crows. His father had owned one for a pet when he was a little boy. It would steal anything shiny that was lying around outside the house. Spoons. Dice. A thimble once. That was in 1937. Everybody from then dead now. Just him and his wife left. And Lucinda. Nobody to carry on his name now with Raif gone. But the storm was fine. He'd been waiting for so long. And now here it was, like a reward for building the pond. He sat there and reveled in it for a long time, an old man, watching it rain, remembering other rains.

19

Jimmy's daddy was riding around by himself that same evening, drinking a little beer. Almost dark. After the rain. Cool wind. The kids were home alone but that was okay. They'd be all right. Watch TV. Cook hot dogs. He was down on Old Union Road and the road was still wet and the rain had made the air look different. Softer or something. He hated like hell that he'd accidentally crushed the shit out of John Wayne Payne. But he didn't think the whole thing was all his fault either. He hadn't been able to make himself go to the funeral, although he'd been told that a lot of people who worked in the plant had. They'd actually shut the plant down for about three hours to let people off with pay for the funeral since so many people who worked there had known John Wayne Payne and how he'd give you a lift on a lunch flat. Of course some of them he knew took the three hours and went home and watched TV with it. Or shelled some peas. Cut the grass instead of having to do it Saturday.

Boy, the weekends just didn't last long enough. You got up and you went to work and you came home and went to bed and you spent all week fixing Towmotors, fixing spot-weld machines, fixing baloney sandwiches, taking breaks, eating lunch, punching in, punching out, and then Friday rolled around and you got your check and drove happily to the beer store and iced down a case and then you had all Friday evening before dark to ride around or cook out and then on Saturday you could sleep late and work on your car or go fishing or ride around and go get something to eat and drink some beer and then Sunday just came down like a nine-pound hammer. You could go fishing, sure. You could ride around a little, yeah. Drink a few beers. But it was tainted with the closing-in feeling of the loss of freedom. Because after the sun went down, it came back up on Monday morning. And you had to go work *five more days*. And it sucked. The '55 was running pretty good now that he'd put a new battery in it and a voltage regulator and new brushes in the generator and a new Bendix for the starter and an exhaust manifold gasket and a new race and bearing for the left spindle and a new set of shocks all the way around and a new harmonic balancing wheel and plugs and points and a Rochester four-barrel. Rusty had set the timing on it with a timing light and she was purring like a kitten at its mama's titty nipple. She had a little Bondo in her, sure, but how many were you going to find this old that didn't? This son of a bitch was about fifty years old almost. He was thinking about a cam, maybe an Isky or a Lunati. Maybe a full race or a three-quarter's. Rusty could order him anything he wanted. Just paying for it was the thing. He got tired of arguing with Johnette about what they ought to spend their money on. She said he drank too much beer. Rode around too much. Didn't stay home with the kids enough. And that when he did, all he did was yell at them. She said he didn't socialize with them. Just because he liked to watch his hunting videos and drink a little beer in the evenings. In the bedroom. By himself.

That's what she said. She said a lot of shit. He was glad he wasn't having to listen to any of it right now. He was about tired of listening to all her shit. He'd like to *socialize* with that big-tittied heifer down on the line was who he'd like to socialize with. Socialize with her knockers. Damn, she had a set. Every man in the whole plant was damn near drooling. All of them chickenshit to even talk to her. He was gonna say something to her. He didn't know what yet. But he was going to. Hell, she might not even talk to him.

Jimmy's daddy had the windows down, listening to his tapes. He had a bunch of good ones. Narvel Felts, Lefty Frizzell, David Frizzell, Ferlin Husky, Roy Drusky, Roy Clark, Guy Clark, Petula Clark, the Dave Clark Five. He wished he knew how to play a guitar. He ought to buy one's what he ought to do. Somebody was selling one on TV the other night for $39.95 or maybe it was three payments of $39.95, which wasn't bad if you thought about it, if the guitar was any good. Be something else Johnette could raise hell about. Playing a guitar. Making some more noise. He guessed he could play it outside. He could play it out on the back porch if he ever got around to building one. Shit. He ought to at least build some steps sometime. What if they had a fire by the front door and they couldn't go out that way? They'd have to jump down from the back door. He wondered if Rusty knew how to build steps. He might. He could build anything. He was damn good on deer stands. He was building a little boat right now. Damn, that's what he needed, was a little boat. Once that old fellow's pond got filled up, and if he put some catfish in it, and if Jimmy's daddy had a little boat, he could drag it through the woods at night and catch the shit out of them while the old man was asleep. Drag it back before daylight. Sneak in, sneak out.

He took another drink of his beer. It was good to get out of the house for a while. Get away from them kids. Drive you batty all that yelling and hollering and raising hell and throwing shit everywhere and arguing over what they were going to watch on the TV and making a mess in the kitchen and tracking up the carpet with their muddy feet whenever it rained and just generally being loud all the time. It was mighty fine to ride around in a '55 Chevy with not just a shitload of Bondo in it after a good rain and listen to those throaty pipes. He'd gone ahead and gotten his inspection sticker with regular mufflers out at Gateway one Saturday and then almost immediately changed to glasspacks in the parking lot of AutoZone on Rusty's lunch hour with Rusty helping him and eating a sandwich at the same time, sometimes holding the entire sandwich in his mouth while he reached for tools, put it up on some jack stands and it only took about seventeen minutes to change both of them out, and now it was pretty throaty. It just kind of lugged a little going from second to fourth. It was aggravating not to have third gear. You had to get up some speed going up hills. He needed to see about that transmission down at Bruce. It might even have a Hurst shifter with it. He wondered how much a complete rolled-and-pleated interior would cost him. No telling. How fine would that be, though? Say blue and white. With those little speckles of glitter in it? Have some matching floor mats. Get some of those big foam dice to hang from the rearview. He knew Jimmy needed to get his teeth fixed. He didn't know how much that was going to cost. Or if they could even afford it. They probably couldn't. He shouldn't eat all that candy. Little shit.

He finished the beer in his hand and threw the empty out the window, then reached to the cooler in the floorboard for a fresh one. Popped the top. Took a drink. Set it between his legs. Reached into the pack in his pocket for a fresh cigarette. Lit it. Turned his parking lamps on and the dash lights didn't come on. What the hell. Son of a bitch. He bumped the dash with his hand and they flickered. Then they came on.

Then they went off. He hit it again. They came on. They went off. Son of a bitch. He hit it again and they flickered. He hit it twice and they came on and then went back off. Piece of *shit!* He heard a horn blaring right in front of him and looked up and saw that he was about to be hit by a big pickup head-on and swerved widely, almost going into the ditch, veering, almost sinking into the soft shoulder, then straightening and fishtailing back out of the ditch, mud on the tires making it slide in the road squealing until he got it back under control, and the pickup, real big, jacked way up, lots of lights, rolled on up the hill past him, red lights fading and climbing. Some damn kid probably. The road was full of them and some of them were barely big enough to see over the steering wheel. Where the hell did they come from? He'd be damned if Jimmy was going to run up and down the road like that burning gas. All these kids had it too soft these days, their parents buying them pickups left and right. If Jimmy wanted a pickup he'd have to work for it. Just like Jimmy's daddy did. In the sawmill with Halter Wellums. Digging five or six splinters out of his hands every day. Walking through the woods to work, walking through the woods back home. You probably couldn't find a kid who would do that now.

Damn that was close. Too close. Like to had a head-on collision. With some kid. He needed to get some insurance on this son of a gun. Get some collision anyway. Comprehensive would be a lot better, but that shit was high. He couldn't really afford it. But he sure needed it. Just in case something happened. Damn that was close. Little bastard like to smeared him all over the road.

Jimmy's daddy calmed back down and drank some more beer and cruised by a turf field and some woods and a place in the road where there was a big pipe that ran under the road. Through the big pipe an endless stream of cold spring water poured, and there was a deep pool off to the left of the road that everybody called the Cold Hole, and he'd seen kids swimming there, and he thought what he ought to do was bring Jimmy down here sometime, get a few of his buddies, maybe Rusty and Seaborn, ice down some beer, ride around a little, then bring Jimmy down here and throw him in. Let him sink or swim. That's the way his old man did him. And he nearly drowned, yeah, but he learned how to swim, didn't he? Jimmy could do the same thing. Kids were kids.

People were people. He wondered how deep that old guy's pond had wound up being. He might walk over there one day and see. That old man was probably senile. Probably went to bed with the chickens. Probably slept like a dead man. Probably be easy to sneak in.

He drank some more beer and listened to some more music and stopped and took a piss in the middle of the road and then rode through a little creek bottom and up a hill and around a curve. He wondered if there were any wild hogs running loose down on the levee tonight. He thought he'd ride down there and see. He'd already seen two big ones, one a huge and hairy black tusker with a ridge down his back, and last summer he'd found three dead wild baby piglets in the road somebody had run over, one of them cut half in two by a tire, the head and two front legs and part of the chest and some guts on one side of the road and the back legs and some guts and the little bitty curly tail on the other, and he'd stopped and picked them up and looked at them, the two whole ones, anyway, and wondered if they were fresh enough to maybe eat, but he figured that with roadkill pork you didn't want to take any chances, because it might have already turned bad, and then somebody had come along while he was standing there holding one of them by the leg and had given him a weird look, and he'd only taken one of them home, just to show Jimmy, and then Jimmy had turned out to be in town getting some tennis shoes and a swimsuit with his mother, so then he'd thrown it off the bridge down below the trailer and didn't even get to show it to Jimmy. Buzzards ate it probably. [. . .]

He wondered what was the matter with Johnette's ass. Ill as a damn hornet here lately. Hell, she wasn't going through menopause, was she? She was too young for that, wasn't she? Hell, she wasn't but thirty-five. But his cousin had to have that hysterectomy when she was thirty. Was all messed up inside, the doctor said. He didn't want any more kids anyway. It was hell to keep them fed, the ones he had. Damn they could eat some stuff. Ate something all the time. Chips and dip, couldn't keep that around. Cokes, couldn't keep them around. Hot dogs, couldn't keep them around. Ice cream, couldn't keep that around. They wouldn't eat vegetables very much, so you could keep them around. Asparagus? Naw. Squash? Wouldn't touch it. Now Jimmy liked a homegrown tomato sandwich. Jimmy's daddy had taught him that, how to make one, showed him how to peel the tomatoes, slice them up, put a little salt on them, spread the mayonnaise on the bread, fixed two one day, gave Jimmy one, poured him a glass of cold milk, sat down in the living room with him and ate and watched wrestling on TV. He didn't get enough times like that with Jimmy, and he didn't mean to stay so damn busy, or be gone riding around like this, drinking either by himself or with Rusty, but it just seemed like too much to stand being cooped up in that trailer with them all the time. It was nice to get out. A man who worked had to get out some. *Deserved* to get out some. This beer was cold as hell. Jimmy's daddy's daddy loved him a cold beer, too. He guessed he needed to go see the old fucker sometime. Old hardass. Still smoking them damned old Camels. Drinking that damned old Heaven Hill. He needed to take Jimmy when he went, he guessed. Let him see the old fucker. Shit. Jimmy hardly knew him. And whose fault was that? It wasn't Jimmy's daddy's. It was Jimmy's daddy's daddy's. He didn't have to sit over there in the woods by himself all the time like a hermit. Walk up and down the road picking up cans.

He rode over a few ridges and then around a few more curves and he saw a pair of green eyes up in a tree and slowed down and looked and saw a raccoon up in a persimmon tree eating green persimmons. He burped. He didn't want any green persimmons. Jimmy's daddy's daddy had talked Jimmy's daddy into biting into one one day and he still remembered how it puckered his mouth and how the awful, bitter taste wouldn't go away for a long time. He never had understood why his daddy had done that to him. And then laughed like hell. He went around another curve and crossed a narrow bridge and went up a hill where some young oaks were growing on each side and the road was so lumpy with repair patches that the '55 bumped even with its new shocks all the way around.

Okay, he shouldn't have married her. Big mistake. Now what? Keep on staying with her or get the fuck out? What did they ever do together? Went over to Algoma, that was about it. And that cost the shit out of money. Spend money. Spend money. That was all she thought about. Working at the bank she ought to make some money since they had all the money. He didn't even like to go in there. Hardly ever did. He didn't like to write checks or have to screw around with an account. He didn't like to be around people who dressed better than he did and probably thought they were better than him.

He wondered what the hell she was doing. Evelyn said she'd gone out with some people from the bank. Some thing she had to go to. Probably a meeting. She had to go to things sometimes, things the bank had. Meetings. Dinners. He didn't know what all. He knew they went out and had drinks sometimes, and that always chapped his ass. She needed to be home with the kids. Yep. That was her job.

He'd tried to call Rusty earlier but he hadn't been home. Probably out at Applebee's eating supper and drinking beer. Rusty went out there a good bit and he knew the bartender out there. Jimmy's daddy had been out there before but it cost money to go out there, too. Married people who worked for a living couldn't eat out like that all the time. Johnette was always bitching that they didn't go out enough to eat. Or at least she used to. She didn't bitch about much anymore. Not like she used to. She seemed sometimes like she'd calmed down a little bit, but that probably wasn't too hard to figure out. She was probably smoking the hell out of that damn shit again. He'd tried to talk to Rusty about it a few times and tell him about all the problems he had with her, but Rusty didn't seem to know what to say about all of it. He'd never been married. He had it made. He could take his paycheck and spend it on whatever he wanted to, wood for a boat or a new 7 mm Mag or a four-wheeler—damn, Jimmy would like one of those, wouldn't he?—and he didn't have to put up with all the shit that Jimmy's daddy had to put up with. Rusty was a bachelor. And Jimmy's daddy remembered when he used to be a bachelor. He had it made back then. Could go out with all the women he wanted to and spend his paycheck on whatever he wanted to. And then he met Johnette with Rusty and Seaborn over at Tupelo at the Gun and Knife Show.

They were hunting for a Henry Golden Boy .17 caliber rifle and she was looking for a pistol because she was a single mother. A divorced mother, actually. They'd helped her pick out a good pistol and then they'd all gone out for beers at the Rib Cage. Turned out her family was from down at Bruce. And yeah, she had two kids. He remembered when he saw them for the first time a long time ago. Both of them cute as hell. Hard to keep from hugging them. He remembered when he used to go over to Johnette's trailer when she was still living down on Old 6, all the nights he'd spent there, back in her bedroom after she'd put the kids to sleep, and then she'd gotten pregnant. Just because he hadn't used a rubber one night. Just because they'd started messing around and she'd gotten hot and before he knew it he had it in her and she'd had her hot thighs wrapped around him and it felt so good he didn't want to stop, and he had gone ahead, and now look where he was. Married to a fatass bitch who wouldn't even stay home and take care of her kids. But he had Jimmy. He had him. He shouldn't have whipped him so hard. Just because he got into his tools. But he wouldn't have whipped him so hard if he hadn't accidentally crushed John Wayne Payne. But he did. Mashed the living shit out of him. [. . .]

He wondered where her fat ass really was.

Probably not out fucking anybody. That was one thing he didn't have to worry about. He knew nobody was shucking his corn. No sir. And she used to be so damn fine. He could hardly get over it, how time changed somebody's ass from fine to not fine.

But he had to admit that he liked his mother-in-law pretty good. Carol was okay. Hell, she'd drink a beer or two with you. If she'd been twenty years younger he probably would have wanted to fuck her. She had a nice ass for an older woman.

He sipped some more, rode some more. And then he got to thinking about selling Jimmy's spear point for fifty bucks of beer back in the spring and felt bad all over again. He wondered if the guy he'd sold it to would sell it back. On the other hand, Jimmy could probably find another one sometime. So he stopped thinking about it. If you wanted to get technical it was just a rock anyway.

20

Jimmy's daddy was about six or seven. He lived then in an old rotted house that leaned slightly to the right, a two-story dogtrot of unpainted boards on the sides and rusted tin on the roof. His daddy was already bad to drink and he was sometimes dangerous to be around because he was likely to hit if you did something that made him mad. Jimmy's daddy didn't want to get up on the stump that day because he was afraid something would happen, like maybe getting hit. The stump was in the backyard by the cistern where they caught rainwater and the stump stuck up six or seven feet high, and it had been left from where some men had sawed it off after a storm came through and tore off most of the big elm's limbs.

He didn't want to get up there, but he did because his daddy told him to. His daddy was standing beside the stump and he was holding a pint bottle of whisky in his hand. Jimmy's daddy climbed not easily up on the stump and then he stood there. His daddy had his arms open, one hand holding the whisky.

"Jump to me, son," he said.

"Jump?" Jimmy's daddy said.

"Jump," his daddy said.

Jimmy's daddy stood there and thought about it. What if he jumped and his daddy moved? But surely his daddy wouldn't move. Would he? He was going to catch him, wasn't he? But what if he hit him in the head with that whisky bottle when he caught him? That wasn't going to feel too good. What if it broke?

"Jump," his daddy said.

Jimmy's daddy stood there. He wanted to jump. He didn't want to jump. He knew he was going to *have* to jump, but that didn't make it any easier. He didn't want to get hit in the head with that whisky bottle. And he didn't want to get a whipping for not jumping. He tried to avoid whippings at all cost because his daddy sometimes went a little crazy when he was whipping him and it was like he lost control of himself for a few minutes and it turned into a beating.

"You gonna catch me?" Jimmy's daddy asked his daddy on that day so long ago.

"Jump to me, son," his daddy said again.

Jimmy's daddy was six or seven. His mother sewed patches on his pants because they couldn't afford new pants for him. He got shoes only when he completely wore out the ones he had. He was sneaking butts out of his mother's ashtrays already. And he was more afraid of his daddy than anything else in the world. So he jumped. And his daddy moved out of the way.

Jimmy's daddy hit the ground hard. He landed on his chest and it knocked the breath out of him and he hurt his arm. He hurt his arm so badly that he started crying. He looked up at his daddy and his daddy told him something. His daddy told him: "There. Now that'll teach you not to trust nobody."

21

It was late, and Tommy was working at his desk in the barn in Arkansas. It was dusty and quiet in there, and they had lots of cats for the rats that came for the fish feed. Audrey had already gone to sleep, and he was working on his bills and making some payments, things that had to be taken care of, feed and fish fertilizer and paychecks for the boys who worked for him and gas bills and oxygen bills and plastic bag bills. It was all squared away for another month. He didn't know what he'd do after that. If he could have just hit that damn seven on that last roll last weekend. But he hadn't. And that was some shit he didn't even need to waste time thinking about, because he hadn't hit it, and he was still down by $137,000, and nothing was going to change that fact. He wasn't going to sell $137,000 worth of fish in the next month. He'd be lucky if he sold ten. Summer was almost over. People didn't stock many fish over the winter. He didn't even raise many fish over the winter, just enough to keep the brood stock going and some Florida bass that he sold to people down in Florida. The busy season for him was almost over. Pretty soon it would slow down. And he'd have the whole winter to take care of things, do maintenance, try to find a way not to gamble. He'd probably have to let Bob and Barry go. Maybe even Bill. He hated to. Bill had been with him a long time.

He didn't want to kill himself. Had no desire to. He'd known people who had and he'd never understood it. If you killed yourself, your life was over. Last chance. But sometimes it seemed there wasn't any other way out. He didn't see any way out of this. Except bankruptcy. And that meant starting all over. He was too old to start over. He was fifty-seven. He ought to be thinking about retiring instead of all this bullshit. Hell. A man got old and tired. He got tired of the things that happened to him on his job. He'd lost count of the times he'd been finned by catfish, but he remembered the worst ones. The one that got him all the way through the thumb that day in Hot Springs. The one he stepped on that day in Batesville, Mississippi, and drove the fin up under his big toenail. He had very nearly shit on himself for real when that one happened. But hell. Everybody had something on their job to worry about. Firemen risked getting burned up. Ironworkers had to deal with the reality of falling to their deaths. Getting finned was a part of Tommy's life. You just tried to minimize it as much as you could. It helped to wear leather gloves.

He had a roll of stamps on his desk and he pulled them out and peeled some off and stuck them to the envelopes for the bills and bundled them all together with a rubber band so that he could take them down to the mailbox in the morning and get them on their way. He could operate for another month. He could go that long. And then. Well shit.

He wasn't dead yet. And if you weren't dead there was always hope, wasn't there?

He stood up and gathered the outgoing bills in his hand and turned off the light over his desk and stepped across the floor he'd laid himself in what had been an old tack room, and turned off the lights in the hall of the barn, and then, like he always did, he stepped back there where the big round tank sat bubbling in the semidark, with only one dim and dusty bulb burning above it, and he stepped up to the side of it, and laid his hand on the cool rim of the concrete curbing that he'd poured himself, and looked down. And she was there. Like always. Floating in the dark water, her fins slowly and gently waving, about a foot off the bottom.

He was very fond of her. She was responsible for everything he had built up, everything he had made. She was almost like some kind of greatgreatgreatgreatgreatgreatgreatgreatgreatgreatgreatgreatgreatgrandmother. How many millions had she caused to be hatched, and how widely spread were they across this whole country, from New Mexico to New Hampshire? And what would happen to her if he went under? How did he know somebody might not wind up just butchering her and eating her? He didn't want that to happen. If he went under, he wouldn't let that happen. He'd turn her loose somewhere first. Some pond out in the country somewhere, some quiet lake. He didn't know where. He could find some place to turn her loose where at least she'd have the chance not to be caught. Or to tear loose if she was hooked. Whoever hung her would have to have some good strong line, at least thirty-pound test, and a good rod and reel, and would have to know how to use the drag. No lucky kid with a cane pole was going to catch her. She'd snap a cane pole. He stood there and envisioned slipping her out of the tank somehow, maybe with a hoist, and hauling her on the truck, and putting her in some dark pond in the middle of one night.

Kind of like turning an old horse out to pasture.

But then there wasn't really any need of thinking about that. Because he wasn't going under. He was going to do something that would pull them out. He didn't know what yet. He'd been trying to think of something specific to pull them out for a long time, but nothing had come to mind. He'd bought some lottery tickets, knowing he was throwing money away. But that was nothing new, throwing money away. *Don't bet the baby shoe money.* Somebody had told him that a long time ago but he couldn't remember who it was now. It might have been his great-uncle LaVert, who'd been dead for over forty years, who had already been old when he'd first come to know him. He still remembered going into his house walled with raw planks on the top of Crowley's Ridge and seeing a bunch of fuzzy yellow chicks in the living room, huddled in a washtub pulled up close to the wood-burning stove, a lightbulb hanging low from the ceiling to help keep them warm, the house filled with their cheeping, owls hooting out in the woods behind the house when he slept in the back bedroom that was always cold because they didn't run the gas heater back there.

So many of his people were gone now. They had all slipped away from him one by one. He wished LaVert could have seen this fish.

He stood there for a while longer, looking down at her, wondering what he was going to do with her. But he'd think of something. He'd have to. He couldn't lose all this. It was unthinkable. Wasn't it?

Ursula. He remembered when he caught her, when she weighed only twenty pounds. She bit a piece of Rod 'n' Reel shrimp. Horsed her in after only about ten minutes on his old solid glass two-piece rod and his [. . .] Zebco 33. But he had new line on it. Thirty-pound test. And he knew how to work his drag. That was a long time ago.

"Take it easy, old girl," he said, and left.

22

The air over the Cold Hole felt hot as Jimmy sailed through it, briefly, for one unforgettable moment of his life, in his new dry swimming suit, the leaves in their trees overhead lending shade down on the rippling pool of water, the edges lapping at the little rocks that lined the pool, the water steadily pouring through the big pipe that ran under the road from the cold spring up the hill. As he plunged into it headfirst and drawn up, crablike, he couldn't help but yell. What? He didn't know. Something. *Umyammahokaywhee!* Then he was under. Drowning his ass off. Mouth full of cold muddy water and gulping more down. He clawed his way to the top and spit it out and took a deep breath, trying to spot his daddy, or call out for help, but he didn't know how to swim or kick his legs correctly and he soon went under again, mouth full of water, swallowing some, coughing, and then he clawed his way back up. His hair was plastered down over his forehead. He felt the doom of death closing over him on such a sunny day. He could hear his daddy yelling something. He knew they were up there on the road above him, drinking beer, his daddy and Mister Rusty and Mister Seaborn, where they'd been standing for a couple of minutes, before his daddy had thrown him in, but he couldn't see much for the water in his eyes and then he was going under again. The water was very cold and he didn't know how deep the pool was, but he didn't touch bottom. Nobody had given him any instructions about holding his breath, but he'd seen some scuba diving on TV one night and thought to pinch his nose closed. Only thing was, now he couldn't seem to get back to the top. He was just hanging under the surface, clawing rapidly at the water with one hand and his air was running out. He knew there were people in distant lands who lived around distant oceans and could dive for pearls or oysters or sponges or tourists, but he just couldn't seem to get back up. He knew his daddy was going to be disappointed, and he tried to get back to the top. Plus he needed another breath of air before he died. But he just couldn't seem to do it. He held his breath as long as he could and then he had to let it out. And when he did, the only natural thing was to draw in another breath, but his mouth filled with water, and he sucked some into his lungs, and then he knew he'd messed up. He felt himself sinking. He heard two big splashes above him. Then the cold cold black closed in. And, for just a few moments, Jimmy died for the first time.

[. . .]

When Jimmy came back to life, his head was on the rough pavement of the road and some people he didn't know had pulled their cars over and were standing around. He was coughing and he was surprised to be alive since he'd been pretty sure he was going to be dead. Mister Rusty was soaking wet and pulling back from him, kind of hovering over him, and Jimmy couldn't get all the water coughed out of his lungs fast enough. He gagged some, too, and tried to puke, but just strings of thick watery stuff came out and that was all. Then he looked over to the left and saw some chunks of the hot dogs he'd eaten for lunch lying in the road beside him. Had evidently puked while unconscious. He didn't know you could do that. He gagged some. He gagged some more and said, *A . . . A . . . Ack!*

He coughed some more and tried to sit up, and then his daddy was kneeling beside him, dry, with a beer in his hand. His daddy put his hand on Jimmy's shoulder. Jimmy's lips felt mashed, his nose pinched.

"Boy," he said. "You all right?"

Mister Rusty looked more than a little pissed when he turned his head to Jimmy's daddy.

"Hell naw, he ain't all right, you like to fucking drowned him."

Jimmy's daddy had some kind of look on his face that Jimmy couldn't say what was. He never had seen him look like that before. He wondered if he was still mad at him about the tools. Then he went dizzy for a moment. It was all too much for his head. [. . .]

Later on, Jimmy was in the backseat of the '55, and they were going down the road passing some turf fields and a big green pump. Pallets piled up in the corners of the fields. Sage grass at the edges of the woods. Jimmy was lying on a wet towel and his head was wet and his hair, his swimming suit. First time he'd worn it besides trying it on after he got it home. He coughed and turned over. The insides of the car smelled like they were rotted and his stomach felt like it was full of water. He wanted to puke but he didn't think he could.

Up front, his daddy at the wheel glanced over his shoulder and said, "How you doing there, Hot Rod?"

Mister Rusty turned his head to look at him, as well as Mister Seaborn, who was sitting in between them. Mister Seaborn had recently had two of his front teeth knocked out by a skunk that made him fall down.

"I'm okay," Jimmy said. He wasn't really okay, but he thought he'd better say that. He didn't want to get his daddy upset any more than he already was.

"You need to stop and throw up?" Jimmy's daddy said. He was still glancing over his shoulder.

"Better watch the goddang road there, Sweet Pea," Mister Seaborn said, and lifted his beer. It made a sucking sound when he drank from it.

"I'm watching the damn road," Jimmy's daddy said. "Say you all right?" Jimmy's daddy turned his head back toward the front after he said that, but Mister Seaborn and Mister Rusty kept looking at him and drinking beer. They were both kind of halfway turned around facing him. Mister Seaborn was wet, too. His hair was plastered down, too, but now in the wind that came through the windows of the '55, sprigs of it were starting to dry out and float around his red balding head.

"I guess so," Jimmy said.

"How you feel?" Mister Seaborn said.

"Kinda sick," Jimmy said.

Mister Seaborn took a drink of his beer. Jimmy's daddy took a drink of his beer. Mister Seaborn said, "Well, I got a good reason for asking. I went to school with a boy that drowned one time. Drowned in his swimming pool. Right there at home. Stayed down about thirty minutes fore anybody seen him. He was cold as a mackerel when they pulled him out. Dead as a damn doornail."

"Maybe it was one of them cold-water drownings," Mister Rusty said. "I've heard of them before."

Mister Seaborn looked like he didn't appreciate Mister Rusty interrupting him. He turned to him briefly.

"Hell naw, it wasn't no cold-water drowning," Mister Seaborn said. "It was a fucking swimming pool. In August."

"Oh," Mister Rusty said.

"How deep was the damn water?" Jimmy's daddy said.

Mister Seaborn didn't turn around or answer Jimmy's daddy because he was focused on Jimmy, and Jimmy was paying attention because hardly anybody ever focused on him and he liked it. He wished more people would focus on him more often.

"And see, back then, they didn't know nothing about all this mouth-to-mouth shit like Rusty done on you. They used to have to like pump your arms up and down. Like this here, up and down. They had to pump all that water out of his lungs and he said when he woke up he felt so damn bad he wished they'd just gone on and let him die. Hell, he was already dead. Dead as a damn doornail. So my question to you is, you feel like that? You wish you'd just gone ahead and died?"

"No sir, I don't reckon," Jimmy said. "I was hoping maybe we'd get to go see Kenny Chesney in Tupelo next month." He looked at his daddy.

That must not have been the answer Mister Seaborn was looking for. He took another drink of his beer and then looked at Jimmy again.

"Well, did you see any of that big white light at the end of a tunnel like they say folks see when they have a near-death experience?"

"No sir, I don't reckon so," Jimmy said. "It just looked muddy."

"See anybody dead you knew, like your great-granddaddy?"

"Aw shit, leave him alone, Seaborn," Jimmy's daddy said. "He feels bad enough as it is."

Mister Rusty turned back around and lit a cigarette. Jimmy sat up in the seat. He coughed a little. Mister Seaborn reached out and patted him on the back, not unkindly. Then he turned back around, too.

"Why don't you send him to the YMCA?" he asked Jimmy's daddy. "They could teach him how to swim."

"Where's a YMCA at around here, dumbass?" Jimmy's daddy said.

"They got one in Memphis," Mister Seaborn said.

"Memphis?" Jimmy's daddy said. "You know how far away that is?"

"Hell yes, it's seventy-five miles," Mister Rusty said.

"It's closer to seventy-eight if you go up Seventy-eight," Mister Seaborn said with a mild chuckle.

"Why don't you get him in the Cub Scouts?" Mister Rusty said. "I think they teach kids how to swim. I know they teach em how to camp out. Start a fire with rocks. All that shit."

"I'll teach him how to swim myself," Jimmy's daddy said. Then he said: "I don't know why it didn't work. It worked for me."

Mister Rusty leaned forward and said, "So, your old man just pitched your ass in and you come up swimming like a duck."

"Hell naw," Jimmy's daddy said. He nodded toward Jimmy in the backseat. "I looked about like he did. They had to come in and get me, too. Four times. They just kept on throwing my little ass in. I didn't have the heart to do it to him."

"Each generation gets weaker," Mister Seaborn said.

"That's the damn truth," Jimmy's daddy said.

Then Mister Rusty said something that was pretty amazing. "Me and you would've fought if you'd throwed him in again."

And everything got a little quieter. The '55 slowed. They passed a guy in the ditch with a garbage bag picking up cans.

"Is that right?" Jimmy's daddy said.

"Yeah, that's right," Mister Rusty said.

"Aw-right now, boys," Mister Seaborn said.

"He ain't your kid, Rusty. He's my kid."

"I know whose kid he is. It ain't right to throw him in like that and him not knowing how to swim. Shit. His heart could have stopped or something. Happens to these kids playing football."

Jimmy's daddy thought it over for a few moments.

"Yeah, it does," he finally said. He turned his head briefly to speak to Jimmy. He looked embarrassed. Jimmy didn't see him look that way very often. He only looked that way whenever he made a mistake.

"Don't tell your mama I throwed you in, all right?"

"No sir, I won't," Jimmy said.

"Raises hell about every damn thing already," Jimmy's daddy said.

Things were quiet for a few more moments. Then Mister Seaborn said, kind of murmured, "Where's that big lake up here got all them bass in it?"

Jimmy's daddy took a drink of his beer.

"It's right on up the road here. He won't let you fish in it, though."

"How you know? You done asked him?"

"Everybody in the country's asked him."

"I heard it's got some big bass in it," Mister Seaborn said.

"Hell yes," Jimmy's daddy said. "Crappie, too."

"I thought crappie wouldn't live in a pond," Mister Seaborn said.

"This ain't a pond," Jimmy's daddy said. "It's a lake."

"How big?" Mister Seaborn said.

"About sixty acres," Jimmy's daddy said. "It's a watershed lake. Government built it about three years ago."

"We could go down on the river and fish," Mister Seaborn said.

"Yeah, if you want to get a bunch of ticks all over you," Mister Rusty said. "Last time I went down there I come back with about fifty on me. Them little bitty ones? Them deer ticks?"

"That's the ones carries that Lyme disease," Jimmy's daddy said.

"That's right," Mister Seaborn said. "I saw it on TV."

Mister Rusty said, "My uncle when he was in World War II was in a infantry company in Texas somewhere and they went out on a bivouac one night and he set his pup tent or whatever it was up in a big grove of pine trees and he got so many ticks on him he even had one go up inside his *dick*."

"Ummmhhhhh!" Jimmy's daddy said.

"Sheeeit!" Mister Seaborn said.

"Hell yeah. Doctor had to take some tweezers and go up in there and get it. He said he like to shit on his self."

They shuddered some more and they all took a drink of their beer and Jimmy just sat in the back on the wet towel and listened to them. He didn't ask any questions or try to interrupt whenever they were talking because he was so well trained about how to act around grown-ups. He could sit there for hours while grown-ups were talking and never say a word. Which is what he did again, riding in the backseat while they kept drinking beer, his wet swimming suit getting colder as the sun went down.

But he was also glad to be alive, and counted himself as very lucky, so he didn't say anything about being cold. He didn't ask them to roll up the windows. It seemed a small price to pay and eventually they'd go back home. There were plenty more hot dogs at home. If Evelyn and Velma hadn't eaten all of them already. Evelyn could eat about six by herself. Raw.

23

[. . .] Out in the barn, there wasn't any light at all except for a kerosene lantern that was hanging by a piece of coat-hanger wire over a wobbly table that held a tray with tools and things, and Cortez Sharp's gun. He was cleaning it. He'd had it a long time. It still worked fine. He shot it only a few times a year since it made so much noise. Plus he didn't want anybody to know he had it because he was pretty sure it was still illegal for him to have it. He didn't want anybody coming over and trying to take it away from him. Somebody would play hell doing that. If there was more than one of them there'd be more than one would play hell.

The wind had stopped sighing through the cracks with the coming of dark. He raised his head from his work and listened, seated at the little table, the faint chirping of crickets leaking through the plank walls. Everything was singing tonight after the rain, frogs in the trees and frogs in the creek, frogs in the grass and frogs in the gravel. And the air smelled different. On it floated all kinds of scents, cow shit and green clover and dried hay from up in the loft and old fertilizer stacked in damp bags in darkened corners and burned oil saved for keeping in milk jugs on the floor of the barn.

Cortez liked cleaning his gun. He cleaned it three times a year whether it needed it or not, and it never had let him down. Never had jammed, never had rusted, never had misfired, never had gotten so hot it cooked off a round in the chamber, never had done anything but exactly what Mister Thompson had designed it to do: shoot and shoot some more.

He wished he could shoot it tonight. Boy, he wished he could shoot it tonight. It would be a good night to shoot it if it wasn't so dark you couldn't see anything. If it wasn't so loud it would probably wake her up. If she was asleep. He hoped she was. She didn't sleep much. Moaned when she did. Like she was having bad dreams. She probably was. They were probably about Raif. He hoped his were over. About him. They seemed to be. He hadn't had one in a long time.

He picked up a gun rag from the tray. It was soft with the grease and oil that had soaked into it over the years and it was limper than a dishrag. He picked up a small plastic squeeze bottle of Remington Rem Oil and squeezed some of it onto the cloth. He also had a spray can of Rusty Duck Premium Gun Action Cleaner. He also had a spray can of Birchwood Casey Gun Scrubber. Some folks would put WD-40 on a gun but not him. Oh, it made one slick and shiny, sure, for a while, but that shit evaporated later and left you without a thin coating of protective oil. Left you high and dry, buddy. That's when they started rusting. They'd rust right there in the gun cabinet. You had to oil a gun. You had to take care of it. You had to love it. A gun loved oil the way a goat loved a gourd.

And Cortez loved this one. He'd owned it for so long that he'd developed a deep fondness for it. And who knew? How did you know that one day you wouldn't be surrounded by government agents with guns intent on taking you away? You didn't. You didn't know from one day to the next what the hell was going to happen with the way the country was going now. Hell, look what they'd done in New York City and Washington. Just flew some airplanes right into a bunch of buildings. Killed all them people. Lucinda flew up there and looked at it. He didn't know why. He didn't want to look at it. The damn world was crazy and sometimes he was not afraid to know that he was somewhere near the end of his life. Maybe. Hell, who knew? He might make it to a hundred. His granddaddy did. Only had one arm. Lost it at Shiloh. Blind, too. He'd been ninety when Cortez was born and Cortez could remember him sitting in a cane-bottomed chair in front of the fire, spitting his snuff at the edge of the bricks, his long white beard stained with snuff juice. He sat there rubbing the gun with the oily rag, in the little circle of light, with straw scattered around, the air still and laden with the rain and the night things calling out there down by the creek. It had rained more than a couple of inches, and the forecast was for more of the same. That sounded pretty good to him. He thought maybe if it would rain for four or five days in a row, it might fill the pond maybe halfway up. He would have gone over this evening and looked if it hadn't rained for so long, and if it hadn't been so muddy. He needed some new ground grips on his truck but he just never had gotten around to getting them put on yet. It didn't matter. He could walk over through the woods in the morning. Put on his rubber boots. See how deep the water was in it. And he needed to ask Toby sometime when was the next time the big red fish truck was coming. He didn't want to get behind. He wanted to be there waiting in line when the pond was ready and the fish truck was in town.

He had a little linseed oil in another can and he unscrewed the metal cap from it and poured some of it on a clean piece of cheesecloth and rubbed some on the stock, sliding the gun across the padded surface of the wobbly table, watching the scratched and dented wood shine under the kerosene lamp. He rubbed some on the fore end as well. Then he put the rag down and pulled the gun over in his lap.

He opened the bolt and checked the tension on it, watching it slam shut when he let it slip off his finger. The round canister clip was sitting there and he stuck it into the belly of the gun and opened the bolt again, watched the brass-cased slug slide up out of rotation, and he let the bolt slip again, sending one into the chamber. He sat there with it on his lap, pointed up. The muzzle had little grooves cut into the end of it to let the excess gases out. It was just like the ones they used to have on *The Untouchables,* that old TV show. Eliott Ness. Now that was a good TV show. Not like this stupid shit now. He put it to his shoulder, aimed at a bag of feed, almost touching the trigger. Then he put the safety on and got up with it. Fully loaded.

He reached up and lifted the kerosene lantern from the coat-hanger hook and used it to light his way to one of the back stalls. His shadow loomed large around him as he walked, throwing scant light into dark corners, the lantern swinging in his hand, the gun heavy with its belly full of lead.

The harness room had a cobwebbed wooden door and Cortez pushed the sliding latch aside and opened it. He stepped up into a walled box that held leather mule collars, his wife's old cracked sidesaddle spewing its stuffing, some singletrees hanging by nails from the walls, and an old trunk of the kind people used to haul around on steamships and trains. He knelt and set the lantern down and opened the trunk.

He started to put the Thompson inside, in the top tray, but then set the gun on the boards of the floor and lifted out the tray instead. It was full of old things: rusted red-and-white bass plugs, a rusted bayonet that was still sharp. He tested its edge with his thumb. Last time he'd used it was to stab a deer to death. Dried blood still showed on the blade. He set it back and looked around in the tray. He always did. There was a small tobacco sack and he lifted it out. The strings that pouched its mouth he drew open with his fingers. And reached in. Caught hold of the chain and drew it out, then the locket followed it. His knees were hurting, so he sat down. The white gold glowed dimly in the wavering light from the lantern, and he heard an owl hoot down in the woods. The chain was supple in his fingers. The cool of the metal. Money he'd spent on her himself. At Elliott's on the square. He didn't need to open the locket. He didn't need to look at what was in it again. But he'd known all along that he would. And he did.

She looked like she always had, smiling stiffly, standing in a South Carolina photographer's parlor in 1946. Just before she moved here to be with her mother and help her work for Cortez's mother. Just down the road. At fourteen. He said to himself, *I loved a nigger. Damn me but I did.*

Cortez sat there for a long time, silent, studying her image, knowing his wife was probably sitting in her wheelchair in the blue glow of the television, wondering where he was. He closed the locket, stuck it back in its little bag, dropped it back in the tray. And started to set it back in there, and then put the gun away, but he didn't. He set the tray aside, and reached into the bottom of the trunk, and pulled a folded quilt up out of the way, and pulled out the long robe. It was yellowing now, and starting to rot, and he brought it closer to his nose, and it still smelled faintly of wood smoke. And pine tar. Maybe even blood. He couldn't tell.

He looked at the once-white hood, its eyepieces making it a vacant mask. It had been a long time since he'd worn it. And he knew he'd never wear it again. Why then did he keep it around? He didn't know. Maybe the same reason he kept the locket. To have something to hold on to. A man needed something to hold on to, even in this world today, which had certainly gone straight to hell.

He sighed, something he hardly ever did. He was hungry and he didn't know if there was anything good to eat in the house. He could have a peanut butter sandwich he guessed. Or a tomato sandwich.

Except he'd fixed one of those for lunch. He could fry some bacon to put on it maybe.

He put everything away and closed the lid of the trunk and shoved it back under the pile of empty feed bags and then scattered some of them over it again. He had money stashed in a bunch of places in the barn. Under bales of hay in fruit jars. Inside old feed bags in Calumet baking powder cans with plastic lids. Hidden from his wife. Inside the house, too. He didn't know how much. Enough.

He got the lantern and shut the door to the harness room and slid the latch closed again. He went out through the hall of the barn, his steps soft in the dry dirt and crushed bits of hay. He slipped out between the two big doors but left the crack open. Wasn't any need to close it. He'd be back out here tomorrow. He had a cow that needed a shot for her cough and he'd have to find the needle in all the shit he had stashed out here. No telling where it was. Then he'd have to get her in the chute and maybe tie her ass up. Sometimes he wished he had a head gate. It would make it a lot easier to fool with one. Especially for something like that. Maybe he ought to just go ahead and get one. He could stick a thermometer up his bull's ass if he had a head gate and there wouldn't be anything the bull could do about it except take it. He had a catalog in the house and he thought he could get a good one for about eight hundred. Then he'd have to get some big posts, dig some post holes, put the posts in the holes, get some concrete, mix it up, pour it in the holes, bolt the head gate to the posts once the concrete set up. It'd be a lot of trouble. Sure would make it a lot easier to give a cow a shot, though. They always liked to try and kick your head off when you did that to them.

The ground was muddy between the house and the barn. Cortez blew the lantern out before he got to the back porch, and he stopped and looked up. The sky was still cloudy and he was hoping the forecast was right. There was some faint rumbling far off in the sky, and he saw blooming yellow light somewhere a long way down the country toward the east. It was very dark. He set the lantern on the back step and went on in.

As soon as he looked at her he knew she was dead. The TV was still playing, and she was still sitting in front of it, but now she was leaned over sideways in the wheelchair, with one of her arms out at an odd angle, and just as still as could be. He leaned over and lowered the volume some.

He walked around in front of her and looked down at her. She was looking at nothing. She wasn't breathing. He could see her scalp plainly through the thin white hair on top of her head. She was seventy-six years old. She had been twenty-two when Cortez married her. And he was only eighteen then. She must have had another stroke.

There was a daybed in the front room and Cortez sat down on it. He glanced at the TV. That old woman with the sex show was telling somebody who had called in how to lubricate somebody with some jelly and Cortez wondered what flavor they used. He looked at his wife and reached out his hand to touch her on the arm. It was cool. He pulled his hand away. Well. She was gone. After all this time. She couldn't cuss him any more or call him to the house on her bullhorn. But now he'd have to bury her.

He didn't know who to call first, Lucinda or the funeral home. Maybe the sheriff's office? No. He didn't want them out here. But they might have to come take pictures. Seemed like they had to whenever somebody died at home. They didn't used to, but he thought now they did.

He wondered how long she'd been dead. He wondered how long he'd stayed out in the barn. Couple of hours. Reading some of those *Hustler* magazines again before he cleaned his gun. Piddling around looking at that stuff. But when was the last time he actually saw her alive? He tried to think. She was alive this afternoon around four, when he stopped in to get a handkerchief. Wasn't she? Hell, he didn't really know. The TV had been going. Which had always meant she was sitting there watching it. But how did he know she wasn't already dead then? He hadn't talked to her. She hardly ever turned around when he walked in the room anyway, so it was hard to say. She might have been dead since lunchtime, since he didn't actually talk to her at lunchtime, figuring she could roll her wheelchair into the kitchen and get something out and microwave it. She kept stuff you could microwave. Macaroni and cheese. Stuffed potato skins.

Why hell. What was the last thing she'd said, and when did she say it? He had to think. He came in here about the middle of the morning and she was alive then, he knew, because he told her he wished to hell it would rain, and she said he'd already said that about a million times and wished he'd shut up about it. And then she'd picked up the remote and flipped the channel over to *Bonanza*. It was one he'd seen before, the one where Hoss went temporarily blind, so he didn't watch it. He went on out into the garden and started picking tomato worms off his tomatoes and pulling suckers [. . .].

Hell. No telling when she died. She might have been dead since this morning. It was about eight o'clock now. If that was true, she might have been dead for ten hours. He touched her again to see if she was stiff. Only a little.

Shit. He didn't know what to do. The sheriff came out when all that happened with Raif. But that was a long time ago. God. Damn near forty years. He didn't know who to call. He'd have to go find Lucinda's number if he called her. And she might not be in. He thought she went out sometimes with that retard. She had an answering machine that usually answered if you called. He never had called much after he found out that she was living in Atlanta with a retard. Afraid he might answer.

And where was the damn number at? No telling. He'd have to look. He got up and walked over to the wall and flipped the switch to turn the overhead light on. His dead wife sat there in her chair. The bottoms of her legs were very dark. He looked at that and understood that it was blood that had drained from her upper body down. It was the same thing that happened to a pig when you hoisted him up by his hind feet and cut his throat, only he was upside down and all the blood ran the other way.

There was a table with a bunch of envelopes and junk mail and a small bound book he thought might hold phone numbers for various businesses and people, emergency numbers, that sort of thing. He never had looked through her stuff. A long time ago she used to order flower bulbs and seeds over the phone from some nursery up in Tennessee. He flipped open the book and started looking through it. He didn't have any idea what Lucinda was going to say. He knew they hadn't been real close. Not close like a mother and daughter ought to be. Lucinda rarely wrote. Rarely called. Didn't much want to come home for Christmas. Sometimes didn't. Just stayed in Atlanta with that retard. Had some excuse or other. And when they were here they made him nervous anyway, because that retard cussed something awful and sometimes he barked like a damn dog and his head jerked and his legs and his feet and he was just a blinking mess. No wonder they didn't have any grandchildren.

He found the old nursery numbers. Some of them had been scratched through. He found some recipes tucked into the pages, one for cat-head biscuits. He pulled that one out and laid it aside. He knew how to make gravy but he never had been able to make biscuits. She could, when she used to be able to cook and get around in the kitchen. Made good ones, too. For about fifty-four years. His wouldn't be worth a shit.

He raised his head and looked at her. And the phone rang. Loudly. Right beside him. Without even thinking he almost picked it up. But then he thought, *Hell, what if it's Lucinda?* It rang again, and he started to pick it up. It was probably just one of her friends. The other old biddies she talked to and checked on throughout the day. They called each other so much that Cortez had gotten to where he almost never answered the phone in his house. It rang again. He had his hand on it. Whoever was calling was going to hang up if he didn't answer it in a few more rings. It wouldn't be Lucinda, surely. Hell, she never called. It rang again and he picked it up.

"Hello?" he said.

"Hey, Daddy," Lucinda said.

"Oh," he said. *Oh crap.* "Uh. Hey."

"What are you doing?" she said. Sounded pretty happy.

"Not much," he said. He sat on the day bed. "Setting on the day bed."

He looked at the TV.

"Watching TV," he added.

He could hear some kind of music in there with Lucinda and he could hear what sounded like a bunch of people talking, too. He didn't know what he was going to say. He didn't know how he could tell her like this, unexpectedly, without being ready, exactly what was going on. He didn't know how to do that. He wasn't good on stuff like that. Never had been.

"Oh," she said. "Well, I just called to check on y'all. What's Mama up to?"

"She's done conked out on me," he said. Okay. There it was. She could pick up on it if she wanted to. But she didn't.

"Oh," Lucinda said. "Kind of early for her, isn't it? I thought she always stayed up half the night watching TV."

"I reckon she was wore out," he said.

"I got you," Lucinda said. Somebody laughed really loudly behind her and somebody else yelled something that sounded like *Bust it open, baby, just bust it open!* Lucinda said, "Well, I hate I missed her. I know I ought to call and check on her more. How's she been doing on that new medicine the doctor gave her?"

"She never did say."

"Tell her I called," Lucinda said.

"Is it hot in Atlanta?" Cortez said.

"Lord yes," Lucinda said. "It's been awful. Albert's gotten a really good tan working in the yard this summer. You and Mama should come visit sometime. You could get somebody to drive you to Memphis and it's only a one-hour flight. It's about fifty minutes, actually. I live ten minutes from the airport and I'd be right there to pick you up when you got off the plane. Albert would love to show you his new paintings."

"I ain't getting on no airplane," Cortez said.

"Oh, Daddy," Lucinda said. "There's nothing to it. I've taken Albert on flights with me before. You know if he can do it, you could, too."

"I thought he threw up on one one time."

"He just had a little bit of an upset tummy that day."

"Why don't you come over here?" Cortez said, not knowing what else to say, trying to decide what to do. It was kind of awkward over the phone like this, because you were having to juggle two things at once: keep up your end of the conversation by listening to whatever she was saying while at the same thing trying to figure out what the hell to do while she was talking. And then you had to come back with something, wham, bam! It didn't leave you enough time to think. He was kind of sorry he'd picked up the phone now. He could have just let it ring.

"I can't right now. We're just too busy. We're having a dinner party tomorrow night and we're getting ready for that. Albert's got a pretty bad cold and we're trying to get him over that. Maybe we can get over at Christmas and see y'all for a few days. Or maybe we could come over sometime around Thanksgiving."

"Well," Cortez said. He started to just go on and blurt it out, but he didn't think he could do that. He wished to hell she hadn't died right before Lucinda called. Lucinda hadn't called in about two months that he knew of. She might have called that he didn't know of. For all he knew his wife might have talked to her every day while he was out of the house because he stayed out of the house all he could. It was tougher in the winter. You could only sit in the barn so much without some kind of heat. It got cold as hell out there in the wintertime. Ice would freeze in a bucket. And in the cows' watering troughs. You had to take a hammer to it and bust it.

"What you been doing?" Lucinda said.

Cortez was glad for that question because he had a ready answer and had secretly been hoping that she'd ask him what he'd been doing. Besides killing flies on the front porch. And picking worms off his tomatoes. And listening to the damn TV screaming night and day like some unwanted houseguest he wasn't allowed to kill.

"I been waiting on my pond to fill up."

"Pond? You mean that old muddy thing down in the pasture the cows wade around in?"

"Naw. This is a new one. I just had it dug this summer. It's up on the hill."

"Whereabouts up on the hill?"

"Up there on the ridge by the road. Up there where all them big white oaks was."

"What did you do with the trees?"

"He bulldozed em down."

"Who did?"

"Newell Naramore."

"All those big white oaks?"

"Yep."

"Oh my God, Daddy. Do you know what that timber was worth?"

"I don't give a shit what it was worth. I wanted a pond built."

"Where did you find this Newell Naramore?"

"Schooner Bottom. He used to live over in Muckaloon."

"Oh. Well, how big is it?"

"It's pretty big. He took out two hundred and sixty-seven cubic yards of dirt."

"I don't know how much that is," Lucinda said. He could hear her blowing the smoke from her cigarette back out in Atlanta. In a bar. No telling who all was in there with her. No telling what they'd do when the bar closed. He figured it was dangerous over there. He didn't figure it was safe to walk the streets.

"It's a shitload," Cortez said. "I'm gonna put some catfish in it soon as it fills up. I just been waiting for it to fill up. We had a big rain today. Supposed to get some more tomorrow."

"You just can't get good catfish in Atlanta," Lucinda said.

It sounded like a whole bunch more people had just come in because it was getting louder in there with her. It sounded like they turned the music up, too. It was getting harder to hear her. Maybe the battery in his hearing aid was getting low. He'd have to check it. But on the other hand, sometimes he didn't mind being almost deaf. If you were almost deaf, there was a lot of shit you didn't have to listen to.

"Maybe you can come fishing later," Cortez said.

"Maybe we can."

"Does he know how to fish?"

"His name is Albert, Daddy. And I can show him how."

"He needs to be careful he don't get finned," Cortez said.

"Albert is very smart, Daddy," Lucinda said. "And I've told you over and over that he can't help what he says sometimes."

"Yeah, but he sure does cuss a lot," Cortez said. "I don't guess you can take him to church much."

"Daddy. I'll hang up on you," she said. Then she muttered, "God-damnit. Call over there to see how you're doing and you start that shit up again."

"Where you at?" he said.

"I'm at the Ritz-Carlton Buckhead. In the bar. We come over here for drinks sometimes."

"You using their phone?" Cortez said.

"Whose phone?" Lucinda said.

"I don't know. Hotel phone, I guess."

"I'm on my cell phone, Daddy."

"Oh," Cortez said. He'd heard of them. Then he couldn't think of anything else to say. It was like his mind was going totally blank. He kept looking at his dead wife sitting there in her wheelchair. He started to ask Lucinda if she was dating any regular men, but he already knew she didn't like that question, so he didn't ask her that. She was strong headed sometimes. Ran away from home once when she was seventeen. Said nobody understood her and nobody could understand what her life was like or how horrible it was. The police picked her up in Memphis and they got her back home. Cortez knew she'd been lucky not to be found naked and raped and stabbed to death in a field out by the airport.

"Okay. I was just calling to check on y'all," Lucinda said. "I guess I was feeling kind of guilty because I hadn't called in a while. I just get busy with everything I'm doing. Work. Albert. You know."

"I don't know nothing," Cortez said. "I know I'm gonna walk over in the morning and see how much it rained in the pond."

"Well. I don't want to get too close to it. I never did learn how to swim. Wish I had. I'd like to take a cruise, but I'd be scared to get on a ship in case it sank."

"They got lifeboats," Cortez said.

"Did you ever see *Titanic?*"

"Naw."

"If you had, you'd know what I'm talking about."

He could tell that she was getting ready to get off the phone and he still didn't know what to do. Just to blurt it out seemed wrong. To have to call her back tomorrow and tell her that her mother had died last night seemed wrong, too.

There was silence on the line, and Cortez couldn't speak. He could hardly hear her with all the shit going on wherever she was.

"Well," she said. "I guess I better let you go."

"Well," Cortez said. "Okay."

"Y'all think about coming over to Atlanta sometime, now."

"I don't know," he said. He wished she'd shut up about it. He wasn't getting on an airplane. Not unless they held a gun on him and tied him down in it. And they'd play hell if he knew they were coming for him and he could get to his Thompson. Splinter the whole damn wall of the barn with that son of a bitch. He could see himself shooting it out with these imaginary people, whoever they were. He wondered if anybody else ever thought of the crazy shit he did. Probably not. But then again, if he did, why didn't other people?

Lucinda spoke to somebody for a moment and he thought how strange it was to be listening to a small part of her life in Atlanta, sitting right here at home with his dead wife. Lucinda was out in a place in Georgia with lights and tables and chairs with some people he didn't even know, drinking. Whooping it up. Probably laughing and telling jokes. Not caring that she didn't have a regular man. Content that she had a retard. And slept in the same bed with him. He heard her say something else and then she was speaking to him again.

"I think we're closing our tab, Daddy, so I guess I'll let you go. You take care of Mama, okay?"

"I'll take care of her," he said.

Then he hung up the phone. Right in her ear. Same way he did everybody. Even Toby Tubby.

24

Lucinda put her cell phone in her purse and reached for the last of her drink. Albert was exhibiting some of his tics and watching her from across the table. His right eye was blinking and he was sniffling from his cold.

"Don't block my dock with your cock," he said.

"I may have one more," Lucinda said. She didn't know what had set him off this time. Sometimes it was a ringing telephone. Sometimes it was a rabbit. Around Easter, it could even be a *picture* of a rabbit.

"I saw Buck fuck a woodchuck," Albert said.

"Maybe I'll just have half of one," Lucinda said, and reached back into her purse for her cigarettes and lighter. "Then we can get on home if you want to. I know you're ready to go, sweetie."

"I'm a hick with a big dick," Albert said, and he got up and headed toward the bar. He had on good slacks and a nice wine Polo shirt.

Lucinda watched him walk away and then looked down at the table and thought about how she needed to go home and see them. Her mother was frail now, had gone downhill fast after the stroke. And she couldn't help but feel guilty about not visiting more often. They'd raised her. Bought her her first car with cows her daddy sold. Sent her to five years of college. And she was grateful for all that. But she just couldn't stand to stay there for more than a day or two. Not when she had Albert with her. Daddy wouldn't even try to communicate with him. She'd tried to explain to him that Albert wasn't retarded, that he had Tourette's syndrome, but Daddy didn't pay any attention to that. He just believed what he wanted to believe. Albert couldn't help it that he'd been born that way.

She sat there and looked around in the dim bar, tapping the filter of her cigarette on the table. She liked coming here after work a few nights a week. It was pretty fancy, with dark wood moldings on the walls and round tables with marble tops and padded chairs. Well-dressed and beautiful people talking and laughing and having drinks. The waiters were polite and soft spoken. The drinks were high in here, but you got what you paid for. You paid for hanging out in a nice place like this, where sometimes some of the Hawks and the Braves and the Falcons hung out. A couple of them had hit on Lucinda a few times, but they always turned away with a puzzled look on their faces when she pointed to Albert and told them she was with him. Especially if he was blinking his eyes at intervals, left then right.

She could see Albert talking to Earl behind the bar and laughing at something he'd said. After you hung around Albert for a while you could see that he was totally harmless. It was true that he got worse in certain social situations, but most times people could see that there was something wrong with him and usually they acted accordingly. Still, you had to look out for him. Two people had punched him out just since she'd known him, once when he'd said something particularly filthy in front of a child in a Burger King and once in front of somebody's girlfriend at a yard sale. It was awful to see somebody hit him, and he wouldn't hit back. She was often afraid that somebody would hit him. But they didn't stay home because of it either. You couldn't. You couldn't just hide from the world.

Tonight had been pretty good. They'd gone to a strip club earlier, a funky place Albert liked near the Margaret Mitchell Center where the girls danced on a dented piece of linoleum to loud heavy metal and hard rock. Some of the girls were kind of heavyset and they were all popular with the crowd, which was mostly a bunch of old drunks and laid-back yuppies. She and Albert had sat there for a couple of hours, she sipping her beer slowly, Albert yelling obscene rhymes at the girls, sipping Cokes. All the girls knew by now that he had Tourette's and they didn't care what anybody said anyway. He couldn't drink very much because of the way it aggravated his condition. At Christmas she let him have a little bourbon in his eggnog and then locked the door. She lit her cigarette just as Albert came back with the drink and set it down and then slid into the chair next to her. He crossed his legs and swung his foot back and forth as steadily as a metronome.

Lucinda pulled the fresh drink closer. She stirred it with the plastic stirrer that was standing up in it. Then she picked it up and sipped it. She thought about her daddy, sitting on the daybed at home, her mother already asleep. They were so old. Lucinda was afraid her mother would have another stroke sometime. And Daddy. He was just . . . Daddy.

"I'd suck muck to fuck a rare Bohemian guck," Albert said.

"How about me when we get home instead?" Lucinda said.

Albert gave her a happy look and smiled.

"I'll need that rubber sock on my cock," he said.

"You always do," Lucinda said. She sipped her drink. "I get tired of using them. Sometimes I'd just like to feel you. You know what I mean?"

He didn't want to talk about that. He didn't want to take a chance on getting her pregnant because he was afraid the child would be like him. She'd been on birth control pills for a long time, but she didn't like what they did to her body, so they'd gone back to condoms. He jerked his head to one side like somebody had pulled it with a rope. He barked and a few people at tables nearby pulled back from their drinks and looked at him.

"I probably shouldn't finish this whole drink," she said.

They sat there for a few moments without talking. She tried not to blow her smoke in Albert's direction. It was the only thing she did that he didn't like. It was the only thing that kept them from being together almost constantly. If Albert was gone, she smoked her head off, smoked in the kitchen, smoked in the bathroom, smoked in the bedroom. And Albert would complain about the smell whenever he came in. But Lucinda wasn't planning on quitting. Her nerves needed cigarettes. She could make it fine whenever she went to the studio downtown for her photo shoots, because they had a smoking lounge just down the hall and she could go down there and have one while they were changing sets or setting up lights.

"Was your father a bother?" Albert said. He was blinking again and he still had his foot going, maybe a little faster now.

"He was watching TV," she said. "He said Mama had already gone to bed."

"I thought Mom was at the prom with Tom."

"He said she was worn out."

"He's a thick prick," Albert said.

"I don't know about going over at Thanksgiving or not," Lucinda said. "I know it's a pain in the ass for you. Just because of Daddy. But it's so hard to get away except on a holiday. And then the airport's jammed, and everybody's trying to fly, and it's such a hassle. But I hate not to go see them."

Albert jerked his head again and she thought about her mother and daddy and how long they had been together. And was this thing with Albert forever? It made her afraid sometimes, to think that there might be a time when Albert wasn't around, if something happened, if they fell apart, if they stopped loving each other, if they got interested in other people. How did you know that a relationship was going to be forever? How did you know? What proof was there? How did love last through years? How had her mother and daddy made it this long? She'd wondered a lot of times if they even loved each other. They never had seemed to act like they did. Maybe things had been different between them before Raif died. Maybe when that happened, something had happened to them, too.

"I heard Bach had a big cock," Albert said. He slid his chair closer and rested his head on Lucinda's shoulder. They sat there.

"I was just thinking about my folks," Lucinda said, and took another sip of her drink. "They've been together so long. I don't know how they've made it this long."

"They fucked like ducks," Albert said gently, and sniffled again.

"I think mainly they just got used to each other," she said. "They got married when Daddy was eighteen and they had Raif and then I didn't come along for ten more years. I only remember a little about him."

Albert turned his head to look at somebody on the other side of the room and then turned back and said, "I saw Dick hit his prick with a brick."

"Mother used to talk about him," Lucinda said. "She'd talk about him more often if Daddy wasn't around. And Daddy wouldn't talk about him at all. He'd get mad if you asked him anything about Raif. He'd tell me to go ask my mother."

Albert waved to somebody and Lucinda turned her head to see who it was. Some woman at the bar was smiling in their direction, then glanced at Lucinda and stopped smiling, just nodded and turned away. Albert fiddled with a loose straw, bending it, unbending it, bending it, unbending it, bending it, unbending it, bending it, unbending it.

"Who's that?" Lucinda said.

"Some chick I dick at a salt lick," Albert said.

"How do you know her?" Lucinda said.

She'd found out a long time ago that you couldn't pay any attention to most of the stuff he said when he was showing his tics because his brain was just making it up. All this stuff he was saying, it was just junk. Just words that didn't really mean anything. She was used to it.

"Just some muff I'd like to stuff," Albert said. "Some ho I'd like to blow."

"Well, I'm just curious when some woman waves at you and I don't know her. Why don't you introduce me to her?"

Albert glanced over that way, then back.

"She fucks on a truck," he said. He stopped swinging his foot and then he barked twice. "Can we flee?" he said.

"Sure, if you want to," Lucinda said, even though most of her drink was still in the glass. "You pay the tab?"

Albert was nodding, starting to swing his foot again.

"I gave Earl a twirl."

"Thank you," Lucinda said. She picked up her drink and took one last sip, then set it back and pushed it away. She got her purse and stood up. "Okay," she said. "I'm ready if you are."

"I hope you scream when you cream," Albert said. He was already up and waiting for her. She held out her hand.

"Come on. Hold my hand now."

They started out through the middle of the tables and Lucinda saw the woman at the bar turn and look at them again. She was still smiling. She was beautiful, slim and black haired, Asian features, maybe some black blood, too. She looked like a movie star. Albert waved at her and they went out through the lobby and the revolving door and she handed their ticket to the valet for him to bring the car around. Lucinda had another quick smoke while he was getting it, standing on the other side of the covered entrance to the hotel, where the polished brass doors kept turning and letting people in and out. Albert was standing away from her, looking up at the sky, trying to see the stars, Lucinda guessed. That was one of the things you gave up when you moved to a city. It wasn't like living out in the country. You couldn't look up and see the stars any old time you wanted to.

There were four or five shiny new luxury cars already parked in front of the hotel and the rich people who drove them were coming out to get them a few at a time, and Lucinda watched them. The women were all as sleek as seals and the men wore expensive suits. Last year, during the PGA tour, people were supposed to have seen Tiger Woods in the hotel.

She stood there and smoked and paced in little steps. They had an agreement that Lucinda wouldn't smoke in the car, and it was twenty minutes home usually, so she was having a last smoke before the ride. But why couldn't he at least stand on this side of the driveway with her?

She could hear Albert barking and he was walking in little circles. Some of the valets were standing there watching him bark and walk. His head jerked out sharply again.

She saw the car coming around, up the ramp, and she stubbed her cigarette out, stepped over beside Albert, then started looking through her purse to see if she had some ones to give to the valet. When the car pulled up and stopped on the bricks in front, she saw that one of the brake lights was out, the right one. Fuck. It was a nice used Lexus and not over three years old. One more thing she'd have to take care of.

The valet got out of the car in his blue uniform and shut the car off, then got out, the chimes inside gently pinging. He was a very nice young black man named Lonzo and he knew Lucinda well enough to tease her and make her laugh. Albert headed around to get in the passenger seat and Lucinda walked over to Lonzo and handed him five folded ones.

"Don't buy PBR with all that, Lonzo," she told him.

His face seemed to light up in the warm breeze that was blowing around the front of the hotel, making the limbs sway in the red-flowered alders that had been planted on the other side of the cobbled driveway. He stuck the money in his pocket and took Lucinda by the arm.

"You better let me help you get in, Miss Lucinda. Earn my pay."

He played lead guitar in a band called Rudy and the Rockets, and she'd heard he was good. He'd been trying to get her to come out to one of the clubs where he played, but Lucinda was afraid to take Albert, so they never had gone. She hated to keep making up excuses.

"When you gonna come out and hear me play?" Lonzo said. "I done asked you about fifty times. Ain't never seen you sitting in the audience yet."

"I don't know," she said. "I've been wanting to. I just haven't gotten around to it."

He tugged on her arm and started over to her car with her. Albert had already closed his door and was looking out the driver's window at them.

"Well, you better hurry up if you want to hear me in Atlanta," he said. "Cause we fixing to cut us a record on the West Coast and rocket on out of here."

She smiled and squeezed his arm with her hand.

"That's great, Lonzo. I'm really glad for you."

"We out at the Motif next weekend if you want to come over," Lonzo said. "I'll put you on the guest list if you'll tell me you coming."

He reached for the door handle and pulled it open, and bowed slightly and swept his hand toward her seat. Albert was sitting there, looking straight ahead. Lucinda hesitated. She hated to just brush him off. He was too nice a person. You didn't just brush nice people off. It didn't matter if they were waiters or valets or whatever. They had a job, didn't they? They weren't slobs who went around on the sidewalks with their palms out, begging the public for money. They weren't bums.

"I'd sure like to, Lonzo. I don't know what we're doing next weekend yet. But thank you for asking me. And good luck."

She got into the car and sat down and stashed her purse. She reached for her seat belt and harness and strapped herself in. Lonzo waited on her. He nodded when she started the car.

"Y'all have a good evening, now," he said, and then he closed the door. He waved and stepped away. Lucinda pulled out, the car surging forward, she shifting gears quickly. She never choked it off at crucial times, like when she was pulling out into traffic, or trying to get started on a hill. She'd learned how to work a clutch on a John Deere tractor.

They drove about twenty feet and then had to stop on a small rise and wait on some people who were getting into a new black Tahoe. You saw a lot of new black Tahoes around the Ritz. Lots of white Jaguars, too.

The people who were blocking their way didn't look like they were in any big hurry to get out of it. Some of them had cups in their hands and they were drinking from them and laughing. A short guy in a golf shirt and slacks and loafers who looked a little drunk had the keys in his hand and he was going around to the driver's side. Then a woman got out of the backseat on the other side and followed him around and they started talking. She was taller than him and wearing a flowered skirt and a sleeveless top and she had a drink and she was pointing up the street with it. Then he grabbed her by the ass and laughed. She shoved him playfully. He came back and acted like he was going to take a bite out of her, and she squealed with laughter and danced away.

"What the hell's going on?" Lucinda said. She had both hands on the wheel and then she reached up and adjusted the rearview mirror.

"Dipshits and nitwits with tits," Albert said.

"I'm gonna blow the horn if they don't move in about two seconds," Lucinda said. She would, too. She didn't have a whole lot of patience sometimes. She'd blow her horn so fast it would make your head swim.

The woman with the drink turned around and snatched at the car keys the guy was holding, but he jerked them out of her reach. Then a man in the backseat got out of the same door the woman had exited and walked behind the Tahoe. The lights of the Lexus were shining on his legs, but he didn't look at Albert and Lucinda when he walked in front of them. As soon as he got around to the other side of the Tahoe, the woman walked over to him and grabbed him by the sleeve, really stretching it out, and said something, and pointed to the guy with the keys, who had stopped his grab-assing and was opening the door and starting to get in.

"I think they're trying to keep him from driving," Lucinda said.

Lucinda blew the horn. The woman and the man whose sleeve she'd grabbed turned and looked at Albert and Lucinda and said something to them that they couldn't hear with their windows rolled up. Lucinda thought the word *fuck* or some variation of it had probably been used.

"Drunk assholes," Lucinda said.

"Fuck his duck with a puck," Albert said.

The guy who was trying to get behind the wheel had gotten back out. He and the drunk woman and the man who'd gotten out of the backseat started waving for Albert and Lucinda to come around.

"I hate going out and seeing these . . . assholes," Lucinda said.

Albert barked and jerked his head out at that odd angle again.

"Rich assholes . . . probably fucking Republicans," Lucinda said.

Albert rubbed his chin and pulled at his ears and then put his finger inside his fist and started sliding it in and out.

"Think they own the goddamn world," Lucinda said. "Maybe they'll move in a minute."

But they didn't. They went back to arguing and pointing fingers in different directions, and now it looked like they were having an argument not about who was driving but where they were going, since they were pointing in all different directions. One of them even pointed up.

Lucinda blew the horn again and then got a sinking feeling in the pit of her stomach. The arguing people stopped arguing and they all looked at Albert and Lucinda again. Then the woman with the drink got a mean look in her eye and walked back to their Lexus.

"Don't roll the window down, honey," Lucinda said. "You don't know these people."

The woman with the drink stopped beside the car and rapped hard on Lucinda's window with a big diamond ring. It was so big that it was stunning. It winked and shot bits of light in all directions even in the semidark outside the car. Lucinda rolled the window down. The woman with the drink leaned down and bent toward the car. She stopped just short of sticking her head inside.

"What's the fucking problem, sister?" she said.

"We'd like to leave," Lucinda said. "That's the problem."

"Well, just go *around*," the woman said, as if Lucinda were the stupidest person on earth.

"We can't go around," Lucinda said. "You all have got the drive completely blocked."

"Aw, we ain't got the damn drive blocked," the woman said, and took another sip of her drink. It was in a clear plastic glass and there was a slice of lime floating around in it.

Lucinda was tapping her fingers on the steering wheel. Then she blew the horn again. Long and loud. Lucinda looked toward the front door of the hotel and could see Lonzo and some of the other valets looking their way. But none of them had walked over yet. They were probably going to keep their noses out of it unless some shit happened.

The woman did put her head inside the car then. She brought her face close to Lucinda's and said, "Why don't you stop blowing that fucking horn?"

"Why don't you make me?" Lucinda said. Then she blew it again. And again. The valets out front were still staring at them.

"Tell them to move the fucking car, lady," Lucinda said.

The woman turned her head to yell at the men, who'd said something.

"What?" she said. "Why don't you let me handle this? I'm quite capable of handling it, okay, Harold?"

"Okay," Lucinda said. "Handle it then."

Then she tried to reason with her. Just as a last resort. Just to try and be reasonable herself.

"Why don't you all take your argument on down the road somewhere and let us out? Please? We've been sitting here a couple of minutes and we're really ready to go."

"We're figuring out where we're going," the woman said, and it was now apparent that she was pretty drunk. "And we're trying to get the keys away from Ron." She stood there beside the car and looked at him. "Drunk son of a bitch. Hung like a horse, though."

She leaned her face down to the car again.

"We're sorry," she said, then looked at Albert, who was still sliding his finger in and out of his fist. "Oh, he's . . . cute. Y'all in the hotel?"

"We just came over for some drinks," Lucinda said. Albert let out a short bark and the woman looked at him again, in out, in out, in out . . .

"Y'all are not guests," the woman said.

"No," Lucinda said. "We're not guests."

"Oh," the woman said, and then she walked back up to the men, who were leaning up against the Tahoe by now, still talking. She said something to them and they looked at the car Albert and Lucinda were sitting in and they said something to the woman and then they all laughed. Lucinda felt her face getting red.

"They're talking about us," Lucinda said. Albert finally stopped all that stuff with his fist. They sat there. The car quietly running.

"I can get Lonzo to get them to move," Lucinda said. She put her hand on the door handle. "Wait just a minute."

But she didn't get out because the drunk woman was walking back to their car. She leaned her face down again, but she didn't get as close as before. The look on her face had changed again.

"What's the matter with you?" she said.

"What do you mean?" Lucinda said.

"You know what I mean," the woman said. She looked at both of them like something was funny. The men up by the Tahoe were yelling at her. The short guy had gone around to the other side and he'd given the keys to the guy who'd gotten out of the backseat.

"I think your ride's leaving," Lucinda said to the woman. But the woman had fixed her eyes on them and was looking at them with something they'd both seen before.

"There's plenty of men in Atlanta," the woman said. "I can introduce you to a couple if you want me to. You could upgrade and fuck somebody besides a retard."

"How fucking dare you," Lucinda said, and tried to open her door. "I'll kick your skinny ass, you drunk bitch."

"Wah!" Albert said, and reached out and grabbed her arm to hold her back. Lucinda snatched her arm away and started out the door, trying to untangle herself from the seat belt and harness.

The drunk woman wobbled back and turned on her heel and made a misstep and then went on back to the Tahoe and got in. The door closed. The Tahoe pulled off and somebody waved an obscene gesture from a back window. Lucinda screeched the gearshift and for the first time choked off the car. Rested her forehead on the steering wheel with her eyes closed, cussing like her daddy used to.

"Suck a puck for luck," Albert said.

So that messed up the rest of the whole night. They went on home, but it wasn't the same. She knew it wasn't going to be the same. As soon as they got into the apartment, Albert went back to his studio and shut the door and stayed in there for a while. They had decided together that Albert's work was too important to be relegated to a broom closet or a spare bathroom, so he'd taken over the extra bedroom, ripped up the carpet, and in general had made one hell of a mess in there and was still making it. There was paint on the walls, paint on the ceiling. Long loopy swirls of it, and spatters here and there, layers of it on the floor.

Lucinda dropped her purse on the kitchen counter and set about making herself a nightcap. But she stopped and walked back to Albert's studio and rapped on the door.

"Hey," she said. "You want a nice cold Hershey's bar?"

Albert mumbled something from behind the door and Lucinda couldn't make out what it was. But he was a known chocoholic.

"Knock once for no and twice for yes," Lucinda said.

There was one faint knock.

"Okay," Lucinda said, and turned away. "Maybe later. I got some fresh sweet milk and Oreos, too, babe."

She went back to the kitchen and got a square crystal glass with a duck embossed on it from the cabinet to the left of the sink and opened the right side of their side-by-side refrigerator/freezer and scooped some cubes from the bin into her glass. She dropped one on the wood-grained vinyl flooring and it went skittering into the base mold. She had to bend over and pick it up or it would melt and be a wet spot in the floor in the morning.

"Shit," she grunted as she bent over. She picked it up and flung it into the sink. But it bounced out and somehow knocked over a wineglass that she had left beside the sink last night, causing it to topple into the metal drain and break. It made a slight *ching!* sound.

"Gosh damn it!" Lucinda said. "Shit!"

She set her unmade drink down and carefully picked up the broken pieces of glass and got them in her hands along with the stem, cradling them until she could drop them in the garbage. She went back to look and see if there were any glass chips she'd missed, but she couldn't see anything. She turned on the cold water and rinsed her hands and then dried them on a fresh towel from the drawer, then hung the towel through one of the drawer pulls and finished making her drink. She found the bottle of Maker's and tipped some of it over the ice cubes. She set the bottle down. She looked at the whisky in the glass. Then she tipped some more in there. About twice as much as what she'd had. Might as well. What in the hell did they go over to the Ritz-Carlton for anyway? Bunch of rich-ass people who didn't have anything in common with them. Maybe they needed to just stay away from there. They were rednecks even if they drove a Tahoe and looked like they had money.

That woman was awful. She wished she'd kicked her ass. But that would have just upset Albert worse.

There were some cold Cokes in the bottom of the icebox and she reached in for one and opened it and poured some of it over the ice and whisky. She watched and waited until the fizz ran down before she added some more and brought it to full. She was going to smoke some, too. She had to if she was going to drink. He'd probably stay back there. She reached across the sink and unfastened the latch on the aluminum window and pushed it up. She felt warm air waft in. It smelled like barbecue. And garbage. And auto exhaust. And there was noise. Distant noise. Some kind of a regular roar that was part of the interstate that wound around the city, the constant roar of trucks and cars that went on all day and all night. Sometimes she wondered what she was doing here and then she looked at Albert and knew. She was taking care of him. She had a purpose, a reason to get up every morning and a reason to come home every night. And she enjoyed her work, modeling large ladies' lingerie. There was a need for what she did because big girls like her loved sexy things to wear, too.

She leaned against the counter and turned her purse around and got her cigarettes and lighter out. She lit one and let the lighter fall to the counter. There was an ashtray in a drawer and she pulled it out. She set it near the stove and pulled one of the high stools across the floor, over close to the window, and sat down in it and reached for her drink. She sipped it. Why did she call her daddy tonight? Because she was afraid something was wrong. But he'd said that her mother was asleep. So if she was asleep, everything was probably okay. She had to stop putting it off and go see them before long. Hell. It wasn't that big a deal. It just took some preparation to get Albert ready for the airport. She always had to pack his bags for him and make sure he wasn't wearing anything that was made of metal, because he'd freaked out one day when he'd set the metal detector off with a fountain pen she hadn't known was in his pocket, and they'd made him take his shoes off and go through the whole body-wand deal.

She tried to blow her smoke out the window, but it kind of pooled in the air and started spreading throughout the kitchen. Fuck it. She paid the rent. And most of the groceries. And did most of the cooking when some cooking got done. But Albert could make the most beautiful cakes if you helped him, preheated the oven for him, mixed the batter, greased the pans, set the timer on the counter and listened to it ticking. Where he shined on cakes was decorating them. He could make lovely red roses, purple wisteria, green vines, blue wildflower petals, all with those little squeeze bottles of icing that came in all those different colors. She guessed it was related to his painting methods. Sometimes he just took a tube of paint and squeezed it from the tube directly onto the canvas. The floor in there was littered with them, but he refused to let her clean it up. His room stayed as cluttered as his mind. And then in one bright shining moment of clarity, whatever drove him to create slipped from where it was imprisoned in his brain into his fingers and together they made a thing of beauty on the canvases he had stretched and tacked himself. There were a lot of tacks in there on the floor. You didn't want to go in there barefooted.

She picked up her drink and sipped from it. It was way too strong, but that was all right. She might just sit up and get drunk and watch a movie. She had some weed left, but it wasn't really good to mix too much of both of them together. Getting drunk was one thing and getting stoned was another thing, but getting drunk along with getting stoned was a whole other thing and not a good thing if you overdid it. She'd gotten to where she really hated to wake up with a hangover, and she knew it made her irritable with Albert when she did. But all he'd do was walk into the kitchen and make her a Bloody Mary and squeeze some fresh limes into it and bring it to her. He was good at *mixing* things somehow. For what he didn't have, to take the place of them, things like normal speech or the ability not to bark involuntarily sometimes, he had other things. Things that let her see that he had many gifts, just slightly out of order.

Lucinda sat there and tried to blow her smoke out the window again and sipped her Maker's and wondered how her daddy's garden was doing this year. He'd always raised so much food, cabbage and onions and Irish potatoes and sweet potatoes and squash and corn and tomatoes and English peas and purple hull peas. His rows were always so clean because he simply refused to let one stem of grass go to seed in his garden. It took lots of work with a hoe, but all her life at home she'd seen him almost every summer evening out there in the orderly dirt, chopping with the hoe, delicately sometimes, vigorously sometimes, keeping it all clean, gathering the okra, bringing in squash in a bucket. The sky growing dark back behind the big pecans and the chinaberry tree where he always hung his post-hole digger. The cows bawling. Sometimes she missed it so badly she could hardly stand it. Like now. She didn't need to keep Albert in Atlanta. She needed him out in the country. But there was Daddy.

Lucinda heard the door on the studio open. He'd turned his radio on. She took another drag on her smoke and sipped her drink. She heard Albert go into the bedroom. She made a move to get up, then stopped. Kept sitting there. Listening to the radio playing back there. Pop tunes from the mid-1980s. Albert listened to the crappiest shit on the radio.

She tapped the ash off the end of her cigarette and crossed her legs on the stool. Albert was bumping around in the bedroom. Drawers were opening and closing. She put her cigarette in the ashtray and went back there.

She poked her head in the door. Albert had already changed out of his clothes and had on a pair of baggy black silk boxer shorts with red hearts printed on them that Lucinda had given him. He was bent over a drawer and he didn't look up. Lucinda could see almost all of his slim tanned body, and it caused a great ache of wanting in her heart. Why couldn't other people just leave them alone? She couldn't understand why people couldn't accept him as he was. He was kind and gentle. He had a lot of good things going for him. He had more talent in one of his little fingers than most people had in their whole bodies.

"Hey," Lucinda said, as softly and as gently as she could. He had to know that she loved him completely as he was.

"Hey."

"How you doing?" she said. She walked on into the bedroom and sat down on the bed. The big pale yellow comforter was already pulled back, exposing just one pillow.

"I'm pretty tired," he said, still going through the drawer.

"I'm sorry," Lucinda said. Albert slammed the drawer crisply and marched past her and out the door. He looked pretty sad.

"Holy fucking shit," she said in a low voice. He went back down the hall, his bare feet making little padded sounds, and the bathroom door slammed shut. Lucinda got up. She stood there for a moment, looking at the bed, and then she raised one foot at a time and slipped her loafers off, then sat back down on the bed and pulled her socks off. She unsnapped her tight designer jeans and slipped them down her legs and kicked them toward a chair. She pulled her red pullover over her head and threw it on the chair and unsnapped her bra and took it off. [. . .] She put the bra on top of the dresser and opened the closet door. She pulled a Waylon Jennings T-shirt over her head, glad to have the bra off. Her breasts were very big and she liked the looseness of them under the T-shirt. [. . .] But Albert was sad and he'd stay sad overnight. And he couldn't make love to her when he was sad. He wasn't physically able to. A doctor they'd seen didn't know why. Something related to his brain. Everything was related to his brain. She'd read up on it. Some doctors thought people with Tourette's had abnormalities in their neurotransmitters. Albert had displayed his first symptoms at age seven, which was usual in people with Tourette's. His parents had pulled him out of the second grade when he'd started disrupting his class so badly and had schooled him at home. That had kept other children from mercilessly mocking him, but Lucinda thought it had also partially deprived him of learning how to function around other people.

There was a pair of pink jogging pants on a hanger and she slipped into them, and found her house shoes on the floor of the closet, and wriggled her feet into them. Then she went back to the kitchen. Her cigarette had burned down almost to the filter and she stubbed it out and almost immediately lit another one. She picked up her drink and sipped it. The whisky was starting to build a warm place inside her and she could sleep as late as she wanted to in the morning.

The radio went off back there. She heard the light click off, and then the padded walking of Albert's feet back into the bedroom. She didn't hear the door shut.

"You going to bed?" Lucinda called from the kitchen.

"Yeah," came the dim answer from Albert. A square of light in the hall went dark. It was like he had flicked a switch on her happiness for the evening. But she knew that he was just feeling bad, and needed to lie awake in the dark for a while and look up at the ceiling, and run through whatever was running through his sweet fucked-up brain.

[. . .] Lucinda wound up getting her pot out of a drawer in the living room and putting some in her pipe and mixing a fresh drink and settling down in front of the television and getting stoned and drunk while watching movies and documentaries about World War II and biographies of minor television stars until about midnight when she went to sleep on the couch.

She dreamed of something she could never remember whenever she was awake. A thing buried, a thing not quite permanently put away. A thing that got dimmer as the years went on but was always there. A memory from maybe a child's fever dream. An enormous silent growing ball that was coming to crash against the earth, taking eternity to get here, she standing between them on a mountaintop pile of rocks, watching in silent space the enormity of what was coming. Not just her death but the death of everything. The death of the world. Of all worlds.

25

The movie started at 8:20 in Tupelo and Johnette dropped the girls off in front of the doors at 8:10 with enough money for admission and Cokes and candy and popcorn. They had her cell phone number if something happened. She was parked near the curb and she watched them walk into the lobby of the Malco from the driver's seat of her Toyota. By 8:29 she was sitting on a bar stool at the Rib Cage downtown, sipping a margarita on the rocks and looking for her date. She didn't have long since she had to be back at the theater by 10:30 to pick up the girls.

He came in after she'd been there only a few minutes and sat down next to her. She turned around and smiled at him because she was very glad to see him. And horny? My God.

"Hey, baby," he said. "How much time we got?"

"A little less than two hours," she said. "I wish it was longer."

"It's long enough on short notice," he said. "You ready to go?"

"Sure," she said, and she picked up the rest of her drink and drained it. He left some money on the bar and took her arm as they went out the door. She'd slipped her wedding ring off. She always did.

The Trace Inn was just up the road and by 8:55 they were in the room and he was mixing himself a drink. She took her pot and her one-hitter from her purse and slipped into the bathroom and changed into a black negligee in between taking tokes off the one-hitter. It was good weed and she needed to get some more of it.

He was already under the covers when she came back in, his clothes hanging neatly folded over a chair. They tried to get together about once a month, but it didn't always work out. Other shit sometimes interfered.

The TV was going, but they didn't watch much of it since it was only showing the war. After a while he turned over and set his drink on the table and reached for her. She pulled him on top of her.

They went at it hard for about an hour and did a little of everything, made her come three times and scream. After that they rested. He'd been trying to talk her into taking a trip with him, but she'd already told him that she couldn't pull that off, that it was hard enough just to meet him in Tupelo or Oxford once in a while.

She got up and went to the bathroom while he fixed himself another drink. When she came back in and started putting on her clothes he was already dressed and standing there sipping from his blue Solo cup.

"I got to run," he said.

"I know," she said. "I do, too."

He put the room key and the money on the bedside table and then walked over to her and kissed her.

"Call me when you can," he said.

"I will," she said, and he went out the door.

She sat on the bed and looked at the money. Then she reached out and picked it up. Six fifties. Always the same. Always pinned together neatly with a regular paper clip. He always said it was just some money to help her out. She'd gotten used to taking it. And God knows she needed it. She stuck it down in her purse.

[. . .]

26

Cortez Sharp slept with his dead wife that night. Not in a literal sense. Not in a figurative sense. In an actual sense. He cut off the lights and curled up on the daybed without his supper, beside her where she had stiffened in her wheelchair, and took off his brogans, drew his knees not quite up to his chest, pulled the little worn bedspread over him, and tried to sleep. But it didn't work. There were too many things going through his mind. One was, what if a doctor looked at her and said she'd been dead longer than what Cortez was going to say when he called them in the morning and what would happen if he did? Another thing was, when was he going to call Lucinda and tell her she was dead? He couldn't call her tonight. It was late. She was probably already asleep. He didn't want to wake her up with bad news. He knew what she'd have to do. She'd have to get up and call in and take a day off work and pack and drive over to that airport she lived close to and stand in line and buy a ticket and fly to Memphis and rent a car, buy some gas, get out of Memphis, drive all the way down here, bring some clothes for a funeral or enough to stay a day or two, and she'd probably bring that retarded guy with her. He was probably one big mess when you had to take him somewhere. Cussing and all. And they'd have luggage. Shitloads of luggage. He didn't know why they needed so much luggage. Most of it looked like it was made out of brown alligators. And they'd probably have to sleep in there in Raif's room again like they did the last time they were here. And he didn't have any idea how long it had been since the sheets had been changed on that bed. He guessed the last time they were here. And when was that? Was it last Christmas? He couldn't remember. It seemed like she'd been here since Christmas. But when was it? Had she been here this year? Yes. Had she been here since it got hot? No. Had she been here when it was cold? Yes. Had it been raining? Yes. Was it March? No. Was it February? Maybe. It might have been. But what would she have been doing here in February? She didn't come for Valentine's, did she? Maybe she did. She usually only came at Christmas. She used to come at Thanksgiving. But it had been three or four years since she'd done that, come for Thanksgiving.

He couldn't remember when she'd been here. It had been a long time since the sheets had been changed anyway. Maybe he needed to go in there and do that. But not right now. Hell no. He wasn't going to get up in the middle of the night just to make up a bed. No way. He had to lie here and figure out what in the hell he was going to do.

And what the hell was he going to say to Lucinda about when she'd died? What if the doctor looked at her and then Lucinda talked to the doctor? Well, he'd just say he didn't know she'd been dead that long, that he'd been out in the garden that afternoon working and that he'd gone in a few times for a drink of water and heard the TV running, which told him that she was still alive, and he hadn't actually checked on her, had just figured she was all right, and that later on he'd been out in the barn piddling around—he wouldn't say anything about the machine gun because he didn't want her to know about it or the Klan robes—and that he just hadn't known she was dead and had gone on to bed. Would she believe that? What if she didn't? What if she asked him point-blank if her mama was dead when she was talking to him that night on the phone, what would he say then, would he lie, would he tell the truth, what would he do? He probably couldn't tell the truth, hell, no. That wouldn't work. She'd have a screaming damn fit if he told her that shit. He'd just have to think of something before then.

But that was really nothing new. He'd had to think of things before. Sometimes pretty fast. Like a long time ago when he'd screwed that woman down the road in the barn one afternoon in hot weather and another woman had come walking by and heard them and walked over and looked through a crack in the barn and had gasped and gone on up the road to probably blab it up at the store. He'd gotten rid of the first woman in a hurry and had gone over to the house and gotten his wife and carried her over to the barn and laid her down on some bales of freshly baled fescue hay and screwed her, too, right away, so that later on, if the woman who had been walking down the road and had peeked through the cracks told Cortez's wife that she'd seen him screwing somebody in his barn, his wife could just cackle and flap her hand and say, "Oh, silly goose, that was me, Cortez wanted him some in the middle of the day and we did it in the barn, hee hee!" Cortez didn't have STUPID written on his forehead.

He was going to have to go to the funeral home and pick out a casket, make arrangements; the grave would have to be dug. He'd have to do all that tomorrow. People would start finding out about it. They'd start calling over here. All her old biddy friends. He'd have to talk to all them. They'd be crying and stuff. It wouldn't be any fun. It'd be pretty unfun. He dreaded all that shit.

Then there would be people over here at the house. They'd bring food. They'd put the food on the kitchen table and the whole house would fill up with people and they'd sit and talk and eat and cry and tell fishing stories and stories about his wife and they'd sit on the furniture and leave napkins on the floor and chicken bones on plates in the kitchen and he'd have to clean all that shit up and take out a couple of bags of garbage and maybe sweep the chicken crumbs off the floor.

He wondered how much the funeral was going to cost. Probably a pretty good bit. It seemed like he had a funeral policy, but he didn't know where in the hell it was. He'd have to start looking through the drawers and try to find it. He didn't know how much it was worth. Probably not much.

He lay there and looked at her. He could remember when her hair was brown. Her remembered one time when they'd gone swimming at night, naked, down on the shoals of the river. They were very young then. They hadn't been married long. She wasn't pregnant with Raif yet. He remembered how she had wandered naked along the banks of the river, getting mud on her feet and laughing, and then how they had lain down on a quilt they'd packed, and had screwed right there on the clean white sand of the river with the frogs calling and the crickets screaming, so loud it almost hurt your ears. That was a long time ago. Everything now for him was a long time ago.

He was awful hungry. He wasn't used to going to bed without his supper. He hadn't done that since he was a little boy, one time when there wasn't any supper, and he still knew what that felt like. It was a scary feeling. His daddy had been gone to the lumber camp working and he hadn't come home with any money and his mother hadn't been able to find anything to fix for their supper. She'd gone out with the rifle that evening and tried to kill some squirrels, but she came back empty handed and said they were too wild, that she hadn't been able to slip up on any of them, and had cried for a while in front of the hearth, with the old man sitting there supperless, too, with his empty sleeve pinned up, and then they'd just gone to bed. When he woke up the next morning it was to the smell of fresh pork tenderloin frying on the woodstove and his daddy had been there and there was coffee brewing and everything had been okay. He'd gotten up and eaten the brown eggs his daddy had bought on the way home, that his mother had fried in lard in a black iron skillet. The man his daddy had been riding with had gotten the wagon stuck in a mud hole because he was drunk and his daddy had gotten down from the wagon and walked the rest of the way home. He had started walking at midnight and he had walked for the rest of the night and had come out the woods down the hill just as day was breaking, carrying the food, his heavy leather boots wet from the dew. That was in the log house, the one his daddy had built from pine logs he'd dropped in the forest with an ax and hauled out with mules and a log chain and a pair of snaking tongs and had set them up in what would become the front yard and had hewed them flat on their sides with an adze and had notched them and laid them together on the corners and had raised the walls with a block and tackle and the mules, and other men, bit by bit, and Cortez could remember how the woods almost steamed on summer mornings with the dew melting off the leaves and the birds calling and the squirrels jumping from limb to limb. The smoke from cooking fires, washing fires.

Back then when people died the women fixed up the bodies and they took down a door and laid the body on it and everybody came over that night and hung around and ate and then the next day the preacher came over and they brought a plank coffin and put the person in it and loaded the person into a wagon and hauled the person over to the graveyard and they had a simple service and then went home.

But it wasn't like that now. Now you had to mess with all these people. You had to make all these decisions. And should he wait for Lucinda to get here before he made all those decisions? What if he went ahead and made all the decisions and then she got here and didn't like any of them? He didn't want to have to fuss with her on top of everything else.

Thinking about all that made his head hurt, so he stopped thinking about it. He just lay there in the dark beside her, looking at her, not knowing what else to do. He didn't want to be doing this but he didn't know what else he could do. So he just lay there. Waiting. For what he did not know. Enlightenment, maybe. The hand of God. A tomato sandwich. But it seemed too dark to venture toward the kitchen. So he just stayed where he was. Curled up on the daybed.

He guessed he'd have to get used to being alone now. But it seemed like he'd been pretty much alone ever since Lucinda moved to Atlanta. And how many years had that been? About fifteen, probably. He could count on his fingers and toes all the times she'd been home since then. And it was fine whenever she came home by herself. But then she started bringing that dirty-mouth retard with her, and that made things different. He didn't feel comfortable sitting around talking about his tomatoes in front of somebody like him. Who was sleeping in the same bed with his daughter. And mostly they just sat around and watched TV. And he didn't care anything about that. They never showed *The Untouchables* anymore, hadn't for years.

He started to get up and get his flashlight and go out to the barn and get his gun and just shoot it. Just shoot it for the hell of it. Just to listen to it. Just to feel it kick. But what good would that do? He'd just have to come right back in here and lie down beside her again.

Maybe he ought to just call the funeral home now. They probably had somebody who sat up and took calls at night. Somebody who was just sitting in a chair waiting for the phone to ring and say that there was somebody dead somewhere who needed to be brought to the funeral home. But the more he thought about that, about calling them now, the more he worried about what they were going to say about her being so stiff and dead for so long. What could he say? Could he say that he'd found her sometime this afternoon and just couldn't bring himself to call until now? Would they buy that? They might. He hadn't done anything criminal. Not to his wife anyway.

He could hear the chains on the swing on the front porch creaking. But why? Why would they be rattling? It was probably Queen. She hadn't been around in a while, but maybe now she was going to come back. Make him pay some more. Stand out there and rattle the chains on the swing and moan through the windows again. His wife never had heard it. Or claimed she hadn't. He'd asked her about it a couple of times, had asked her the next morning several times if she'd heard anything during the night, when he had, and she'd said no, she hadn't. Maybe he was the only one who could hear it. Maybe he was the only one meant to hear it.

Shit. He'd just call them early in the morning. Tell them he hadn't been able to do it last night, and what would it matter anyway? There was plenty of time. But he had to call Lucinda. That was the thing he was dreading the most. Telling her. She was probably going to take it hard, even though she and her mother hadn't been that close. Not in these last years.

Boy. It looked like stuff could go right in your life, but a lot of times it didn't. He wondered if it was like that for everybody. Probably so. It was probably tough for everybody. Even those people down the road in the trailer. What was it going to hurt if those kids came on his land? Would it hurt one thing? Probably not.

And then he thought about the pond. About the rain that had fallen into it. He was dying to know how much water it had in it.

So he got up. He didn't turn the light on in there. He went up the hall and turned the light on out there and got his rubber boots from the closet and found his flashlight and turned the porch light on and went out, through the front yard, up the hill toward the new pond. Lighting his dim yellow way. The little hidden wet frogs cheeping. His boots slurping in the fresh mud. A big cow bawling to a little cow baby and a hoot owl hooting harmony backup, *Hoot hoot, who, who?*

27

Jimmy's daddy was standing at the vending machine getting his lunch since he hadn't gotten up early enough to fix a baloney sandwich, which is what he sometimes had. He'd noticed that lots of people at the plant ate baloney. Sometimes Vienna sausage and crackers. Or sardines and crackers. Potted meat and crackers. You had to switch it up so you didn't get burned out like a dog eating the same kind of dog food 365 days a year. [. . .] He was about to go sit down with Seaborn and some guys from the Tool-and-Die Department when the new girl down on the line walked in with two other girls, both of them kind of short and to his way of thinking *dumpy*. He'd heard that one of them had given somebody a blow job in the parking lot one day, which was pretty interesting, but he didn't know which one since they looked pretty similar.

He tried not to stare at them, so he just kind of watched them out the corner of his eye to see where they were going to sit while he was digging his change out of his pocket. The break room was pretty filled up with people, but there were always a few open tables, since they'd expanded it. It looked like they were heading toward the back. Jimmy's daddy got out some quarters and dimes and shoved some of them into the machine and punched R6 for a small can of Castleberry's chili, and he watched a metal arm slowly push it off a shelf, where it rattled down through the machine and hit a little door at the bottom. Jimmy's daddy reached in and got it. He ate it pretty often, since it was easy and quick, which helped him smoke a few more cigarettes before he had to get back to work. [. . .]

He couldn't remember how many times he'd begged his mama to make him some chili. But she wouldn't do it. She always said she didn't know how to make it. Then she'd make some more of that fucking meat loaf. Shit. He could think about it now and almost get indigestion.

He leaned to one side and looked past Hootie Pearson, who always had a baloney-and-cheese sandwich that he had to microwave, to see if he could see where that big-tittied heifer and her buddies were sitting.

He couldn't see them. Maybe they were behind the Coke machine. Sometimes some of the girls and women sat back there and grouped up and gossiped.

He wished the damn line would hurry up. He looked to see who was up front. It was Garson, who worked down on the line, had some glasses that looked like they were about half an inch thick, and he was evidently roasting his lunch, because the microwave had been running for about a minute at least, because that was how long he'd been standing in line, he figured. He looked toward the back of the break room again and just then saw the new girl walk across the room, throw something in the garbage, and walk back. She was wearing a tight light blue T-shirt with LYNYRD SKYNYRD written across the front of it and he didn't know they still had a band. He got a pretty good look at her breastworks as she made her way back to the table. Then, while he was watching her, not noticing that Garson had gotten his turkey pot pie from the microwave steaming hot and had turned away with it, carrying it on a pot holder he had evidently brought from home, and let the next guy up to the microwave, which caused Hootie to take another few steps forward, leaving a gap between himself and Jimmy's daddy, she turned and looked straight at Jimmy's daddy and gave him a look that was definitely not friendly. It was actually a look that let Jimmy's daddy know that she knew he was looking at her breasts when she caught him. She stared coldly at him for a few seconds while she was walking and then disappeared back behind the Coke machine.

Damn. She didn't look too friendly, did she? Kind of looked at him like she was thinking, *Eat some shit and die!*

"Come on, we ain't got but twenty-seven minutes left," somebody said behind Jimmy's daddy, and he turned around to see who it was. It was Snuffy Smith, who worked down on the line, wrapping insulation around stove liners all day long, and he was holding what looked like a damp and thawed-out Lean Cuisine of beef tips and noodles in his hands. Jimmy's daddy turned back around and saw that there was about six feet between himself and Hootie Pearson, who was just sticking his baloney-and-cheese into the microwave, and Jimmy's daddy knew that he only warmed it for thirty seconds. Every time. Dependable as clockwork. He had it down to a science. Jimmy's daddy closed the gap between them and when Hootie finished, Jimmy's daddy walked on up and stuck his chili in and twisted the dial over to get it piping hot.

While his chili warmed, Jimmy's daddy stuck the spoon in his mouth and held it there, his fingers slipped into his front pockets. He looked over at Seaborn and them. They were talking and eating. He knew that Seaborn was probably telling them some lie. He'd been knowing Seaborn for a long time and knew that he'd rather climb a tree and tell a lie than stand on the ground and tell the truth.

Forty-five seconds later the bell dinged on the microwave and Jimmy's daddy reached in for it. It was hot, so he had to hold it gingerly and he set it down on the edge of the counter for a moment while he grabbed some napkins from a dispenser and wrapped them around it.

"Now I got twenty-six minutes left," Snuffy Smith said, standing there watching his watch and waiting for him to get out of the way.

"She's all yours, Snuffy," Jimmy's daddy said, around the plastic spoon, and scooped up his chili and made his way over to where Seaborn and them were sitting. They'd left a hole for him to sit in and he set his chili and napkins down with the spoon and told them he had to get a drink and then walked over to the Coke machine. He could see the back of the big-tittied heifer's blue shirt and her long light brown hair, and he dug down in his pocket for some more change. Shit. He didn't have but thirty-seven cents left. He had to step over to the dollar changer then. First he had to root through his billfold and look among the crumpled and sweat-soaked ones to try and find one that might be accepted by the machine. This one here in the break room had gotten to where you had to have a pretty dadgum smooth dollar bill or it would spit it back on you. Sometimes you had to put one down on the counter and try to smooth some of the wrinkles out of it, and this was the case with the one Jimmy's daddy pulled out. He worked on it for a while, unbending the corners, flattening it with his hand and running his hand over it, and by then, when he finally got it to looking a little better, somebody else had already stepped around him and stuck a bill into the machine, which promptly spit it back out. It was Miss Cricket, from down on the line, who put screws into stove parts all day long, hinges and self-cleaning door covers mostly. She was tiny and white haired, couldn't possibly have weighed over sixty-five pounds and looked mummified.

She had a high, nasal voice like somebody on helium. Smoked the hell out of some cigarettes, worked with one in her toothless mouth, blew the fumes out her nose like a small dragon. Favorite footwear: slip-on tennis shoes.

"Cheap son of a bitch," she said, and looked up at Jimmy's daddy. "Why don't y'all fix this piece a shit?"

"I don't know how to fix it," Jimmy's daddy said. This was true. Jimmy's daddy didn't know how to fix anything much. Collums could probably fix it if he stared at it long enough.

The old lady worked on her bill some, straightening it in her veined and knobby hands, smoothing it, stretching the wrinkles from it. Then she looked back up at him, her watery blue eyes enormous behind her glasses.

"Why not? You in Maintenance, ain't you?"

She stuck the bill back in the machine.

"Yes'm," Jimmy's daddy said, "but I don't know how to fix no dollar changer."

The machine spit the bill back out. Jimmy's daddy looked up and saw the big-tittied heifer eating a spoonful of what looked like maybe vegetable soup. She chewed and then laughed at something one of the dumpy girls was saying. He wondered how long they'd all known each other.

"Have you got change of a dollar?" Miss Cricket said. She was looking at Jimmy's daddy with a hopeful expression.

"Not me," Jimmy's daddy said. "If I had change of a dollar I wouldn't be standing here in line to get change of a dollar."

"Well shit," she said. "Have you got a good dollar bill you can swap out with me?"

Jimmy's daddy held out the one he was holding. It was pretty sad.

"This one's about the best one I got. And it ain't good."

Miss Cricket leaned over and looked at it. She examined it closely and then looked at hers. Then back again.

"Dang, looks like somebody's wiped their ass with that one. I'll just go get fifty cents from Doris."

She stuck her dollar in her pocket and hurried away. Jimmy's daddy walked up to the dollar changer and very carefully started threading it in. The whole idea, he thought, was to keep it good and flat until the rollers kicked in and caught it and pulled it on in. He felt the pull. He held on to it for a second, just to put a little tension on the bill while the rollers were pulling on it, and then he turned loose. The bill rolled right on into the machine and it spit four quarters back out. Jimmy's daddy grinned and got them in his hand and walked around the corner to the Coke machine, which happened to be directly behind the big-tittied heifer who was now laughing and telling some story that sounded like it was about a picnic. Jimmy's daddy didn't look at her this time. He wasn't going to stare at her this time. He was just going to listen to her. He put two of the quarters into the coin slot and stood there for a few moments, acting like he was trying to make up his mind what kind of drink he wanted and listening to the new girl.

"And so we went up this dirt road, and it had all these funky-looking . . . I don't know what they were. Buildings," she said, and laughed again. "But I'm telling you, I was glad to get the hell out of there."

Jimmy's daddy wondered who *we* was and wondered if she had a boyfriend and heard the two dumpy girls laughing and he pushed the button for a Coke. Nothing happened. He pushed it again. Zero. Piece of shit! He looked at his watch. He'd already been in the break room for almost ten minutes and now he only had about twenty-something minutes left to eat and smoke and shoot the shit with Seaborn and them. And his damn chili was getting cold.

He mashed the button for the coin return and his two quarters rattled down into the plastic tray. He instantly put them back in, like a sucker feeding a slot machine. He pushed the button for a Coke and nothing came out.

"Son of a bitch," he muttered, and he heard a girl laugh behind him. He didn't look around, though, because he didn't have any way of knowing if they were laughing at him not being able to get a Coke out of the machine or not. They might be laughing at something they were talking about. Hell, they might be laughing about something that happened last summer. Or at the senior prom. His face turned red anyway and he felt it. Damn it, he *hated* for his face to turn red!

He waited until his face turned back to not red and pushed the Coke button and nothing happened again. So he pushed the button for the coin return. Nothing happened. Son of a bitch! He whammed it pretty good a couple of times with his fist.

"That old machine don't work half the time," somebody said behind him, and he looked around to see who was talking. It was one of the dumpy girls. She was sitting beside the new girl, and both of them were turned around looking at him. The new girl was chewing, and she looked at Jimmy's daddy with what he saw as thinly veiled disgust. [. . .]

"It won't gimme me my money back," he said, looking at the new girl while he said it. She was still chewing, and then she swallowed. Then she turned back around. The dumpy girl got up and came over. Jimmy's daddy wasn't sure what her name was. She worked down in Porcelain, kept a mask over her face most of the day, and sprayed liquid porcelain on stove interiors that were coming by hanging on hooks. He saw her down there pretty often since he had to walk all over the plant to work on this or that.

"It took my money last week," she said. "But the Coke man'll give you your money back if you leave him a note."

She looked up at Jimmy's daddy. Her hair was kind of frizzy and long and she had a wide face that was powdered heavily. She looked like she had painted her lips on.

"I got a pen in my purse. You want to leave him a note?"

Jimmy's daddy cut his eyes past her briefly to see if the big-tittied heifer had turned her head to listen to their conversation, but she hadn't. She didn't appear to be interested in what was being said between Jimmy's daddy and the dumpy girl. But the dumpy girl was smiling up at him in a way that made him wonder if she was the one they were talking about who had given somebody the blow job in the parking lot. How the hell would he find out? And would she be able maybe to introduce him to the heifer? Because he saw now that her beauty was so great that he wouldn't be able to work up the guts to just nonchalantly walk up to her and toss off some bullshit. He needed an introduction.

"Yeah, I guess so," Jimmy's daddy said.

The dumpy girl never had stopped smiling and she stepped back over to the table and said something to the other girls and they giggled, the heifer, too, then the dumpy girl picked up her purse and brought it over and started digging through its contents. Jimmy's daddy was looking

A Miracle of Catfish 135

over the top of her head at the back of the new girl. She was still eating and now she was listening to some story the other dumpy girl was telling, and nodding a lot, and saying, "Um hum," and picking up some cookies and biting into them. She had a box of milk. She had a blue purse with red and yellow cloth flowers sewn onto it. She had tight blue jeans and sandals. Maybe she was a college woman.

"Here's the pen," the dumpy girl said, and pulled out a black-and-white Bic missing the cap. She handed it to Jimmy's daddy and he stood there watching her paw through her purse.

"I need to get on and eat," Jimmy's daddy said, and the dumpy girl looked up while still pawing.

"I got a piece of paper in here I know," she said. "I see you around the plant a lot," she said. "You used to be in Spot-Welding, didn't you?"

"Yeah," Jimmy's daddy said. "I'm in Maintenance now."

"I know," she said. "I see you working on them Towmotors and things. I bet you know a lot about lubrication. That sure was bad about John Wayne Payne, wasn't it?"

"Yeah, it was," Jimmy's daddy said. He wished to hell people would stop mentioning it to him, about how bad it was. About fifty people had already said something to him about him accidentally crushing John Wayne Payne, although almost all of them said how they understood that it wasn't totally his fault. But none of that made a shit. By then he was wishing to hell he never had come over here and gotten into all this. She was still looking through her purse and pushing things aside.

"He gimme a lift one time," she said.

"Do what?"

She looked up. "Gimme a lift. On my Mercury. I had a flat at lunch one day and he drove his lift right out in the parking lot and picked it up while some fellers changed it for me. Ate his baloney sandwich with one hand. I know I got a piece of paper in here."

"That's okay," Jimmy's daddy said, and tried to hand her back the pen. "I got to go eat before my lunch break gets over."

She stopped pawing through her purse and took the pen back and stuck it in there.

"What about your fifty cents?" she said. "Don't you want it back?"

"I'll just get it from the Coke guy next time I see him," Jimmy's daddy said, and started to turn away.

"Well," she said. "It was nice talking to you."

And then she stuck her hand out.

"My name's Lacey," she said. "I already know your name."

"Aw yeah?" Jimmy's daddy said. He shook her hand and then dropped it. "How'd you know my name?"

"Asked somebody," she said. "I live down at Water Valley. You ever get down there?"

"Well, naw," Jimmy's daddy said. "I don't get down there much. I went to the Watermelon Festival one time back when I was a kid. Did you ever go to it?"

"Shoot. My sister Loretta was Watermelon Queen one year. I live on Church Street," she said. "One eleven Church. I always have some cold beer around if you ever down there and want to come by for some."

Some what? Jimmy's daddy wondered. "Uh. Well," he said.

"My house is easy to find. It's on Church and if you going up from Main Street it's the fifth house on the right."

"Oh yeah?" he said. Damn. She wasn't shy, was she?

"I'd be glad to draw some directions. If I could find some paper."

She grinned. She had a few teeth missing, but the ones she had were okay. Jimmy's daddy didn't have a whole set of teeth himself.

"We could drank five or six beers." She giggled slightly.

"Well, uh," Jimmy's daddy said. Did she say *111 Church*?

"I stay up late," she said.

He would have talked to her some more, but he had to go eat.

"Specially on the weekends," she added.

"Okay. Well. Maybe I'll see you sometime," Jimmy's daddy said.

"I sure hope so," she said. She wasn't making any effort to move. Then she said, "But I'll let you go eat your lunch. I wouldn't want you to get hungry and go all weak on me."

"Okay. Take it easy."

"You, too."

By the time Jimmy's daddy got back to the table where Seaborn and the Tool-and-Die guys were sitting, he figured his chili was cold and he still didn't have a Coke. He was kind of pissed off. He sat down and looked at his watch and saw that he only had seventeen minutes left on his lunch break.

"What the hell you doing?" Seaborn said.

"Aw, the damn Coke machine," Jimmy's daddy said, and picked up his spoon. He stirred his chili a little and dipped his spoon in and took a bite. It was barely warm. Some orange grease was standing in tiny puddles in there. And now three or four people were standing in front of the microwave, maybe warming up pies they'd brought from home. Some of the ladies in the plant did that, brought cakes or pies from home and warmed the pies up in the microwave and shared them with the other ladies in the plant who worked in their sections, or even just people they knew. He didn't think it was worth getting in line and waiting all over again.

"Looked to me like you's over there tryin to get you some," Seaborn said with a grin, and the Tool-and-Die guys grinned across the table, too.

"I don't think so," Jimmy's daddy said, and took another halfway warm bite of his chili. He was about to get pissed off now. If he had a goddamn wife who'd get up and fix him some lunch, he wouldn't be going through this shit right now. But hell naw, she couldn't do that. She had to go back to bed for another hour after she got the kids off to school. And they weren't even in school now. So she didn't even get up as early as she did the other nine months of the year. She just slept later all summer, like she was doing now. Didn't have to be at the bank until nine. So she stayed up later. Watched HBO and Showtime and Cinemax and he didn't know what all else. He had to go to bed. But she didn't. Couldn't get up and fix him a nice lunch that he could sit down and enjoy. Oh no. He had to get some chili from a machine. In a can about big enough to feed a small dog. And chili just wasn't good if it wasn't hot. It didn't taste the same.

He sat there and ate it anyway. Seaborn was telling the Tool-and-Die guys the story about the skunk causing him to knock his front teeth out, and he wished to hell he had a Coke. A glass of lemonade. Water. Anything.

It looked like most people had already finished eating. Lots of them were throwing their empty lunch sacks into the garbage cans and pushing open the double glass doors to go outside in the parking lot and sit in their cars for a few minutes or smoke or talk to people. He looked down at the little can of chili. He didn't even want the shit now. Cold as hell. The whole damn thing was about to put him in a bad mood. And he hated to get in a bad mood at work. If he got in a bad mood at work, it always meant he'd be in a bad mood when he got home. And he hated to be in a bad mood when he got home. It messed everything up. [. . .]

He didn't finish his chili. He just dropped the spoon in the can and wiped his mouth with one of the napkins and reached into his pocket for a cigarette while reaching for one of the butt-strewn ashtrays sitting nearby on the table. He stuck the cigarette in his mouth and pulled his disposable cheapo lighter from his shirt pocket and struck it, but it didn't light. He struck it again. And again and again and again. It didn't light.

"Son of a bitch," he said. This son of a bitch ought not be out of lighter fluid already. He'd just bought it down at the store the other day. They'd had a whole plastic bucket of them sitting on the counter for fifty cents apiece. It was one day when he'd come by and there weren't over two or three vehicles sitting out there, no delivery trucks, and he'd turned in just to grab some smokes without having to go to town. He'd grabbed one while he was getting some smokes and a cheeseburger. Last weekend was when it was. Oh. It was right before he went and picked up Seaborn and Rusty. Just before they'd taken Jimmy swimming.

He struck it again. Son of a bitch. He held it up and looked at it. It still had fluid in it. He could see it. Why wouldn't it light then? Off-brand son of a bitch probably. Made in fucking Japan or somewhere probably. People would work for thirty-seven cents an hour over there. He'd heard Rusty talk about it. He said it was why everything in the world now was made in China. [. . .]

Jimmy's daddy looked around, wondering where in the hell he could find some matches. What he ought to start doing was carrying two lighters, a used one and a new one, so that he'd always have a spare. And as soon as the used one ran out, go get a new one. That way he could be perpetually replenished in lighters.

The Tool-and-Die guys started laughing when Seaborn finished his story, and Jimmy's daddy waited for a moment and then said: "Y'all ain't got a light have you?"

They shook their heads, still grinning, and started getting up from the table.

"Don't smoke," one of them said.

"I can give you a chew," the other one said.

"Thanks," Jimmy's daddy said, and he turned to Seaborn. "You ain't got any matches on you, have you?"

"Naw," Seaborn said, and rolled up his lunch sack into a ball like he did every day. Most days he'd shoot it like a basketball into a garbage can that was sitting about twenty feet away, and most days he'd make it. He'd always wait until the lunch crowd thinned out somewhat, like now, then shoot it, which is what he did. It arched up and bounced off the back of the Coke machine and hit the floor.

"Shit," Seaborn said, and got up to go get it, but some lady walking by saw it and picked it up for him and dropped it into the garbage can and he did a wave of thanks toward her and walked back to the table and sat down next to Jimmy's daddy, who was getting up.

"Where you going?" Seaborn said.

"Get me a light," Jimmy's daddy said.

"You ain't got but about five minutes," Seaborn said, as Jimmy's daddy was walking away, looking for somebody who might have a light. Just about everybody had cleared out now, except for the big-tittied heifer and her buddies, who were sitting back there smoking. He stopped. He could see a pack of cigarettes and a lighter lying right beside the elbow of the dumpy girl who wanted to drink some beer with him. Hell. It didn't sound like that was all she wanted.

The dumpy girl, Lacey he remembered her name was, looked up and saw him and smiled real big at him. He smiled back and went over there with his cigarette held out in his hand.

"Could I get a light off you?" he said.

He'd figured she'd just probably smile and nod and hand him her lighter, but she didn't. She got up and came right up to him and got real close.

"Course you can," she said, and struck the lighter for him.

Jimmy's daddy put the cigarette in his mouth and leaned over toward the fire, and for just a moment, as he leaned his head down to it, he looked over at the big-tittied heifer, who was watching him. Holy shit, what a set. Then he had to turn his eyes back to what he was doing, which was getting his cigarette lit. He did. He puffed.

"Thanks," he said. "Mine run out a fluid a while ago. Just bought the son of a bitch last Saturday."

The dumpy girl was more than glad to hear it.

"They just don't last long enough, do they?" she said.

"Naw, they don't," Jimmy's daddy said. He started to look at his Timex but he thought that might be rude. They'd sound the buzzer at one minute till. "I used to carry a Zippo all the time but the damn things are so bad about leaking and blistering your leg with that fluid, I quit them."

"Them Zippos is nice," the dumpy girl said. Now that he was up close to her again, he could tell that she had a pretty hefty set of breastworks herself. She just wore these loose clothes that ill defined her figure, he saw. She was a little broad in the ass, but so was Johnette.

"Yeah," Jimmy's daddy said, blowing smoke toward the ceiling, casually glancing toward the new girl, then looking back to the dumpy girl. "Then I carried matches for a while. But if you out in the wind you can't hardly get a light off a match."

"Ain't that the truth," she said. She was looking up at him with a smile again, and Jimmy's daddy wondered if she was wanting to, like, maybe *go* with him or something. He knew there were a lot of plant romances, most of them between married people who were constantly messing around or looking for somebody to mess around with, as close as he could tell. There was a man who worked down in Shipping named Hornwell who was married and wore a wedding ring, but always ate lunch with a woman named Jones who worked at the end of the line, packing stoves into cardboard cartons and sealing them with a glue gun. Sometimes they left together at lunch and came back wearing different clothes. They never left together after work. She was married, too.

"Well, thanks for the light," Jimmy's daddy said, and started to turn away from her again, but she held out the lighter.

"Why don't you just take this one?" she said. "I got three or four more in my purse."

"You sure?" Jimmy's daddy said. He kind of hated to take a lighter from her, but it was going to be a pain in the ass to smoke for the rest of the day until he could get to a store and get a lighter. Or some matches.

"Sure I'm sure," she said. "Honey, you can flick my Bic all day long."

She turned a little red in the face after she said that, and giggled again, and Jimmy's daddy took the lighter and dropped it in his shirt pocket.

"Well thanks," he said, and then the one-minute warning buzzer sounded in the break room.

"You welcome," she said, and kept standing there.

"I guess I better get going," he said. "Collums'll get his panties in a wad if I ain't got my head up under a lift when he walks back in the shop."

She laughed like he'd said the funniest thing in the world and turned away to get her purse off the table. The new girl and the other dumpy girl had already gone.

"Yeah," she said. "I got to get back in there and punch in, too. I'll just walk back to the time clock with you if you don't care."

Jimmy's daddy was puffing on his cigarette and didn't know how he could say no, seeing as how he'd accepted a light and a lighter from her.

"I don't care," he said, and the next thing he knew he was walking beside her, past Seaborn, who was getting up with a shit-eating grin on his face. Jimmy's daddy shot him a murderous look and pushed open one half of the double doors while the dumpy girl pushed open the other one. They went outside together and stepped across the ten feet of concrete and sunshine that separated the break room from the front entrance of the plant and walked in under the overhanging roof and inside to the darker light of the plant. Workers were punching their time cards and sticking them back into a rack and then hurrying toward their jobs. Jimmy's daddy and the dumpy girl moved forward, him behind her, got their cards, and punched back in.

"I'll see you," he said, and slipped his card back into the rack. He turned away to leave a last time.

"I sure hope so," she said.

He just waved at her and started walking back toward Maintenance. Then the main whistle blew for them to get back to work. He started down the aisle and he turned to look back at her. She turned, too, and waved, and since he thought it would be impolite not to wave back, he did.

28

It poured down for the whole funeral. That was on Sunday. It had been raining for three days and it didn't look like it was going to stop any time soon. There was mud on the ladies' shoes, mud on the tires of the cars, mud on the truck that brought the tent for the shade they didn't need.

Lucinda had taken some tranquilizers for her nerves. Albert had to help her away from the grave site once the service was over, her daddy in his starched shirt and tie and suit looking somehow sharp as a tack. Looking like she'd never seen him look before. The suit was new. So were the shiny brown shoes. Somehow the suit and the shoes had made him look about ten years younger. He had a fresh haircut. And he didn't smell like a cow. He was like some new daddy she didn't know. A daddy who could have been someone else. A businessman. A jeweler. A maker of fine cars.

There had been all the people to thank and to say hello and good-bye to, and there had been the walks from the cars into buildings and the walks back out and the picking out of the casket and the ordering of the flowers and the selection of the music and the preacher and the pallbearers and everything, every awful bit of it. It had all been a blur, still was. She was so glad that he'd waited on her to get here before he did any of those things. And it wasn't over yet. They still had to go back to the house and talk to people. And eat. And try to get some rest. And try to figure out what they were going to do. Hell. What was there to do? She was gone.

People were starting to drift back to their cars. It had been raining in Atlanta when they drove to the airport, when they boarded, raining in Memphis when she walked out of the airport with Albert and their bags and caught the bus for the car rental agency. Raining all the way down I-78 into Holly Springs and on down Route 7 South to Oxford. Out Old 6 to Yocona, down DeLay Road, across the river, and then up over all the hills and down to the road her daddy lived on. There was a shortcut you could take. An old dirt road everybody called the Cutoff. Muddy as hell in the winter. That was one reason she'd left: mud. She'd gotten sick of mud. And smelling cow shit. And working in a big vegetable garden in the summertime when it was hot. And chasing cows. And getting kicked. She knew a farmer's life was a hard one. It was hard on everybody around him. He'd worked for fifty years to get what he had. Worked her hard, too. And Mama. And Queen. She could remember playing jacks with Queen on the kitchen floor. And picking peas with her. Once, behind the barn, she had seen Daddy kiss her on the mouth. She had never believed that Queen had gone back home without saying good-bye. For years she'd thought she was still here, just hiding somewhere. Now she thought she was probably dead.

She stood there looking at the flowers they had mounded over her mother. So many people had sent flowers. And Lucinda had seen more people she knew from her childhood, some she'd forgotten about, some she remembered. Like Mister Toby. And he still looked just like he always had. A little grayer. Maybe a little bit smaller. New teeth. Different teeth. He was standing over there next to her daddy in the rain, just at the edge of the tent, and she knew they needed to go and let the workers who were hanging around the trucks with their shovels go on and do their work.

"You want to sit down?" Albert said.

"Yeah. I think it's about time for that," Lucinda said. So they walked over to the car and opened the doors and sat down. It wasn't that hot, just humid, but Lucinda cranked it up and let the air conditioner vents blow on them anyway. She sat with her legs out the door, hating the black dress she was wearing and the fake pearls that were all she had. The stupid hat. The awkward shoes.

She was wanting a cigarette, but people kept walking by the car and saying they were sorry, or that they were headed over to the house, where some other women had already put out the food neighbors had brought and had put out paper plates and napkins and plastic knives and forks and spoons and were waiting for the mourners to show up. Lucinda knew how it was. She'd grown up with that. It was what they did in the country.

"I'm sorry," she said, after some more of them went on by. She reached for her purse and opened it. "I know we're sitting in the cemetery, but I've got to have a smoke."

"I know you do," Albert said, and smiled at her. He'd been so good. So understanding. He had helped her decide things and she had driven around with him to get the things she needed, up to Kroger in Oxford to get stuff for supper last night and down to Fred's Dollar Store for candles and napkins and plastic forks and things. The funeral had seemed to calm him, and now you couldn't tell that there was anything wrong with him.

She lit her cigarette and dropped the lighter on the seat and crossed her arms over her breasts and sat there with the door open and spoke to people as they kept going by. She could see her daddy and Mister Toby slowly making their way from the tent, coming down the gravel in the light rain, what had slowed to less than a drizzle now in the last few minutes. But his suit was wet in spots. She could see that from here. What she couldn't see was how he felt. He hadn't cried. He hadn't said that he was going to miss her. He was vague about when she'd died. Sometime during the night. After they'd talked on the phone. It was mildly troubling for some reason. Like maybe he was lying. But she didn't know that. She could see him laughing at something Mister Toby was saying. She wished she were closer to him. But it wasn't like she hadn't tried. And tried and tried.

"Who's that guy with your daddy, again?" Albert said.

"That's Toby Tubby," Lucinda said. "I've known him all my life. Him and Daddy have been friends since they were little boys. One of them was born one day and one the next. They're one day apart."

"Which one's older?" Albert said.

Lucinda laughed and took a drag of her smoke. "I can't ever remember. Mister Toby used to bring these catfish up to the house that he'd caught with his bare hands out of these logs. They were monsters. Him and Daddy used to fish a lot. I don't know if they still do or not."

"He's excited about that new pond," Albert said.

Lucinda flicked her ashes out on the gravel and scratched her leg.

"Oh yeah, we got to go see the pond. Maybe when everybody leaves this afternoon we can walk over there. It's not far. You mind?"

"Naw, babe, I don't mind."

"Great. Well let me get up and go see if he's ready to go. God knows I am."

She dropped her cigarette on the gravel and stood up and stepped on it, and walked over to her daddy and Mister Toby where they had stopped just short of her daddy's truck and Mister Toby's minivan. Her daddy was so much taller than him that it still looked funny. They'd always been like Mutt and Jeff. She'd be so glad to get these shoes off.

"You ready to go?" her daddy said.

"I guess so," she said. Then she looked at Mister Toby. "You're coming over to the house, aren't you, Mister Toby?"

Mister Toby nodded.

"Aw yeah. I'm coming. I want to see that catfish pond later on."

"Good," she said. She walked up closer to her daddy and stood in front of him. She didn't know what she was wanting him to do, but she wanted him to do something. Maybe say something. He'd held her elbow during the whole graveside service, seated in the draped chairs right in front of the casket, but she never had seen a tear in his eye. Not today. Not any day. He didn't seem to have any. But that was old news, too.

"Are you okay?" she said.

"I'm all right, I reckon," he said.

"Well," she said. "Okay. I guess we'll see y'all there then."

"Yep," he said, and turned away toward his truck. She watched him get in and start it up. It was just as rusty and dented as it had ever been, and he never would listen to her at all about buying a nice car so that her mother would have something to ride in besides a truck whenever she needed to go to the doctor or wherever, said it was a waste of money. He backed the truck up and started to turn around, craning his head out the window to see. Always poor-mouthing about how broke he was. Her whole life. She knew better than that. Her mother had told her that he had money hidden in the barn, that he always had. Lucinda wondered if it was true, if he still had money hidden out there somewhere in the hay. He got the truck backed up and then turned the wheel and pulled forward. She didn't have any idea how much he had in the bank. But he had all the land. The house. All the cows. And a new pond she hadn't seen yet. He pulled out and headed toward the highway. Mister Toby had gotten into his minivan and he was pulling out. She waved and got in the car and shut the door.

"Okay now, we're ready," Lucinda said. "Thanks for being patient."

Albert reached out and touched her on the arm.

"I'm here for whatever you need," he said.

"I know you are," Lucinda said, and reached for another smoke. She lit it and rolled her window down and hung her arm out the window. She looked back to see the men coming with their shovels to the tent. Then she looked away. She put the car in gear and started down the drive. It was hard not to look in the rearview mirror at the men. But she kept her eyes on the dirt driveway and stopped at the highway and looked both ways before she pulled out. There were woods across the road, deep hollows studded with white oaks and hickories and beeches. It was shady down in there. It looked cool and inviting.

"Those are the prettiest woods there," she said. "Daddy's got some woods like that. Up on the other side of the place. I'm looking forward to seeing the pond. I guess you could swim in it once it gets filled up."

"Maybe if he puts in a diving board," Albert said.

"I was always so scared of the water," Lucinda said. "We used to go over to Wall Doxey State Park for family reunions and Mother was always scared to death I was going to drown. I can hear her now. 'Don't wade in off past your knees!' Stuff like that. Boy."

They went around the curve at a gentle speed. The road went past a couple of houses. One carport held a Jeep up on jack stands with the back axle missing. Both houses had big vegetable gardens, one with rows of red tomatoes hanging thick and heavy. Beans staked with cane poles in big Xs. The vines tied with twine. She could remember doing that with her daddy and her mother. The long days out in the sun. How brown she'd be in the summers. Except for the white places left by her swimming suit.

"I wish Daddy had something to drink at the house," Lucinda said. "But I bet he doesn't have anything."

"You wanting a drink?" Albert said.

"I wish I had a beer. A glass of wine. Anything. You holding out okay on Cokes?"

"I've got a few left," Albert said.

"We'll get some more. I know there's going to be a bunch of people over there. But don't be nervous. I'm going to stay right beside you the whole time. You okay?"

She glanced at him and he was nodding. She could tell he was fine. He'd rolled his window down, too, and the wind was blowing through his hair. He picked up one leg and raised the bottom of his trousers and scratched at his ankle. Then he set his leg back down and peeled off a butter rum Life Saver from a roll on the seat beside him and slipped it into his mouth.

"Something bite you?" she said.

"Yeah. Some kind of a damn little old bug," he said.

"Probably a red bug," she said. "I used to get them on me all the time when I picked blackberries."

Albert slid over in the seat and sat close to her, touching his hip against hers. It made her feel better for him to be sitting so close to her. He was what she was leaning on. She couldn't lean on Daddy. He wouldn't let her.

She glanced at him again. His tanned hands were muscular and strong. He liked the new suit she'd bought him a few months back. Black suit, black tie, black shirt, black belt, black shoes, black socks. It was what he'd wanted. And she had already learned that there wasn't any use in arguing with him, because another thing he had in great supply when he needed it was patience. She'd seen him work two days straight in his room and go without eating. Or sleeping. And then he'd eat a bucket of KFC dark meat and sleep for nineteen hours. And then he'd want to make love for a couple of days. He was ravenous in his appetites.

She patted him on the leg and he patted her on the leg. She started slowing down when she saw the roof of the church through the trees on the side of the road, and put on her blinker to turn left where the road split. An old guy in the ditch with a garbage bag was picking up cans.

They stopped at the STOP sign and Lucinda looked past the church, where people were pulled up in their cars, cleaning the church, she guessed. They still did that. People cleaned the church and fed the preacher and somebody came and fixed the water pipes when they were broken or vacuumed the carpet once a week.

She pulled out. They went around another curve and Lucinda saw that things hadn't changed that much in London Hill. But the store was closed. She hated to see that, see it dark and empty, a big FOR SALE sign hanging out front, with some realtor's phone number in town written on it.

"I wonder when the store closed," she said. She looked over her shoulder as it receded in the distance. "I can remember coming up here with Daddy and being scared to death of all these old men who sat around outside on these benches and chewed tobacco and dipped snuff."

They went past a couple of houses and a trailer with a deck where some Toyota pickups were parked. A group of young men drinking beer in the yard waved at them and Lucinda waved back. It felt good being home except for the reason she was here. She hadn't moved quick enough. She'd assed around and waited too long.

Albert pointed to an old barn they were passing, tall and crumbling, rusted sheets of tin with trees coming through them, the whole thing leaning slightly toward the road.

"Thing's about to fall down," he said.

"I know," Lucinda said. "It's been that way a long time."

The rain had washed the air clean and Lucinda looked at the high clumps of wisteria they were passing, their light purple flowers strung among honeysuckle and thorny vines. Cedar trees standing beside the road in little copses, rusted wire strung in front of them on broken posts. It hadn't been that many years since cows had grazed in that pasture, and she could remember her daddy and Mister Toby going down to the catalpa trees there for fish bait and knocking the fat green-and-black caterpillars from the undersides of the leaves with a long cane pole. That was back when they ran set hooks in the river. She took a drag from her smoke and let the smoke slip out the window. She remembered how good that fish was. Queen used to cook it. Where had she gone to? Would she ever know? Had they been lovers? Had he done something to her? As long as she'd stayed here, why had they never heard from her again? It was easier not to think about these things in Atlanta. It was hard not to think about them here, where you could look around and see where your childhood had taken place.

"Why don't you loosen your tie," she said to Albert. "I know that thing must be choking you."

Albert just shook his head. She had to admit that the black suit and the black shirt and tie made him look Hollywood. She'd seen lots of women looking at him. Wondering who he was. Wondering who Lucinda Sharp had brought home from Atlanta. She was glad for that. She was glad for them to wonder just who it was she had. Because for a very long time she hadn't had anybody. Nobody. Zero. Zilch. A lonely life. TV. Pizza. Always thinking she was too fat for anybody to want her.

They went over a hill and met a car. The driver waved and then Albert did, too, after the car was already past. He bent his head and stuck just the tip of his tongue into her ear and she jumped slightly in the seat.

"Ooooo, sweetie!" she said. She put her hand on his leg. Albert put his warm fingers on the back of her neck. He rubbed the muscles there gently. He'd learned somewhere in his life how to do massages and he could work on you until you were completely limp and drifting off into sleep. He could take every muscle and bend it and twang it until it was whimpering with happiness, could rub his strong fingers deep into the fibers of the muscles and almost make them cry with pleasure and relief. She stayed tensed up too much. She worried too much. What about? About everything. About what *might* happen.

"I'd better watch it," she said. "I'll run off the road."

He smiled and scooted over a little toward his side of the car and she slowed again near an orchard of pecan trees where a little girl was in a swing, swinging, her ponytail flying out behind her on the downstroke. Some little dog was standing there watching her. It was almost too small to be a dog, and she slowed the car a little more to take a look, glancing back at the road to make sure nothing was coming. Then some bushes obscured the little girl and the dog and she sped back up, put on her blinker, and turned down the hill onto her daddy's road.

"Did you see that dog?" she said.

Albert was nodding and still looking back that way.

"I thought it was a rabbit at first," he said. They were going past a trailer home that had a nice garden with some of the tallest tomato plants she'd seen. Somebody had put a storm house into the bank in front of it, and there were some boats propped up against trees in the yard. An old couple was sitting in front of it, looked like they were shelling peas with their dishpans in their laps and their paper sacks for the hulls beside their chairs. They waved and Lucinda waved at them. She used to know the man who lived there, Mister Roscoe Sparks, but he'd been dead now for three or four years. She didn't know these new people. Maybe his sister or somebody. It was plain after not even two days here that more people had moved in. There were more trailers, more new houses, new driveways going off the highway. When she was a kid she knew everybody who lived around here. But it was changing. Here were some horses in a lot and a small barn where woods once stood.

It seemed that the only thing that hadn't changed very much was her parents' place. The barn, the house, the yard all looked about like they had when she was growing up and riding her bicycle up to the store. And riding the school bus. And working in the garden. And running cows from one pasture to another. And driving a tractor in a cotton field under the burning sun. He had worked her just like she was a boy. And she didn't really hold it against him, even though sometimes it had been pretty rough. Pulling calves. Building fences. Catching cows and putting tags in their ears. But she still couldn't understand why it had been necessary. Cleve had been around for some of those years. It was like her daddy had wanted her to know how the sun felt when you had to be under it all day or how tired your legs and arms were when you chopped cotton for eight hours. None of the people she knew in Atlanta had ever worked the way she had worked when she was a child, a teenager, almost a grown woman. And when she told things like that, they looked at her as if she were from another planet.

They drove past a new house in a hollow and then wound through a stand of woods, and the shiny green leaves were hanging thick and washed clean from the rain. The road whispered gently beneath the tires as she drove carefully around the curves and past the gas pipeline where a fifty-foot swath from Texas to Mississippi had been cut across the country. She had walked that pipeline one time, where it crossed a creek on the other side of her daddy's place. It was six feet in diameter and you could stand on it and see where the line ran up through the woods, a clear-cut channel. She drove past where the Cutoff road intersected with this one. She'd already noticed that somebody had put a trailer down there above Queen's old house. Somebody with a '55 Chevy, looked like a junker.

"I've got to hit that bathroom," Albert said.

"Okay," she said. "We're almost there."

She slowed when she saw the barn. It was set a little off the road, just beyond the steel cattle gap that had been there as long as she could remember. Albert was fascinated by the thing and wanted to get out of the car and look at it every time they drove over it, but he didn't ask her to stop now. And he was funny about going to the bathroom when he was in a place where he didn't know the people. Like in a restaurant, if they were sitting at the table and he had to go, she always had to get up and go with him and stand outside the men's room door while he went inside and did his business. He was so much like a child in so many ways. He didn't like storms, would want to sit very close to her and hold on to her when it thundered and rained hard. She had always liked storms and she liked them even better now.

She could see the cars and trucks parked in the yard and in the drive once they got past the barn. A lot of them. And they were probably going to make Albert's condition worse, if he got packed in there among them. Some of them had already been shocked. Some more would probably get shocked this afternoon. Too bad. It wouldn't be forever. He was who she had and she was sticking by him.

"It's a pretty good many folks, looks like," she said.

"Wharm quark," Albert said. "You so go slow." Already starting up and God knows why.

"I'm *hurrying*, honey," she said.

She could see some people standing in the yard and a few people sitting in the rockers on the front porch, probably eating. She pulled down the drive between the cars and trucks and found an open place beside the house and pulled in there and shut off the car. She got the keys and dropped them in her purse. Albert was already out and waiting when she shut her door.

"Harm quarm farm," he said.

"It's all right," she said. "You want me to hold your hand?"

He nodded and grabbed her hand and pulled her close to him as he started for the front porch. She looked down and her feet were squishing in the wet grass.

"I hate these damn shoes," she said. Then she stopped. "Let's go in the back door. We might not run into as many people that way and we'll get you to the bathroom quicker."

Albert stopped and turned and then she stopped again.

"Actually let's just walk behind the equipment shed," she said. "I won't be able to get through that crowd inside for five minutes probably. You can pee behind the equipment shed. Come on."

Albert nodded and held on to her hand and kept up with her as she went across the backyard, waving to a few men who were standing back there smoking, and they walked across the wet pea gravel that had always been there. The openings in the equipment shed were high and wide, and her daddy's last cotton picker sat in one of the stalls, the tires all flat, some of the red paint rusted away, the whole thing bent and crumpled like a cheap toy that had been played with too much. His big John Deere 4020 was in another stall with a chisel plow hooked to it, the green paint faded, but she knew it was probably still running like a champion. She worried about him being on it, old as he was. What if he rolled it over on himself?

"You can walk right around the corner, baby," she said, and turned loose of his hand. Albert nodded and went down the trail alongside the building and turned the corner and disappeared. Lucinda dug into her purse for her smokes, lit one, and then set her purse down on the ground. She stood there holding her elbow and smoking, listening to the people in the house. She could see some of them in the kitchen, and a few people were coming out the back door. The pecan trees were already big when she was a girl, and now they were simply giants. The entire backyard was engulfed in their massive shade in the summer, and the trees made the heat bearable. Most days, there was always at least a whiff of a cool breeze under there. All those leaves blocking away the sun. How many purple hull peas had she shelled out here? Thousands upon thousands. Thumbs purple for days.

A cow bawled down in the pasture and she turned her head to look. She didn't know how many mama cows he had now. Looked like maybe fifteen or twenty. She stood there thinking about him being on the tractor in the winter, in January and February, driving those big round bales of hay around and dropping them off for his cows. He had a plywood kind of a cage he'd built that he could set over the tractor seat in the winter and get inside it and she guessed the heat from the motor warmed him a little. She didn't know why he was still messing with cows, old as he was. But he'd always done it. She knew it would be hard to give up things even if you were old.

Good God, Albert, are you still peeing? she thought. She walked on over to the cotton picker and looked at it. Nothing but a great big pile of junk now, but she could remember the day they delivered it from Pontotoc. She didn't know what year it was. Late sixties maybe. She was probably about eight. Thank God her mother wouldn't let him or he would have made her learn how to drive it, too. But that job always fell to Cleve. When he was here and not in the pen. She wondered where he was. It had been a very long time since she'd seen him, but she knew he still remembered her. Besides Queen, he was the only black person her daddy would let her around when she was a kid. She guessed her daddy trusted him. He always called her Miss Lucinda. Even back when she was a little bitty thing. He'd tip his hat to her. Like an old familiar thing he'd been trained to do, automatically, without thinking. He must have been in his twenties when he first worked for her daddy. And then he went away to prison and was older when he came back. And then he went away again and looked much older when he came back that time. But her daddy had always said that Cleve was the best hand he ever had. It was the only praise she had ever heard him say about a black person. He just hated them. But he didn't hate Queen, did he? And he wouldn't talk about her, would he? Oh no. That subject would only get you a cold look and silence. Maybe a little admonition to mind your own business or go do your homework.

Somebody slipped his hands over her eyes and she smiled.

"Now I wonder who that is," she said, thinking it was Albert. And then she smelled Old Spice and knew it wasn't. He hadn't done that in a long time. She pulled the hands away and turned around and looked at her daddy.

"Hey," she said. She took a last drag from her smoke and then dropped it and stepped on it.

"What you doing?" he said. He was loosening his tie and unbuttoning the tight collar. He undid the tie and pulled it by the small end until it slid around under the collar of his shirt and came out in his hand. He rolled it up carefully and put it in his pocket.

"I'm waiting on Albert," she said. "He's going to the bathroom behind the equipment shed."

Her daddy looked back that way. Then he turned back around to her.

"You all right?" he said. He acted like he was afraid to touch her. He was just standing there watching her.

"I'm okay," she said. "You gonna go in and eat?"

He put his hands in his pockets and toed at a pebble.

"Yeah, I reckon so," he said. "Your mama had got to where she didn't cook much no more."

"I'd think it would be kind of hard to cook in a wheelchair."

"She said it was easier to use the stove since she didn't have to bend over. She could roll it right over and stick a pan of biscuits in."

Lucinda saw Albert walking out from the side of the equipment shed and she smiled at him. He smiled back and then he stopped. Her daddy turned and looked at him. Lucinda spoke up.

"It's okay, Albert. Come on over."

So he did. He'd tried to talk to her daddy a few times when they first got there, but as usual her daddy didn't have any patience with him, which had made him nervous and started his tics up. He looked up at her daddy and stuck out his hand to be shaken. Her daddy looked down at it, and then looked up at him, and then looked at Lucinda, and then slowly took Albert's hand and shook it. But instead of turning loose after the handshake, Albert held on. Her daddy tried to pull his hand back, but Albert just held on.

"You can turn loose now," her daddy said. Albert smiled at him, agreeing with him, but he didn't turn him loose. His head jerked.

"Lucinda?" her daddy said. "Can you make him turn loose of me?"

"I don't know," she said. "Sometimes he finds somebody he likes and just won't turn loose. That's how he got me. When we going to look at the pond?"

"After we eat," he said. "If I can get in the house to eat."

"Harm quarm farm," Albert said to him, and then turned loose of his hand.

Albert had gotten the fishing pole in a snarl and he was down on his knees in jeans working on it, trying to untangle it.

"Piss fuck cock shit dick," he said.

"I done told him they wasn't no fish in this pond yet," her daddy said to Mister Toby, who had come back in his overalls and was periodically spitting into a small white cup his viscous liquid tobacco discharges. "But wouldn't nothing do him but bring the rod and reel. That old thing needs some new line on it anyway."

"It's a beautiful pond, Daddy," Lucinda said, standing beside him. She'd put on some shorts and sandals and a button-up shirt of Albert's. All the people had finally gone and there was so much food left over that she'd had a hard time fitting it all into the refrigerator, which hadn't been very well stocked. Canned biscuits and bacon and eggs and some jelly and some sliced baloney. Now it was crammed with deviled eggs and sliced hams and chicken and dressing and fried chicken and casseroles and even some fried quail.

"It's about halfway full," her daddy said, looking out over the muddy water. "I figure if I get three or four more good rains it'll fill on up."

"I believe it's deep enough to where you can go ahead and get your fish and put em in, Cortez," Mister Toby said.

"How often does the fish man come?" her daddy said.

"Every month or two in the summer. He was just here, let's see . . . this is . . . He was here third week in July. So he ought to be back fore long. I can find out when I get back to work in the morning for you. I'll ask Richard. He'll know."

"Reckon how many I ought to get?" her daddy said.

"I don't know. The fish guy can tell you, though. Deep as this thing's gonna be I'd say it would hold a lot. You gonna feed em, ain't you?"

"Oh yes, I'm gonna feed em," her daddy said. "I'm gonna get me some feed the same day I get the fish."

He looked over at Albert, still messing with the tangled reel. Then he looked at Lucinda.

"He gets into something, he just kind of sticks with it, don't he?"

"Yeah, he does," she said. "I don't know what makes him that way, but that's how he is. Albert? Why don't you quit messing with that rod and reel? We'll come back and fish when it has some fish in it, okay?"

"Fuck a goat's ass," Albert said, but he calmly nodded. He stood up with the rod and reel and walked over to them. He leaned the rod against his shoulder and his head did that jerking motion. Lucinda couldn't get over how nicely shaped the pond was. Whoever had built it had taken his time and done it right. It was over an acre of water and the banks were gently sloped and smoothly finished. It looked so natural that only the big pile of trees down near the levee revealed what had been here before. Over the fall the remaining trees would layer the banks with shed leaves, and in spring and summer it would be a nice place to come and fish. Sit with Albert and show him how to do it.

Albert handed her the rod and reel and she took it. She couldn't wait to get him back home. She was afraid to make love with him here, back in her old bedroom. She knew she was over forty years old and all that, but she just couldn't do it. She was afraid her daddy would hear them. Especially with the kind of noises Albert made when he got excited.

She wished now that she'd booked their plane tickets for Tuesday instead of tomorrow. Now that she was here, and the funeral was over, and all the people were gone from the house, it would have been nice to stay around, work in the garden some, bring a blanket and some suntan oil and lie out in the sun beside the pond. And there were so many things she needed to talk over with her daddy. One of them was what to do with all her mama's things. She knew what he'd do. He'd box everything up and stick it in the barn probably. The wheelchair would be folded up and crammed somewhere. And he would be here all by himself. Maybe she was more worried about that than anything. What he was going to do with himself. What he was going to eat.

"Where's Cleve these days, Daddy?" she said.

Her daddy scratched his ear and then cut a faint fart.

"Daddy," she said.

"He's still over there in Old Dallas. That girl of his finally come home with some soldier."

"How old's Cleve now?"

"I don't know. I think he was in his twenties when he went to the pen the first time. Stayed nine years and then he come back and he was fifty when he went back again. I think he did eight years then. He ain't been out but three years. I'd guess he's about sixty."

"You think he remembers me?"

Her daddy nodded and looked out across the water.

"I imagine he does."

"I wish I could go see him."

Her daddy turned around and stared at her.

"What the hell you want to go see him for?"

He was looking at her hard and it was difficult for her to say what she felt. It always had been, in front of him.

"I don't know. I just remember when he used to work around the place. He was always nice to me."

"He ain't nice if you cross him when he's drunk. That's how come he did two stretches in Parchman for manslaughter."

She stood there, nodding.

"I just wondered how he was doing," she said.

"He's doing about like he always has."

She could tell that was the end of that. And it was getting close to late evening anyway. She'd toyed with the idea of driving across the river for some beer with Albert and then come back and maybe make some sandwiches for supper. There was so much food in there.

A bat had come out of the woods and was swooping low across the water, not quite touching the surface with its wingtips. It skittered and jerked across the air, returning, flying off, coming back.

"Well," her daddy said. "We better get on back before it gets dark."

"It's sure nice, Daddy," she said.

"It's mighty fine, Cortez," Mister Toby said. "I'll find out about that fish guy for you in the morning."

"Good," her daddy said.

The Tallahatchie River bridge was long rusted and the wheels made a rushing sound when you went between the guardrails. It was almost dark and the rental car's lights were bright. Lucinda hadn't made a run across the river to the beer store in a long time. It used to be a thing to do on Sunday afternoons, with some of her friends, back when she was going to Ole Miss. She didn't have any idea where all those people were now. Most of them probably had children by now. At forty-three, she'd realized that the clock had run out for her. Her daddy didn't mention it anymore, but she knew he was disappointed not to have any grand-children. She'd failed him. He hadn't said that, but she knew that's what he thought. He didn't think much of her living in Atlanta either, but she couldn't live her life just to please him. She had a good job modeling. It paid for nice things.

Albert was asleep in the seat beside her. She guessed he was worn out from everything. She had the radio playing at a low level that maybe wouldn't wake him up. By tomorrow night they'd be back home, to sleep in their own bed, wear their comfortable clothes, watch their own TV. Daddy hadn't even turned his on since she'd been home. He'd mentioned how loudly her mother used to play it. But it was all the entertainment she'd had. He stayed outside all the time, working at one thing and another. He didn't seem to be slowing down a whole lot, even at his age.

She glanced over at Albert. He was relaxed in the seat, his face turned toward her, his hands composed in his lap and lit by the green glow of the dash lights. Sleeping as peacefully as a baby.

The traffic was fairly light. She met one state trooper who flashed his blue lights at her because she was speeding. She let off the gas and looked in the rearview to see if he'd hit his brake lights. He hadn't. She guessed she'd better slow down, especially on the way back. The cops had always been bad on this highway.

Marshall County. She knew there were dirt roads that led all through the woods on the other side of the railroad tracks and that little juke joints were scattered all up and down them, places where people gathered on weekend nights to listen to electric guitars and drink homemade whisky and Budweiser. A long time ago she'd gone to Junior Kimbrough's place one Sunday evening and had heard him play. But there weren't many white faces in there. Nobody had acted ugly to her, but more than a few of the men had hit on her. That was a long time ago. But she still remembered what it felt like in there, the smoke and the dim lights and the screaming guitar Junior had played, one of his boys drumming for him, another one playing bass, everybody drinking and laughing and dancing. It was another world. And now Junior was dead and his place had burned down. [. . .]

She started slowing down just this side of the county line and she put on her blinker to turn left, even though there was only one car way back behind her. It had rained over here, too, and the dirt drive she turned onto was still a little muddy, but it had plenty of gravel on it. The tires made a crunching sound rolling over it. She reached out and touched Albert.

"We're here, babe," she said, and he stirred in the seat. He put out his arms straight ahead of him before he opened his eyes and he squinched his face up into a contortion and made a grunting noise deep in his chest and then twined his fingers together and turned them backward and flexed his knuckles so that they popped. Then he opened his eyes and looked around.

"This the place?" he said.

"This is it. Best barbecue around. And they got cold beer."

The place was called Betty Davis's and it was a little shack that was perched on a low hill. Rusty roof, beer signs all over. Smoke was always rising from the cooker in back. The clay gravel parking lot was one Lucinda had never seen empty. She drove slowly and a rabbit ran across the road. Oh shit. She stopped just short of the joint to let out a car that was backing up, a black Lexus, new, muddy, what looked like some college students driving it. They had their interior light on and Lucinda stopped to let them do whatever they were doing. Laughing. Getting beer out of the paper sack. They turned and straightened up and went past her, waving as they went. She waved back and eased up the hill into the slot they had vacated, parked and shut it off.

"You ready to go in?" she said.

Albert's head jerked. He was already taking his seat belt off. She hoped nothing would happen in here, but he was starting to blink.

She got out and put the keys in her pocket and waited for Albert to get out and come around. There was a car parked beside her and a big black kid with a paper sack came out the door, heading toward it. He was dressed all in clean starched denim, a Raiders cap turned backward on his head, tremendous Nikes on his outsized feet. He was boogeying his head to some internal rhythm as he came out, almost dancing as he walked.

"Whassup?" he said, flashing a big smile, one gold tooth showing.

"How you doing?" Lucinda said.

"Suck a duck, Buck," Albert said.

The black kid stopped. He weighed close to three hundred. Big enough to be a linebacker at Ole Miss. Might have been.

"Say what?" he said. He had put a look of concern on his face.

"Come *here*, Albert," Lucinda said to him. "He has something wrong with him," she said to the big black kid.

"He gonna have something wrong he don't watch that mouth," the kid said.

"It's all right," Lucinda said. "Come here, Albert, and hold my hand."

Albert walked obediently between the rental car and the big kid, who was looking at him curiously. His ride was a superclean '68 Chevy two-door sedan, chrome spoker rims on narrow sidewall tires. He went ahead and got into it. Lucinda took Albert's hand and opened the front door and pulled him in.

It hadn't changed any. There were still packs of pigskins in racks in the middle of the floor and the glass-door beer coolers were on the left. There was a big warmer on the right where they kept the ribs and buns and sauce and pulled pork, and a high counter ran down the length of the room. There was a small dining room in back where you could sit down and eat if you wanted to, behind some nicely sewn curtains.

A big-bellied black guy behind the counter said, "Hey. How y'all doing this evening?"

"Pretty good," Lucinda said.

"Arm quarm farm," Albert said. He was blinking a little and Lucinda saw the guy behind the counter see it. A couple of women back there with stained aprons looked at Albert. One said something to the other one.

"We just need some beer," Lucinda said, and pulled Albert toward the beer coolers. "And some Cokes if you've got em."

"Y'all better get you some ribs while you here," the man sang out. "Fatten him up a little bit."

Lucinda turned back to speak to him.

"We're gonna eat when we get home," she said. "I know y'all have some good barbecue, though. I used to come over here when I went to Ole Miss. It's the best."

"Aw yes'm," the man said. "We feed all them Ole Miss kids."

She turned back to the beer coolers and found a six-pack of Bud tall boys and opened the glass door and reached in for one of them.

"Let me see if we can find you some Cokes, honey," she said, still holding Albert's hand. But she dropped it and handed him the beer. "Hold this," she said, and Albert took it and held it to his chest.

She saw some Pepsis. Some Mountain Dews. Some Dr Peppers. Down near the bottom she found the Cokes and reached in for a sixer.

"Okay, sweetie. We'll just get me some cigarettes and pay for this and we can go."

Albert followed her over to the counter, pausing to look at the racks of pigskins. He reached out and touched a bag of Brim's barbecued.

"Kwaka?" he said. "Kwaka."

Lucinda turned and looked at him. She walked back over there beside him.

"You want some pigskins?" she said.

Albert had a puzzled look on his face.

"Kwaka?" he said.

"No, honey, it's not a cracker. It's pigskins. You want some?"

"Ate shits?" he said.

"No, honey, it's pigskins. They make them out of hogs. They're like cracklings. Here, let's get you a bag, you might like them. Let's get some barbecued ones. They're the best."

She showed him how to pull the bag from the clip on the rack and then they went to the counter. She set his Cokes down and Albert, after watching her, set her beer up there beside them. Then he moved over to a large jar of pickled eggs and studied them as if they were some kind of exhibit in a carnival sideshow. Then his eye caught the pickled pigs' feet in another jar and he moved to it and stabbed it with his finger.

"Pig dick," he said excitedly.

"We live in Atlanta," Lucinda said to the big man behind the counter, smiling at him. "He doesn't see stuff like this in Atlanta."

She pulled some money from her pocket and the guy started ringing up the stuff on the register, looking at Albert warily.

"And let me have a pack of Virginia Slims Lights, too," she said.

"Hock his cock!" Albert said, and then he walked over and caught her by the arm.

"Hold it just a minute," Lucinda said to the guy behind the counter.

Her face was turning red but she went over to the jar with Albert. He kept poking it with his finger.

"Those are pigs' feet, Albert. I don't think you want any of them."

"Ain't nothin wrong with my pigs' feet," the man said, offended.

"Well, no, I didn't say there was anything wrong with them," she said, glancing up at the man. "He just doesn't know what they are."

"He act like he want some," the man said.

And Albert did. He kept tugging on her sleeve.

"Okay," she said. "Can you get him a couple?"

One of the women came up with a long pair of stainless steel tongs and a little white paper tray. She took the top off the big jar and reached in for one pig's foot, holding it and shaking the pink juice from it for a moment before she pulled it out and put it in the tray, and then she got another one and put it beside the first one. She dropped some napkins over them and put the tongs down and put the lid back on the jar and handed the paper tray to the man, who put it in a paper bag and set it up beside their beer. He raised his face to search the cigarette rack above him.

"How much em pigskins?" he said.

Lucinda looked at the bag in Albert's hand.

"Fifty-nine cents," she said.

The man wasn't having any luck finding her cigarettes. The door opened and the bell over it jangled and two more young black guys came in, wearing denim jeans and jackets, black bandannas on their heads. What happened next happened fast.

"I done told you two sons of bitches not to come back in here no more," the man behind the counter said, and the next thing Lucinda knew he had pulled a sawed-off shotgun from behind the counter and thrown down on both of them. One of the women back there screamed. Both of them ducked down. But the young men only backed against the door and stopped. They put their hands up.

"Hell, Pop," one of them said.

"Don't you Pop me, motherfucker," the man behind the counter said, and Lucinda could see murder in his eyes. She was frozen and she didn't know where Albert was. "I'll blow your goddamn head off."

One of them put a surly look on his face and lowered his hands.

"We ain't wanting nothing but some Miller, old man. Why don't you chill your ass out?"

The man behind the counter cocked the hammer and put his finger on the trigger.

"Marvis, I swear fore God I'll blow you and that punkass nigger with you half in two if you don't turn around and walk out that door right now."

Lucinda had to admit they had some balls. Both of them spit on the floor, then one of them snatched the door open and they slouched out, mumbling about jive-ass niggers as they went. She heard a car that had been left running rev up, then the motor noise receded. She was scared to look out the door and turned to find Albert back behind the counter with the women. He was looking over the top at her.

The man behind the counter was watching through the window glass as the car with the two young men left. She watched him put the hammer back down and rest the butt of the gun on the counter beside her beer. His face was intent, peering out the dirty glass past a neon SCHLITZ sign.

"Raymond," one of the women said, and nodded her head toward Lucinda. It was only then that the man seemed to remember where he was.

"Punkass," he said, and put the gun away under the counter. Then he looked up at Lucinda.

"Sorry about the language. But them two thiefs right there—"

"Hush, Raymond," the woman said. "Don't you get your blood pressure up. Go on and ring their stuff up."

"Yes, thank you," Lucinda said, since she didn't know what else to say. She was hoping Albert wouldn't say anything. And for once he didn't.

"Yes'm, let's see now, where was I?" the man said, and he looked at his machine as if he didn't know what it was. Then he looked up at Lucinda and pointed toward the window.

"You see them two fools right there?"

"Yes sir," Lucinda said. She could see now that he was older than he looked. There were twinges of gray hair on the side of his head.

"That one on the left, one I was talking to, that's my cousin's boy. Raised in Chicago. Him and that other one, they robbed Mister Jones up here four years ago and beat him with a pistol. Now they done home from the pen and running loose again."

"I'm sorry," Lucinda said.

"Hell, I don't know what I'm doing," the man said, shook his head, and turned away from the register. He went back behind the warmer and somewhere in the back and he didn't come out again. The woman who had been talking to him walked over to the register and reached up for Lucinda's cigarettes and handed them to her. She finished ringing their stuff and Albert walked up and looked over her shoulder as she worked. He had opened the pigskins and was eating some, crunching them happily.

"Albert, I think maybe you'd better come back from around there," Lucinda said, and pulled a twenty-dollar bill from her front pocket. Her fingers were trembling just a little. The woman must have seen it.

"It's all right," she said. "That's twelve dollars and forty cents."

Lucinda gave her the twenty and Albert took his time wandering out from behind the warmer. The lady gave Lucinda her change and put the beer and Cokes in a paper sack and dropped the pigs' feet in on top of them. She pushed the sack toward Lucinda.

"Y'all come back," she said. "We sorry about the trouble."

"Yes ma'am. Thank you," Lucinda said. "Let's go, Albert."

She got him out the door and back in the car and then locked the doors after she got the car started.

And late that night, long after supper, long after Albert was asleep beside her, snoring very gently, she was still lying awake, the last empty can on the bedside table, having a cigarette before she turned in.

She turned on her side and took the last drag from the smoke, then dropped it in the Budweiser can. It made a slight hiss.

She rolled over onto her back and put out her hand to find Albert's. It was partially stuck under his leg and she rubbed his thumb with her fingers. He was warm beside her and he smelled very clean. When they got back home they would rent some movies and buy some steaks and cook them on the grill on the patio and they would resume their lives. She would call and check on her daddy often. She wouldn't lose touch with him the way she had with her mother. She'd been trying to hold it in, but now, with a six-pack in her and Albert sleeping beside her, in a bed she was afraid to make love with him in because she thought her daddy might hear, she began to cry, very softly, shaking the bed gently, not wanting to wake him up, because he was sleeping so peacefully, curled on his side, his fingers clenched in hers.

[. . .]

29

Jimmy was sitting in the dark, out on the trailer steps, listening to the things in the night. There were plenty of them. He'd been trying to catch lightning bugs earlier, but it looked like a lot of them were gone.

He could sit out there on the steps and be almost hypnotized by the sounds of the crickets in the weeds and the trees, a constant roar of noise after dark that filled him with wonder. He liked sitting out there and listening to that a lot better than sitting in the living room watching TV with the girls and his mama. It looked like all his mama wanted to do these days was watch TV. And eat. She ate all the time. She ate ice cream and hot dogs and pizza she'd brought from town and she ate big sandwiches she made from ham and cheese and baloney and salami and she used thick slices of bread she got somewhere. Large bags of Cheetos. Fritos. Doritos.

He didn't know where his daddy was. Off somewhere was all.

He stayed gone a lot at night. Even on the weeknights. And Jimmy couldn't help but wish his daddy would stay home a little more. It was kind of comforting to know that he was home, even if he was back in his room watching his hunting videos. At least you knew he was home. When he wasn't home, it didn't feel right. And he thought that was why his mama just ate and ate. And sometimes cried and cried. But he didn't ask.

You could hear a car coming down the gravel road he lived on for a long time before it got here. And he'd been listening for the sound of his daddy's car. The sound traveled a long way at night. From here he could hear a car down on the levee crossing the three bridges, because there was something about the tires rolling over the joints that made a distinctive noise. Once you heard it you couldn't mistake it for something else. Two cars had come down the gravel road since he'd been sitting out here, but neither one of them had been his daddy's.

He decided he'd just sit here and wait on him. He knew it might take a long time. But he didn't really have anything else to do, with the go-kart chain all messed up. He hadn't asked his daddy about fixing it anymore. It was plain his daddy didn't want to mess with it. But he wished he would. He wished he'd fix it for him so he could run it a little more before he had to start back to school next week.

And he didn't know if they were going to get to go see Kenny Chesney in concert in Tupelo or not. He'd asked his mama, and his mama had said she was afraid they couldn't afford it. He wished they could. He'd give anything to see Kenny Chesney. He'd asked his mother why they couldn't afford it, and she'd said for him to ask his daddy. But he wasn't doing that. Oh no. He'd learned his lessons pretty well by then.

Then he heard that dead black lady crying again and went on inside.

30

Those peas down by the creek took on a growing spurt after the rain fell on them for several days in a row. Their pods started filling out and Cortez took the tractor down there and plowed between the rows with the scratchers, dragging the grass out and turning the caked earth over to fresh brown dirt that piled up nicely against the plants so that his rows when he climbed down from the 4020 and looked at them were nice and straight and clean. He knew it wouldn't be long now. He mowed his yard.

Two days after Lucinda left he got in his truck and drove down the Cutoff road and looked at the trailer where those people lived. He didn't see anybody outside except a little girl who was sitting on the trailer steps reading a book. She was a strange-looking child, he thought, a long purple dress and some crazy glasses. When he passed she looked up and waved. He didn't wave back. He guessed she was that little boy's sister. He wondered what that little boy's name was. Then he went on down the road into the creek bottom and over the bridge on the other side of where Queen used to live. He didn't look at it much anymore, but he used to go and sit down on the cracked linoleum inside it and cry. It was just rotted wood and rusted tin, what was left of it. He still owned it.

He slowed and turned off onto a field road just past there and eased the truck down a slight incline and drove around the edge of the cotton that had been planted there and around the curve of the creek where cane was growing. He slowed to a crawl and looked. He wanted some that wasn't too tall. Some of this was tall enough to use for set hooks. A long time ago he used to bring Lucinda down here to help him cut bean poles for the garden. He'd noticed she took a whole sack full of tomatoes back home.

He could remember when they cleared this patch of land. It was back in the forties sometime, he thought. A crew had come in and cut the trees and snaked the logs out with mules, and people had come from miles around to get the limbs that were left for firewood, thousands of them, all piled up everywhere.

He drove on around the curve of the creek and then he was out of sight of the road. There was a patch of smaller cane back there and he drove up beside it and stopped the truck. It was still a little muddy, but he didn't think he'd get stuck. He shut the truck off and got out and left the door open. He had a sharp machete in the back end and he reached in for his gloves and put them on, then grabbed the machete. The trick with cane was to cut it at an angle with something sharp, in one whack, which would give you a pointed end that was easy to stick into the ground or the bank of the river, depending on what you were using it for.

The sun was hot and the humidity was up again, but it didn't take him long to cut twenty canes about eight feet high and whack off the leaves, put them in the back end of his truck. He let the tailgate down and fixed the two chains to it. He wouldn't be going very fast. He never did.

After he finished he tossed the gloves and the machete back there again and pulled his water jug from its resting place in the floorboard and opened the drinking spout. He took a long drink of ice water and sat there for a few minutes, wiping a little sweat off his forehead, listening to the water running in the creek, watching red-winged blackbirds flitting about. He saw a hawk circling out over the field and he watched it turn and flare the undersides of its wings, rising on a thermal until it went out of sight beyond the tree line. He took another drink of water and then got back in the truck and left.

The next day he took the canes and went down to the pea patch and looked at all the tracks and the peas that had already been eaten, even though they weren't quite ready. There were some little bitty tracks in there, too. Well. They weren't cute when they were eating your peas. They'd get their little asses shot, too.

He started sticking the canes into the ground, standing them up straight and gripping them hard with his hands and pushing them into the soft earth as deeply as he could get them, twisting them, making sure they would stand on their own. He put them in a circle about six or seven feet wide. When he finished that he pulled an old tarp from the back end of the truck and then stood up on the tailgate and draped it over the canes so that it resembled an Indian teepee sort of. He left an opening in the front and then duct-taped it in place. He placed a straight-backed chair inside it. Then he stepped back and looked at it. Shit, you could live in it.

When he got home he went out in the garden and picked a five-gallon bucket full of tomatoes and threw some bad ones over the fence. He took the fresh tomatoes to the rickety table that was sitting under the chinaberry tree and set them out, not letting them touch each other, and then he picked through the ones on the table that were getting soft on the bottom and tossed them over the fence. More tomatoes than he knew what to do with. If those kids down the road hadn't pissed him off messing around his pond he might have taken some down there and offered them to them. He stood there looking at the tomatoes. They were perfect, fat, beautiful. Nobody to eat them but him. He looked up at the tree. Did he miss his wife? He shook his head. No. Not yet. Would he ever? Who knew?

Then he had to go cut his okra. It had been a few days since he'd been down the rows and some of it was too big to eat. These big ones he just cut off and left on the ground, but the young and tender pods he put in a small bucket that he kept hanging out there and took a few dozen of them into the house and set them on the kitchen table. It was cool in the house and very quiet. He looked at his watch. It was five o'clock. He needed to water the heifers before he ate supper. Get done with everything and then he could wash his hands and eat.

He pushed open the screen door and walked across the yard under the big pecans and across the driveway and up to the heifer pen. He turned on the water hydrant. The hose was already in the watering tank and he looked at it to make sure it wasn't going to kick itself out of the tank from the pressure. Sometimes it did.

He stood there holding on to the wire at the top of the fence and looked at the heifers. He had fourteen of them in there and they were fat and fine. They'd been riding each other and he guessed he'd turn them in with one of his bulls before long. September October November December January February March April May, they'd calve in May. Good.

He didn't like to have to deliver calves in February or January when it was so rainy and cold. He'd gotten too old for that shit. Especially at night.

He noticed that their salt block had gotten worn down to a nub and he went over to the barn and got a fresh one and set it down and unlatched the gate and carried it in and put it in the feed trough. Some of the heifers had come up to the watering tank and were drinking from it. They lifted their shiny muzzles, water dripping from them. There was an old apple tree out there that they used for shade, but they'd just about worn all the bark off it rubbing their hides against it. It looked like it was going to die and he didn't know what they'd do for shade then. He guessed he could open that stall in the barn back up and let them in there. It beat nothing. They needed some shade in this sun.

"Sook, baby, sook," he said, and then he went on back to the house.

There was still plenty of ham left and he got some of it out and found some bread and a plate and made a sandwich and poured himself a glass of cold milk and carried it all into the room where his wife used to watch TV. He sat down and put his milk on the side table and bit into his sandwich, then lowered it to his lap. The TV remote was lying there and he reached and got it and turned on the TV. News. He didn't know how to operate the thing very well, but he could learn. One thing he'd found out over the last few nights was that there was a station or two that showed movies of people screwing and messing around naked and stuff, and he tried to find one of those, but there didn't seem to be any of those on right now. He guessed maybe they didn't show them at a time when kids might see them. Maybe there would be one on later tonight, when he came back. He hoped so. He hadn't been able to have that dream about those angel girls again and he needed something to look at.

After he finished eating he decided he'd take a nap before it got dark. Just in case he had to wait a while. But he probably wouldn't. The dumb sons of bitches would probably be in there as soon as it got dark.

He stretched out on the daybed and closed his eyes. He didn't take his shoes off. He could do whatever he wanted to now. Lie on the bed with his shoes on. Watch dirty movies as much as he liked. Maybe he could even get a video machine now and send off for one of those tapes with those college girls showing their bosoms.

When he woke the sun was going down. He had to hurry. He got up and turned on the porch light, then went out to the barn.

A fox barked up in the woods and the moon was shining a pale cast over the rows. The creek was whispering as the water surged past the banks. Then they came.

They were like apparitions that appeared in pieces, unmelting out of the darkness and their feet sometimes making little crunching sounds. They moved slowly, halting to sniff the wind, push their ears in different directions to hear what was around them. Sometimes they snorted or made little grunting sounds in their throats. Deer language. Maybe *Ain't these some fine fat peas?* Or *My aren't these juicy pods particularly juicy?* The crickets were screaming and the night was warm and the little tree frogs were calling out there, too.

The deer came almost single file from a wall of cane he would have thought they couldn't have gotten through. Like ghosts they materialized from the pale night into things that had legs and heads and moved with the rhythms of the woods. Now that his eyes had become adjusted to the darkness and his pupils had enlarged, gathering the available light, he could see them very clearly as they entered the patch and lowered their heads and began to feed. The question was always how much to let them feed. He didn't want to wait until they'd nearly eaten the whole patch, but he wanted more than this before he started shooting, too. He decided he would wait a few minutes and see if more came.

More did. They started drifting in from the sides and they joined the ones already there and pretty soon their bodies were a solid mass in front of him, the little ones whisking their tails and then he put it to his shoulder and didn't aim, just pointed, and the red fire began pouring from the barrel and the rounds were chattering through the magazine and they were falling and running and falling and running and kicking on the ground and he kept raking the rows and the gun kept barking, *Brupbrupbrupbrupbrupbrupbrupbrupbrupbrupbrupbrupbrupbrup!* until he was out of ammo. By then the makeshift teepee was full of smoke.

He got up from the chair and touched the barrel with the tip of his finger. It was very hot. He pushed aside the flap of tarp and stepped out. Most of them were dead. He didn't have a flashlight. He didn't need one. He knew what it would look like. Dead eyes shining into the beam. Blood soaking into the ground between the rows. The hair the bullets had cut lying over everything like cotton lint.

A few were kicking. They didn't kick long. Their heaving sides stopped moving and they stretched their necks out on the ground and were still. He wondered if those people up in that trailer had heard the shots. It was early yet. Those kids were out of school for the summer and they might be outside. And then again they might be inside with the TV on.

When he saw that nothing else was moving he put the safety on and rested the butt of the stock against his hip while he counted them. Nine. Seven big ones and two little ones. He thought a few ran off that were hit. He'd probably see some buzzards circling for them in a few days. Last summer he had an old cow that got down and sick and waded off halfway into the old pond down in the bottom and couldn't get back out and he didn't know she was in there until she'd been dead for two or three days, was already swollen up when he found her, and she stank so bad already that instead of tying a log chain around her hind feet and hooking her to the bumper of his truck and dragging her out of there, he just left her, hoping the buzzards would clean her up, and they did. Eventually. Took about a week. He thought even some coyotes tried to get in on the act because he saw tracks all around the edge of the pond.

He stood there looking at what he'd done. What would it hurt to let the kid come over and fish once he got some fish? Nothing. It wouldn't hurt a damn thing. How could it hurt anything?

He'd parked his truck near the road and he had to walk back to it. He took the Thompson with him and stuck it under the seat. He dropped it off at the barn and hid it in the trunk again, and then he turned the truck toward Old Dallas and drove that way. It wasn't even nine o'clock yet. He knew he was still up, this early. He just hoped he wasn't drinking. But there was a pistol in the glove box just in case.

He could see a light on inside the house when he drove up in the yard and turned his headlights off and shut off the truck. The pistol was a little .32 and he stuck it in the pocket of his overalls when he got out.

He wasn't ever going to clean all this shit up. That '59 Chevy had been sitting there with chickens nesting in it for at least twenty years.

And a tree had grown out through the windshield of that Dodge pickup. Old refrigerators. Fifty-five-gallon barrels crammed full of trash. Rotten cardboard boxes full of bottles and fruit jars. Old tires piled up for safe-keeping. Firewood long rotted stacked against trees in the yard. It was a wonder he didn't have termites. He probably did.

Two dogs growled at him from beneath the porch and he heard some-body inside the house say something. Then the door opened and he could see Cleve standing there in his undershirt and overalls, peering out at him. He was a very small man.

"You up?" Cortez said, and stopped just short of the porch.

"Hey, is that . . . ? Yes sir, I'm up, Mister Cortez."

And he came on out on the porch and pulled the door partway shut behind him.

"Shut up, dogs," he said, and they hushed.

Cortez stood there waiting. Cleve's little pickup and a strange car were parked beside the house. And the house wasn't really a house, just something Cleve had made to live in. Part of it was made of blocks and part of it was made from sheets of tin, and the roof was patched together from asphalt shingles and wood shingles and some of it had a couple of sheets of Visqueen tacked over it. He wondered if that soldier was here.

"What you know?" Cleve said. He leaned up against a post and struck a match to his cigarette. Cortez saw it light the stubble on his chin and then he blew the match out and tossed it into the yard.

"You want some fresh deer meat?" Cortez said.

"Yes sir," Cleve said. "I been looking for you. I figured it was about time."

"They down there in the pea patch," Cortez said. "It ain't too bad wet."

"How many is it?" Cleve said, and Cortez saw the tip of his cigarette glow red when he drew on it.

"Seven big ones and two little ones," he said.

"Good Godamighty," Cleve said. He sat down in a chair and reached for the boots he'd left beside the door and started pulling them on.

"They won't last long in this hot weather," Cortez said.

"Yes sir. That's right. I'll get em on out a there right now," Cleve said.

"I know a guy's got a big cooler we can hang em in till I can get em all skint. I'll make Montrel get up and help me."

Cortez stood there. He didn't know what else to say. He'd been knowing Cleve since he was a kid. And Cleve didn't know about the things he'd done. He didn't think he knew about Queen. Why of course he didn't. Nobody knew all that but Cortez. Maybe God, if God knew all things. God was who he was going to have to answer to. He knew that. If there was a hell, Cortez was absolutely sure that he was going there. That's where they sent people like him.

He turned to go and stopped. He turned back around and spoke toward the porch.

"You don't know nobody that needs a good wheelchair do you?"

31

Lord God, this weather was fine for riding around. If it just wasn't Sunday again. It had been a pretty good weekend, though. Johnette had been gone somewhere, which was fine. He'd caught three crappie and four bream and one catfish out of a pond that he and Seaborn had snuck into. They'd tried to get Rusty to go with them, but he'd said he was going up to Memphis to see the Boat and Tractor Show at the Mid-South Coliseum.

He guessed he should have carried Jimmy fishing with him. But hell. You didn't want a bunch of kids hanging around and talking and needing help baiting their hooks and taking fish off and asking a million questions when you were trying to just take it easy and drink some beer and hang out with one of your buddies. He'd take Jimmy when the old man's pond filled up and he got some fish in there. Johnette said the old man's wife had died.

Jimmy's daddy tossed an empty beer can over the roof of the car with his left arm, trying to hit a road sign, but he missed it by six feet. He got a fresh one from the cooler and popped the top on it. He was running kind of low on cigarettes, but he hadn't wanted to stop by the store. He'd driven by there earlier in the evening, and it had been so crowded he hadn't wanted to pull in. Four or five cars lined up on each side of the gas pumps. Jeeps and pickups parked everywhere. Folks standing around out front. It might have taken twenty or thirty minutes to get a pack of cigarettes. So what he'd done was just pace himself on his smokes. He'd only allowed himself one every fifteen minutes, which wasn't easy when you were drinking beer, and that had lasted for a long time, but now he had only four left, and he was going to have to make a decision about where to go get some more. It was a long way to town. And the cops sometimes had those roadblocks put up. He didn't want to drive through a roadblock because he'd been drinking all afternoon and didn't really know how many he'd sipped his way through. Maybe seven or eight. Maybe nine or ten. He wasn't drunk, no sir, no way, but still.

The cops were strict about that shit. They'd say you were drunk when you really weren't. And they had the law on their side. If you tried to argue with them, that would just make it worse. And if you got in court, it was your word against theirs. Plus now they had those video cameras on the dashboards of their patrol cars. He sipped again. It was hard to stop thinking about John Wayne Payne. Especially the blood.

He'd been toying with the idea of riding down to Water Valley. Find a store down there and get some cigarettes. And while he was down there, he thought he might just cruise up Church Street and look around. What was her name? *Lacey.* Hell. Why not?

He knew there was a store down on Highway 315 because he'd stopped in there one time and gotten some fried chicken gizzards and a big fountain Pepsi. They didn't sell beer down there. Dry county. You had to drive on down 315 to Panola County and they'd sell you all you wanted down there, just across the county line. That was probably where Lacey bought her beer. The next closest place for cold beer was Grenada, in Grenada County, but you had to get on I-55 to get down there and he didn't like to get on I-55 when he was drinking because that was where all the state troopers hung out. You had to stay on the back roads. You had to drink and drive responsibly if you were going to drink and drive.

He wondered what she looked like with her clothes off. A lot of times, you couldn't really tell what somebody looked like with her clothes off until you got them off and could take a good look at her. [. . .]

He lit another cigarette, which left him only three. He was going to have to do something pretty fast. Point this son of a bitch toward some place that had his brand of cigarettes. He couldn't stand to wake up in the morning and not have a cigarette.

Fucking Monday morning. He wished he was rich and didn't have to work. Didn't have to fuck with Collums. The son of a bitch. He wasn't any better than anybody else. He knew how to fix a lot of shit, yeah, but he wasn't any better than anybody else. Jimmy's daddy had just about given up now on getting to meet the big-tittied heifer. He'd about convinced himself that somebody as fine as her was out of his reach. If she was a college student, she was probably fucking some college student. And if she wasn't a college student, she probably had some boyfriend anyway. Anybody as fine as her wouldn't be wanting for men. Shit no. Anybody as fine as her would probably have men drooling all over her. He knew she was too fine for somebody like him.

Jimmy's daddy turned the '55 around at Old Union Baptist Church, and they were having church. He could see through the glass doors some people sitting in the pews, and somebody in a white shirt and tie standing at the front of the sanctuary talking to them, holding a Bible. Sometimes Jimmy's daddy had a little voice that whispered inside his head and most times he didn't pay any attention to it, because it was usually telling him that he was messing up in some way or another. Like right now, while he was turning around in front of the church, the little voice said, *Yeah, look at you, riding around drinking beer while other people are in church. And not only that, but you're also thinking about screwing somebody. And you don't treat your kid right. Give him shit about drinking the last Coke. Why don't you just buy some more Cokes, asshole?*

Jimmy's daddy turned off the voice and made it shut up and just as he was about to pull back into the road, he was nearly run over by a jacked-up pickup that came hurtling over the hill, big speakers blasting, whip antennas waving, chrome bumpers and roll bar shining, lights mounted all over with yellow smiley face covers, Yosemite Sam mud flaps that said BACK OFF!, a winch on the front, a metal step hanging from the bottom of the driver's door, some kid who looked like he was about seven behind the wheel. Jimmy's daddy slammed on the brakes and skidded in the loose gravel at the edge of the church parking lot, and the truck didn't even slow down, just kept on hurtling down the road. Where did these damn kids come from? Who bought those big trucks for them?

He watched the truck roll on up the road and then he looked to make sure nothing was coming before he pulled back out. Then he pulled back out. He thought he'd ride down toward Water Valley. He could be there in twenty minutes. If he only smoked one cigarette every ten minutes he could still have one left by the time he got to the store.

Lacey answered the door on the first knock. He guessed maybe she'd seen him come up the street in the '55, since he'd had to drive up and down it a few times before he saw 111 on the front post. He'd pulled the car in beside the house where her Mercury was sitting.

Jimmy's daddy thought maybe she was wearing a red negligee before she opened the door because it was one of those with glass in the top half and a thin curtain was hanging over it. So he had a vision of her coming hurrying down the hall in something red, and when she got closer, he was pretty damn sure it was a negligee, and when she pulled the door open he saw that he'd been right. [. . .]

"I thought I's gonna have to run out on the front porch to stop you," she said, and kissed him. To Jimmy's daddy's pleasant surprise she was a very good kisser. Her tongue working against his was warm and fat, like a well-fed snake. And then he had a revelation. She was *seductive* was what she was. He stood there kissing her for a while, and then he pulled back and took a sip of his beer.

"I still got three twelve-packs of Bud in the fridge if you need one," she said, looking up at him, pulling his cap off.

"I think I do," he said, and kissed her again.

One a.m. Jimmy's daddy rolls slowly down the road he lives on with his lights off, guiding it carefully, turning the last curve and turning into his driveway. [. . .] He parks the '55 and shuts it off. He rolls up his window. The other one is already up. He gets out and doesn't make a whole lot of noise closing the door. The main thing he's wondering is if the trailer door is locked. It probably is. It's a good thing he's got a key.

The little dogs come moiling from their little doghouse under the trailer and they hop against his legs, so that he's wading through dogs, and one thing he's fearing among many others is that Johnette is going to be sitting up waiting for him, watching TV or something. He hopes she's in the bed, sound asleep, preferably snoring. If he can just get in the bed without waking her, he won't have to talk to her until tomorrow afternoon, which will give him some time to rehearse in his mind what he's going to say about where he's been tonight.

He crunches across the gravel and takes the last drink of beer from the can and then tosses it over beside Jimmy's go-kart, which is pulled up at the corner of the trailer. Jimmy's not running it now because the chain won't stay on at all. He needs to fix it. He needs to build a back porch with steps. He needs to get Jimmy's rotten teeth fixed. And he probably needs to get divorced. But all that shit will have to wait until later. Right now what he needs worse than anything is sleep.

He goes up the steps. The door is not locked. He goes inside, closes it, locks it. He stands for a moment in the darkness of the living room. There's not even a lamp on. He can't hear anything. So he goes down the hall toward his bedroom. The door to that room is open, too. He steps in. Johnette is a dark lump in a dark bed and she's snoring gently. He takes his cap off and drops it on the floor and then takes his boots off without sitting down, which is hard to do because he's been drinking so much beer and because he's tired and because the boots are about half a size too small, but they're Tony Lama ostrich and he thought they'd stretch eventually, only they didn't. They hurt his feet every single time he wears them, but they look so damn good on him that he hates not to. Lacey likes them.

He takes off his shirt, drops it, undoes his belt and his jeans, drops them, steps out of them, and peels off his socks. He kind of needs to pee, but he doesn't want to make any noise going to the bathroom, so he just slips in under the covers next to her and settles his head carefully on the pillow, listening to her. She's not moving. Then she does. She rolls over and flings one forearm across his forehead, and he reaches up and moves it. He puts it down by her side. Then he rolls over on his side, away from her. He can hear the little dogs whining underneath the trailer. He wonders if Lacey is asleep. He wonders if she's dreaming about him.

He rolls over onto his back and looks at the ceiling. It has those glowing stars plastered over it, but they're very dim now. He wishes he didn't have to get up in four and a half more hours. He knows he's going to be hurting for certain. But it's unthinkable to miss work. Then he wonders if the alarm clock's set. Oh shit. What if it's not? Surely it is. Surely she went ahead and set it before she went to sleep. She sets it every Sunday night so that he can get up in time on Monday morning.

He lies there and thinks about it. He'll have to turn on the lamp to see if it's set or not. He doesn't want to do that. He doesn't want to take a chance on waking her up right now. He hasn't had time to rest. He hasn't had time to think about what he's going to say. And he's too tired to move. So he doesn't get up and check it. He just lies there until he doesn't know that he's lying there anymore.

The amplified voice of Kenny Chesney singing with Uncle Kracker erupts beside Jimmy's daddy's bed in such a volt of surprise that he nearly leaps from under the covers. He gropes for the snooze button and slams his hand down on it, then groans aloud to the blessed silence that follows. It will only stay off for two minutes, and then it will come back on. They're selling tickets on the radio this week for that concert in Tupelo and Jimmy's daddy knows how badly Jimmy and the girls want to go. He lies there, trying to go back to sleep. But he has to get up. Go to work. To hell with breakfast. Just getting there on time will be job enough. He moans.

He doesn't feel very good. He wishes he didn't have to get up. He wishes now that he hadn't drunk all that beer yesterday afternoon and evening. And then the sudden memories of Lacey's naked body and all the things they did for hours come rushing in. He groans again. It's still dark in the trailer. He looks at Johnette. She's asleep on her back, her face turned away from him. What if she wants to eat lunch with him?

"Two big shows!" the radio screams. *"At the Bancorp South Center! Kenny Chesney! Live!"*

Jimmy's daddy hits the snooze button again and closes his eyes. Oh my God. If he had known he was going to feel like this he would have just stayed home yesterday. All day long. He groans and turns on his side. He's going to have to get up. He's going to have to go into the bathroom and turn the light on and piss and shave and find his work clothes and his work boots and put them on and get in the car and go. He isn't going to have time to make a baloney sandwich. He'll have to eat another can of that chili. But they've put in a sandwich machine now. He thinks it has hamburgers and ham and cheese. Maybe hot dogs. He doesn't know what else. Salads? With those little packets of dressing? Sausage and biscuits.

He lies there. Johnette is not moving beside him. He's going to have to fix his life somehow because it's not working the way it is. But what's he going to do? What's the first move he's going to make? What's he going to do today that's going to be different from yesterday? Why couldn't he have been born rich?

Jimmy's daddy can hear the waking birds when the central air stops running. There's going to be dew all over the windshield of the '55, and he'll have to run his headlights for a while on the way to work. The road will be filled with other cars, in them people all hurrying to town, to work, to jobs, to steady employment, and some of them will be going to the same place he's going. They'll be coming from College Hill, from Paris, from Dogtown, from Yocona, from Tula, from Potlockney, from Bay Springs, from Cambridge, from Bruce, from Water Valley. All of them rushing to punch their clocks, start up their machines, work away their lives. He's doing it, too, and already can feel his life seeping away, one day at a time. It's enough to make him sick. But it's nothing new.

[. . .]

Jimmy's daddy punched in at 6:59 and saw Collums eyeing him when he walked into the Maintenance Department, which had a big table with a lot of disassembled tools and loose nuts and bolts and welding rags and rods lying on it, and a bunch of metal cabinets hung on the walls with tools in them, air hoses, work lights, air wrenches, and a cleared space on the grease-soaked concrete floor for parking Towmotors that needed work. And they all needed work. Just about every day. Because every one of them was a piece of shit. Because the company wouldn't get any new ones and just kept buying parts for whatever tore up on them, and getting Collums and Jimmy's daddy and a few other guys who worked in Maintenance to fix them. It got old. Crawling around on the floor.

"What's up?" Jimmy's daddy said to Collums, who was sitting on an upturned five-gallon plastic bucket, sipping a smoking cup of coffee.

"You look like you had a rough night," Collums said. "And the damn toilet in the ladies' pisser's stopped up again. So you better get on up there and fix it."

"Aw *shit*," Jimmy's daddy said. "I done fixed that son of a bitch eight times already." Well, he'd unplugged it eight times anyway.

Collums sat there sipping his coffee in what looked like utter comfort. He brought it from home every morning, piping hot, and sat there sipping it, and it never failed to chap Jimmy's daddy's ass. And the son of a bitch never offered him any either. Like right now, Jimmy's daddy couldn't think of any one thing that would be better than a hot cup of coffee, but do you think the son of a bitch would offer him any? Hell no. Stingy bastard.

"I think they using the wrong kind of toilet paper in it," Collums said. "I thought toilet paper was toilet paper," Jimmy's daddy said, wondering if there was any way he could sneak into the break room for a cup of that watered-down coffee that was sold from a machine. And then he stopped thinking about it. He knew there was no way he could because somebody would see him and nobody was supposed to be in the break room unless it was break time except for the people who took care of the break room, swept it up, emptied the trash cans, wiped off the tables, emptied the ashtrays. He'd bet they snuck a cup of coffee sometimes. Lucky bastards.

And how did Collums get away with sitting on his ass on a five-gallon bucket and sipping coffee after 7 a.m.? That was easy. They were scared to make him mad. Afraid he'd quit. The people in the front office wouldn't say shit to him. They needed him too badly. And the plant manager knew it, too. Even *he* wouldn't say anything to Collums. But it looked like the son of a bitch could at least offer Jimmy's daddy a little coffee.

But he didn't. So Jimmy's daddy grabbed his tool pouch and a pipe wrench in case he needed it—he didn't know why he would, but it might be better to take it just in case—and a rubber plunger and headed down the aisle toward the assembly line, first past the Spot-Welding Department and then the Porcelain Department, where Lacey worked, and hoped maybe she'd have her back turned when he walked by.

And she did. She was spraying a stove liner with liquid porcelain. She had her mask on and she had her right arm raised holding the spray gun and the liners were coming by her on hooks and she was concentrating on what she was doing. That was real good. That was terrific. He had no time to talk. Up ahead he could see the brightly lit cavern of the two assembly lines, where the stoves were built up from the porcelain-coated liners. Then the insulation was wrapped around them. Then wires were put in. Hinges. Handles. Heating elements. Thermostats. Dials. Broiler pans. Each person stood there all day on the concrete and put one or two things on the stove and sent it on down the line, where somebody kept doing something to it until it was all pretty and new and finished and ready to be boxed up by the people holding the glue guns down on the very end, who rolled them down a little ramp to a waiting pallet, where eventually somebody on a forklift would come to get it and all the others and store them in the warehouse on the other side of the tall block wall until they were put into trailers by people in the Shipping Department. Some days they made hoods. Some days they made self-cleaning double ovens, some days non-self-cleaning single ovens. Nobody seemed to know why they built what they built on any given day. It all came down from the front office through some mysterious process. Jimmy's daddy knew he could have run the whole thing if they would just let him. But of course they wouldn't.

Here was going to be the tricky part, turning the corner, going right, and walking down the side of the first line, right past the edge of the Porcelain Department, where if Lacey was looking up for the six or seven seconds he'd be in sight, headed to the stairs to the women's bathroom, she'd see him going by with his bag of tools and his plunger and his pipe wrench. And the big question was, Should he turn his head and see if she was seeing him? Or should he just ignore her and walk on past? What if he turned and looked at her and just waved and kept going? There wouldn't be anything she could do about it because the liners were coming through and she couldn't stop what they were doing because somebody on the other end was loading them onto the hooks from a long rolling cart that held about twenty of them, with some more lined up behind it. And they'd keep coming until the baking booth was full of them.

He got closer and he could begin to see all the people scattered up and down the line, men and women, old and young, pleasant and skanky, dark hair and gray, spectacled and unspectacled, fat and skinny, all shapes and sizes. They were all busy working and some of them were wearing safety glasses that were just cheap plastic things like you wear to run a Weed Eater. The line was rolling slowly along and a boy on a forklift was lowering a long pallet of insulation to the end of the line where the workers were wearing gloves against the itch of the rock wool they were wrapping around the stove liners. The foreman was walking around and smoking a cigar, his tiny desk set up in the middle of all the bustle, air hoses hanging from the ceiling, and the noise: clanking and whirring and talking and shouting and laughing, the high whine of the air wrenches and the hundred little *zipzipzips* of screws going into stoves destined for the kitchens of America. [. . .]

He went on down the aisle beside the assembly line and over to the metal stairs that led up to the second floor and clanged on up there. He stopped outside the door. He couldn't just barge in. He had to wait for a woman to come out or a woman to head in. If one was coming out he'd have to ask her if anybody else was in there and if one was going in he'd have to ask her when she came out if anybody else was in there. Then after he'd made sure there were no women in there, he'd have to prop the door open with a MAINTENANCE WORKING sign that was stored in the broom closet just around the corner. He went and got the sign and then he stood at the rail overlooking the assembly line while he waited. He could see all of the line from here, and there were eighty or ninety people working down there. He could see the edge of the Porcelain Department but not the spot where Lacey was standing since it was hidden by the baking booth.

He stood up there for a long time. If he didn't fix the damn thing pretty quick and get on back, Collums would say something about him taking so long. He was about tired of Collums's shit. He was damn sure tired of fixing those ragged-ass Towmotors all the time. One of them had gotten in such bad shape that it wouldn't even think about cranking without a shot of ether in the mornings, like an old man needing a shot of whisky.

He went over to the door of the bathroom and knocked on it with his knuckles, but it was made of metal and hurt his knuckles, so he stopped. Well shit. He guessed he might as well have a cigarette while he was waiting. Somebody would have to take a piss sooner or later. If Collums said something to him about it taking so long to fix the toilet, he'd just say, *Well, Collums, I can't make em piss, you know.* That'd shut his ass up.

Jimmy's daddy lit a cigarette and stood there at the rail smoking it. He wondered if the Shipping Department boys had any coffee back there. They had a nice big office with a desk and a couple of chairs and even a radio and they had some big glass windows and he wouldn't be surprised at all if the foreman had a little private Mr. Coffee or something back there. It wouldn't take him two minutes to walk back there and see.

Nah. He'd better wait. Some woman might come up the stairs at any minute. Or out the door at any minute. Then he got to wondering how a woman down there on the line took a piss without getting behind on all her stoves. Did she get somebody to cover for her, do her job as well as theirs while she went to the bathroom? Did the foreman take over for her? Maybe he did. Hell, he probably knew every assembly procedure on the line. Kind of like one of those orchestra conductors who has to be able to play every instrument in the orchestra before he can conduct it. Jimmy's daddy figured it was the same kind of deal: orchestra, factory.

He looked at his watch. He'd already been at work for twelve minutes. Break wasn't until nine thirty. What he was going to do was kind of ease away from whatever he was doing about a minute before break and be somewhere poised to bolt out the door and into the break room and hopefully be the first one in line to put some money in the coffee machine, sip it, have a few cigarettes, maybe a sausage and biscuit if that new machine had any. Maybe what he could do was be the first in line at the coffee machine, put his money in, punch the buttons for the kind of coffee he wanted, with cream and sugar, extra sugar, extra creamer, wait until the cup rattled down, then rush over to the new sandwich machine and put the money in and push the buttons for a sausage and biscuit, get it out, then rush back to the coffee machine in time to take his cup out. But then he'd probably have to microwave the sausage and biscuit because all that shit in the sandwich machine was cold. He damn sure didn't want a salad for his morning break. And he damn sure wasn't going to drink any beer this afternoon when he got off. He saw where that shit got him.

And too he had to figure out what he was going to tell Johnette about where he'd been last night for all that time. Missed supper again. He could say he was out with Seaborn, he guessed. Or he could just say he'd been riding around. For about seven and a half hours. Was that believable? Or would she call bullshit on him? Hell. He could say he'd been down to the VFW in Calhoun County drinking beer. Since she didn't know anybody down there, there was no way she could check to see if he was lying. Or hell. Maybe she didn't give a shit where he'd been.

[. . .]

Then Jimmy's daddy heard some feet on the metal stairs and he turned around to see who it was, hoping it wasn't Lacey. It was Lacey. Her head rose vertically as she climbed the last step and she was already grinning. He figured she'd seen him walk by.

Jimmy's daddy flicked the ashes off the end of his cigarette and leaned against the rail. She walked up next to him and stopped.

"Well hey," she said. She looked like she had more than a little makeup on. A different color lipstick. She was wearing a pretty nice blouse and pants outfit, too. He wondered if she had done this for him.

"Hey," he said. "How you?"

"Pretty good." She looked out over the line and then looked back at him. Then she lowered her voice as if someone were listening. "I sure did enjoy last night. Damn, baby."

"Me too," Jimmy's daddy said. He glanced around. Nervous.

"When you coming back?" she said. She was looking up at him and he could remember what she'd done with that mouth. [. . .]

"I don't know," he said. "I didn't get in till one."

"You didn't get in no trouble, did you?" she said.

"I don't know," he said. "I didn't talk to her yet."

"What you gonna tell her?" she said.

"I don't know. I'll figure it out before I get home, I guess."

She was looking up at him with some kind of shine in her eyes. She looked damn near delirious with happiness.

"What you doing?" she said. "I seen you walk by."

"I got to go in here and fix the toilet," Jimmy's daddy said. "I been waiting on somebody to come by. How bout going in and see if they's any women in there for me?"

"Okay. How you gonna fix it?" she said, still smiling.

He lifted his plunger.

"I'm gonna plunge it," he said. "That's what I usually do. I done fixed this son of a bitch eight times."

"They's one in there that's always stopped up."

"That's the one I'm gonna fix."

Jimmy's daddy took a last pull on his cigarette and then dropped it on the concrete and stepped on it. Then he looked up at her. She was still watching him and smiling, and it began to dawn on Jimmy's daddy to wonder if she was going goofy over him. He hoped to God she wasn't going to ask him to eat lunch with her. In front of everybody.

"You want to eat lunch with me?" she said.

And Jimmy's daddy just lied right off the top of his head because he didn't want to. He didn't even know if he wanted to go back to Water Valley anymore if he had to put up with this shit at work.

"Aw well, naw, I got to run to town on my lunch break."

He didn't know why he said that. He *never* went to town on his lunch break, even though they were very close to town. They were down on Old Taylor Road, which wasn't far from the bypass that went around Oxford. You could be on the square in five minutes if the traffic wasn't bad. But it was hard to get something to eat in town and then have time to eat it in only thirty minutes. And if the traffic *was* bad, you might be screwed. You might be late punching back in. And you didn't want to do that. They frowned on that big-time. They might even say something to you. Shit. They probably *would* say something to you.

"Oh yeah?" she said. She looked a little defeated, and nodded a few times, but then she looked at him again with a brave smile.

"What you got to go to town for?"

"Parts," he said, not thinking, just any bullshit he could feed her.

"I like that fifty-five," she said. "My brother had a fifty-six and people always thought it was a fifty-five. I don't know how many times he had to tell somebody it was a fifty-six instead of a fifty-five cause you know they look almost exactly alike cept for the tail fins and the taillights."

"Yeah," Jimmy's daddy said, and then looked around again to see if anybody was watching them. A few people down on the line were. One of them was the big-tittied heifer. He looked back at Lacey. "Well, look here, I got to get in here and fix this thing and then get on back to Maintenance fore Collums comes looking for me. Can you go in there and see if they's anybody in there for me so I can put this sign up?"

"I'd be glad to," she said, and turned and pushed open the door. She stayed gone for a few seconds and then she came back to the door. Stuck just her head out.

"Did you know you can't see this door from the line?" she said.

"Naw. I don't guess I ever noticed."

She kept standing there with just her head stuck out. She was doing something with her hand and he couldn't tell what it was. And then she pulled the door open and backed up and held on to it and lifted the front of her blouse and showed him her big tits. She was smiling. Then she ran her tongue around her lips very slowly. Then she smooched a kiss toward him, dropped the front of her blouse, and disappeared behind the door. He stood there waiting. He heard steps and then another woman came up the stairs. It was that Jones woman who had that plant romance going. She was smiling, too. He coughed and reached for another cigarette.

By lunchtime, Jimmy's daddy was really pissed. Since he'd told Lacey that he had to run to town on his lunch hour, he actually had to leave the plant. And he really didn't want to go. For one thing, he didn't know what he was going to eat for lunch or how he was going to get it and get back with it in thirty minutes and still eat it. Since he was going to have to leave the plant, he wasn't going to be able to get a can of chili, probably, not unless he just left the plant for ten minutes or something and then came back . . . hell, that wouldn't work. She'd know he couldn't go to the parts store and back in ten minutes. And what if she asked him again tomorrow about eating lunch? He could see a problem growing already. But he'd just have to deal with it later. Right now it was 11:58 and he was washing some of the black grease off his hands with some Go-Jo they kept beside the sink in the men's bathroom. He washed his hands good and then dried them on some paper towels and dropped them in the trash and went out the door. He looked at his watch: 11:59. What the hell did he tell her he was going to town for? What else could he have told her to avoid eating lunch with her, though? That he usually ate with Seaborn? That would have worked. That he didn't want everybody in the whole plant to know he had a plant romance going? That would have worked, too. If she couldn't deal with it, tough titty. She knew he was married. She knew he had to be careful. And now he was going to have to leave the damn plant because of her.

The buzzer rang and Jimmy's daddy rushed over to the rack of time cards and grabbed his from its slot. He could see the plant manager watching him through the glass in the window of his office, which was planted squarely across from the time clock so that he could watch everybody punching in in the morning and punching out at lunch and then back in after lunch and then out at three thirty. He didn't miss a thing, and he'd probably noticed how fast Jimmy's daddy had made it over to the time clock. Fuck him. He was just the plant manager.

Jimmy's daddy punched his card and stuck it into the rack on the other side of the time clock just as a whole herd of people started filling up the aisles, all headed toward the time clock. He walked fast out the front door and dug his keys from his pocket, hoping like hell she wasn't going to follow him out to the parking lot. [. . .]

32

A Tommy's Big Red Fish Truck sat in front of the fancy double-wide, whose neat deck and shady porch held thick leafy ferns in pots and a variety of tropical plants. All the flower beds were mulched and free of grass, and the big red truck was dusty from the road. The left front tire was almost halfway down.

There was some kind of notice on a flimsy piece of pink paper tucked beneath one of the windshield wipers, but it had been rained on and the ink had smeared and there were rain spots in the dust on the truck.

On a hill behind the trailer, five well-manicured ponds were scattered down its length, each of them connected to the other by pipes and pumps. The big hatchery barn down below them stood quiet under the sun. A lot of white fluffy clouds were drifting very slowly in the sky.

Inside the double-wide, muffled by the walls, the phone rang. It was shrill and insistent, and it sat there ringing, maybe twenty times. It stopped. In the front lawn were some ten-year-old pecan trees, mere babies compared with the leafy giants standing down behind the trailer.

The phone started ringing again and it kept ringing constantly until it had been ringing for ten minutes. It finally stopped and then there was nothing to hear again but the something-like-whispering noise green leaves made from breeze in the trees.

Up in the sky above all this a bald eagle soared in the blue void, its wide brown wings white tipped and flared for the thermal updraft he was surfing. He circled as he soared, ever lifting, so small he became not much more than a speck. And then he leveled off and began a gradual glide that curved and came back over the land behind the trailer. He was coming fast and he was getting lower all the time. He untucked his talons just before he touched the top of the bream pond, making a thin splash, and without actually slowing down much he flapped his wings and pulled back up, droplets of shiny water falling from the fat and still-flopping bluegill, little diamonds of just a wink of light as the eagle climbed with him, the long feathers gliding them through the air, until they became smaller and smaller and then flew away into the solid blue above the green line of trees that overlooked that part of Arkansas.

33

Cortez sat there and listened to the phone ring. After it rang four times, somebody picked up and said hello. A man.

"Uh, yeah," Cortez said. "This is Cortez Sharp over here in Oxford, Mississippi, and I wanted to talk to the fish man if I could."

The man on the other end laughed just a little.

"This is him," he said. "Or what's left of him. I'm Tommy Bright, but I'm just about out of business."

Cortez was alarmed to hear that. He'd been calling for a couple of days, trying to get somebody to answer the phone number Toby Tubby had given him, and this was the first time somebody had.

"Well dang, I hate to hear that," Cortez said. "I got your number from a friend of mine who works at the Co-op in town. They said they didn't know when you's gonna come back."

Cortez heard some kind of noise on the other end of the phone. It sounded like a door slamming.

"Yes sir, well, I've had some trouble and it looks like the bank's gonna foreclose on me next week. I've done let most of my help go. All I've got on hand is some small catfish right now. Are you interested in some of them?"

"Some little catfish is exactly what I need," Cortez said, and some hope began to rise in his heart. He didn't want to ask the man why he was going out of business because that wasn't any of his business. All he wanted was some fish. He didn't give a shit about the rest of it.

"How many you got?" Cortez said.

The man paused for a moment as he thought.

"I think I got two thousand four inch and a thousand eight inch left. I got em in some tanks in my barn. How many catfish were you wanting, Mr. Sharp?"

"I don't rightly know," Cortez said. "My friend said you can put a thousand to an acre. Is that right?"

"Yes sir, that's how we figure it when we custom stock a large pond. How many acres is yours?"

"It's about a acre and a half," Cortez said. "But it ain't filled all the way up yet. It's a new pond."

"How deep's your water?"

"It's nine foot or better in the middle."

"Aw, why, you're okay," Tommy Bright said. "Let me figure just a minute. You sure called at a good time cause I need to get rid of these last fish. Let me . . . just a second."

"Okay," Cortez said, and just listened. There wasn't much to hear. There was a radio or a TV playing. Some music. Shitfire. He might wind up with some fish after all. He was going to have to get the guy to bring them, though. He wondered what a custom pond was. Maybe he customized the fish to fit the pond. He wondered how soon he could come and bring the fish. It'd be nice if he could do it today. But he probably couldn't do it today.

"You need any bream, Mr. Sharp? I got some in one of my ponds and I need to get rid of them. They're hybrid, grow to a pound and a half in about a year or two. They're great fish for grandkids."

"I ain't got no grandkids," Cortez said, wishing like hell he did.

"I see," Tommy Bright said. "I'll tell you what I'll do, Mr. Sharp. Uh. I hate to ask you this, but can you pay me in cash?"

"Shit yeah," Cortez said, thinking of the barn dough, stashed.

"Okay. I get twenty-nine dollars a hundred for my four-inch catfish. That'd be . . . five eighty if you want all those four-inchers. On the big ones, the eight inch, I get seventy-nine dollars a hundred on them. That'd . . . be . . . seven ninety on them . . . say eight hundred and six hundred. These eight inch, now, if you'll get you some feed and feed em regular, you'll have some big enough to eat before long. I got to charge you a little something to deliver from Arkansas. It's six hours. But I'll do you right. So let's see. Mr. Sharp, I'll bring these fish right to your pond and put em in for fifteen hundred dollars cash. That's two thousand four-inch, one thousand eight-inch channel catfish. If your pond's going to be eighteen feet deep it won't hurt to put that many in there. What do you say?"

"I say bring em on," Cortez said. "When can you come?"

"How about Friday?" Tommy Bright said.

"Friday's fine," Cortez said.

"Okay. Now let me ask you this. Have you got a good road going to your pond? My truck's really heavy when it's loaded with water and I hate to get it stuck. Last time I stuck it I had to get a dozer in there and we snapped three log chains before we got it out."

Shit. He hadn't thought about that. Of course it was heavy. Water was heavy as hell. And he'd have a lot of it for three thousand fish. Three thousand catfish! Imagine what that was going to look like!

"Well, I ain't got much of a road in there to it," Cortez said. "It's just a old log road that goes up through the woods. If it's dry I can drive my pickup in there to it."

"Is it muddy now?"

Was it muddy now? After all this rain? Shit, yeah, it was muddy.

"It is right now," Cortez said.

"Well," Tommy Bright said, and Cortez could almost see him maybe thinking about backing out. "That ain't good."

"I tell you what I'll do," Cortez said. "I'll call the gravel company right now and tell em to bring me out some pit run and grade it smooth. You won't get stuck on that stuff."

"You think they could do it by Friday?" Tommy Bright said.

"They will if they want any of my money," Cortez said. "I aim to have them fish. My daughter wants to come over and catch some of em. She lives in Atlanta." He started to add, *And lives with a retard*. But he didn't. Wasn't any need in getting too personal with this fish guy.

"Okay, then, Mr. Sharp. I'll plan on being there sometime Friday afternoon. I've made that run to Oxford plenty of times, but if you'll give me directions to your house, I'll call you on my cell phone when I get to Oxford and let you know I'm there, and if I have any trouble finding your place, I'll just call, okay?"

"That sounds mighty good," Cortez said.

"Okay, then. I got my pencil. Tell me how to get there."

Cortez told him. Promised to be sitting by the phone Friday.

As soon as he hung up with the fish man, Cortez got out the phone book and started looking through the yellow pages. Dirt. Sand. Gravel. That's what he was looking for. What he was really looking for was a picture of a dump truck. When he found one, he folded the pages back and set it down and dialed the number. It rang three times and then some woman answered. She had a very sexy voice.

"Rebel Gravel, this is Reba," she said lazily. "How may I help you?"

"Y'all got any pit run over there?" Cortez said.

"Pardon me?" the woman said.

"Pit run," Cortez said. "I need some pit-run gravel."

"I don't think I've ever heard of that," the woman said. There was a lot of noise behind her and Cortez could plainly hear some guy yelling, "Warren? Y'all git out of them goddamn culverts fore you crawl up on a snake! I done told you little shits!"

"Y'all don't sell that?" Cortez said.

"Well we sell sand and gravel and clay gravel and washed gravel and pea gravel but I don't think we've got any pit-run gravel. I never heard of it if we do."

"It's that stuff that sets up like concrete," Cortez said.

"Oh you mean *clay* gravel?" the woman said.

"Does it set up hard like concrete?" Cortez said.

"Yes, it does," the woman said. "Excuse me just a minute."

It sounded like she put her hand over the phone, but she must not have put it over it very well because Cortez could hear her yelling, "Clay, would you get him off that backhoe before he kills himself?"

"I'm sorry," she said, when she took her hand off the phone. "My sister's kids are here from Peoria and they're about to drive my husband crazy. Now you want some clay gravel, right?"

"If it sets up like concrete I do," Cortez said.

"How much do you need?" she said.

"I don't know. Enough to build a road."

"How long of a road?"

Cortez had to think. More than a hundred feet. Might be close to two hundred feet. Enough to come from the dirt road where the dozer dude had unloaded down the hill to the pond.

"I'm just guessing," Cortez said. "I'd say maybe two hundred feet. Enough to come down to my pond. I need a road built for the fish guy to come on Friday."

"Maybe I'd better let you talk to my husband," the woman said. "Hold on just a minute, please."

It sounded like she put the phone down. He could hear some kids screaming and the woman yelling at them and the man yelling at them and then he heard the woman say, "If you gonna take that tone with me I'll go my ass straight to the house and watch TV and you can answer your own damn phone!" and then the phone was picked up and a man said, "This is Clay."

"Hey," Cortez said. "This is Cortez Sharp and I need some clay gravel brought over and put out on the road to my pond. And I need it by Friday. Can you do that?"

"Yes sir, I sure can," the man said. "How much you need?"

"I don't know," Cortez said. "I'd say it's about two hundred feet long."

"Well, give me some directions to your house," the man said, and Cortez did.

Cortez had to tear down his little hog-wire go-kart barrier to let the dirt men in, and it took six truckloads to do it right, but by late afternoon they were nearly done. Cortez stood under the shade of the last monster white oak and watched the man on the dozer shaping and smoothing the new red road that snaked its way down from the dirt road that fronted his property to the pond. The man and his nephew had made a good sort of parking lot at the lip of the pond, so that it was easy to park right beside the bank.

When they finished he paid the man, and they loaded their dozer, and the man got back into his dump truck, and his nephew climbed into the truck pulling the low boy that held the dozer, and they left, black smoke pouring from their exhaust pipes.

Cortez stood there, looking at it. It was mighty fine. He'd have to put a gate up to keep people from being able to drive in to it. Later.

Here's what he'd do: He'd go get one of those steel garbage cans with a tight-fitting lid and he'd put it right here next to the bank. Then he'd go to the Co-op and get some fish feed. It might be a good idea to just go ahead and go to town tomorrow and get the feed so that Friday when the fish man got here and put all the fish in, he could go ahead and start feeding them right away. Make them feel welcome.

He was so excited about the fish coming that he wanted to talk to somebody about it when he got back home, but he didn't know who to call. He'd already called Toby and told him. He thought about calling

Lucinda and telling her, but he didn't know if it would make him look bad to be so excited about some catfish he was getting when they'd just buried his wife and her mother a few weeks back. So he didn't call her.

Ham didn't ruin very fast and he was still eating some of it from the fridge, although he'd whittled his way through most of it. He fried a few pieces of it for supper and fried some potatoes that he peeled and cut up. He used a Fry Daddy he found with some cooking oil already in it in a cabinet. He sliced a pretty tomato. He mixed a glass of instant iced tea and then took his supper into the living room to eat it while he watched TV. It was strange. As much as he used to hate the TV, probably from hearing it played so loudly all the time, day and night, now, when he could pick and choose whatever he wanted to watch, he was getting to where he liked the TV. There was a lot of good stuff on it. They had hunting and fishing shows. He'd already watched one bass show and one elk show.

He sat down with his plate in his lap and set his tea on the table and picked up the remote. He was getting pretty good with it, too. He was starting to learn the names of the channels and the numbers that represented them. The Western Channel was 326. The guy who used to play Chester on *Gunsmoke* was the host on that channel. Then they had all those *National Geographic* shows. They had snake shows, lion shows, elephant shows, crocodile shows, all kinds of shows. There was a lot to choose from, and there was rarely a channel that didn't have anything on it. It wasn't like the old days, when stations went off the air late at night. Now there was always something on. It might not be something you wanted to watch, like people selling jewelry, but if you kept pushing the button on the remote, you could eventually find something to watch no matter what time it was.

Shit. He forgot to get a knife to cut up his ham. But he hadn't sliced it very thick and could cut it with his fork so he did, and held the remote out in front of him and aimed it at the TV. He pushed the button and it came on. CNN News. More shit getting blowed up. More killing. He pushed the button and then took a bite of ham. He cut off a piece of tomato.

He was kind of looking for that old woman's sex show, because sometimes women called in and asked interesting questions. [. . .] There was some man speaking at a podium. There was some sports news. A baseball game. Some baseball scores. An old World War II movie. A World War II documentary on Hitler. A documentary on Vietnam. A naked man and a naked woman on a couch. Cortez stopped right there. He took a sip of his tea. This was the channel he'd been looking for. What number was it? He backed up the remote to check: 517. Okay. He'd remember that. Then he flipped it forward again and kept eating his supper while he watched the man and the woman panting and rocking against each other. The woman was slinging her hair around. He raised the volume a little.

"Oh *baby*," the woman was saying. She was blonde and had some kind of bosoms that didn't look exactly natural. They were way too big for her, for one thing, and the skin on them looked like it was stretched so tight they might explode. They didn't look like real bosoms to Cortez, who'd seen a lot of them.

"Oh *yeah*," the man was saying. He was a muscleman and he was whamming at her from behind. He didn't look too excited.

"Holy shit," Cortez said, chewing his ham. He watched them until they finished and then it switched to an office scene where everybody had their clothes on, so he picked up the remote and started looking for something else to watch. He was getting kind of full although he hadn't put that much on his plate. It seemed like the older he got, the less he could eat. He could remember a time when he could sit down and polish off almost two whole plates of catfish and hush puppies and green onions, but that was when he had been a young man and needed a young man's intake. Back when he was still plowing a pair of mules, before he ever bought his first tractor. And it hadn't been much. A little old John Deere 40, a two-cylinder, but it had planters and a disk and you could raise a cotton crop with it. He raised four before he traded for a bigger one. And he never had bought another brand of tractor. He'd owned six and every one of them had been a John Deere. He took one more bite of ham and then put his fork in his plate and set it on the table. He took another sip of his tea.

[. . .]

He turned the volume down and got up with his plate and his glass and carried them back to the kitchen. He raked the food off the plate into the garbage and poured the rest of the watery tea down the drain and set the glass and the plate and fork in the sink.

He went out the back door and looked at the sky. It was clear, gray fading to black, a few pink streaks fading along with it. The leaves on the big pecans were still and he could hear a bobwhite calling. Some lightning bugs were dancing in the air out by the equipment shed and he pulled up a chair to sit in the yard for a while. The days were already shortening and he knew those kids down the road would be going back to school pretty soon. A long time ago when Raif was a kid, the county would let the kids out of school so they could help their parents pick cotton. But those days were long gone. Now they taught schoolkids with computers. He couldn't believe how much the world had changed.

He heard a dog bark somewhere far off and in the distance a gun fired. What was somebody shooting at this time of day? Evening? Kids probably. He saw them running up and down the roads on their four-wheelers. He'd seen some of them come up his road in a line.

A cow bawled down in the pasture and he dreaded putting that milk tube up that bitch's teat again, but her bag was so swollen it looked like it was going to burst. He'd already drained it once, two or three weeks back. Now it had stopped up again. He'd have to get her up first thing in the morning in his old catch pen and try to tie her to where she couldn't kill him. He had the milk tube in a clean little cloth bag in the bib of his overalls, and he needed to sterilize it again. And he needed some lubricant. Seemed like he had some somewhere. And it was dark now, so he got up and went into the house to see if he could find it. [. . .]

The back door slammed behind him. The light over the yard went off. The dog kept barking.

34

Tommy sometimes has to draw the things he sees in his head in order to be able to see how to make them. He'd had to draw a design for his five ponds that were all connected to each other through the pipes and pumps so that he could show the dirt man who built them exactly what he wanted. He is at his table in the brood house, drawing different types of slings on clean white paper with a freshly sharpened pencil. One he makes looks like a sleeping bag. Another looks like an insect's abdomen. Then he thinks, *Tarpaulin,* and quickly draws a rectangle with grommets in it. How long? How long is she? About five feet. Is three feet wide enough? Probably not. Better make it four. The main thing is not to drop her on the concrete. That might kill her. It sure won't do her any good. Is he going to tell the old man what he's doing? How's he going to slip her in if he doesn't tell him? Can he make up something that will send the old man to his house for a few minutes to give him enough time to unload her? Is it going to be physically possible to carry her some distance? What is the distance? What does she weigh now? Is there any way to weigh her by himself? Probably not. The last time they weighed her he had Bill helping him and they made pictures and now Bill's gone back to Marked Tree to live with his brother until he can find another job and where are the pictures? Maybe Audrey's got them. Wherever she is. Maybe she's gone back to her mama in Dallas. She hasn't called. She's pretty pissed. No wonder. The question is whether she'll get over it or not. Maybe she will and maybe she won't. All the money borrowed. All the promises made and broken. He imagines spouses go through something like the same thing with their drunk husbands and wives.

Tommy keeps drawing. He adds short lengths of rope that can be put through the grommets and then the sides can be drawn up around her. Or maybe he should just hire some kid to ride to Mississippi with him to help him unload her in the old man's pond. Why is he obsessed with figuring out how things work? What makes a roulette wheel work? What makes it sometimes stop on red and sometimes black? Why won't

Audrey call him? Is she going to stay pissed off forever this time? Has he finally pushed things too far? Was all this shit the last straw? Is the last straw the same straw that broke the camel's back? Was that from the Bible?

Hell. Can he even keep her alive by herself in one tank for a six-hour ride? Why couldn't he stop every twenty minutes and check her? Maybe make some kind of a dry run first. What if an aerator quits? How will he transfer her to another tank on the side of the road? Is the whole thing stupid? Should he just put a rope stringer through her jaw and put her on a piece of cardboard and skid her down to the bream pond and turn her loose and forget about her? Hope for the best? Let her take her chances with whoever buys this place from the bank?

The answer to that is still no. He figures he owes her this. He knows she's only a fish. She can't think. She doesn't have feelings. She's meat to be eaten. People who catch them her size while they're grabbling skin them and freeze them and then run them through a band saw and slice them into steaks like a hind leg of beef. A slice of deep-fried catfish as big as your plate.

But he keeps drawing a sling for a big catfish. He can get a small canvas tarp and cut it down to size and buy one of those grommet-putter-inners and get some grommets and he can lash it around her and he'll need to have some ropes or something that will join together at the top so that he can put some kind of ring in it that will hold all the ropes together so that he can hook the chain hoist to it and lift her with that. Maybe two rings would be better, one on each end. It'll be along the same lines as the way they move those killer whales, or dolphins. A safe transport. Once she's in the tank he'll take the sling off.

But he doesn't want her to fall out, so he keeps drawing. He adds a latch at the front that will close over her head and a drawstring at the back that won't let her slide backward. He stops and looks down at it. He can make it in a few hours. How much oxygen does she need in an hour? What's her consumption? What if he gets halfway to Mississippi and she rolls belly up? Will he have the heart to go on and deliver the little catfish? He'll have to. He needs the fifteen hundred. If he's careful, if he bets carefully, he can take one third of it and play cautiously until he builds up some capital, and then he can hit the roulette tables.

If he could just hit, then maybe he could work everything out, pay everything off, call Audrey at her mother's and tell her to come back, that everything's changed, that everything's going to be all right, that all this has been just another temporary setback. Wouldn't that be a fine thing to be able to do?

And then he wonders why he's kidding himself. It's all gone to shit now. It's too late. It's all over. Katie barred the door. That's all she wrote.

Fish. Why did he think they were the answer? For a long time they had been. Fish were part of the real beauty of the natural world. It was good clean fun to fish. Kids could do it. Anybody could eat it. Even old folks. Some of his fondest memories were of fish fries at Uncle LaVert's house back when he was a kid. Crisp hush puppies, fried golden brown, and fat cut potatoes that were fried in the same oil, and fish. Mounds of fish: bream, crappie, bass, catfish, all crispy in browned meal, piled high on the plate. Wedges of lemon lying on the side. The cabbage slaw Aunt Addie made and kept in the icebox until time to eat so it would be good and cold.

He wished he could go back to that time and live there again. But that world was gone. He raised his head and looked around. Just like this one was about to be.

35

The days were cooler now. School was starting back pretty soon and that's why there was nobody home that afternoon. Johnette had taken the kids over to one of the malls at Tupelo to start getting them some notebooks and pencils and backpacks and tennis shoes and underwear and shorts and blouses, and Jimmy's daddy knew there was no telling how much money she'd spend. Put it on a credit card. He wondered how much they owed on that damn credit card. He was scared to even find out, so he never asked. He'd been waiting for Johnette to ask him a bunch of questions about why he'd been out so late that night he'd been down at Lacey's and she never had. But he had several stories ready in case she did. One involved a couple of flat tires. One involved running out of gas on a dirt road and having to walk a long way to Toccopola and wake a guy up. Another involved fishing and getting drunk with Seaborn. He wasn't real sure about this last one because he didn't remember if he'd been carrying his rod and reel with him that night or not. But he could always say he'd borrowed a cane pole from Seaborn.

He'd been kind of avoiding Lacey at work. Well not really *avoiding* her, just not sitting in the same area of the break room she did, and concentrating on talking to other people at break and lunch, and trying to make sure he didn't make eye contact with her, although it had happened a few times. Maybe three or four. He'd just smiled and nodded and then quickly looked away. He'd thought some more about not using rubbers with her. He hoped she wasn't pregnant. That would be too bad to even think about. He already had to think about John Wayne Payne all the time.

Jimmy's daddy wanted to check the brake shoes on the back left because he'd heard something squealing this morning heading in to work, and it was a nice afternoon, so he got the jack from the trunk and found a piece of board and set the base of the jack on that. The car was pretty level where it was sitting and the hand brake didn't work very well, so he didn't set it. But he didn't think it would fall. He jacked it up a little and then got the lug wrench and started loosening the nuts on the wheel. What he needed as soon as he could afford them were some really nice mag wheels. Maybe some chrome-plated Keystones. He'd checked the price on them at Gateway and they were $118 apiece plus tax, but they'd mount them for free, they said. It would probably be just a shade over five hundred. But damn, wouldn't they look fine?

And if he did get divorced, where in the hell was he going to live? Would she want the trailer? What would happen to Jimmy? What if she married some other son of a bitch? Who would raise him? And those girls of hers. They'd run wild. Wind up pregnant by the time they were seventeen or something. Jimmy might fall in with the wrong crowd. Some of those kids in big pickups. And Jimmy's daddy would miss him.

He guessed what he needed to do this fall was take him hunting. Maybe he could buy him a shotgun. A little single shot .410. That was a good beginner gun for a kid. Jimmy's daddy could gather up some beer cans and take him down to the dump or the creek and let him get in some target practice. Blast a few beer cans.

When he got to thinking about stuff like that, stuff like teaching Jimmy how to use a gun and taking him hunting, and maybe one day starting to take him fishing, he didn't want to get divorced so much. Sometimes, when he thought about it, he realized how good he had it. He got his clothes washed. He got his meals fixed. He got all his banking done for him. He had a nice bed to lie on while he watched his hunting videos and he only had to work forty hours a week. He had the '55. He had Jimmy. He didn't have much of a sex life with Johnette, true, but he had Lacey now. If he wanted her. He knew he was going back sometime, he just didn't know when. He didn't want everybody in the whole plant to know he was messing around with her. He guessed he'd have to explain that to her sometime. Surely she ought to be able to understand that. Women were funny, though. They got things in their heads. Like love.

He got four of the lug nuts off and then jacked the car on up until the wheel cleared the ground. Then he sat down next to the wheel and took off the last lug nut. He put it beside the others and started pulling the wheel off and before he knew it the car had come sideways toward him because the jack and the board he had set it on had slipped in the loose gravel and the wheel started to slip off and he tried to shove it back on to keep the car from falling all the way and it came down on top of his hands, pinning his hands between the wheel well and the tire tread and mashing the shit out of his fingers.

Jimmy's daddy closed his eyes and screamed. "Oh shit!"

He tried to pull his hands loose, but it felt like it was going to tear the skin off them. The car had stopped moving. He tried to stretch his leg out and kick the jack erect, but nothing doing. He had his face up against the rear fender, and he had to scream again.

"Hey!" he screamed. "Hey!"

Son of a bitch! It was breaking his fucking hands! Oh my God! Jimmy's daddy panted hard and tried again to pull them out. He could feel the blood getting squeezed out of his fingers. It hurt so bad he didn't know what he was going to do. He knew one thing he was going to do if he couldn't get his fingers out from under that wheel well. He was going to shit in his britches. His stomach hadn't been in very good shape for the last few days, because he'd been drinking beer every evening for the last few days, and he'd had a light bout of diarrhea just after lunch today. And he'd meant to take a couple of Imodium before now, but he'd forgotten about it. And he'd felt another twinge of it just before he came out of the trailer with a cold beer to start jacking up the car, and it was just one of those little slips you make, not taking something when you needed to, planning on doing it later. It was bad timing. Which would get you every time.

"Hey!" he screamed. "Hey somebody! I need some help!"

Nobody answered. Nobody showed up. There was just the silent gravel road beside him. And how long would it take for somebody to come by? What if they didn't stop? What if they saw him yelling and still didn't stop? Oh God. His stomach was hurting and he was afraid he was going to shit on himself. He really didn't want to do that.

"Hey! Hey! Heyyyyyyyyyyyyyyy!"

Oh Jesus. It was breaking his fingers. Tears squeezed from his eyes, as hard as he tried not to let them. Oh shit. He couldn't shit on himself and let somebody find him like this. What if he had to stay here until Johnette and them came back? No telling when that would be. It was only about five thirty. They probably weren't nearly through shopping yet. Oh God it hurt. What he had to do was concentrate on not shitting on himself. What if the girls saw him like this? What would they think? How ridiculous did he look?

"Heyyyyyyyyyy!" A yelp for help lost in the wilderness.

And then they'd probably go eat. Maybe even at Seafood Junction. He thought they were open on Wednesdays. She'd probably eat two or three desserts. Shit. They might not be back until nine. That would be after dark. He didn't think he could sit here that long, with the car mashing the shit out of his hands. But did he really have a choice?

"Please!" he yelled. "Somebody!"

He tried again to pull his hands loose. He could feel the rough metal of the wheel well cutting into his hands. Rusty. He'd probably need a tetanus shot. He was trying to think of other things to maybe keep from shitting on himself and he wondered how long it had been since he'd had a tetanus shot. He'd gotten one when he'd stepped on that rusty nail about six or seven years ago. He didn't know how long tetanus shots lasted.

Jimmy's daddy didn't think he could take it any longer, but he didn't know what he could do about it. His stomach was hurting worse and he needed to get to the bathroom pretty soon. He was going to have an accident if he didn't. And if he had an accident he was going to have to sit here with his own shit smeared all over his ass until somebody came along who could reset the jack and get the car off his hands. If that old man who lived up the road could hear him, maybe he could jack it up. He looked like a farmer. He probably knew how to operate a jack.

He looked at the driver's door. He wished he'd left it open. If he had left it open, he might have been able to reach out with his leg and maybe get to the steering wheel and start blowing the horn with his foot. If his leg was long enough. Hell, his leg wasn't that long. He didn't think. He stretched his leg out to see if it would reach, but he couldn't make it go very far past the closing edge of the door.

What was he going to do? Just stay here? Hell. The blood in his hands was getting cut off. He might have gangrene to worry about. What if he lost his fingers? Why hell, he wouldn't be able to work then. He'd be disabled. He'd have to go on disability. He wondered how much that paid.

Probably not enough. How would he hunt? With no fingers he wouldn't be able to pull the triggers on his guns. How would you throw the line out on your rod and reel? Or learn to play the guitar if you had one?

His stomach was hurting now. All this pain in his hands wasn't helping anything. His stomach was letting him know that if he didn't get to a bathroom pretty quick, something was going to happen to him that hadn't happened to him since he'd been wearing a diaper. And he didn't even remember any of that. He knew it must have happened, but he just couldn't remember any of it. Oh Lordy. He couldn't stand it much longer.

He couldn't even scream anymore. There wasn't anybody to hear. And sometimes hours passed before anybody came up or down this road. In a way that was good. Sometimes. Right now it wasn't. Right now he felt like he was going to have a nasty accident in his pants. He didn't think there was going to be anything he could do about it. He was trying not to. But he was afraid that trying wasn't going to get it. His stomach was hurting too bad. Something had to give. Oh God. Oh God! And then it happened. Jimmy's daddy cried while he shit on himself. He couldn't get his hands loose to wipe his tears away, so he just wiped them on the shoulder of his shirt, the way he did sweat when he was too busy with his hands to mop it with them.

An hour later he was still there. He could see his watch just fine and it was six thirty. [. . .] Nobody had come down the road in all that time. He'd been hoping that maybe some kid would come rolling down the road in one of those big pickups, but there hadn't been a soul. He'd been hoping that maybe one of those caravans of four-wheelers would come down the road, but they hadn't come by either. Now his hands just felt dead. There wasn't much feeling in them at all. He was surely going to lose both of them.

By then he'd gotten to wondering if he was going to die. What if he had a heart attack while he was sitting here so stressed out? He wouldn't even be able to get loose to go inside and call 911 for an ambulance. They'd find him here, dead, when they came in from shopping at Tupelo, and he could imagine how Jimmy would cry. He knew Jimmy loved him. And he loved Jimmy. He told himself one thing. If he got out of this alive, he was going to start treating Jimmy a lot better. Hell. How long would it take to take the chain off the go-kart and find a small-engine shop and get another chain? It wouldn't take very long. He knew how much Jimmy loved driving that go-kart. And no wonder. What else did he have to do around here? Watch TV? Hang out with the girls?

Yes sir. A thing like this could make a man take a look at his life and see what all was wrong with it. And he'd been doing that already. Only now he was doing it a lot harder. He could do better. He could cut back on his beer drinking. It cost the shit out of him anyway. It was an expensive habit. You smoked about twice as many cigarettes when you were drinking. Burned twice as much gas because you were constantly riding around. Which wore your tires out quicker. Made you need an oil change sooner. Things snowballed on you.

Man, what he'd give for a cigarette. They were right there in his pocket. Not even six inches away from his chin, but they might as well have been on the moon.

Inside the trailer, the phone rang. It was probably Seaborn or Rusty. It was probably one of them calling to see what he was doing.

"I can't come to the phone!" he yelled. It kept ringing. It rang and rang. Maybe it was one of the girls' friends. They had friends who called them on the phone. But they never came over. Jimmy's daddy had made it plain that he didn't want a bunch of kids over at his trailer drinking up all the Cokes and messing the trailer up and talking on the phone to other kids and all that shit. Jimmy's daddy liked peace and quiet. But maybe if he got out of this okay he should lighten up a little there, too. Jimmy's daddy's daddy and Jimmy's daddy's mother never would let him have company over when he was growing up. They just didn't allow it. And Jimmy's daddy never did get to go home with a friend and spend the night like other kids he knew did. What would that have hurt? The phone stopped ringing.

Jimmy's daddy thought maybe something was happening to his brain to help him deal with his situation. The pain had eased, numbed itself, really, he guessed, and he was more peaceful than he would have thought he'd be. He guessed he'd accepted it. He'd had to. He'd shit on himself, yeah, but it wasn't the end of the world, was it? It probably happened to people every day. And how long did the circulation have to be cut off before you'd lose one or more of your fingers? He had a little feeling in them, just not a whole lot. So that was probably a good sign. That probably meant that there was still at least a little bit of blood circulating through them. Maybe.

If he could have just gotten one hand loose, he could have done something. He could have at least smoked. This way he couldn't do anything but sit here and hope for somebody to come along. And it didn't look like anybody was going to come along.

And then somebody did. He heard the gravel crunching under the tires long before he saw the car, partly because it was going so slowly, partly because he couldn't see past the fender of the '55. So he waited. He got ready to give out a really big yell just as the car or truck or whatever it was passed the trailer. He didn't care who it was. He didn't care that he'd shit on himself and was sitting in it and that somebody might see it. He just wanted some help.

The gravel kept crunching and it got louder and he wondered why the person driving was going so slowly. He turned his head toward the gravel road, waiting, getting ready to suck in a big breath of air so that he could yell plenty loud, and he waited. And waited. And then the nose of a Mercury nosed past the front of his '55 and he saw Lacey looking out at him from behind the wheel of the car. She grinned and waved. She was creeping at about one mile per hour. Maybe two.

"Stop!" he screamed, and she slammed on the brakes.

"Hey!" she said gaily, leaning her head out the window. She lifted a beer and took a drink. "What you doing?"

Jimmy's daddy closed his eyes and shook his head. Could she not see what he was doing? Could she not see that he had shit on himself?

"Come here and help me!" he yelled.

"What about your wife?" she said. "She not home right now?"

"Get your ass over here and jack this fucking car up off me!" he screamed, and damn near fainted when she backed up and stopped and then pulled on in and got out to help him. She set her beer on her fender.

It almost hurt worse when it came back up. Lacey seemed pretty expert at setting up jacks because she took the base of the jack and scraped away the loose gravel down to hard ground and set it on that, and then she hunted around until she found a chunk of wood and set it behind the other rear tire to keep it from rolling. Then she jacked it up. Jimmy's daddy winced as he felt the rough metal slowly releasing his hands, and it was such a relief that he almost cried again.

"Oh God," he kept saying, over and over, and he looked back at Lacey to see that she was almost crying, too.

"Hold on, baby," she said, pumping on the jack, her big boobs swinging. The fender well lifted off his hands and Jimmy's daddy slammed himself backward, flat on his back on the gravel, and he was afraid to look at his hands. They felt all crabbed up. Finally he looked at them. Both his palms had tire tracks printed in them. They looked swollen. They were slightly purple. But miraculously, nothing seemed to be broken. He could wriggle his fingers.

He dragged himself backward, away from the car, and he rubbed his hands together. His thumbs felt numb. But in them there was starting up that little tingling feeling like a thousand needle points sticking him, just like it did when his legs went to sleep on a deer stand from not moving for so long. When he felt that, he knew he was going to be all right.

"Help me up," he said, and she did.

She waited in the living room while he cleaned himself up in the bathroom. He was a nervous wreck because he knew he had to get her the *hell* out of here before Johnette and the kids came home. Hell. He'd just say he didn't know who in the hell she was but that after she'd been good enough to stop and get the car off him, he'd invited her in for a beer.

His underwear and his pants were lying in the bathtub and he got some clean shorts from the drawer in his bedroom, then pulled a clean pair of jeans off a hanger in the closet. He walked into the kitchen and went to a cabinet at the side of the stove and opened the cabinet door. He got a Hefty garbage bag with yellow ties and looked at Lacey where she was sitting on the couch, having a smoke and drinking a fresh beer that she'd gotten from her Mercury. She looked pretty comfortable. Would she tell anybody that he'd shit on himself? He sure hoped not. They hadn't talked about it. She'd seen what had happened to him. Couldn't help but see. But she hadn't said anything about it. Thank God.

"You got a nice trailer," she said.

"Thank you," he said. "I'll be done in a minute. Then we got to get you the hell out a here."

"I know it," she said. "If she comes in while I'm setting here, just tell her you don't know me from Adam and I just happened to come by."

"That sounds like a good idea," Jimmy's daddy said, and took the garbage bag back to the bathroom and put the soiled underwear and pants inside it, rolled it up tightly, turned on the water in the tub and washed out the inside of it, then took the rolled-up garbage bag back to the kitchen and put it inside another garbage bag that was inside the garbage can. Then he bagged up the trash and took it outside and stuffed it down inside one of the metal garbage cans he kept out there and closed the lid over it. What the hell did she mean coming by here? And how in the hell had she found out where he lived? He was going to have to have a talk with her. But not today. And damn sure not here.

When he stepped back inside the trailer she was sitting there looking at some pictures of the kids and just generally checking everything out in the living room. She looked up at him and smiled.

"Let me get my boots on," he said.

"I ain't in no hurry," she said.

"Yeah, but I am."

He went back to the bedroom and put his boots back on and got his cap and went to the bathroom and popped a couple of Imodium from a bottle Johnette kept in the medicine cabinet. Then he went back out to the living room. But Lacey wasn't in there.

"Lacey?" he called.

"I'm back here," her dim voice called. Where the hell was she?

Holy shit. Was she in the back bathroom? "Back here in the bathroom."

Back in the *bathroom*? Fuck! What if Johnette came in now?

"What are you *doing*?" he yelled.

"Taking a leak," she called. "That dang beer runs right through me."

"Well, hurry up," he called. "You got to go!"

"I know it," she said, and he heard the toilet flush.

Jimmy's daddy's hands were feeling better now, but they still had the tire tracks on them. They looked like they'd been imprinted on his skin.

He'd already tried washing them and it wouldn't come off. He didn't know what he was going to tell anybody who asked. What was he going to tell Johnette if she asked? Who was he going to say got the car off him? Some passing kid in a big truck? Maybe so.

Lacey came up the hall, smoothing her black pants over her hips, straightening the bottom of her flowery blouse, and she walked up to him and stopped. He opened his mouth to say something and she raised one of her hands and placed her fingers over his lips.

"I know already what you're gonna say," she said. "I know I ain't supposed to be in here. But I'm glad I come by when I did."

"I'm glad you did, too," Jimmy's daddy said. And he really was.

"Don't be mad cause I come driving by," she said. "I was just out riding around, having a few beers. I wouldn't have got you in no trouble. I'm heading home now. I'll see you tomorrow at work."

"Okay," Jimmy's daddy said. He could see love in her eyes for sure now. And he could see the hurt in her eyes, too. He didn't know what it was from, only that she had it. She leaned a little closer.

"I'd give anything to kiss you right now," she said.

Jimmy's daddy stood there. He didn't say anything because he didn't know what to say. But he didn't want to kiss her here. He was afraid he might not be able to stop himself from going ahead with her right here. Or taking her down the road somewhere. And maybe getting caught.

"But I know I got to go."

"Yeah," Jimmy's daddy said. "I guess you'd better."

"I don't need to be here when your family comes in," she said.

Then you better get your ass in the road, he thought.

"Bye," she said, and she opened the door, stepped down the steps, then closed the door. Jimmy's daddy sat down in a chair. He heard her open her door, heard the door close, heard the car start, heard the car pull out, heard the car go on down the road until the sound of it died away. He got up and went to the door and opened it. Lacey had put the wheel back on while he'd cleaned himself up. She had even put the jack and the lug wrench away. It looked like nothing had happened except for his tire-tracked hands.

36

Cortez got up early in the morning like he always did and shaved care-fully like he always did. He made some coffee and he made pancakes from a box of Aunt Jemima mix and poured some Johnny Fair syrup all over the stack and sat down alone at the kitchen table and ate while the birds sang outside the screen windows. Since his wife died, Cortez had raised all the windows and had kept the air conditioner turned off most of the time. It got warm sometimes in the afternoons and he ran it then if he was in the house, but he liked to sleep with the windows up at night now since he was alone and could do whatever he wanted to at long last. It was kind of like having a brand-new life. He guessed he could even date now if he wanted to.

But who would he date? He'd probably have to go to church to find somebody, and he didn't want to go to church. All the old women he knew around here his age looked like they were all dried up. If he *did* decide to date somebody, he might want somebody a little bit younger. Say maybe somebody who was about sixty-five or so. Somebody who still had some meat on her bones. He wasn't sure he could still do it, but he was thinking about finding out. He knew he still thought about it. Even more so now that he'd been watching those dirty movies on the TV. They had kind of recharged his batteries.

He washed his dishes after he got through eating so he wouldn't have to do it later. He'd been keeping the house clean, too. Dusted one day, swept and mopped another. He put his rubber boots on and went up to the barn and then he closed the lot gate and turned the heifers out into the north pasture where the grass was belly high and left them there. He got into his truck and drove down past the equipment shed and opened the gate there, drove through, then got out and closed it behind him.

The sun was bright on the dew in a million points of light and he could see the sun striking the droplets of moisture on the fresh webs of spiders strung here and there, knitted overnight. The cows were down in the bottom pasture and he started blowing the horn when he saw them. They started walking toward him and he turned around and stopped to see if they were coming on. They were. It was a wonder. If there was anything dumber than a cow he didn't know what it was. They had to be the dumbest animals God ever put on the face of the earth. He blew the horn a few more times and then drove on up behind the barn and parked the truck and got out and opened the south gate and left it open. He walked into the barn and got a bucket and filled it with some sweet feed and carried it back out. The cows were starting to trot toward the trough and he dumped the sweet feed on the rough boards, spreading it in a long row. The cows hurried forward, and he went around the edge of them and waited for the old Brahman to get herself in and then he shut the gate, leaving the rest of them and their calves out there bawling to get in. [. . .]

He put the bucket back in the barn and shut the door, and then he went over and opened the gate to the catch pen and started shooing them toward it. A couple darted out past him and he let them go back to the trough. But he got the old Brahman and nine other cows with their calves into the loading chute and started letting them out the side gate one by one until he had just the old cow in there. He hemmed her in front and back with some fence posts he'd left lying there just for that. He slid the posts through the six-inch cracks between the boards, rested each of them against a post. He put three in front of her and three in back, too high to jump over. She couldn't back up or go forward. She didn't like it and tried to get out, but unless she broke something, he thought he had her. He wondered if he ought to tie her feet. He didn't want to get kicked in the mouth. With a hoof full of fresh shit. But it wouldn't be the first time.

He squatted down outside the wide boards of the catch pen and looked at her bag. It looked like it was holding about five or six gallons of milk. She'd been a good cow and had delivered a big healthy calf every year for the last nine years. He stretched out a hand for one of her teats, the biggest one, to see if he could squeeze some milk from it, but quick as lightning she kicked his hand and then kicked again and almost hurt him before he could get his hand back.

He looked up at her head. She had rolled one baleful eye back toward him and she was trying to twist her head around to see how to kick him better.

"I'm trying to help you, you stupid son of a bitch," he said.

She bowed up and kicked and tried to heave herself up out of the chute, but the boards were eight feet high and she couldn't get that high. She could kick the shit out of him whenever he reached in for that teat, though. He was going to have to tie her feet. So he went into the barn, hunting some rope. He didn't want to get crippled by a cow at his age. Then *he'd* be in a damn wheelchair. How much dating could you do in one of them? Not much, probably. Unless maybe they had a club for people in wheelchairs.

He opened the big side door so that he'd have some light. He seemed to remember having some rope somewhere, but there was so much stuff in the barn that it was hard to find anything specific. A lot of stuff was hung on nails, most of it coated with fuzzy dust and the spider webs of years.

He walked back toward the stalls and stopped beside the door where the trunk was stashed and opened it and looked inside, but he didn't see any rope hanging on a nail there. He closed it back and latched it.

Maybe it was upstairs. He went on down the hall in his rubber boots and walked over to the ladder and started up it very slowly. Old as he was, he had to be careful about climbing stuff. And some of the steps were loose, needed replacing. It was hard for a man to take care of everything that needed taking care of. Especially by himself. A long time ago when he'd had Cleve helping him, it seemed that everything got taken care of: fences fixed, tin roofs painted, tomatoes staked, hay cut and baled and hauled, calves castrated, gates repaired, stock all watered. He had a lot more cows then, though. He didn't want to mess with more than twenty head now. And a day would come when he wouldn't be able to take care of even one. He knew that. But that day hadn't come yet. And as long as he could walk and get around and climb up and down from his tractor, he was going to have some cows. There was nothing better than standing at the fence on a summer afternoon and watching them graze. It made a man feel good to look at them and know they were his. No matter what else had happened.

He went on up the steps, careful of his footing and his grip. His head rose above the floor and he stopped with the top half of himself sticking up into the loft. He hadn't been up here in a while. The peak of the rafters was twenty feet above his head and he had nailed every one of them on. It had taken two months and six men to build this barn. That was in 1958. And the son of a bitch was still solid. It didn't even have any leaks in the roof that he knew of. He didn't see any rope. There were forty or fifty small bales of hay stacked against the back wall and some baling twine was looped around some nails sticking out of the rafters. But that stuff wasn't strong enough. Or it might cut her. What he needed was some rope. And he couldn't remember where in the hell he'd put it.

He climbed on up and pulled himself up onto the floor of the loft and stood up and walked across the boards. He looked around for the rope, but he didn't see it anywhere. He had spent a bunch of hot June afternoons up here, stacking hay amid buzzing red wasps while men below on trucks threw it up through the opened loft door, which was closed now and hadn't been used in a while, since he'd switched to large bales he could move around with his tractor. It was easier. Let the tractor do the work. He guessed the world got better in some ways as it went along. And in lots of ways it got worse.

He remembered screwing his wife up here. That was a long time ago. He'd done a lot of screwing in this barn. He'd done so much he couldn't remember all of it. It was so big and had so many places to hide somebody that it had been almost easy to get away with it. Somebody could walk in off the road and come in the back door and nobody at the house would even see her. That was how he used to meet Queen. How many times had they done it in this barn? Hundreds. At night. In the middle of the day. On cold and frozen days, wrapped in blankets and lying in the hay. Up here, too. Why in God's name did he do it? Why didn't he just run off with her? Would he do the same thing if he had the chance again? He hoped Lucinda never found out about it.

He looked above him and could still see the saw marks in some of the rafters. Halter Wellums had sawed every piece of this wood out of some longleaf pines that Cortez and Toby had cut on Coy Patton's place. Those were some mighty fine logs. And they had made some mighty fine timber. In its height and width, the sheer size of it, the loft had always reminded Cortez of pictures he'd seen of cathedrals. And it always smelled the same. It always smelled like hay. But there wasn't any rope up here. And what was done with Queen was done.

He climbed back down and went out the back door of the barn and opened the door on the corn crib and looked in there. There it was. It was nylon rope and he remembered sticking it in here now. He'd bought it up at Sneed's, twenty feet of it, in a plastic bag. It was eight-hundred-pound test, dark blue, very soft. He grabbed it and went back through the barn, up the hall, out the big door and over to the chute. She was knocking her head against the boards of the chute and she was bawling. Her calf was bawling, down on the other side of the barn.

"All right, you son of a bitch," he said, and pulled out his pocketknife. He cut two pieces about four feet long from the rope and bent down next to her. He looked up at her. She had her foot right next to a post and Cortez threaded the end of the rope through the boards and around her foot just above the hock. She didn't raise hell and she let him pull the rope back out through the boards and then he made an overhead knot, tying it twice. She tried to move her foot and couldn't and she went crazy, jerking her whole body and trying to lift her foot. The chute was shaking. Cortez got up and went around and let himself into the catch pen and walked around to the other leg. He squatted down.

Three times he tried to tie that leg and three times she kicked at him. One time she nearly smashed his finger against the post. He just squatted there and waited for her to calm down. She was gentle as a lamb unless you had her hemmed up. Or tied up. She was a good cow, but she was getting old. She probably wouldn't have but one or two more calves. When one started having bag trouble, they were about like an old car: time to trade for a new one. Make some baloney out of her. Potted meat. Vienna sausage.

He tried twice more before he got the rope around her leg. He didn't get it up as high as he would have liked, but he had to settle for it. He made the same knot he'd made on the other side and then he opened the bib of his overalls and pulled the milk tube from its little cloth bag. He stuck it lightly between his lips while he twisted the top from the small tube of lubricant and then he squeezed some of it onto the tube, making sure the tip was coated with it. He set the lubricant on the ground and leaned toward the cow with the milk tube. It was hollow, made of aluminum, with a rounded end that would open up the teat and let the stopped-up, curded milk flow out through it. Get all that mess out of there. Let the calf nurse and keep her from getting her bag messed up. Teat might rot off or something. You didn't want that.

"All right, baby," he said softly. "You let me get this up in you and you'll feel better."

He put his hand around the swollen teat and pushed the tip of the milk tube up in it and things went wrong. She heaved backward toward him and he heard a post crack, and then she slammed herself forward and tried to break the posts in front of her. Cortez dropped the milk tube and she stepped on it, mashing it into the mud and cowshit in the bottom of the chute. She kept trying to kick, slamming herself against the boards.

"You crazy son of a bitch," Cortez said, trying to find the milk tube in the mud. He caught a glimpse of it and then she stepped on it again. She was spattering shit all over him with her lunging feet. But he stayed calm. Cortez was kind of like a doctor with a cow, is how he thought of it. You had to have patience. You already knew that you were smarter than the cow, who was a lot bigger than you, but the thing about it was that a cow, being one of the dumbest animals there was, might hurt you accidentally trying to get away from you because of something you were doing to it that maybe didn't feel so good. Like punching holes in your ears to put in plastic identification tags. Sticking a pointed trocar into your abdomen wall to let out deadly fescue gas. Or cutting your balls off with a really sharp knife if you happened to be a bull. So you had to outsmart the animal, and you had to make sure that the animal couldn't get loose until you were through doing whatever you were doing to it. This foot-tying business wasn't the best idea in the world, but it was all he had right now until something better came along. They probably made leather hobbles for something like this. He could check in one of his catalogs and see.

He had to reach in with his hand and go through the mud and the shit, squeezing gobs of it between his fingers, searching mostly by feel for the little aluminum tube. Which would have to be taken back inside the house now and washed and sterilized again. He'd have to stick a straw down through it to make sure it wasn't plugged up. But he hadn't even found it yet. He kept feeling around for it and finally got it back in his fingers.

There was a man gate built into his fence on the side of the barn that faced the driveway and he went through it and walked back down the driveway to the house. He left his boots at the back door and went to the kitchen sink and washed the milk tube with soap and hot water. He turned a burner on under the pot of water that was still sitting there from when he'd sterilized the milk tube last night. He made sure it was clean on the inside and then he dropped it into the water on the stove and sat down at the kitchen table to wait.

It was only about seven o'clock. Maybe he ought to just load her up when he got done with her and take her to Pontotoc and let her out at the sale barn and they could sell her for him Saturday. She wasn't going to bring much, old as she was, but he could probably find another one to take her place. He could look in the *Mississippi Market Bulletin,* which he read religiously each month, from front to back.

He sat there and waited for the water to boil and thought about going up to the Co-op this afternoon after lunch and see Toby and get a couple of bags of catfish feed. And then he probably needed to run by Sneed's and get a steel garbage can with a tight-fitting lid to keep the feed in. And he had to remember to be sitting by the phone Friday, waiting for the fish guy to call. He couldn't imagine why the fish guy would be getting out of the business since it looked like a pretty interesting business. He wondered how the guy raised them. Maybe he could ask him when he got here. He had to go get the money from the barn. He'd do that Thursday night and have it ready for him.

He heard the Brahman bawl out in the chute. He wished he had somebody to help him. She'd already cracked one of the posts and that wasn't good. He didn't think she could get out. She probably weighed twelve hundred pounds, though. Some of that old rotten wood might not hold. But there was nothing to do but wait and see.

He got up and went over to the refrigerator and opened the door, wondering what he was going to have for lunch. Just about all the food from the funeral was gone. Even the ham, which had lasted a pretty long time. He wished he had some more of it. Maybe he needed to go buy a few groceries this afternoon after he got the catfish feed. He thought he wouldn't mind having some bacon for his breakfast since he was getting tired of pancakes. Or maybe he needed some cereal. Cereal was easy. Just pour some milk on it. He didn't much like cereal, though. It didn't seem like it filled you up very much.

He shut the refrigerator door and walked back over to the stove and looked at the pan. Some small bubbles were starting to arrange themselves in rings at the bottom of the water. He saw one little piece of shit float out of the milk tube and he reached in with just the tip of his finger and dipped it out, wiped it on his pants. Then he sat down at the kitchen table again. He played with the salt and pepper shakers. He pushed one this way, one the other way. He wished the water would hurry up and boil. Get this shit over with. He wondered if his wife had gone to heaven. He hoped so. She'd always wanted to.

When the water finally boiled he turned off the burner and took the pot over to the sink and poured out the hot water and reached in for the milk tube and wrapped it in a paper towel because it was hot. He went ahead and lubricated it and then stepped back outside and put his boots back on and walked back up to the barn.

Then he stopped. He stood there for a minute, looking at the cow, who was watching him. He knew as well as he knew his own name that she was going to kick him again. And he didn't intend to keep washing and sterilizing that milk tube half the day.

So he went back inside the barn and walked back to the harness room and unlatched it and went in and pulled the feed sacks off the trunk and raised the lid. He lifted the tray and didn't take time to look at the locket again because he had more important things to do. He took the Thompson out and walked through the hall of the barn with the butt of the stock resting on his hip and he walked out into the bright sunshine and looked at the cow. She turned her head to watch him.

"You son of a bitch," he said. "If you kick me again, I'm gonna shoot you with this damn machine gun. I swear fore God."

That did it. He couldn't back out now. It wasn't even up to him anymore. He put the gun on the ground and walked over to her.

She was still standing there waiting for him. He looked at her and started right that minute to go back to his truck and back it around to his cattle trailer and hook it up and pull it up to the end of the loading chute and load her, just take her on to Pontotoc. The calf was plenty old enough to be weaned. But he didn't. He went ahead and squatted next to her back end again and reached in and got his hand around the swollen teat and then pushed the milk tube inside it. Blood and mucus came out first, then some chunks of white matter, then some stuff that looked like bits of butter came out, and the old cow stood there and let it drain. He looked up at her.

She had her head turned again, watching him with a big round peaceful eye.

"See there?" he said. He looked back down at the milk tube. Pure white milk was flowing now. He let it keep draining. Taking the pressure off her bag. He didn't care that he was wasting her milk. Her calf didn't need that much milk now. But that milk was why that calf was so big. Why all hers had been so big. She was a good one. Maybe he wouldn't sell her after all.

He squatted there, letting the white milk spatter in the greenish mud between her hind feet, until it made a puddle she was standing in, and then, finally, after what seemed to be several gallons of milk, it began to ebb.

When he got done with her he untied her feet, took the posts from in front of her and turned her out the side gate and let her go back to her calf. He opened the gate to the heifer pen so that they could get back in to their water and then he went back to his truck and drove it down to the house and parked it. He thought he might watch a little TV before he went to town.

Floating catfish feed was eleven dollars per bag, and Cortez got two. He'd already backed his truck around to the side of the warehouse and Toby walked out with him, holding his green sales slip, and handed it to a sleepy black guy who was in a chair with a fan blowing lots of hot air on him.

"Two bags of catfish feed, Sam," Toby said, and they waited while the guy took his two-wheeler and pushed it into the shadows of the big tin-covered building. Cortez wondered if they'd killed any more woodchucks in there lately. He saw some guy across the road picking up cans.

"I think I'm fixing to retire," Toby said, and leaned against the wall in the shade. Cortez leaned with him.

"Shit. You done retired three times," Cortez said.

"I know it. My old leg gets to hurting, though. It's walking on this concrete all day's what it is. Lurlene has to rub my leg with liniment at night it hurts so bad sometimes."

They stood there in the heat. Cars and trucks were passing out on the street and there were lots of pickups parked at the Beacon Restaurant just up from there. A colorful sign on a brick house said LOCAL COLOR.

"You heard from Lucinda?" Toby said.

"Naw. She ain't called. I don't reckon."

"She might of called while you's gone," Toby said.

"I guess she could have," Cortez said.

"Maybe you ought to get you one of them answering machines," Toby said. "That way you wouldn't miss any calls. We got one."

"You do?"

"Yep. Plus if it's somebody you don't want to talk to, you can just let the machine catch it."

"Well how you know who it is?" Cortez said.

"Caller ID," Toby said.

"What's that?" Cortez said.

"It's a little screen on your phone that lights up and shows you who's calling. Like if it's one of them asshole telemarketers trying to sell you something over the phone, you don't have to answer it."

"My phone ain't got no little screen on it," Cortez said.

"You got to get a new phone that's got one," Toby said.

"Oh," Cortez said.

The warehouse guy came back out with two big blue paper bags on his two-wheeler and Cortez walked over to his truck and let down the tailgate so the guy could slide them in. Each bag had a picture of a catfish on it. The guy looked like he was about to keel over from sleepiness.

"How much is that, fifty pounds?" Cortez said.

"Yes sir," the guy said. "You must a got you some catfish."

"I'm fixing to," Cortez said.

When the bags of feed were in, he raised the tailgate and fastened it shut and told Toby he'd see him later, then he got back in his truck and left. He drove through town and up to the square and had to wait for the traffic to clear before he could pull out. Somebody behind him blew their horn and he looked into the rearview mirror to see some person looking at the back of his head.

"Don't you be blowing at me," he said.

It was very hot already and his truck didn't have air conditioning. That had always seemed like a waste of money, to pay extra for air conditioning in a vehicle since you could always just roll the windows down. But Lucinda couldn't drive one without it. Refused to. She damn sure hadn't been raised like that. He hadn't agreed to buy a window unit for the house until 1973, but he had to admit it was nice when the weather was really humid, like it was now. But he still liked sleeping with the windows up. He thought that night air was probably good for you. The traffic kept coming around the square and there wasn't any way to pull out. The person behind him honked the horn again and Cortez pushed his truck into neutral and pulled out the hand brake, opened the door, and walked back to the car behind him. More horns started blowing. He didn't pay them any attention. Some kid was behind the wheel of the car and Cortez knocked on the window. You could bet he had air conditioning.

The window slid down just a crack. It was a boy about nineteen, and he looked a little scared. His car was shiny and new.

"Yes sir?" he said.

"What you blowing that damn horn at me for?" Cortez said.

"I don't know," the kid said.

"Don't know?" Cortez said. He was about to get riled.

Some more horns blew and Cortez looked up briefly. Some people in cars were staring at him. He looked back down at the boy.

"I'll pull out when all this traffic lets me out, all right?"

"Yes sir," the boy said.

"But don't blow that damn horn at me no more. I'll pull you out of there and jerk a nanny goat in your ass. You understand me?"

"Yes sir!" the boy said, and rolled his window back up fast.

Cortez walked back to this truck and got in and released the hand brake and pushed in the clutch and pulled it down in first. There was a big break in the traffic and he pulled right on out.

Some people were mowing the grass around the courthouse and a lot of people were out walking around. Things had changed a lot around the square but they were still kind of the same. Most of the stores were different. He remembered the hardware stores and dime stores that used to be on the square. A long time ago he used to bring his cotton to town to get it ginned just off the square, down on Fourteenth. That was one of Lucinda's favorite things to do when she was a kid, come to town with him in the fall to get the cotton ginned. He could remember a time when they were close and he could talk to her and all that had changed one day. He didn't know what all her mother had told her about him. He felt like she'd told her *some* things about him. He just didn't know what. Mostly he wondered if she knew about Queen. But he couldn't ask her that.

[. . .]

He drove out the other side of the square and followed the traffic down to the red light on University Avenue and sat in a line of cars and trucks waiting for the green arrow. He didn't get to town very much these days and every time he did, something new had been added. A new business, a new place to eat, some kind of shop. More traffic. More people. He guessed it was like that everywhere. He was sure glad he lived out in the country and didn't have to put up with all this every day.

The line was so long that he had to wait for a second light and by then he was ready to get on home, just as soon as he got a few groceries. He finally got to turn and he went down the hill, past Sneed's, and he glanced out that way to see if they had any steel garbage cans sitting out there. They did, and he put on his blinker to turn right and pulled into the parking lot. He parked and got out and put the keys in his pocket.

They had some picnic tables and some grills set up outside under a big metal awning and he walked over to the garbage cans and looked at them. They had the prices posted on some cardboard signs. A thirty-gallon steel garbage can with a tight-fitting lid was $16.95 and one about half that size was $12.95. He stood there looking at them. He didn't think the little can would hold both bags of catfish feed, so he grabbed one of the big ones and carried it over close to the front door and set it down and left it there and went inside.

He'd always liked coming to the hardware store. Back in the old days you could buy steel traps and you could still buy pocketknives and screen wire and hinges and paintbrushes and screws and plumbing supplies. The store had been up on the square for years, right there at the corner of Jackson Avenue, with a plank floor and wooden barrels of sixteen penny nails. This new place was brightly lit and the people who worked there wore red vests that said ACE and now they had hummingbird feeders and electric bug killers and air-conditioner filters and shiny new log chains.

[. . .]

"Is there something I can help you with?" a kid working there said.

"Naw. I just need to pay y'all for a garbage can is all."

The kid pointed toward the register where a few people were waiting with copper tubing and paint rollers and sandpaper and PVC glue.

"She'll take you right there," the kid said, and Cortez nodded and got in line. He didn't notice her at first because he was looking at the screwdrivers and cans of WD-40 and small plastic bins of fingernail clippers they had displayed near the checkout so that people would hopefully grab something else on their way out. Then he looked toward the register and saw her. Damn. One of the best-looking black women he'd ever seen in his whole life was laughing and talking to the customer she was ringing up. He was close enough to read the letters on the name tag she had pinned to her red vest: Zula.

She looked like she was about twenty-five. Tall. Shiny black hair and a big smile and a mouthful of clean white teeth. She was a big girl and Queen had been a big girl. Big breasts, big legs, a big behind. He realized he was staring at her and stopped. But it was hard not to look at her. He hadn't been with a woman since he'd buried Queen behind the pea patch, all those years ago. He hadn't been with his wife ever again. He hadn't wanted to. Had no desire to. Not after Queen. How did you go back to what you'd had before you had the best thing you ever had? And how long had that been? He knew exactly. It was thirty-seven years come September 17. All that time. How had it passed so quickly? Thirty-seven winters and thirty-seven springs and thirty-seven hay cuttings and thirty-seven gardens and all the work all that took. Lucinda had been six then. She had been in the first grade. [. . .]

The first customer in the line paid for his stuff and picked up his bag and walked out and the line moved forward. Cortez very much enjoyed listening to the girl's voice while she talked to the next customer. It was a voice that was rich and husky, one that laughed easily. It was the kind of voice you wouldn't get tired of listening to your whole life.

He stood there and looked at some garden hose and squirrel feeders while he was waiting. Somebody was making some keys on the key-making machine and he could hear the machine grinding. He was going to take the garbage can and the feed straight over to the pond when he got in and set the can next to a tree and then open both bags and pour them in and it would be ready when the fish got there.

She finished with that customer and the guy in front of Cortez moved on up and set down his rollers and his PVC glue and a few sheaves of sandpaper. Cortez noticed that he had both rough and fine, figured he was sanding down some furniture. He glanced at the girl again. She had big brown eyes that were so dark they shone. Her skin was beautiful to him. Under the bright lights of the hardware store, surrounded by things he didn't need, he remembered undressing her so many times, and the way her breath would catch in her throat when he caught her nipple between his thumb and finger. And being inside her. With his mouth on her throat and her pushing back against him, moving her hips, her breath getting faster.

He snapped himself out of it. He was a crazy man. Only a crazy man would do what he had done. He needed to be in the penitentiary was where he needed to be. Rotting away in Sunflower County one day at a time.

The guy in front of him finishing paying and then it was just him. He moved on up and the pretty black girl smiled happily at him.

"How you doing today?" she said.

"Pretty good," Cortez said, reaching for his billfold. "I need to pay you for one of them steel garbage cans out front," he said.

"Okay," she said, and reached beneath the counter for a bound notebook with a plastic cover which she opened.

"I think it's sixteen ninety-five," Cortez said.

She looked up.

"Is it a big one?" she said.

"Yeah, big one," Cortez said, pulling a weathered twenty out and putting it on the counter. She closed the notebook and put it away and rang it up. She told him how much it was with tax and he shoved the twenty across.

"I had to get me one of them steel garbage cans," she said, and picked up the twenty. She turned to the register and started punching buttons.

"You did?" Cortez said.

"I sure did. I had to get me something where them coons wouldn't get in my garbage ever night. They got to where they'd wake me and my husband up when we's trying to sleep. Come right up on the back porch."

Cortez looked down and saw the tiny diamond on her finger then.

"My daddy had a pet crow that would steal anything he could carry off," Cortez said.

"Is that right?" she said, and rolled open the cash drawer on the register. She put the twenty in and started getting his change.

"I'm gonna put my fish feed in this garbage can," Cortez said. "I thought maybe that would keep the fire ants out of it."

She shook her head and handed him his change and his ticket.

"I don't know," she said. "Them fire ants get in just about everthing. I just hate them things. Reckon where they come from anyway?"

"They come from South America," Cortez said.

She looked up at him and her big brown eyes got bigger.

"They *did*? How'd they get way up here?"

"They brought em in on a ship loaded with dirt for ballast. I think it was the Port of Mobile. Back in the thirties."

"Well I swear," she said. "Somebody messed up, didn't they?"

"They sure did," Cortez said, folding his little paper and folding his dollar bill and sliding them and his change back into his overall pocket. "They'll eat the eyes out of a calf if his mama has him close to one of them mounds."

She let out a little shiver of revulsion.

"*Eyes*," she said.

"Yep," Cortez said. He wished he could stay here and talk to her, but he knew he couldn't. There was somebody already behind him.

"I know they hurt when they bite," she said.

"Some people's allergic to em," Cortez said.

"That's right," she said. "My auntie's allergic to em. You have a nice day okay, now?"

"I sure will," Cortez said. "You watch out for them coons."

She smiled at him and turned to the next customer. He went on out through the glass door and picked up his garbage can and carried it over to his truck and set it in. Then he took the lid off and dropped it in the floorboard and laid the can on its side so it wouldn't maybe blow out on the way home.

He went on down the street and caught the light at the bottom of the hill on green and drove past the new Walgreen's they were building. The bricklayers were up on scaffolds with their water coolers beside them and there was heavy equipment moving around on what he guessed would be the parking lot. One thing about his wife dying was he didn't have to go to the drugstore any more. Not unless he needed a thermometer or something. And he thought he had one of those somewhere.

He went past McDonald's and turned right at the light and went up the hill past the bank and through the parking lot and parked down near the end, away from most of the other cars. The parking lot was pretty full and there were lots of people walking in and out of Big Star and Fred's.

As soon as he got inside he saw that they had changed everything around and he didn't know where anything was. But surely they hadn't moved the meat market. He walked down an aisle and came out the other end looking at some chicken. He looked right, left, then went right.

He saw a whole rack of baloney and sliced ham and salami and stuff like that and knew he was close to the bacon. Was he out of milk? Shit. Where was it? Over there on the far wall. He guessed he'd better get some milk. Now that his wife was dead he'd let the cleaning woman go and she used to bring the groceries evidently too because these days there was almost nothing in the refrigerator and he guessed he hadn't paid too much attention to where the groceries had come from. Now that he was in here he realized that maybe he needed a shopping cart to get a few things to eat. So he went back up front for one.

He didn't need any tomatoes. The ones they had didn't look nearly as good as his anyway, and he picked up a few of them just to make sure, then set them back and picked up a bunch of bananas. He'd get some cereal and some milk and he could slice the bananas over the cereal. He got some eggs. Did he have butter? Better get some. Cheese? Did he want some cheese? He got a chunk of cheddar. He got some milk and orange juice.

Some other people were drifting up and down the aisles. Old women with their old women friends and young women with their children. He wondered if those kids down the road who lived in that trailer had started back to school yet. He hadn't seen the school bus come down the road. He wondered what grade that little boy was in. Third or fourth?

He walked by some young black man in a long white apron who was stocking shelves from a cart. He looked up and smiled as Cortez went by.

"Hi," he said. "How you doing today, sir?"

Cortez just looked at him and went on by.

They had what looked like some homemade chocolate-chip cookies down at the end of the aisle and he got a pack of them. He slowed down at the meat market again, gazing over the chicken. He got a pack of wings for frying. Even he could fry chicken. They had some tasty-looking, thick-sliced ham, and he got a pack of that. Could fix that with eggs for breakfast. Or cook with french fries for supper. He got a six-pack of Cokes. He got a big pack of the cheap bacon. A pack of hot dogs. A package of sliced baloney. He went up the cereal aisle and got some cornflakes.

Over on the far side they had some cakes in a cooler and he reached in for a small German chocolate and put it in his cart. He got some bread and dinner rolls, and then he went back the other way and found the ice cream and got a half gallon of black walnut. Then he stood there for another minute looking and reached in for a pack of grape Popsicles. Did he even have any mustard and mayonnaise? The cupboard had looked pretty bare last time he'd looked. He guessed he have to make a list the next time he came for groceries. He turned his cart and went back the other way and looked for a couple of minutes until he found the mustard and mayonnaise and got a jar of each. He saw olives. He liked them. He got a jar. Then he saw a big jar of dill pickles and got them, too.

"That's enough," he said out loud, and some woman he hadn't seen who was looking at the rice raised her head and looked at him funny.

"Harm quarm farm," Cortez told her, and pushed his cart on up toward the checkout.

When he got home he parked the truck close to the back door so he wouldn't have to carry his groceries very far. He had three bags and the little bit of stuff he got cost about forty dollars. But he had plenty to eat. He'd already picked some peas and put them in the deep freeze. It was too bad he didn't like deer meat or he could have eaten it year round.

He put everything away and then got the milk back out and set it on the kitchen table and got a glass and poured some in it. He sat down at the table with the pack of cookies and opened them and ate a few of them, washing them down with the milk, and it was cool and quiet in there. Slowly he had been getting rid of the things that had belonged to her, some old clothes, the police bullhorn, pincushions and heating pads and her teeth that had stayed in a glass of water in the bathroom every night for over twenty years. He sat there and bit into a cookie and was glad he still had some of his. But hers had never been good. He'd spent thousands of dollars on her mouth. And then she'd wound up having them all pulled anyway. Might as well have thrown that money down a hole in the ground for all the good it did.

He put the cookies away and finished the milk and set the glass in the sink, put the rest of the jug back in the refrigerator. Then he went back out and got in his truck and drove out his driveway and up the dirt road to the front corner of his property and down the new road to the new pond, and pulled his truck over next to the big white oak. The new road looked great, and now he only had to wait two more days. He could hardly believe that fish guy was going to drive a truck full of catfish right up beside this pond and dump three thousand of them in here. It was going to be something to see.

Cortez was happy with the way the pond looked, even though it was only half full. The muddiness had settled out of it and it was calm and had a dark tone to it. A lot of grass had already grown up across the dirt that had been shaved off by the dozer blade, most of it on the sloping sides of the banks where it was kind of steep. He might need to bring his Bush Hog up here and mow it sometime. He just needed to be careful on that slope. He could bring the Bush Hog up here before long and cut it, make it look nice and neat. What he'd do, next year, when the fish got bigger, was bring a lawn chair up here and maybe some cold drinks and sit under this white oak and fish in the afternoons. Sit in the shade and reel them in. Fry up a mess for supper that night. Just like he used to do when he was a boy. There was nothing better than fresh fish you'd caught for supper.

He unloaded the garbage can and set it under the tree and then he took the bags one at a time and pulled the sewn strip of tape from the tops and poured both of them into the garbage can. For a minute there it looked like it might not hold both of them, but he mounded up the last bag over the top of what he'd poured in there and was just barely able to squeeze the lid down over it. There. That'd keep the rain out of it. And it would be right here every day, to feed them. He'd make some kind of signal the fish would understand, to let them know it was feeding time. Bang the lid on the side of the garbage can or something. Maybe a whistle? Shit. Blow the truck horn. He needed to bring a quart fruit jar up here, too, to scoop the feed out.

He sat on the ground under the tree, looking out at the pond. He hadn't seen that little boy up here again. Come to think of it, he hadn't seen the go-kart running up and down the dirt road in a long time now. He wondered if they'd sold it, or if it had torn up. He oughtn't to have yelled at that kid that way. Probably scared him clean off. He probably wouldn't be back. Reckon what his name was?

It was hot and Cortez could feel the sun peeking down between the leaves above him to warm his neck. It was almost lunchtime but he wasn't that hungry. A baloney sandwich might be good, though. He could take a piece and fry it in the skillet and put some mustard on the bread and slice some slices off one of those dill pickles and put them on it. He thought there were still some potato chips that Lucinda had bought in one of the cabinets. Then he could take a nap. Go down there and see if there were any more peas left. He could pick them if there were any left. And if the deer had come back and gotten the rest of them, it wouldn't be any big deal. He had plenty to eat and plenty of money to buy some more. And he was already thinking about how good that ham was going to be for supper.

Two more days. Two days and three thousand fish. He'd bet that kid down the road would like to see that.

37

Cleve was trying to get the son of a bitch out of his house and down to the river was what he was trying to do, but it wasn't working. He knew if he ever got him down to the river he could take care of him, but the two of them were making it hard for him. She probably knew what he had on his mind. And if she did, what the hell did she bring him back here for anyway? And how did a son of a bitch who was supposed to be in the army get so much time off? Why wasn't he over there fighting with the rest of them? They had a war going on, didn't they? They showed it on TV every night, didn't they? He was AWOL was what he was. Had to be.

Cleve was in his rocking chair on the front porch, rocking a little and watching the wind blow through the catalpa trees in his front yard. They'd had a good crop of worms this year. Back in June he'd taken his cane pole and knocked twenty or thirty down and put them in a bucket with a piece of screen wire over the top of it to keep them from crawling out and he'd gone down on Mister Bramlett's place on the river and parked on the side of the levee. It had grown up a lot from what it used to be and he'd had to watch for snakes while he waded the briars and mud holes until he could get over to the bank and then pick his way up the river, around a couple of bends, almost up to the pipeline where there was a deep hole under a big old beech that spread its shade out over the muddy river. He'd taken his seat on a chunk of wood, in the midst of dead brown leaves and little green vines and creepers, easing the half pint of whisky out and his pistol with it. He sat there with his cane pole and caught nine nice catfish in a couple of hours, one of them a four-pounder. And had they been good for supper that night? Shoot. But he didn't like that son of a bitch eating his food.

Now it was too hot to fish, but that fool probably didn't know that. Army wasn't going to miss him. Wasn't nobody going to miss him but Seretha, and he'd done turned her head clean around anyway, taking her to Memphis and buying her clothes and where did he get the money for that? He was stealing or selling dope, one. Had to be.

He had his guitar in his lap and he slid his old bottleneck down the strings and made it wail. He picked in the box some, going up and down with his slide, and the old Fender amp beside him growled gently. Usually this guitar would bring him out. But it sounded like they'd been fighting. He'd heard some yelling back there where they stayed. Best thing would be just get rid of him. Before she turned up pregnant. She needed a decent man. Not somebody who wouldn't even stay in the army.

He put his pick on a little table that stayed beside his chair and rummaged in the cooler beside him and pulled out a dripping Budweiser tall boy and opened it. Usually the sound of a beer opening would bring him out, too. He sat there and sipped it and then set it down. He reached for his Swisher Sweet cigarillos and lit one of them, then sat there smoking it for a bit, picking up his beer once in a while, not worrying about it dripping on the guitar since the Epiphone was old and cracked and wouldn't be hurt any worse than it already was.

He wished he had some weed. He hadn't had any weed in so long. Whisky made you mean, he knew that. But some shit a man just had to take care of himself. Like some Yankee nigger son of a bitch coming down here and turning your daughter's head around and taking her to Memphis and putting ideas in her head, ideas like Chicago was a good place to live, Atlanta's a good place to live. What was wrong with this place? It was good enough for him. Always had been. Never would have left them two times if it hadn't been for smart sons of bitches who didn't understand nothing but a bullet in the mouth. Dumbass niggers. Just what he had in the house right now. She wouldn't know what happened to him. He'd just be gone. The only thing was, he'd have to listen to her crying.

He heard them go out the back door and he could hear them talking. Then she laughed. Then he laughed. And the son of a bitch ate everything in the house. Didn't bring nothing in. Nothing. Not even a can of sardines. And his ragged-ass car wouldn't run half the time. It had a blown head gasket is what it was. Get hot halfway to town every time. He'd ridden in it one time and he wasn't going to ride in it anymore. Long as his pickup was sitting there he wouldn't. Car had that nigger perfume all in it. Whew.

He set his Swisher in the ashtray and picked up his pick and his slide.

He heard them stop talking. They were listening. Maybe they'd come on around here. He could dig some red worms. He could scratch up some night crawlers right under those oak trees out by the crib. What was he going to tell her? Tell her anything. Tell her somebody came by and her boyfriend caught a ride to town. *Where's he at? Damn if I know.*

The sun was still pretty high in the sky, but it was starting to slant in on him, so he moved his chair back a little, sipped his beer some more, and played. After a few minutes they came around the side of the house and stood there looking at him. He stopped playing and pointed to the cooler.

"I got some beer if y'all want a cold one," he said.

Seretha shook her head, but her boyfriend walked around to the front of the porch and grinned with his two gold teeth. He had on some fancy shirt. Starched jeans and pointy shoes. Kind of shit a pimp wore.

"I think I'll take you up on that," he said. His name was Montrel and Cleve didn't even like his name. He didn't like anything about him. And he never had. Talked so fancy. Been to thirty-three states. So fucking what?

Montrel reached into the cooler for one of the beers and put the top back on the cooler. He opened the beer and stood there sipping it.

"You want to go fishing?" Cleve said.

Montrel took a sip of his beer and looked around in the direction of the sun. He appeared to be judging it.

"Awful hot," he said, then lowered his face to the beer, slinging drops of water off his fingers like a woman might.

"I know where they's a good hole at," Cleve said. "Full of catfish. I mean *full* of catfish."

"Maybe later," Montrel said. "We were thinking about going to town after while."

"What in?" Cleve said. "That raggedy-ass Buick ain't gone make it to town without getting hot."

Montrel looked at Seretha and she spoke up then.

"Can we use your pickup?" she said. "We won't be gone long."

They were up to something. He could tell. The way they talked. The way they looked. The two of them. Plotting together.

"Where you going?" he said.

"Just up to Wal-Mart."

"What you need at Wal-Mart?" he said.

She chewed on her bottom lip. Ever since she'd been a kid she always chewed on her bottom lip before she told a lie.

"I need some women's stuff," she said.

"Oh."

He looked back down at his guitar. Then he looked up. Okay. He'd wait. He'd wait like a spider waits. In prison you learned patience.

"I guess so," he said. "Don't burn up all my gas."

"We won't," Montrel said, and turned up his beer. When he took it down he said, "You mind if I get one more for the road?"

"Help yourself," Cleve told him, and went back to playing.

It was past dark when they came in. He'd already fixed his supper and eaten and he was lying on the couch, watching the black-and-white television. The picture was fuzzy and he wished he had one of those satellite dishes, but he didn't want one bad enough to have to pay for it. He was about ready to go to bed anyway. He needed to get up in the morning and go down to Banner and see that guy about that puppy. He wasn't going to pay over a hundred dollars for it.

They went around to the back and went through the kitchen and on into her room. So they wouldn't have to see him. But where were his keys? He didn't want to have to get up and go back there and ask for them, but he would if he had to. Women's stuff? Huh.

He lay there. If her mama hadn't left, maybe things would have been different. You couldn't go off for that long and not have things be different. He sure didn't want to go back to the pen over this simple son of a bitch. Honky-ass white motherfuckers and their horses. Call you *old thang*. Let that horse slobber on your back while you were bent over picking their cotton. Chopping out their corn. Loading their watermelons.

He heard some music come on. What kind of women's stuff did they sell at Wal-Mart? And what had taken them so long?

He lifted his whisky bottle and pulled the last dregs from it. Then he capped it and put it on the floor. If it hadn't been so late, he might have gone to town and gotten another bottle. But he thought he had another one stashed somewhere. Just remembering where it was was the thing.

He thought he might have put one out in the pickup in back. Maybe in the floorboard. He didn't want to lie here and listen to their bedsprings start creaking, like he did so many nights. So he got up in his undershirt and pants and walked to the back door and out into the yard. He stopped and stood there with his bare toes feeling the damp grass.

Lightning bugs were poking little green holes in the dark out beyond the trees that fringed the yard. It was very clear, and the stars were bright in the black sky. A dog yapped somewhere far off and he unbuttoned his trousers and took a leak in the yard, trying not to listen to them in there. They had their music going and that was good for killing their noise.

He walked over to the old pickup once he'd finished and the door squealed when he opened it. He felt around in the glove box but didn't come up with a half pint of whisky. Maybe he'd already finished it all off. Where else would he have put one? A long time ago when he'd gotten out of the pen for the second time he'd bought a whole case of half pints of Canadian Mist and had stashed them all over the yard, in the hay beneath the chickens' nests, under the back doorstep, in this old truck. It was hell to go that long without a drink of whisky, and he hadn't wanted for that to happen again. So he'd stashed some. The same way everybody said Mister Cortez stashed his money in the barn. Talk about a mean-ass white man. That was one son of a bitch you better not cross.

He shut the door on the truck and looked toward the bedroom window. He could see Seretha, and he could see that she was talking. He took a seat on an old chair he sat in sometimes in the afternoons and watched her. She was talking to Montrel, but he couldn't see him. Then she moved to somewhere else in the room and he couldn't see her.

She was the last one. The baby. Nineteen. Tyrone wouldn't never come back here. Neither would Woodrow. He'd lost touch with both of them. Or maybe that was the way they'd wanted it. He missed them, though. A man missed his sons. He remembered when they were little boys, when he took them fishing. They were good boys. It was probably good that they weren't here now, to see what he was dealing with.

He kept sitting there in the yard, just listening to the things around him. There were whippoorwills calling out near the road and there were crickets chirping everywhere. Far off somewhere he could hear a vehicle on his road, the road that ran through all the way to Old Dallas.

And then he heard crying. Seretha. What was it now? It was that damn fool. He had to go. Maybe even tomorrow. He'd see. He'd wait. But not too long. He was tired of his shit.

38

Tommy had all the lights turned on in the barn and he had on his apron and rubber boots because he always got wet transferring them out of where they'd been raised. He was putting them in big buckets, about fifty at a time, pulling them out of the bright blue concrete tanks with a long-handled net, and he was trying not to think about them being the last batch. But it wasn't the end of the world. His life would go on in some form or other. He just wouldn't be living here anymore. And raising fish. And if he wasn't raising fish, what would he be doing? Assuming he lost the fifteen hundred. Driving a truck? Framing houses? He had to allow for the possibility of losing. He had to at least be able to eat.

He'd dropped a few of the little catfish on the floor and they were flopping around on the wet concrete, and it would have been nice if he'd had some help. But he'd started on his first delivery by himself. He guessed he could finish his last one the same way.

It was slow like this, by himself, taking them a bucket at a time to the truck and setting the bucket on the tailgate and then climbing up and pouring them into the metal tanks where the aerators were running. He had eight tanks on the truck and he was going to use six for the little fish, one for Ursula, and leave one empty for a spare, just in case something happened in her tank on the way. But he didn't think anything would. As far as he knew, everything was working the way it was supposed to. At five hundred per tank the little fish wouldn't be any more crowded than they'd been in here all their short lives.

[...] He was going to call Mister Sharp on his cell phone before he left, to let him know he was on his way. It would take him a while to get out to the old man's pond and unload, and then he guessed he'd spend the night over there somewhere, get a good night's rest, and bring the truck on back here the next day and leave it. He'd hated to let his new pickup go back, but his old one would run if he put a new battery in it. The last fish truck belonged to the bank now. And they might not like it if they knew he was about to drive it to Mississippi, but that was just tough shit. He still hadn't figured out how he was going to slip Ursula into the old man's pond, but he figured he'd come up with something by the time he got over there. Maybe he'd just tell him.

He kept working, going in and out, dipping the buckets full of water, dipping the net full of baby catfish, taking them out, dumping them in the tanks. And how many times had he done this? A thousand? And was Audrey not ever going to call? He would have thought she'd have called by now. And said something. Anything. But she hadn't. The phone was disconnected now and unless she called him on his cell, she wouldn't be able to get him. He didn't know where he was going to go yet. Somebody from the realty office had come out and walked around and looked at everything and appraised all of it, but the man wouldn't tell him how much it was worth. Said he couldn't. Bullshit.

Well, he didn't have anybody to blame but himself. And all the begging she'd done had just been wasted on his ears. She never should have gotten hooked up with him. She deserved somebody better. Somebody who wouldn't take the chances he had with their money and lose everything. Somebody who wouldn't promise and promise and promise.

By nine he had all the fish on the truck except for one. He checked them in their tanks, made sure the aerators were working, closed the lids and latched them. He'd stop about an hour down the road and check them, make sure they were all right. His generator had plenty of fuel in it. The truck was washed and full of gas. The low tire on the left front was fixed.

He opened the side doors on the brood house and backed the truck in very carefully and left it running. He had already pushed a sturdy table next to Ursula's tank and now he got his chain hoist out and grabbed his clawhammer and climbed up on the table and hooked the cable on the hoist over a joist, slanting the braided steel line and then fastening it to the joist on top with some fence staples so that when she came out of the tank and cleared the edge of it she'd swing back over the table, and then he got his sling out and hooked the ropes on one side to the hook on the hoist. A hanging rectangle of canvas. He'd done a lot of work on it, for several nights, working from his drawings. He knew it would work if he could just get it under her and then pull up the other side and fasten it.

There was a drawstring at each end, to close it around her. He climbed down and reached to the bottom outside edge of the tank for the drain plug. It was rusted, and he had to get a pipe wrench off the truck to loosen it. But when he took it out, water started flowing and it drained all over the floor and the flopping little catfish he wasn't going to pick up. He didn't care. It wasn't going to be his mess to clean up anymore. He walked over to the wall and flipped the light switch that killed her aerator. Then it was quiet. Just the water pouring out and lowering in the tank. Oh, the sleepless nights.

He leaned there with his forearms on the top edge of the tank and looked in at her. As big as the tank was, it would take it a while to drain. He went ahead and climbed back up on the truck and opened one of the back tanks, propped the lid open with a stick. Then he climbed back down and waited for the water to drain on down. He'd have to get in there with her. And she was *going* to raise some hell. He just hoped he could put her in the pond by himself. She'd eat a few of these little ones at first.

When the water level was down to a foot and a half, and her dorsal fin was sticking out, he put the drain plug back in and picked up two short lengths of rubber hose and got into the tank with her. She was splashing a lot of water and it was hard to get her to stay still, but he finally got down on his knees and held her that way while he slipped the rubber hoses over her side fins. He had it in his head to use them for handles to release her.

He stood up and lowered his sling with the chain hoist way down into the bottom of the tank and bent over her again. He started trying to slip it under her, but she splashed mightily and got him soaking wet. He just ignored that and kept working until he slid the canvas beneath her. She splashed water everywhere. He pulled up the other side and laced the ropes together and pulled the drawstrings snug against her on each end. Her side fins folded back and she was in.

He had to stand there and pull on the chain on the hoist with both hands to make her rise vertically against the side of the tank. She did a lot of flopping and slapping at the wall of the tank with her tail, but she was somewhat restricted in her movements by the sling, and all he had to do was keep pulling on the chain. He hoped nobody from the bank drove down here and asked him what the hell he was doing. Somebody would have to get told that it wasn't any of their business.

He kept working at it and noticed that it was fifteen till ten. She was almost up to the top of the tank and he eyed the table, judging how wide she'd swing when she cleared the edge. He put one hand against the side of the tank and gave the chain a few more pulls, and she lifted dripping from the tank and swung over the table, swaying gently a few times, wriggling, her big wide tail sticking out, and making a grinding noise with her mouth. He raised her a few more inches and then pulled the table out of the way. It had only been there to catch her just in case he dropped her. But she looked like she was safe. He went back and got on the chain with both hands, raising her ever higher, until she was about a foot or two below the joist. He stopped. He tore a couple of paper towels off a roll that was mounted on the wall and wiped his hands. Then he walked around to the door of the truck and climbed up behind the wheel.

He put it in reverse and looked through the back glass. She was not quite centered over the tank but he could sway her a little either way. He backed up slowly, hands and feet careful on the wheel and the clutch and the brake. The thought crossed his mind that if Audrey could see this shit she'd think he'd lost his mind.

He backed up cautiously, letting the raised lid on the truck tank be his guide. It was brushing her a little, but not enough to hurt anything. He stopped when he thought she was right over the truck tank, and then he put it into neutral and pulled out the hand brake. He got out and climbed up on the back of the truck. Could he lift her out of the tank by himself?

She was a little off center, but that was all right. The chain on the hoist was hanging down the side of the truck, and he reached out for it and got it on the inside of the tank wall. He flipped the trigger to reverse it and started lowering her. The cold water was bubbling in the tank. He wasn't going to feed her while she was in there. He'd take some feed with him. He'd already told the old man to get some feed, so maybe he had. And hell. Once the old man started throwing feed out, she was going to come up to eat, and he was going to see her. He could always tell the old man to feed them at night. That might work. It didn't matter. He'd be gone by then.

It only took a few minutes to get her into the water, and as soon as he did he released the drawstrings front and back. He kept lowering her and when her whole back was under the surface of the water he reached up and unfastened the ropes on the side facing him, and she rolled out, splashed mightily, throwing water up to the joists, and then she was in. Lying there pulling cold water into her gills. Opening and closing her mouth.

He stood there for just a moment, watching her, and then he closed the lid on her tank, latched it, and climbed down off the truck. He got back behind the wheel and pulled the truck out from under the chain hoist and left it hanging. He drove the truck back outside and stopped it again and then went back and shut off all the lights and closed the two side doors. He'd drain her tank, lift her out, set her on the back of the truck.

He didn't waste any time looking at everything that had been his. He just pulled out his cell phone and consulted a little tablet he carried around in his pocket all the time and called Cortez Sharp in Mississippi. When he answered, Tommy told him that he was on his way with his fish. And the eager happiness in the old man's voice was a real good thing to hear. It almost made it all worth it.

But not quite.

39

Another thing that wasn't fair among all the things that weren't fair as far as school went was all the homework they gave you to do as soon as school started. It was like maybe the teachers had worked on all this stuff all summer long while they were off so that they'd be ready to load you down with enough arithmetic and Mississippi history and science and English and social studies homework to make sure you didn't have time to go out and ride your go-kart any before dark if you had a go-kart. Jimmy couldn't believe how much homework he had the very first night and how long it took to do it, sitting on the living-room couch with his books and his tablets, trying to get it done while the girls talked on the portable phone and watched TV and his mama fixed herself sandwiches and leaned over into the refrigerator for a container of french onion dip and took it and a big bag of potato chips back to her room and lay down on the bed and flipped through the channels looking for something to watch. She was also tugging on those funny-looking cigarettes she smoked sometimes that smelled odd. Tangy. Sweet. He'd noticed that she never did this when his daddy was around, but she apparently didn't mind doing it while Jimmy and the girls were around. He'd asked Evelyn one time what was that stuff Mama was smoking and Evelyn said it was weed. Jimmy asked her what weed was and she said it was boo. He asked her what boo was and she said it was shit. He asked her what shit was and she said it was tea. He asked her what tea was and she said, *Don't ask so many questions, you little rotten-tooth son of a bitch, she's getting stoned.* When Jimmy told her she was calling her own mother a bitch, that shut her up for a while.

Jimmy in his homework had been reading about all the Indians who used to live in Mississippi, mainly Choctaws and Chickasaws. He wished they still did. He liked anything about Indians. Arrowheads, for instance. He had a couple of real good dark red ones he hadn't shown his daddy that he'd found in the fields below the old rotted house where he'd seen the dead black lady, before he'd seen the dead black lady. Some kid at school, a boy named Herschel Horowitz with big glasses, had told Jimmy during a conversation they were having about arrowheads that his daddy, Herman Horowitz, was pretty crazy about going out and hunting arrowheads and often took Herschel along with him and that the best time and place to find arrowheads was in a field that had just been broken up in the spring, right after a rain. Herschel said what happened was a natural thing, that the rain washed the dirt away from the arrowheads and made it easier to find them. And it turned out that Herschel had been right. Jimmy had gone down in the field below the rotted house back in the spring to see if the men who worked the land had their tractors in the field yet, and he had to go a couple of times, hanging around and waiting on the side of the road, looking for snakes, wishing he could wade in the creek, seeing how many birds he could see, looking for turtles, but eventually he saw a big green tractor plowing the ground and then he just waited for a good rain, which was only two days later, since it was April, and he'd walked out in the muddy field with his tennis shoes getting soggy and had looked for a long time and just saw mud and mud and mud and mud and walked some more and looked some more and just saw mud and mud and walked some more and looked some more, saw more mud, looked and walked and saw more mud and then a point sticking up that was chiseled, Stone Age, handmade, sharp enough to cut meat. He reached and plucked it like a flower and it was not an arrowhead, it was a spear point, a nearly perfect one, and Jimmy had gotten really really *really* excited and had taken it back home to show his daddy, and his daddy had borrowed it to show it to somebody at work and never had given it back, and now Jimmy didn't know where it was. He'd asked his daddy about it a couple of times and the second time he asked him his daddy got madder than he had the first time so Jimmy didn't ask him anymore. He had gone so far as to complain to his mother, but she just said she couldn't do anything with him and that if Jimmy would be good and not cause any more trouble than there already was in the trailer, then maybe the next time Kenny Chesney scheduled a concert for Tupelo *maybe* they could go. Now she was saying they definitely didn't have the money. She was backing out. Crawfishing. They'd already argued about it some, a couple of times. He said he never got to go anywhere and had to stay home all the time with the girls and she said that she'd only said *maybe* and Jimmy said that school was fixing to start back up and talked a little about how nice it would be if they could all go to a Kenny Chesney concert together and she said they never would be able to get his daddy to go over there because he didn't like to go anywhere except to work and hunting and fishing and riding around drinking beer with his buddies and Jimmy said he didn't think his daddy liked to go to work. He mouthed off a little bit more and even whined some but pretty much gave up when he realized it was a question of money, which was something he could do nothing about. But tonight while he was doing his homework he still had a few questions going through his head. One of them was, How much did big fat sandwiches cost? Another one was, What about those great big bags of chips? And, How come the girls got CDs and he didn't? And, Where was his daddy again tonight? Wasn't he hungry? Didn't he want some supper? How come he stayed gone so much? Jimmy had already eaten some hot dogs. And he had a tooth that was hurting. It wasn't hurting bad. It was just kind of hurting. This had been a problem for a while, his rotten front teeth, and having to look at them in the mirror and be ashamed of them. And he was. Had been for a long time. Jimmy sure hoped he wouldn't have to go to the dentist. He was kind of scared of the dentist after listening to his daddy tell some horror stories about what some dentist had done to him when he was a kid. Jimmy had already decided that he didn't want to meet any dentists.

Jimmy did some arithmetic homework and some science homework and watched part of *Back to the Future* and part of *Conan the Barbarian* and the tail end of *Jaws* while the girls changed channels and talked some more on the phone. His mama came in and fixed herself a chocolate milkshake and got a handful of Oreos and turned to go back to her room. Jimmy raised his head.

"Where's Daddy?" he said.

"I don't know," his mama said.

"He's off drinking beer," Evelyn said.

"Or riding around," Velma said. "In his ragged-out fifty-five he thinks is so cool."

"Y'all's guess is as good as mine," Jimmy's mama said, and went on back to her room. She shut the door.

"I'm gonna go take a bath," Velma said, and got up. She was in the fifth this year. She had hardly any homework at all, looked like. If she had some, she wasn't doing it. She wasn't doing anything except looking at a *Seventeen* magazine and talking on the phone whenever Evelyn wasn't talking on it.

"Don't use all the hot water up," Evelyn said.

"Oh shut up," Velma said.

"Don't you tell me to shut up," Evelyn said, and got up.

"I'll tell you to shut up any time I want to," Velma said.

"No you won't," Evelyn said.

"Yes I will," Velma said.

"You might get the shit slapped out of you, too," Evelyn said.

"You might shit and fall back in it, too," Velma said.

Jimmy laughed. Evelyn looked at him.

"What you laughing at, you little fucker?" Evelyn said. "I'll slap the shit out of you, too."

"I'd like to see you try it," Jimmy said.

Jimmy's mama came storming out of her room and she was mad.

"All right!" she said. "I heard all that. Evelyn, I'm gonna wash your mouth out with soap if you don't stop talking to your brother and your sister that way! You think I'm kidding, Missy? Try me!"

"He ain't my brother, he's my half brother," Evelyn said in a pouty way. "And she ain't my sister, she's my half sister."

"I don't care," Jimmy's mama said. "Just stop all that. I don't want to listen to it tonight," she said, and went back to her room.

Evelyn waited until she heard her mother's door shut and then she walked over to Jimmy and leaned down in his face. She had on a V-neck shirt and when she leaned over Jimmy could see part of her breasts, which were growing and already pretty big for somebody who was only in the seventh grade. He'd noticed over the summer that they'd been growing some the same way he'd noticed that his feet were getting too big for his shoes. He figured Evelyn was probably going to be a whore. He didn't know exactly what a whore was but he figured she was a good candidate for being one.

Evelyn said: "You little smart son of a bitch, just wait till they're both gone sometime. I'll call my boyfriend over here and he'll beat the dog shit out of you."

"No he won't," Jimmy said. "I'll tell Daddy if he does."

Evelyn gave him a hateful smirk. "That redneck? What's he gonna do?"

"Don't you call my daddy a redneck," Jimmy said, and he stood up and put his schoolbook down on the couch.

"Redneck redneck redneck," Evelyn said.

"Shut up, Evelyn!" Jimmy said.

"You're Redneck Junior," Evelyn said.

"Mama!" Jimmy yelled. "Evelyn's calling Daddy a redneck!"

"I'm gonna take a bath," Velma said.

"Don't use up all the hot water, you little whore," Evelyn said, and then sat back down and called up somebody on the phone.

Jimmy sat back down, too, and tried to finish the rest of his homework. He thought school would be pretty cool if all you had to do was read about Indians. He was planning on taking his arrowheads to school one day for Show and Tell whenever they had it. Last year for Show and Tell he'd taken a shed deer horn that his daddy had found in the woods, one that had been gnawed on by animals for the minerals in it, with gouge marks like a beaver had been ahold of it, but his teacher said it was probably squirrels and mice. A lot of the kids in the class had laughed at Jimmy for bringing in an old gnawed-up deer horn that had turned partly green from lying out in the woods for so long, but it was about the best thing that Jimmy had been able to come up with. He'd bet they wouldn't laugh at his arrowheads because none of them probably had anything nearly that cool.

He did his arithmetic and listened to Evelyn talking to her boyfriend on the phone. She was giggling a lot and talking about the movies she'd seen and she kept lowering her voice and talking in whispers, then laughing out loud. That kind of got on Jimmy's nerves because he couldn't sit there and concentrate on his homework while he was wondering what they were talking about. He heard the tub draining. Evelyn got up with the phone to her ear and went into the kitchen and opened the refrigerator and Jimmy turned his head to see what she was getting and it was another raw hot dog. She brought it over to the couch and ate it a bite at a time while she was talking on the phone. The bathroom door opened and Velma came out in her white bathrobe and went down the hall to her room and then came back with a brush and sat down on the couch beside Jimmy and started brushing her hair. She looked at the TV. One of those shows was on where people redo a house. She looked over at Jimmy.

"You watching this?" she said.

"Naw," Jimmy said, without raising his head. "I'm working on my homework. How much you got?"

"I ain't got none," Velma said, brushing her hair. It was long and pretty and black. Jimmy liked her better than he liked Evelyn, which wasn't saying much. He kind of felt sorry for Velma because of the way Evelyn treated her, and he'd seen her cry a lot of times from it. It seemed to Jimmy that Velma tried to be nice to Evelyn, because he'd seen her do stuff like bring Evelyn a cold Coke from the refrigerator or loan her some barrettes. But it looked like Evelyn just wanted to be a bully to Velma and make her cry. He wondered sometimes if it had something to do with them having two different daddies. He didn't even know who Velma's daddy was, and he'd only heard about Evelyn's, the Corvette thief. Jimmy wondered sometimes about the history of his family. He knew he had a dead grandmother, but he never had seen a picture of her. That was his daddy's mama. He knew he had a dead grandfather, who was his mama's daddy, and he'd seen pictures of him, but he'd only met his daddy's daddy a few times, and Mama Carol, his mama's mama, lived down close to Bruce, and he used to go down there sometimes and eat hot dogs on Saturday nights while his mama and daddy went to Seafood Junction at Algoma. But it had been a long time now since they'd gone over there.

"You got the remote there, partner?" Velma said.

Jimmy picked it up and handed it to her, then got back on his science homework. This one was explaining about the needle on a compass and why it always pointed north. Then he got to reading about earthquakes and magma and tectonic plates and geysers and hot springs and the Richter scale. Velma flipped it over on Cinemax and a naked man and a naked woman were in a bed.

"Gross," Velma said, and Jimmy looked up at the TV. He'd seen stuff like that before. He'd gotten up one night in the middle of the night for a drink of water from the bathroom and hadn't been trying to sneak up on his daddy or anything, had simply gotten out of bed and walked down the hall and had to go through the back part of the living room to get to the bathroom, and his daddy had been sitting in a chair in the dark, with no lights on, only the light from the TV, drinking beer and watching a movie like that. Jimmy was starting to get an idea about things like that, about what men and women did when they took their clothes off and got into a bed. He'd heard kids at school talk. He thought he was beginning to get the picture. Velma changed the channel. Evelyn giggled sexily on the phone.

Jimmy was lying in bed when he heard his daddy come in. It wasn't even ten o'clock, but his mama always made him go to bed early on school nights. She always said a growing boy needed his rest. A long time ago, when Jimmy was younger, he might have gotten up to see his daddy if he'd been lying in the bed and heard him come in and hadn't seen him all day. Not now. The missing spear point. The ass whipping he'd taken for getting into his daddy's tools. The near drowning. The torc-up go-kart. Never actually getting to go fishing. *You little shit.*

He heard the car pull up in front of the trailer, heard it die, heard his daddy's car door open, heard it slam. Then nothing. The front door didn't open. He didn't hear his daddy's steps. His daddy was still outside, and Jimmy figured he was probably going to the bathroom. He did that a lot, went to the bathroom in the yard, but Jimmy's mama had told Jimmy's daddy that nice people didn't do that sort of thing, at least not around other people. Another thing she absolutely hated was for Jimmy's daddy to go to the bathroom inside the trailer, but then leave the door open, so that if you walked by you could hear him peeing in the toilet. Jimmy had heard his mama ask his daddy to please not do that anymore, that surely he hadn't been raised in a barn, and that it wasn't the right thing to do, especially in front of the girls, and his daddy had said that if they never had seen one, they wouldn't know what the hell it was.

Jimmy kept lying there, waiting to hear the door open, his daddy's steps inside the trailer. He hoped his mama was asleep, because sometimes when his daddy came in late on a weeknight and she was still up, they had fights. And Jimmy hated to have to listen to their fights. It made it hard to go to sleep if you were already in bed and trying to go to sleep. He was pretty sure the girls hated to listen to them, too, because whenever a fight started, you could hear the volume come up on the TV in the girls' room, like they were trying to drown out the noise.

One of the things that Jimmy hated most about the fact that they didn't have the money to go to the Kenny Chesney concert in Tupelo was that it meant he wouldn't get to go to Tupelo Buffalo Park either. He'd been kind of hoping that if they got to go to see Kenny Chesney in concert, maybe they could go over to Tupelo a little early and swing by Tupelo Buffalo Park. He'd heard about it from advertisements on the radio. It sounded like they had buffaloes you could ride, and they also had the tallest giraffe in the world over there. Jimmy had asked his mother if they could go to Tupelo Buffalo Park sometime, and she'd said maybe they could when they were over at Tupelo sometime, but they'd gone shopping for school clothes a while back, and he'd asked her that day, while they were over there, if they could go to Tupelo Buffalo Park, and his mother had said they didn't have time. He could imagine himself riding a buffalo. He imagined the buffalo had some kind of a buffalo saddle.

Jimmy rolled over in his bed. [. . .] He lay there and thought about Evelyn's breasts. He wondered what they looked like. Then he rolled over on his other side. The door didn't open. His daddy's footsteps didn't walk across the trailer floor. He wondered what was taking him so long. Then he heard his mother's door open. The TV went off. He heard her steps down the hall, and then there was silence.

40

Cortez was sitting by the phone when it rang. It was Friday afternoon, about three. He'd been sitting there watching the TV, but there weren't any sex shows on at that time of the day. He'd flipped through the channels looking for something good, and the best thing he'd been able to find was a rerun of *Rawhide*. So he'd watched that, waiting for the phone to ring. Cortez picked it up. He knew it was probably the fish man, and he hoped he was just down the road somewhere. He turned down the TV.

"Hello?" Cortez said.

"Mister Sharp?" a voice said.

"Yeah. This is him," Cortez said.

"Tommy Bright, Mister Sharp," the fish man said. "How you doing today?"

"I'm doing good," Cortez said. "What about you?"

"I'm doing all right," Tommy said. "I'm setting up here on the Mississippi River bridge at Memphis. They got all the traffic stopped both ways."

Memphis. Cortez hadn't been up there in a long time. He knew what the bridge over the river looked like, though. How high it was. How muddy the water was and how wide.

"Aw yeah?" Cortez said.

"Yeah," the fish man said. "They got some idiot who's trying to jump off, I think. Cops everywhere. I thought I'd be there by four but I've been sitting here for a half hour already and I thought I'd better call. I'll be on down there soon as they let me by."

"Well," Cortez said. He thought about the fish on the truck, how many thousands of them there were. "You still got them fish?"

"Oh, yes sir," Tommy said. "I still got the fish. I stopped outside of Blytheville and checked em and they're fine. I ought to be there by five if they let me on through."

"Well," Cortez said. He wished the son of a bitch on the bridge who was thinking about jumping off it would make up his mind and either do it or not so his fish could get on out here and he could feed them.

"I'll give you another call when I get rolling again, Mister Sharp," Tommy Bright said. "Sorry about the delay. I left in plenty of time."

"That's okay," Cortez said. "You think you know how to get out to my place?"

"Yes sir, I think so," the fish man said. "I see a cop waving people through. I'll talk to you later," he said, and then the phone went silent.

"Okay," Cortez said, and hung up.

It was five thirty before he rolled into the driveway and Cortez was sitting on the front porch about to have a fit waiting for him. The big red truck rolled to a stop out at the mailbox and then backed up. Cortez waved. The wheels turned toward the driveway and Cortez got up. He could see the fish man inside the cab and then the truck was rolling down toward his front porch. He wished Lucinda could be here to see this. He stepped down from the porch as the truck pulled up and he walked around to the driver's door. The fish man left it running and it rolled an inch or two until he pulled out the brake and Cortez heard the wheels crunch in the gravel. The fish man got down and shook hands. He'd called again an hour ago, on his way.

"Mister Sharp?" he said. He had a head full of white hair but he didn't look that old. Cortez wondered about that. What would turn a man's hair that white at his age?

"That's me," Cortez said. "Come on up here and set down and rest. You have any trouble finding my place?"

"A little. But I saw a boy just down the road here at a trailer and stopped and asked him and he knew where you lived."

That was the kid with the go-kart. The one he'd yelled at.

"I can fix you some tea if you want some," Cortez said. "My daughter left some Diet Cokes over here but I don't never drink them."

"Some tea'd be fine," the fish man said, so Cortez took him in the house to get him some. Cortez told him he could fix him a sandwich if he wanted one but the fish man said he was all right for now, that he'd gotten a cheeseburger at the Waffle House in Senatobia.

So they sat on the porch for a few minutes. Just talking. The shiny red truck sitting there running. The sky had evened out into a solid blue hue with some fluffy white clouds drifting in it and they talked about cows and fish and cotton. The fish man said they'd had a lot of rain over in Arkansas. Cortez said it had been so dry here that his corn hadn't made much corn. The fish man said that the fish would be big enough to eat next year if Cortez fed them through the fall until October and started again in March, or as soon as the water warmed up. It took two weeks to train them to feed. You fed them at night. He finished his tea and set his glass down.

"You ready to see em?" he said. "I can raise the lids on the tanks if you want to get up on the truck and take a look."

"I sure would," Cortez said, and they went down the steps and over to the truck. Cortez hated he couldn't feed them in the daytime.

"It's a big step up," Tommy Bright said, and he climbed up on the back of the truck first and then extended a hand down to Cortez. Cortez took the hand and felt the strength in the fish man's arm as he pulled him up. Then he was standing between two banks of stainless steel rectangular tanks. A wood floor between them. Things were humming and bubbling. There were two round canisters marked OXYGEN strapped to the back. Tommy Bright opened one of the fish tanks and told Cortez to look in. What he saw in there thrilled him. The clean bubbling water was black with tiny catfish, a moving herd. They hovered in the water singly and in masses, and he could see them swimming beneath the rippling water, their little tails waving. Their tiny side fins and their small whiskers. He looked up at the fish man.

"Is this three thousand in here?" he said.

Tommy Bright smiled and opened the hatches on two more tanks.

"Oh no," he said. "That's five hundred of your four inch. I've got five more tanks with the rest of them and your eight inch. Come on over and look at these, Mister Sharp."

Cortez couldn't remember being any happier in a long time as he stepped up to the next tank. The fish man had picked up a long-handled dip net and he dipped into the swimming mass and lifted a net full of them.

"These are the ones I was telling you would be maybe big enough to eat some this year if you feed em good," he said. "They grow fast."

Cortez looked down into the dip net. The fish were squirming against each other and dripping water down onto the planks of the truck bed. The catfish were slick and gray with small black spots on them.

"Will they bite already?" Cortez said. "I mean bite a hook?"

"Hell yes, they'll bite. If you've got some red worms you could catch some this afternoon after we put em in. And they will strictly fin the hell out of you, too."

"Aw, I know," Cortez said. "I had one fin me all through the web of my hand right here one time," he said, and he touched the round scar on his wrinkled hand. He'd never forgotten how bad it hurt.

Tommy Bright turned the net upside down over the tank and started dumping them back into the water. One or two hung, their side fins caught in the nylon mesh. He was trying to shake them loose.

"This is how I usually get finned, trying to get em loose from this dip net," he said, and he got them loose and closed the lid on the tank and put the dip net away.

"You got fish in all them tanks?" Cortez said.

"I got one spare that's empty," Tommy Bright said.

"I see," Cortez said. "It's always good to have a spare, I guess."

"It sure is," the fish man said. "Well, if you're ready, you can just get in with me and ride over to the pond if you want to. Which way is it?"

"Right out the driveway and turn left," Cortez said, pointing.

"Okay then."

"And here's your money," Cortez said, pulling the roll of bills out of his pocket and handing it to him. The fish man wiped his hands on his pants before he took it.

"I counted it twice, but you count it again," Cortez said.

"I'm sure it's all there, Mister Sharp," the fish man said, and stuck it in his pocket without looking at it much.

They climbed down and Cortez got up into the cab. Tommy Bright climbed in behind the wheel and released the brake and started turning around.

"You got a pretty place here, Mister Sharp," he said, looking out over the pasture and the hills behind it. Cortez's cows were black dots in the tall green grass. White egrets flew among them and landed on their backs.

"Thank you," Cortez said.

"I guess you've lived here a long time," the fish man said.

"I bought this place when I was twenty-five," Cortez said. "And it looked like shit."

"It don't now," Tommy Bright said, and he started up the driveway. "I think I told you I'm losing my place over in Arkansas. I had it twelve years."

"That's a damn shame," Cortez said.

"Yes it is," the fish man said. "It's my own fault. I can't blame it on a soul but me."

Cortez looked out the window as they drove up the driveway. This fellow seemed like an honest, hardworking man. It was bad to hear that he was losing his place.

"How big a pond does it take to raise them fish?" Cortez said.

"I had fourteen altogether that I used," Tommy Bright said. "I've got five right behind my trailer that I had built myself and then I had nine more down the road that I leased. They're all different sizes."

The heifers were all standing at the fence looking at them as they rolled by and the fish man turned his head and looked at them briefly.

"That's as fine a bunch of heifers as I've seen in a while."

"They fat," Cortez said. "I'm fixin to turn em in with one of my bulls in a day or two."

"How many mama cows you run on your place?"

To somebody else Cortez might have answered that it wasn't any of their business. Coming from somebody else it might have seemed like asking how much money he had in the bank. But he liked the fish man, and in truth, he was starting to get a little lonely sometimes, and he was glad for the company. Besides, they were talking about business: the cattle business, the fish business. The fish man wasn't being nosy. He was just talking.

"Aw, I ain't running but twenty head," Cortez said. "Them's their heifers and I sold my bull calves earlier. I'm seventy-two and that's all I want to fool with now. I used to run about eighty head."

The fish man pulled up beside Cortez's mailbox and stopped. He was grinning.

"I wouldn't have believed you's that old, Mr. Sharp. You sure don't look it."

"Born in nineteen thirty-two," Cortez said.

"You got any kids?"

"I got a girl lives in Atlanta."

"That's right. You told me."

"I had a boy one time. He tripped and fell at the back step with a twenty-two rifle. Was fixing to shoot us a chicken for supper and it shot him through the neck. He wasn't but fourteen."

"I'm sorry to hear that," the fish man said.

"Aw, that's all right," Cortez said. "It was a long time ago."

It wasn't like Cortez to talk about Raif, and especially not to a stranger. But what did it hurt to talk about him? He wasn't asking for sympathy. He wasn't asking anybody to look at what happened to him and see how bad it was. He was just telling him what happened to his boy, why he didn't have him anymore. He didn't tell about the sight of his screaming wife trying to plug the hole in his boy's neck with mud she scooped up from the yard, mud that turned as red as the blood that was spouting out of his neck until it ebbed away and there was no more left. He didn't tell any of that. He didn't tell about the things she screamed up to God or the names she called him. Maybe she didn't go to heaven after all.

Tommy Bright turned left out of the driveway and shifted into second.

"It ain't but a little ways," Cortez said, and the fish man nodded. Just at the curve, some of the red clay gravel was spilled out into the dirt road and the fish man slowed the truck. From there you could see the new road going down through the shady woods. And beyond that, through the green leaves, a patch of calm dark water. Tommy Bright feathered the brake pedal with his foot and turned the truck down into the hollow.

"I feel bad about making you build me a road," he said.

"I needed one anyway," Cortez said.

"It's a mighty good one. They don't give that clay gravel away, do they?"

"Naw they don't," Cortez said, noticing again how nicely packed it was. They rolled past a couple of the POSTED signs he had nailed to some trees beside the new road.

"You have trouble with people trespassing on your property, Mister Sharp?"

"It's just some kids down the road," Cortez said.

"Well, I hate to tell you this, since I'm fixing to turn loose three thousand on you, and I'm not trying to tell you your business, but it's been my experience that the quieter you keep it about having these catfish in here, the better off you'll be. I mean unless you don't mind the general public coming down here and catching most of em for you once you get em up to eating size."

Cortez had already been worried about how to keep people out once the fish started growing. There was no fence up here. Anybody could walk right down through the woods to it. And the kid down the road had seen the fish truck already. He'd probably tell his daddy or his friends. He hated the fish man had asked the kid for directions.

The catfish man steered the truck carefully down the new road and the woods shaded them.

"I'm gonna hang a gate up there at the road," Cortez said. "I think that'll keep most ever body out."

The fish man nodded and reached for a lower gear. They were coming out of the woods now and they could see the whole pond and the farmhouse and the barn and the equipment shed and the yard and the fenced pastures below them.

"Yes sir, you're right. A gate and a POSTED sign will keep out an honest man. But it's just like a lock. That's all it'll keep out. I've had more people tell me that after they got some catfish from me and put em in their ponds, folks would come from miles around to sneak in there at night. Run trotlines. I tell you what, I shot a guy with bird shot who kept getting into one of my ponds at night and catching my brood catfish."

"The hell you did," Cortez said.

"I had to. He was coming in there at two o'clock in the morning while I was asleep and putting out a throw line and catching fish I'd been raising for four years. Ten-pounders. He ain't been back."

"I guess not," Cortez said.

"Now we want to park as close to the pond as we can, Mister Sharp," the fish man said. He stopped the truck near the shallow end. Then he pulled it on over to the wide graded place and stopped it again there.

"This ought to be fine," he said. He pushed it up into neutral and pulled out the hand brake. He reached to another key in the dash and turned it on, then pushed a button beside it, and Cortez heard an outside generator rattle for a few moments while it was starting and then kick on with a steady roar. The fish man put the truck in gear and shut off the ignition.

"Okay," he said, and opened his door.

Cortez opened his and stepped down and shut the door behind him. It was still pretty hot and he couldn't see any breeze blowing through the leaves of the trees. He heard the other door slam and then the fish man walked over to him.

"You sure got a good view from up here," he said, and turned his head to look down on Cortez's place. He looked at the pile of tree trunks that were already overgrown with weeds and tall grass.

"That the trees he took out?" he said.

"Yeah," Cortez said. "I've been wanting to build a pond up here for years. I had this natural hollow here already. And he dug it out some more when he was building his levee."

"It's a fine pond," Tommy Bright said. "Say it's about halfway full?"

"It's over my head, I know," Cortez said. "I may build me a boat dock right over here before it fills up all the way."

"That'd be nice," the fish man said. He went over to a side compartment on the truck and reached in for a rolled-up rubber apron that he slipped over his head and started tying around his back. It hung down below his knees in front. He slipped his leather boots off and set them on the ground beside the back wheels and got a pair of white rubber boots from the compartment and put them on.

"One thing about messing with fish," he said. "You always know you're gonna get wet. And I usually bring some dry clothes with me and ran clean off and forgot em this trip."

Cortez nodded and stood there watching him. He wished it would rain some more and fill the pond on up whether he got a boat dock built or not.

"Can I help you with anything?" Cortez said.

Tommy Bright opened another compartment door and took out a stack of five-gallon plastic buckets. He set them on the ground and pulled out some gloves and put them on.

"Yes sir, if you don't mind, once I get some of em in these buckets, you can start turning em loose for me. Now they've been in this cold water for about seven or eight hours and it's probably colder than your pond water, so they need to get acclimated."

He set the stack of buckets on the back of the truck and then he climbed up.

"You need me up there to help you?" Cortez said.

"No sir, I'm fine," the fish man said, and reached for the dip net again. "It'll go easier if I just hand em down to you."

He raised the lid on the first tank and then took two of the buckets from the stack. He set one on the floor close to him and with the other one he dipped water from the tank into it.

"I ain't gonna need this water no more," he said. He set a few more buckets from the stack on the floor and kept pouring water into them.

"Is that just plain water?" Cortez said. He thought it might be some kind of special water.

"It's Arkansas spring water," Tommy Bright said, and kept working. "It's the cleanest water I can find. Now what we'll do, Mr. Sharp, I'll get you three or four buckets ready and then you can take em right to the bank of the pond. Pour some of that cold water out and then just take the bucket and ease it down in the pond and let some of that pond water run in there. Then set it up on the bank and do the next one. And let em swim around in that bucket for about five minutes and then just pour the whole thing in. It's just so it won't shock em."

"Are they all still alive?" Cortez said.

"I ain't seen a dead one yet."

That was good. He was going to get everything he'd paid for. He wondered if maybe the fish man might like a good tomato sandwich after they got through putting the fish in.

When Tommy Bright had five buckets full of water he started dipping up little catfish and putting them in the buckets.

"It ain't gonna take that long," he said. "Usually I have to count em when I'm somewhere like the Co-op in Oxford. But I counted these when they were just hatched and I know how many there are. You probably got about thirty-three hundred fish. I always tried to be generous to my customers whenever I counted fish. Some die."

"I appreciate it," Cortez said. "I'll be glad to pay you for them extra fish."

"My treat, Mister Sharp," the fish man said.

Tommy Bright kept dipping fish and Cortez stood there and watched him. He couldn't help but think about what a good job the fish man had, getting to mess with fish all the time. He wished he could go see his place, his fish operation in Arkansas. But didn't he say the bank was foreclosing next week? It was a damn shame. Hell. He'd give him a whole bag of tomatoes. He could take them back to Arkansas with him. Maybe his wife liked a good tomato sandwich. He'd noticed the fish man's wedding ring. He could see him sweating under the sun.

"Okay, Mister Sharp," the fish man said, and leaned his dip net against the side of a tank. He picked up two of the buckets and set them at the very back of the truck. Cortez reached and lifted the first one down and set it on the ground. It looked like it had about forty or fifty fish in it. He reached for another.

They worked like that in tandem for a while, not talking much, the fish man scooping out the fish and putting them in the buckets and then setting them on the rear of the truck. Cortez started carrying them to the edge of the pond and pouring some water out of each one, then letting some pond water in. Tommy Bright asked for another stack of buckets and Cortez got them. The generator kept running.

"I should have brought us some ice water," Cortez said.

Tommy Bright mopped the sweat from his forehead with the back of his glove. His shirt was already soaked.

"It'd be nice," he said. Then he turned back to work.

It wasn't long before Cortez had ten buckets lined up on the edge of the bank and he'd already put pond water in all of them. He walked the row of them, looking down, and he couldn't see any dead fish at all. He looked up at Tommy Bright.

"You think I can pour em in now?"

"Yes sir, I'm sure they'll be fine. Can I have those buckets back up here when you get done? I'll take me a little break for a minute here if you don't care."

"Shoot naw. Get on down and get under one of these trees. I tell you what I'll do when I get these poured out," Cortez said. "I'll walk down to the house and fix us some ice water and get in my truck and bring it back up here."

And the fish man smiled as he got down from the truck.

"That'd be real good, Mister Sharp," he said. "That'd be mighty nice. If you could wait till I get the rest of em in the buckets, I can get some pond water in em and let you put the rest of em in when you get back."

"Sure," Cortez said, and he went over to the first bucket in the row and squatted down beside it. He looked at the fish man.

"Just pour em in?"

"Just pour em in."

Something magical happened to Cortez when he picked up the bucket and tilted it over the water and started tipping it. The water came flowing out in a wide tongue and the little catfish came swimming with it, fins and tails and whiskers, splashing into the pond and muddying the bottom. He upended it until they were all gone. He looked down into the water. They were swimming around. Some were taking off. But others were hanging around at the very edge of the pond. He reached down and touched one with his finger and it sluggishly swam away into the depths. He turned around and looked at the fish man, who was sitting beneath a nearby tree mopping his face with his handkerchief.

"How come they keep hanging around the bank?"

"They don't know what to do yet," Tommy Bright said. "They'll finally go on off in deep water. You see any dead ones?"

"Not a one," Cortez said.

"They're afraid a big one's gonna eat em," Tommy Bright said. "It's instinct. They'll hide until they figure it's safe to go out."

"Well, they safe in here," Cortez said. "Since there ain't nothing else in here but them."

The fish man pulled at his ear, leaning against the bark on the tree. A little breeze had picked up and it stirred a few strands of his white hair. He looked out across the water and smiled.

"You know, people ask me all the time about this and that. How much you feed em, when you feed em. If they want to raise crappie I tell em they need fathead minnows. If they've got too many bluegills I tell em they better buy some Florida bass. I been messing with fish for almost twenty years and if things had gone better for me — or if I'd done better, I should say — I'd keep right on doing what I'm doing. But it don't matter what kind of pond or lake you've got or what's in it. There ain't but one rule in a pond. You know what that one is, Mister Sharp?"

Cortez picked up another bucket and turned his head to Tommy Bright.

"What's that?" he said.

"The big ones eat the little ones."

Cortez kept pouring them in and the fish man took the empty buckets to the back of the truck and climbed up again. He started working with the dip net again and handing the buckets to Cortez and Cortez kept putting pond water in them and then pouring them into the pond. After another fifteen minutes or so, Cortez figured they were about halfway through. Tommy Bright was working on the fourth tank by then.

"You sure you don't want me to go on and get that ice water?" Cortez said.

"Let me get these last ones out, Mister Sharp. We don't have too many more. Then I'll cool off while you get the water if that's okay."

"Okay," Cortez said. They kept working and working and finally the fish man raised the lid on the sixth tank. It was getting close to seven o'clock by then but it was still hot.

It took more buckets for the eight-inch fish since he could put fewer in each. But finally he had them all sitting on the back of the truck and he was dipping out the last stragglers with the net. He'd been draining the tanks as he went and now there was water soaked all into the red-clay gravel around the truck. He plucked one last remaining catfish from the net and dropped it into a bucket and put away the dip net. He started taking off his gloves.

"That's it," he said, and dropped his gloves on the planks. He took off his apron while he was still standing on the truck and then he climbed down and opened the driver's door and reached in and killed the generator. He shut the door and walked around and started helping Cortez set the buckets on the edge of the bank. "I'll take care of these if you want to go get that water for us."

"Okay," Cortez said. "But I want you to stop by the house before you take off. I want to give you some fresh homegrown tomatoes."

Tommy Bright reached up with the back of his hand and wiped some sweat from his cheek. Then he smiled again.

"That's mighty nice of you, Mister Sharp. I'll take care of these fish for you and they ought to be ready to put in by the time you get back."

"It won't take me but about ten minutes," Cortez said. "I'm just gonna head across the pasture."

"I'll be here when you get back," the fish man said, and Cortez took off down the hill. Damn, he was excited. The grass had really sprouted out after the rain and he needed to get up here with his 4020 and his Bush Hog and Bush Hog it all down. He could do that tomorrow if it wasn't too wet on the sides of the hills. This old clay ground around here was bad to hold water.

He walked on down the hill and looked at his house. He didn't think it was going to need painting again this year. The boys who'd done it last year had done a real good job. And maybe when it cooled off a little more, maybe next month, he'd get down there and fix that rotted section of fence by the pea patch. He'd have to go to Bruce for some posts and some more barbed wire. He had part of a roll in the barn but not enough.

He opened the gate at the foot of the hill and let himself into the back pasture and then closed it behind him. Then he walked along the edge of the fence past the old pond which was muddy. Some of the cows were wading around in it, lifting the flies from their backs. One cow was standing with her heavy black bag in the water and a bream was jumping for the blood-bloated ticks hanging there. The others had moved under the big oaks and were lying in the shade, chewing their cuds, swatting at horseflies with their tails. Clusters of houseflies lay resting on them.

He stopped at the next gate and looked back up the hill to where the fish truck was sitting beside the pond. The fish man was up on the truck, and he looked like he was raising the lid on another tank. Putting all his stuff away, probably. Cortez turned and went on.

41

As soon as Ursula got in there she started eating some of those little catfish. Must have been hungry from her trip. Needed a few snacks. She was kind of like a killer whale, bringing part of her head out of the water to scoop them up in mouthfuls in the shallow end where hundreds of them had gathered to hover in dumb anticipation of nothing.

She scooped them and bit them and swallowed them and chomped them, chasing and catching them, working her way around the edge of the bank, muddying the water, picking up two and three here, one or two there. Most fled. Her stomach fluids would dissolve fins and little bony heads. Mere tidbits of fish. She kept chasing them and eating them until she was full, which only took about five minutes, and then she swam to the deeper end, where the water was colder, and slowly slanted off into the borrow pit and then found its smooth clay bottom with her belly, and there she settled, mouth opening and closing, her gills smoothly working, the water washing out of them on each side, red-laced cartilage as delicately scalloped as snowflakes. The rubber-hose handles on her side fins were gone. Her whiskers were waving gently in the water.

And there she lay, waiting, seeing the small fish dart by, no end of food in sight. But she wouldn't come up again until she was ready to feed again. In the daytime, the bottom was where she'd stay most of the time. Unless she found something interesting to eat. Catfish were like that.

42

The big red truck didn't stop at a motel in Oxford. It passed under the green light at the bypass on 6 just outside of town and barreled west toward the turnoff for I-55 at Batesville. It passed farms and houses and fields and furniture stores, mobile home dealers, little barbecue joints, used-car lots, and places where people sold rocks. Or bathtubs. Wrought-iron gate work. People in the ditches with plastic bags picking up cans. The sun was slanting low in the western sky and the truck rolled on down the road like it was trying to meet it. It went by white fences that kept in horses and it went by trailers that sat treeless under the sun day by day and it went by houses under construction, pale two by fours in rows with headers framed in for doors and windows, stacks of asphalt shingles and long lumber wrapped in sheets of Visqueen and awaiting the saw, the hammer.

It crossed the county line at Rick's beer store and rolled past the entrance to Sardis Lake. It passed a cemetery filled with flowers where a blue tent stood abandoned, a mound of earth heaped with carnations and daisies, fragile lilies already wilted from the heat.

The sun dipped beneath a distant ridge of dark green pines and the truck's headlights came on. It rolled past some business offices and Tri-County Marine outside Batesville, the offices empty, the boats inside the six-foot chain-link fence covered with snugly fitted custom tarps. It rolled past a Lowe's and a Shell gas station and then it moved to the exit and turned right with its blinker flashing until it joined the flow of eighteen-wheelers and cars and pickups and station wagons and motorcycles and campers towing ski rigs going north toward Memphis.

The sun dropped out of sight and the truck rolled between tall stands of pines planted years ago on both sides of the highway, and black Peterbilts and green Kenworths passed it, smoke pouring briefly from their chrome pipes as their drivers grabbed another gear. It climbed the long hills, the highway lit now only by the headlights of the vehicles that moved in groups and by ones, yellow orbs lancing through the bugs that danced in their beams.

The right blinker came on again at the town of Sardis, and it took the exit and came to a stop at the bottom of the hill. The left blinker flashed and the truck sat there at the STOP sign for less than ten seconds, long enough for two cars to pass in front of it going west. The truck pulled out behind them and went up another hill past an abandoned motel with its gangrenous swimming pool, its rotting garden hoses. It pulled in at the Sonic and sat there for ten minutes and then it circled the red-roofed building and came back out on the street and drove on up the interstate to Hernando, through town, past the library and the courthouse, past old magnificent homes with yellow lights showing through the windows.

When it left town it went into more valleys but not so many hills, horse farms with board fences, the posts skimming by like spokes on a slow-turning wheel. By and by the hills leveled out and the trees diminished and there were fields so gigantic they ran to absolute black out beyond the moving beams of the big red truck. The air laden with the sorry smell of insecticides. The land was flat and some of it was growing rice, other parts of it cotton. The truck rolled forward deeper into the blackness of a Mississippi Delta night.

At Robinsonville the truck slowed and turned onto the new highway that was well lighted from the lamps that hung on the concrete poles. Out there in the darkness there rose up a searchlight that tracked a white arc across the black sky and then returned to its start. The lights of the casinos cast the night back like a whole city newly arrived and fully formed from the belly of some monstrous mother ship.

43

Jimmy's daddy, in an effort to be a better daddy to Jimmy, decided to take him to Ripley, to Trade Day, to what folks all over North Mississippi called First Monday, since that's when it happened, the first of every month, winter and summer, spring and fall. But neither of those names was accurate, because it actually started on the weekend, on Saturday, and then went through Sunday, and then Monday. So actually you didn't have to wait until the first Monday to go to First Monday, but Jimmy's daddy didn't understand why they didn't call it Last Saturday, or Trade *Days*. They got up early on Saturday—Jimmy's daddy had consciously avoided overdrinking the night before and had polished off only a six-pack along with a supper of lighter-fluid-flavored hamburgers and watched a little TV before going to bed—in order to get there in plenty of time and have all the time in the world to wander around the old fairgrounds among the booths and stalls and open pickup beds and horse trailers and tables with tents over them and look at everything that was for sale: guns, chickens, chicken cages, chicken grit, pottery, tractors, toys, ponies, mules, donkeys, burros, horses, dogs, quilts, homemade jellies and jams and preserves, ribbon cane syrup, tomato relish to put on your peas, cookware of all types, including rusty cast-iron skillets and dutch ovens, candles, musical instruments, ironwork, new tools, old tools, trailers, antiques of every kind, furniture, knick-knacks, rabbits, rabbit cages, rabbit feed, rabbit feeders, rabbit waterers, frozen pen-raised quail, fishing equipment, tillers, lawn mowers, chain saws, stump grinders, portable sheds, portable water pumps, portable generators, portable sawmills, anvils, harnesses, plows, hand-painted mailboxes, handmade-and-hand-painted birdhouses, embroidery, rocking chairs, porch swings, belt buckles and belts, used military insignia, Bowie knives, swords, hunting videos, hunting equipment, baseball cards, trapping equipment, used paperbacks by the box, fake floral arrangements, hot dogs, hamburgers, chicken-on-a-stick, corn pups, ribs and chicken, slushes, hand-dipped ice cream, wholesale home remedies, audiotapes and CDs, rugs, pet monkeys, coin collections, arrowhead collections, and lots of other things. Plenty of it cheap. It took a whole day to look at everything if you gave everything a good looking over and you could spend the whole day entertained and get food, too.

That morning, Jimmy was shaken awake with the words "Come on, Hot Rod." Jimmy dressed quickly and they ate on the road. Jimmy's daddy knew a place out on Highway 30 and they pulled the '55 in there by eight o'clock. They went in and sat down to a red-checkered tablecloth and the sounds of country radio playing and the smells of coffee freshly brewed and succulent meat sizzling, ordered big breakfasts of ham and eggs and french toast and regular toast and molasses and strawberry preserves, hot coffee for Jimmy's daddy, orange juice and milk for Jimmy.

Jimmy thought it was about the coolest thing his daddy had ever done for him. It went a long way toward stifling most of the feelings of ambiguity he'd been feeling about his daddy ever since he'd almost drowned him. He would have eventually gotten over it anyway, just because he loved his daddy so much, but this hastened the process. The eggs were cooked the way he liked them with the yellows runny and the french toast was sweet and crunchy at the same time, smothered in lots of Aunt Jemima syrup, something Jimmy rarely got at home. Why? Because Aunt Jemima cost too much to buy, according to Jimmy's daddy.

And another thing was that Jimmy's daddy seemed to be in a really good mood, that's how it appeared to Jimmy. He was telling Jimmy jokes and stories about the stuff he did when he was growing up, like working in Halter Wellums's sawmill and digging big splinters out of his fingers in the evenings and walking home through the woods, saving his money to buy his first car. And he went on to tell him what a piece of shit it turned out to be, about all the rattles it had in the dash. Jimmy cut off some more french toast and asked his daddy a few questions about motors just because he knew his daddy liked to talk about motors, and his daddy talked about Edelbrock intakes and Isky cams some. He confided in Jimmy that he was going to have to fix the transmission in the '55, or maybe get a new one, maybe with a Hurst shifter. Jimmy immediately wondered how much that would cost. He'd pretty much given up on the Kenny Chesney concert, but there was still a little piece of hidden mythical pasture in the dreamy back part of his mind that was labeled Tupelo Buffalo Park.

"How far's Tupelo from Ripley, Daddy?" Jimmy said.

His daddy had finished eating now, but the waitress had brought him some more coffee and taken away his plate of egg scraps and puddled syrup and one last piece of country ham he hadn't been able to eat.

"I don't know," he said. "I ain't never drove from Ripley to Tupelo. I wouldn't think it'd be over a hour."

Jimmy's daddy lit a cigarette and the waitress smiled and brought over a clean metal ashtray.

"Thanks, baby," he said, and winked at her. Jimmy saw it. He'd seen his daddy do that before, wink at women. Like there was some secret he was sharing with them.

"I'll tell you what else I'm gonna do. This fall," Jimmy's daddy said.

"What's that?" Jimmy said. He was about to get full. And he was so glad the girls didn't get to come with them that he didn't know what to do. It was just the two of them, Jimmy and his daddy. No stinking girls allowed. He wondered if he ought to tell his daddy that he'd already seen Evelyn messing around again with some of the thugs on the school bus, but then decided that he might ought to withhold that information for now and possibly use it later as some form of leverage against Evelyn if she continued to get meaner and more trashy mouthed and bigger and stronger and might actually try to slap the shit out of him or send her thug boyfriend over to beat the crap out of him. He wondered if he ought to tell his daddy that a guy driving a big red truck that said TOMMY'S BIG RED FISH TRUCK had stopped by the trailer the other day asking for directions for an old man who'd just built a pond. Jimmy's daddy fairly beamed at him.

"I'm gonna take you over to the Gun and Knife Show. How'd you like that?"

"I'd like that a lot, Daddy," Jimmy said, and put his fork in his plate and wiped his mouth with his napkin. He just said that. He didn't really mean it. He was still a little uncomfortable every time he thought about that videotape his daddy had where those dogs chased down those hogs and the men with the dogs stabbed the hogs to death. All that blood and squealing. Jimmy never had shot a gun and didn't know if he'd be too scared to or not. But he knew his daddy expected him to sometime. But maybe he'd enjoy the Gun and Knife Show. He sure wasn't going to tell his daddy that he *didn't* want to go. Lots of things were hinging. He might still get his go-kart fixed one day. And it was entirely possible that Tupelo Buffalo Park might be right across the street from the Gun and Knife Show, so that they could just walk over. Jimmy didn't want to limit his options on travel opportunities.

"Let me see them teeth," his daddy said, and Jimmy opened his mouth. His daddy leaned closer for a better look. He had a serious look on his face when he pulled back.

"You need to get them teeth fixed. You need to go to the dentist."

That struck fear into Jimmy's heart. He'd already heard all those horror stories his daddy had told him about what some dentists had done to him when he was little. Pulling his teeth. Drilling holes. *Root canals!*

"I don't want to go to the dentist, Daddy," he said, and closed his mouth.

"You gonna have to," his daddy said, and stubbed out his smoke. He grabbed the ticket off the table and told Jimmy to come on. He paid up front and didn't go back to the table to leave any money for the waitress. They went back out and got in the '55 and took off again. The windows were down and the wind rippled Jimmy's T-shirt, a red one with a pocket. He had on shorts and tennis shoes to try and stay cool.

Jimmy's daddy pulled a cigarette from his pocket and rolled his window up long enough to get it lit. Then he rolled it back down and told Jimmy to reach back there in that cooler in the rear floorboard that was under that blanket and hand him a cold beer.

Jimmy got up on his knees and turned around on the seat and reached way down behind the front seat and pushed the old green blanket off the cooler. He opened the lid and looked in. It was full of ice and beer. He shoved some of the ice aside and looked around in there to see if maybe there were some Cokes in there, but there didn't appear to be any. A nice cold Coke would have been good after breakfast. Wash it all down. Burp a few times. But Jimmy didn't say anything about there not being any Cokes in there. Even though it looked like if his daddy could go to all the trouble to ice himself down some beer for a trip they were taking together, he could stick a few Cokes from the refrigerator in there for Jimmy. How long would that have taken? Twenty seconds? Jimmy had been hoping that if things went really good today and his daddy stayed in a good mood all day, then maybe he could ask him again about the spear point. And hopefully get it back. How cool would that be for Show and Tell? With his two red arrowheads, he could have a nice little set. Maybe put them in some kind of frame on a background of green velvet. Herschel Horowitz had said he had all his arrowheads fixed up like that.

"Now be sure to put that top back on that cooler and stick that blanket back over it," Jimmy's daddy said. "That way if a cop stops us he won't see my beer. We in a dry county now."

Jimmy handed his daddy a beer. He knew what a dry county was. A dry county was a place Jimmy's daddy didn't like to visit, simply because they didn't sell cold beer there. Whenever Jimmy's daddy knew he was going to pass through a dry county, he took his cooler and packed it with ice and beer. And covered it up with that old green blanket.

Jimmy's daddy opened his beer and took a sip. He nodded to himself.

"Let's turn on the radio," he said, and did. "I usually listen to this station over at Ripley. Kudzu one oh two? They play some pretty good country music. Bluegrass on Sunday mornings. Course I ain't never up much on Sunday mornings." And he laughed. Jimmy was glad to hear him laugh. He wondered again what had happened at the stove factory. The day his daddy whipped him so hard. Nobody had ever told him, but sometimes he caught his daddy staring off into the distance, even if he was inside.

Jimmy's daddy turned the volume up and they listened to the last half of "Diggin' Up Bones" by Randy Travis, and then a commercial for mobile homes came on and Jimmy's daddy turned it down.

"That's the only thing about listening to the radio," he said. "You got to listen to all them goddamn commercials. They just play em over and over. Trying to sell you all their shit."

Jimmy's daddy drank some more of his beer and they rode along. After a while, Jimmy's daddy finished that beer and threw the can out the window and told Jimmy to get him another one, which he did.

"You ever heard that commercial for Tupelo Buffalo Park?" Jimmy said, as his daddy popped the top.

"Naw," Jimmy's daddy said.

The commercials finished and Jimmy's daddy turned the volume back up. The announcer said that there was a Merle Six-Pack coming up within the hour, and that there was going to be a benefit for Bud and Hazel over at the community center at Ripley next Saturday evening, to bring your lawn chairs. Then they started playing "Mama Tried."

"You like old Merle?" Jimmy's daddy said.

"Sure," Jimmy said. Who was Merle?

"He's one of my favorites of all time," Jimmy's daddy said, and then he started singing along with the radio. He sang right along, and knew a lot of the words, but he had to just hum when he didn't know them. He broke back out on the chorus pretty strong and nodded his head and tapped his left foot on the floorboard beside the clutch pedal. Jimmy didn't think his daddy could sing very good, but he didn't say anything since he much preferred being with his daddy and him trying to sing than to not be with his daddy at all.

The song finished and Jimmy's daddy drank some more of his beer. He smoked another cigarette while a rest home commercial ran. Then a body shop commercial ran. Then a feed store commercial ran. Then a commercial for Crawl Daddy's in New Albany. They sold stuff for four-wheelers and big jacked-up pickups. Then a commercial ran for a product that grew hair because it stopped the body's production of DHT.

"That's horse shit," Jimmy's daddy said. "That shit ain't gonna grow no hair. Look at me," he said, and pulled his cap off for a moment. Jimmy gazed onto the bald dome of his daddy, his long streaks of gray hair. Jimmy's daddy put his cap back on. "That shit wouldn't grow no hair up there. Not unless it'll grow hair on a bowling ball."

Jimmy chuckled a little bit, mostly for his daddy's benefit, and then he stopped and got serious.

"What's a motherfucker?" he said, and Jimmy's daddy almost coughed his cigarette out. Then he did cough. He shoved his beer between his legs in a fast move and caught the steering wheel with that hand and took the cigarette from his mouth with the other hand and coughed hard.

"Damn," he said. "I think some of that beer went down the wrong swallow pipe." He cleared his throat and took another drink and set his beer back between his legs. "Where'd you hear a word like that?" he said.

"From Evelyn," Jimmy said immediately.

"Oh yeah?" Jimmy's daddy said. It looked like it pissed him off. He took another sip of beer. "She's about a little smartass. What she needs is a good ass whupping ever once in a while. Course your mama don't want me to lay a hand on her. That's what's wrong with her right now, Johnette won't whup her ass. Did, she wouldn't do all that sassing she does. Iron some damn clothes once in a while or something. 'Stead of talking on the phone ten hours a day."

Jimmy didn't say anything, and he kind of hated that he'd just lied to his daddy about Evelyn, since *he* was the one who'd said he knew what a motherfucker was that day at the empty pond, back when the go-kart was running. And Jimmy wondered if now was the right time to tell his daddy about the dead black lady he'd seen on the bridge that night. And about how he kept seeing her, sometimes at night around the trailer, and that ever since he'd almost drowned that day, he'd seemed to be able to see her more often. He was afraid his daddy wouldn't believe him.

"Evelyn lies down on the bus seat with the big boys and they do things with her," Jimmy said instead. He almost said, *Evelyn lies down on the bus seat with the big boys and kisses them,* and that's what he *would* have said if it had been back in the spring, when she *was* just kissing them, but now that school had started Jimmy had looked toward the back of the bus a few times and had seen Evelyn lying across one of the big boys' laps, with her head out of sight, and the big boy with his eyes closed and his face red, straining and grunting like he was picking up something heavy. The bus driver had already stopped the bus one time and had gotten up and gone back there, but by then Evelyn had straightened back up in the seat and was wiping her mouth with a tissue.

"That little whore," Jimmy's daddy said, and Jimmy nodded to himself. He'd been right about her all along.

"Ain't that just a fine kiss-my-ass?" Jimmy's daddy said. "Buy damn clothes for her and feed her, and then she does *that* on the school bus?"

"Does what?" Jimmy said. "What's she doing?"

"Never mind," Jimmy's daddy said. "I'll talk to your mama about it."

"Tell her not to tell Evelyn I told it, Daddy. Please?"

"Okay. I'll tell her not to tell her."

They rode along for a while and Jimmy looked at the farms and fields they were passing. He saw a farmer out mowing his pasture with a Bush Hog. He saw some hogs in a pen. One of them was stretched out pretty comfortably sleeping on a couch. Then they went by some fish ponds where people were fishing. It sure looked like fun. What if that mean old man up the road *had* put catfish in his pond? How would you know? How would you know if you didn't go down there with a rod and a reel and some bait and see?

"Holy fucking shit," Jimmy's daddy said, and he let off the gas.

Jimmy didn't even have to ask *what*. He could see the blue lights blinking down the road, and a lot of cars pulled over on the sides of the highway.

"It's a damn wreck," Jimmy's daddy said, and started drinking his beer really fast. He took a breath and said, "And damn cops all over the place."

There was a line of traffic in front of them that was slowing down and Jimmy could see all the brake lights of the vehicles in front of them coming on. Jimmy looked over at his daddy. His daddy had the beer can turned straight up against his mouth. He took it down and handed it to Jimmy.

"Here," he said. "Stick this son of a bitch under the seat." Then he burped.

Jimmy did what he was told. He stuck it under the seat and acted like nothing was happening in case the cops were watching him.

"Make sure that blanket's over that cooler good," his daddy said.

Jimmy turned around and checked it. It looked okay to him.

"It's covered up," he said, looking over at his daddy. He didn't want his daddy to get caught by the cops and mess up the trip to Ripley. His daddy had told him they had pony rides over there and Jimmy was wanting one of them, maybe two. If his daddy had enough money. Maybe a few cheeseburgers. Ice cream? His tooth was hurting.

"All right then," his daddy said. "Turn back around and set back down."

As they got closer, Jimmy could see two smashed cars, both on one side of the highway. There was a narrow open space where cars and trucks were creeping through, and Jimmy could see some highway cops in the highway directing the traffic. There was broken glass in the road and what looked like red pieces of plastic. One of the cars was red.

"We can probably just slide right on through," Jimmy's daddy said.

"I bet we can," Jimmy said.

"I just don't want these sons of bitches to catch me with that beer in a dry county," Jimmy's daddy said.

"What would they do if they did?" Jimmy said.

"I don't know. They might take me to jail."

"Jail?" Jimmy said.

"You can't ever tell with some of these assholes."

Jimmy could tell that his daddy was getting nervous. He was already lighting another cigarette and he just had put one out.

"Look over there in that glove box and see if there's any gum in there," Jimmy's daddy said.

Jimmy looked. He didn't see any gum. He did see some small square packets that were stuffed behind some papers and rubber bands and things. He pulled one out and looked at it. It was fat, padded, slick. Jimmy started reading the label and the label said it was a latex c-o-n-d-o . . . condo? There was a wrinkle in the pack. Hiding an *m.* Condom. Con*dom?*

"This ain't gum," Jimmy said.

Jimmy's daddy looked over and alarm suddenly showed on his face.

"Gimme that," he said, and grabbed it. Then he stuffed it in his shirt pocket. Then he reached over and slammed the glove box shut.

"What is it?" Jimmy said.

"Don't you worry about what it is," Jimmy's daddy said.

They had come to a complete halt now since the highway cops were letting some traffic through from the other side and halting the ones in their lane. There was also another trooper who was talking to people in the cars in their lane, leaning down to speak to some of them. It looked like he was checking drivers' licenses, since Jimmy could see a man three cars in front of them handing his out the window. The trooper glanced at it and handed it back and nodded and another trooper on the other side of the wreck stopped the traffic coming from that direction and the one who'd been checking the licenses started waving them on. Jimmy's daddy pressed the gas and eased out on the clutch and they crept forward. Two cars went through and then they were stopped again.

"Son of a bitch," Jimmy's daddy said.

"What is it?" Jimmy said.

"The son of a bitch is checking licenses. Why are they checking licenses at a damn wreck? He's gonna look right in the damn car. Let me get mine out and have it ready."

Jimmy's daddy leaned toward the left and reached for his billfold with his right hand, pulled it out, retrieved his license from it, and laid the billfold on the seat.

"Goddamn it," he muttered under his breath. The trooper was checking the car in front of him.

Jimmy just sat there, saying nothing. He knew this was one of those times when he should say nothing. His daddy was nervous and this was no time to engage him in conversation. He'd just wait until later to tell him about the guy in the big red fish truck. Sometime when he was back in a good mood. And they were at home. And safe. This was trouble.

"You sure that cooler's covered up good?" Jimmy's daddy said.

"Yes sir," Jimmy said.

"And you shoved that beer can up under the seat good?"

"Pretty good," Jimmy said.

And then the trooper was walking back to their car. He had his hat off and he looked like some of the soldiers Jimmy had seen on the television, the ones who were over there fighting the war, in that he looked like he wouldn't put up with much foolishness. He had on sunglasses and his hair was clipped short. His uniform was full of sharp creases. He was wearing a black gun in a black holster.

He leaned down just a bit as he came up beside the window, and he put his hand on the roof.

"Morning," he said.

"Morning," Jimmy's daddy said.

"May I see your driver's license, please," the trooper said. He looked at Jimmy, but he didn't smile.

"Yes sir," Jimmy's daddy said, and handed it out the window. The trooper leaned a little closer before he took it, and then he leaned back and looked toward the wreck. He looked down at the license and then he dropped his hand, the one that was holding the license. Then he leaned in very close to Jimmy's daddy.

"I think I detect a slight smell of alcohol on your breath, sir," he said. "Have you been drinking this morning?"

"Naw," Jimmy's daddy said. "I ain't drank a drop."

The trooper nodded toward Jimmy.

"Is this your son here, sir?" the trooper said.

"Yeah," Jimmy's daddy said.

"Where y'all headed?" the trooper said, and he turned his attention away from them for a moment to look at the '55. He seemed to be studying it. Then he focused on them again. Jimmy felt like he was in a movie where you couldn't tell what was going to happen next.

"We headed to Ripley," Jimmy's daddy said. "We going to First Monday."

The trooper nodded, and he seemed to be thinking something over. He had a look on his face that said maybe he was about to do something he didn't really want to. He moved his head past Jimmy's daddy and looked in the back floorboard.

"What you got under that blanket back there, sir?" he said. "It looks like it might be a cooler."

"Well yeah it is," Jimmy's daddy said, and Jimmy's daddy was kind of wincing in the bright sunlight of the morning. Jimmy saw how gray and ragged was his father's hair. And how nervous he was.

And then there was that moment of truth.

"What you got in it?" the trooper said.

And even Jimmy could figure out that his daddy wasn't going to be able to lie his way out of this. And his daddy must have known it, too, but it didn't stop him from trying.

"It's just some Cokes and stuff for him," Jimmy's daddy said, nodding toward Jimmy.

"Really? That sure looks like a beer can over there under your son's feet," the trooper said, and Jimmy looked down, horrified to see the Old Milwaukee can that had rolled from under the seat the last time they'd stopped. And when Jimmy looked at his daddy, his daddy's face had turned red. And he turned his face very slowly to Jimmy. The look he gave Jimmy was one he'd given him before. It said plainly: *You little shit.*

"You want to get out of the car and open it up for me?" the trooper said, in a bored way. And that was the end of the first trip to First Monday. Since they were in a dry county. Any hopes of possibly riding a buffalo that day were dashed as well.

44

Cleve fried up some of the deer meat the night before he took Montrel down to the river. He'd had to wake up the guy who owned the meat locker that night, after Mister Cortez had come over, after Cleve had hauled the dead deer out of the pea patch under a tarpaulin, and then he had to give the guy three of the deer for the storage fee and for helping him skin them. Montrel wouldn't get up and help him. Laid up there next to his daughter. The little ones didn't take as long as the big ones, and besides that, it was nice and cool in the cooler they used to hang the deer and skin them.

Some parts had to be thrown away: a shattered shoulder here, white bones pulverized by flattened lead slugs still in there and the meat around the bullet holes bloodshot and not fit to eat, a bullet-riddled hindquarter there. But he wound up with almost two hundred pounds of meat anyway.

The guy who owned the meat locker lived up on Bell River Road and he'd sliced up some of the hindquarters into round steak with his band saw that night while Cleve watched. Then he took some yellow foam trays from a stack of them on his bloody worktable and wrapped the steaks nicely in clear wrap just like you'd get at Kroger except without a price tag. Cleve took eight packs home to stick in the little freezer section of his refrigerator and the meat-locker guy froze the rest of it for him in his walk-in locker. Cleve said he'd be back for some more later and the guy who owned the meat locker said he wished he'd bring a few more of those little ones since they were so tender.

They were gone somewhere again tonight, the two of them, he didn't know where. Somebody had worked on Montrel's car and done something to it, but it was still getting hot sometimes. Maybe they were broke down somewhere. She'd find her way home eventually. He wasn't worried about her. She had her razor in her shoe and she was too damn mean for anybody to mess with her. He was glad to be here almost by himself. He was going to do a little drinking and he was going to do a little cooking and he was happy that it was quiet in the house for a change, just him and the little brown-and-white spotted feist puppy he'd bought. It was sleeping on a ragged rug over by the pantry curtain. The puppy was small like him.

He'd already made his biscuit dough and now he lifted the half pint from the kitchen table and took a fiery sip. Then he picked up an empty quart beer bottle and rolled his dough out nice and smooth. There was a clean tin can sitting there and he cut his biscuits out with that. Perfect circles of dough. They'd rise up fluffy and light, so good you could eat them by themselves. One more thing he'd learned in prison. He cut five and stood there and looked at them. He couldn't eat any more than that, not with deer meat and gravy. Seretha might want some when she came in. He cut three more. He'd leave the rest of the biscuits and the meat on the stove in a plate and the gravy in a bowl, and if she wanted to eat, she could eat. Montrel had already turned his nose up earlier to some good fresh deer meat. Said he preferred *fillay min yon,* whatever the hell that was. Always talking with his mouth full. He'd get a mouthful.

He squatted in the floor with a few scraps of the dough and the puppy woke up and walked over, licking at Cleve's hands. He wasn't as big as a rabbit yet and he was already four months old. Cleve petted him and gave him some of the biscuit dough and then he stood up and washed his hands at the battered sink, then wiped his fingers dry. He unwrapped the thawed deer steak from its package and put the package in the garbage.

He had a cutting board that he used for this and he put the meat on it and carried it to the kitchen table. The steak was dark red, thickly sliced, and he picked up a sharp knife and started trimming the sinew from it, putting each piece aside as he finished with it. Made a small pile of meat. Very lean, almost no fat. This meat was from one of the little ones. He'd be able to cut it on his plate with a fork.

He cut off a few good scraps and threw them to the puppy, who had to be constantly with him. He'd never let a dog sleep with him his entire life, but he was letting this one. He had to. There was just something about him. He called him Peter Rabbit and you could talk to him, tell him what a good squirrel dog he was going to be, how many he was going to tree, and he'd prick up his ears and seem to know what you were saying. He definitely knew his name. And if you didn't let him in the bed with you, he'd scratch and whine at the door all night long and never would shut up. And if you got pissed off because he wouldn't stop scratching and whining, and got up in your drawers and took him out on the back porch and closed the door on him, he'd go up under the house and get directly under the planks the bed was sitting on, and stand under there whining and yapping and jumping up, bumping his little head against the boards, and he wouldn't quit because he knew exactly where you were somehow. He'd do it all night. And keep whining. And the other dogs would growl at him.

Open the door and let him get up in the bed with you and he'd curl up and go right to sleep on top of the covers. Hadn't even peed in the floor one time. Four months old and he'd scratch at the door for you to let him out. Acted like he had all kinds of sense. And loved to ride in the truck. Stand there in your lap and put his head out the window and hold on to the door with his feet. Purebred squirrel dogs like this one brought $150 at Ripley, but he'd gone down to the man's kennel below Banner and had talked him down from $100 to $80. He'd already bought him some heartworm pills, and he'd taken him to town for all his shots. Hit the liquor store while he was up there. Save another trip to town. When you didn't have a driver's license you kind of had to watch it. Whitey would have your black ass back in jail.

He grabbed a short green glass Coke bottle and started pounding the first piece of meat with the small end, a steady banging that made the fly-coated fly strips hanging from the smoked-up ceiling boards sway lightly. The puppy dozed. Cleve stopped and took another drink of whisky and walked over to the pantry, stepped inside the curtain, and came out with a black iron skillet that he set on the stove. He turned on the oven and poured a little Crisco into the skillet, then turned the burner beneath it on medium.

While the skillet was heating he took a few more drinks and kept pounding the deer meat with the Coke bottle. He tenderized both sides of the meat. When he'd finished, the steaks were flattened out, much bigger than they had been, the tissue separated, fragile cutlets now. He dredged them in flour, salted and peppered them, and started laying them in the hot oil. They sizzled lightly along their edges, and bits of flour floated away into the oil and settled on the bottom and started browning. Red juice began to rise from the centers of the steaks where the white flour was dusted with black pepper. He kept putting them in as the ones frying began to contract back to their original shapes. And finally there was no more room in the skillet. They were starting to brown, but they didn't stick. Another thing he knew how to do was season a black iron skillet. But he didn't learn that in prison. His mother had taught him that. Corn bread. Cracklings. Catfish.

He looked at the puppy.

"Hey, little man," he said.

The puppy stretched out on his belly and wagged his stub of a tail and wiped one paw over an eye and then put his head back down on the rug and closed his eyes with a deep and satisfied sigh. *You it,* he seemed to say.

When the oven was ready he greased a blackened baking sheet and put the biscuits on it and shoved them into the oven. Then he sat down in a chair that he pulled from the table and reached for the whisky. He took a sip and held it in his hand. He watched steam rise from the skillet, a wavering wisp in the dim room. He heard the thermostat in the electric oven kick on. Last winter the power had gone out which meant his electric heaters had gone out and he'd had to keep himself and Seretha warm with an old woodstove that he and she had to get back inside the house, just the two of them struggling with the heavy son of a bitch across the iced-over grass and up the back steps and in through the door, and then he had to find the old stovepipes and take out a window and run the pipe through the hole and then nail boards and plywood around it to keep the wind out. He had plenty of wood. Some of it was rotten, but it would still burn. They'd hovered around the stove trying to stay warm for three days while the power crews crept down the icy dirt roads and fixed the lines that had been torn down from the weight of the ice. He and Seretha eating soup from cans they'd open and heat on the stove. Playing Go Fish. That was before she met that son of a bitch. And they'd done all right by themselves for those three days. They had spring water and they had Kool-Aid and instant tea and even hot chocolate in those little packs. Sardines on the shelves and plenty of crackers. Hot sauce. Then he shot a rabbit down by the creek with his .22

and skinned it and cut it up and chopped up some carrots and onions and a few potatoes and poured in some canned tomatoes and put it all in a small cast-iron pot on top of the stove and built the fire up and let it simmer there for five or six hours, and that night when they ate it with some warmed-up and buttered loaf bread Seretha said it was the best thing she'd ever had. Now look where they were. He took another drink. Yankee nigger son of a bitch. Think you gonna come down here and knock up my daughter? In *my* house?

He got up and turned the meat over and put a few paper towels on a clean plate. He stood there at the stove with his whisky and a fork, pushing the meat around in the skillet, checking the biscuits from time to time. When the meat was done he took it out and put it all on the plate with the paper towels and then he picked up the plate that still held some flour and he took the fork and raked some of the flour into the bottom of the skillet. He stood there and worked it into the oil with a circular motion. It started browning a little and he turned up the heat a bit. Not too much. If you burned it, you might as well just throw it out. Now if he had a can of sliced mushrooms to throw in there it would be good. Or a can of mushroom soup. But he didn't have either, so he kept stirring. When he judged it to be nearly right he went to the sink and drew a tall glass of cold water, then went back to the skillet and poured some in. The gravy hissed and rose up in bubbles. He started stirring it hard, working it back down, adding more water a little at a time until it was thick but not too thick. When he had about an inch of smooth brown gravy made and it was gently smoking, he put the meat back into it and lowered the heat. He took the biscuits out. They were brown on top, pale on the sides. He slid them off the baking sheet onto a plate and set them on the kitchen table.

He dipped up a little of the gravy with a spoon and poured it into a cracked saucer and set it down beside the puppy. The puppy woke and stood up and lowered his face to the saucer, and his tongue came out and he started licking it up. Cleve stood there watching him.

"You the man, little man," he said, and then he got another plate from the cupboard and filled it with meat and gravy and biscuits and then dipped gravy all over everything, and sat down at the table to eat. Moths were batting against the lightbulb hanging from a cord in the ceiling.

Out there in the night past the windows, the things of the night called to each other.

He heard them come in after he was already in his bed, the walls dark and the puppy silently sleeping on the covers close enough to where he could put his hand on the slick little hairs of his head. The lights rose up outside the window and he heard the sound of the motor running, and then it died and the lights went off. He lay there. He hadn't wanted to get drunk because he didn't want a hangover in the morning. He could get drunk tomorrow night if he wanted to. Play some. Sit on the porch and listen to her crying. Her belly was swollen just a bit now. Just enough to tell.

He lay there in the blackness of his room and heard them come in through the front door. There was some talking and then he heard them in the kitchen. Seretha came to his door and knocked, but he didn't say anything. She turned the knob and the door opened, but he'd closed his eyes to slits against the slice of dim light from the kitchen.

"Pappy?" she said, but he pretended to be fast asleep. There wasn't any need in talking to her tonight. He should have left when he had the chance.

As soon as he got Montrel down to the river the next morning, he set out the fishing poles and the red worms he'd dug two days before and he got out a cooler of cold beer and a fresh pint of whisky. The good stuff. Canadian Club. Cleve carried the fishing poles and the bait and the whisky, and Montrel carried the cooler. They went down a cut in the bank that people had been using for years to a spot shaded by willows and covered in clean white sand. You could just barely see the spot from the bridge on DeLay Road. Cleve told him to throw his line just out at the curve, that there was a hole there where the catfish stayed in the deeper water. He squatted beside him and twisted the top off his whisky. He drank deeply and then offered the bottle to Montrel. Who took it gladly.

Cleve didn't even unroll his rod and reel. Didn't even make a pretense. He just sat in the sand and watched Montrel fish and drink beer. Sat there and thought about how bad the crying was going to be.

It was awful hot. It was only about ten o'clock. They kept sitting there fishing and drinking. Montrel's line in the water was as unmoving as the bank he sat on. The water in the river was falling. Any dumbass knew they didn't bite that good when it was falling.

He kept passing his whisky bottle to Montrel and encouraging him to drink from it, and Montrel obliged him. He was sitting on the cooler and whenever he needed another beer he just rose up on his legs long enough to get the lid up and got another one and then closed it back and sat down on it again. Threw his cans in the river. Litterbug, too.

Cleve sat there and listened to him talk. He listened to him talk about basic training and he listened to him talk about the blues clubs in Chicago and he listened to him talk about all the women he'd fucked, and the drunker he got the more he talked about how smart he was and how bad he was and how he was going to make a fortune wheeling and dealing. Maybe even rapping, like LL Cool J. Cleve kept offering him the bottle and he kept taking it and finally when Montrel was weaving on the cooler, Cleve told him he had to go back up to the truck for a minute.

Montrel asked him what he needed to go to the truck for, but Cleve didn't answer. He went back up the cut like a goat, pulling himself up the loose dirt banks with his hands sometimes, and he emerged in the high grass along the top of the bank and walked through wildflowers that were fading in the heat and opened the door of his truck and reached under the seat for his pistol. He stuck it in his back pocket and then he turned back toward the river. He stood there on the bank and gazed down on what he was about to do. How it would look from there.

When he got back down to the river, Montrel had quit fishing and was just sitting under a tree with his eyes red. He was holding what was left of the whisky in his hand. Cleve didn't speak to him. He just rolled up the rod and reel and gathered up the bait can and picked up the other rod and reel and took it all back up to the truck. Then he went back down and got the cooler. He carried it over to the bottom of the cut in the bank and then he turned back toward Montrel. Montrel was sitting there looking at him, weaving. He looked like he was trying to figure out what was going on. And he didn't really understand until Cleve pulled the pistol from his back pocket and walked over to stand in front of him, looking down on him, and whatever Montrel saw in that sweat-shiny black face must have been the worst thing ever, because he started to scream just before Cleve shot him in the mouth. And again. And again. And again.

The smoke from the pistol drifted out over the river in a little cloud that soon was gone. And there was nothing to hear but the water moving against the bank, going slowly on its way down to the mouth of Enid. He, too, remembered when the white men from town had killed all the fish. Assholes.

He dragged Montrel up under a stand of river birches and kicked some leaves and sand over him. He drank the rest of the whisky and pitched the bottle into the river and left him there. He took the cooler back up to the truck and then he drove home. Seretha was asleep. That was good.

45

The September weeds were hot and dusty where Jimmy's daddy sat on an upturned five-gallon bucket, holding his shotgun and trying to hide behind a few browned cornstalks. The bucket had a padded plastic camo seat. He'd gone out to Wal-Mart one afternoon after work and had gotten a few things for today, the opening day of dove season. He'd bought a camo game vest with shell loops, and a folding camo stool he hadn't used yet. Plenty of bird shot, number 8s. But he wasn't getting to use the shells much. He'd only shot at three birds so far and he hadn't hit any of them.

He could hear Rusty and Seaborn shooting across the field fairly often and then yelling at each other. The guy who owned the field had Bush Hogged down some long strips through the corn so that there were shooting lanes, and it sounded like Rusty and Seaborn had the better spots. He didn't know why they'd stuck him over here by this fence. And the parked pickups. Hell, a bird probably wasn't going to fly over a damn pickup.

It was hard to concentrate on hunting when so many other things were on his mind, but he was doing his best. He didn't even know the man who owned this piece of land, but Seaborn did. It was a baited field, with a couple of hundred pounds of shelled corn scattered over the just-disked land, and it wasn't legal, was actually illegal as hell, but Seaborn had told him that if the game wardens came down and checked it, they could just run off into the woods and hide for a while and let Rusty pay the ticket since they were riding with him. It had taken Jimmy's daddy two days to get his '55 back from the Union County Sheriff's Office, and now it was sitting at home with an unexpected flat he hadn't wanted to change this morning.

Damn it was hot. It was probably just as well that he hadn't brought Jimmy. By now he would have probably been fidgeting and wanting to ask questions and getting on his nerves. Maybe next year he could take him. Buy him a gun. That little .410. Maybe they'd find one at the Gun and Knife Show in November. If they got to go. If he was still married in November. And could even see Jimmy.

Out across the field two doves winged over the broken cornstalks, and shotguns barked at them. One flew on and one tumbled, wings shattered and feathers trailing, in an almost graceful arc to the ground. He heard Rusty yell something at Seaborn. He wished he was over there with them. They were sitting right in the middle of where the corn hadn't been cut down, and they were much better camouflaged by it. On the other hand, Jimmy's daddy had a better view of the whole field where he was. And he had all the beer. Both coolers were sitting next to him. He was having his fourth or fifth, he didn't know which. He'd had to temporarily abandon his drinking-less-beer idea for a while because there was too much going on. Too much he had to deal with. Like the trouble with the cop at the wreck. It had been pretty embarrassing, having to call Johnette on her cell phone from the jail in New Albany and tell her to come get him and Jimmy at the jail because they'd temporarily impounded his car. It had also been pretty embarrassing for Jimmy's daddy to have to see Jimmy riding in the back of a patrol car for the trip over to the jail, even though Jimmy had seemed to enjoy it a pretty good bit. The trooper who'd arrested him hadn't been real nice to Jimmy's daddy, but he'd treated Jimmy kindly, let him play with his gun after he'd unloaded it, even let him up into the front seat and let him run the siren on a deserted stretch of road on the way to jail.

Jimmy's daddy had to be in court over there on October 15. That was a weekday and he'd have to take off from work. Collums would want to know why he was taking off. The plant manager would want to know why he was taking off. The trooper had told him that the fine for having beer in a dry county was probably going to be about two hundred dollars. And he'd had to listen to Johnette bitch about it all the way home. With Jimmy sitting in the backseat just listening. And finally just lying down out of sight on the backseat. That had been a bad day. [. . .]

The sun was bright and it was hot. Damn birds weren't going to fly in the middle of the day like this. And the sons of bitches were so hard to hit if they did fly. This time last year he'd sat in a field and fired seventy-nine times and didn't bring down a bird. That was three boxes of shells. He had decided there was something wrong with his gun and had traded it off for this one, and it wasn't doing any better. He didn't know what was wrong. Maybe he needed to get one of those clay-pigeon shooting rigs and practice up some with that. But a clay pigeon didn't swerve and twist in flight the way a mourning dove did. So what good would it do to shoot at some of them?

[. . .]

He had plenty of cigarettes for a change. He wasn't going to run out of them. He stuck one in his mouth and pulled out his lighter and realized it was the same one Lacey had given him, and that it was still working somehow. He lit his smoke and put the lighter back in his pocket. He didn't know what in the hell to do about her. He was scared and he was sick and he was worried. But he damn sure couldn't sit around the trailer. No way. It was like being in jail. At least out here you had sunshine and air and nature. You weren't cooped up the way you were five days a week inside a concrete box.

He had replayed it over and over in his mind like one of his hunting videos that he could rewind or fast forward with his remote. Lacey coming up to him, right there in the break room, in front of everybody, and telling him she had to talk to him before lunch break was over. There was a look on her face. It was part happiness, part pride, part worry. And he'd known what it was before they'd even stepped outside to sit down in his car for a few minutes so that she could tell him her news. She was pregnant. And it was his since she hadn't been with anybody besides him in three months.

Sitting there on the hot seat with her, knowing the time was ticking away on lunch break, and having to come up with an answer about what they were going to do. Not that she was so worried about that just yet. She mainly wanted him to know that he was going to be a father. Jimmy's daddy had told her that he didn't want to be a father again. And that was where he'd messed up. He hadn't been prepared to see her bury her face in her hands and start crying. And talking to her did no good. She just kept on. A few people walked by and saw them. Nosy sons of bitches. And it had gone on and on. Until almost time for the buzzer that always called them back to work. He hadn't even gotten to finish eating. And her with her face red from crying, and him following her, people leaving the break room and going back into the factory looking out at them, wondering what was going on. A plant romance where everybody knew. The last thing he'd wanted.

Hell. There weren't but two choices, were there? Either have it or not have it. Either have it or have an abortion. He couldn't tell Johnette. And how could he have a kid that would be running around in Water Valley one day? A kid who would be Jimmy's half brother.

If he just hadn't gone down there that first time, he wouldn't be in this mess now. And he'd only gone down to see her three times altogether. He'd used rubbers both other times. But the one that had stuck was the first time. That was five or six weeks ago now. She hadn't been to the doctor to get it confirmed yet, but she'd gotten a pregnancy test from Wal-mart and had tried it three times, and three times it had turned blue. She'd said there was no doubt about it, she was knocked up.

He sat there and sipped his beer and wondered what he was going to do. Get divorced from Johnette and marry Lacey? Hell no. He was already tired of her, of her wanting to be with him all the time, and wanting to eat with him at work, and he was tired of the hurt glances she gave him when he wouldn't just fall all over himself to acknowledge her at the Coke machine or in one of the aisles while he was working. Get divorced and stay divorced? Maybe. He wished he had somebody to talk to about it. He'd thought about telling Seaborn and Rusty, but neither one of them had ever had any experience dealing with something like this, and their first reaction would probably be to make some joke. It was no joke and he didn't want to hear any jokes about it. He believed she meant to have it. [. . .]

So what did that leave? That didn't leave but one thing. Talk her into getting rid of it and take her to Memphis. Find one of those abortion clinics. He couldn't take care of another kid. He could barely take care of the ones he had. And only one of them was his. And Evelyn. The little whore. Sucking off boys on the school bus. He wondered what kind of white trash her daddy had been. Or what kind Johnette was.

He wondered what Jimmy was doing at home. Hell. He should have brought him. Kids his age didn't have to have a hunting license. He could have iced him down some Cokes and sat him down beside him on the folding camo stool he hadn't used yet. He could have talked to Jimmy instead of sitting here worrying over what he was going to do about Lacey. But he couldn't stop thinking about it. In a few months she'd be showing. If she kept going to work, everybody at work would know it. And he knew how people talked. It wouldn't be any secret. The word would get out that it was his baby she was going to have. And then what was he going to do? What if she did have it? Was he going to show up at the hospital and wait around in the waiting room like a dork? Would there be a baby birth announcement in the paper? What was it going to say? Hell.

[. . .]

He heard a flurry of shots across the way, and he saw a dove fall. Somewhere over there close to Rusty and Seaborn. And then he saw Rusty coming across the field with his gun in one hand and three or four dead birds in another. He probably wanted some beer. But he was going to scare all the birds off coming across the field in the wide open like that. He wasn't even crouching. He was just walking.

Jimmy's daddy sat there and waited for him. He wondered if he could tell him. Maybe ask Rusty for some advice, even if he'd never had to deal with anything like this before. He needed to talk to somebody. He'd even thought about going and talking to his daddy. He hadn't talked to him in about six months.

Rusty was grinning when he walked up, wearing his shooter's glasses and carrying a nice 12-gauge Beretta semiauto. About an eight-hundred-dollar gun. All Jimmy's daddy could afford was this Mossberg pump. But it was still a damn good gun. He just needed to learn how to shoot it. Or maybe he needed to get a double barrel.

"Hot damn," Rusty said as he sat down beside him. "Open that cooler and give me one of them cold beers."

Jimmy's daddy raised the lid on the cooler and got him one out and Rusty took off his game vest and started stuffing the dead birds into it. He looked up.

"You killed anything?" he said, and took the beer Jimmy's daddy handed him.

"Nothing but some time," Jimmy's daddy said. "Y'all sound like y'all tearing their ass up over there."

Rusty popped the top on the can and stretched his lanky frame out on the ground and propped his head up with one hand and sipped from the beer.

"I think we got fourteen or fifteen," he said.

"I ain't killed shit," Jimmy's daddy said. He sat there and sipped his own beer. It was starting to get warm and Jimmy's daddy wished he'd remembered to bring one of his little foam Koozies. But they were all in the trunk of the '55 or inside the trailer.

"How many times you shot?" Rusty said. He sat up and crossed his legs and lit a cigarette.

"Five," Jimmy's daddy said. "I had one coming straight at me and missed him head on and then he turned and I must not have led him enough."

"You got to lead em about three foot," Rusty said. Then he looked out across the field. "How come you didn't bring Jimmy?"

"I don't know," Jimmy's daddy said. "He ain't got no gun."

"Well shitfire, I can get him a gun. I got a four ten I ain't used in twenty years in my closet. You oughta said something. He don't even need a license at his age. We could a got him some shells."

"I know it," Jimmy's daddy said, and he decided he'd just go ahead and bring up his problem to Rusty while he was here. While it was just the two of them sitting here in the dove field.

"All right," Rusty said, and he stood up. "Let me have a few more of them beers and I'll take a couple to Seaborn. He's about to go nuts over there without one."

So Jimmy's daddy just opened the cooler for him so he could reach in and stick four beers in his game vest next to the dead birds. Then he walked back across the field. And disappeared into the corn.

After just a few minutes, the shooting started up again. It sounded like they were having a really good time.

It was already dark when Jimmy's daddy got in. Johnette and the girls were gone to a skating party at Skateland in town and Jimmy was watching TV in the living room by himself in his pajama bottoms.

"Hey Daddy," he said.

"Hey Little Buddy," he said. He'd been trying to use more terms of endearment with Jimmy lately. He'd always used Hot Rod but now he'd added Little Buddy. Sometimes Sport. He hadn't whipped Jimmy for letting the beer can roll out from under his seat, which was partly what caused him to get gagged by the Union County cops, and he thought he'd shown pretty good restraint there. He could have blown up once they got back home, but he didn't. Maybe he was improving.

He carried his gun to the closet and put it away. He dumped his shell vest and his shells and then he had to go back outside for his folding stool and he dumped it in there, too. Then he sat down on the couch beside Jimmy and took off his cap. He opened a beer he'd brought in.

"Is your mama still at Skateland?" he said. Her car was gone. The '55 was sitting out there, but if he wanted to ride around in it any tonight, he'd have to get out there and change that flat with a flashlight. He didn't know if he wanted to do that or not.

"I don't know," Jimmy said.

"I thought she took the girls to Skateland," Jimmy's daddy said.

"She did," Jimmy said.

"Well, I guess she's still at Skateland then," Jimmy's daddy said. He put his feet up on the coffee table.

"That's a lock-in," Jimmy said.

"What's a lock-in?"

"The skating party," Jimmy said. "It goes on all night and they lock em in. They can't get out."

Jimmy was watching a show about bears, but he suddenly switched it over to one about lions. A whole pride was killing a baby elephant. It was horrible. Jimmy's daddy didn't know what Jimmy was talking about.

"What do you mean they can't get out?"

"It's a all-night skating party, Daddy. You can have one for your birthday. Invite all your friends over and skate all night long."

"All night long?" Jimmy's daddy said.

"All night long," Jimmy said.

Oh yeah? Well well. He sure didn't know you could do that. It sounded more like all-night babysitting. Right up Johnette's alley.

"You want to do me a favor, there, Sport?"

"Sure, Daddy," Jimmy said.

"Flip it over there on CMT and see if old Jeff Foxworthy's on. I like the shit out of him."

"Okay," Jimmy said, and started running through the channels on the remote looking for CMT.

"Well, why do you think your mama's not still at Skateland?" Jimmy's daddy said.

"Cause. She was going to a movie after she dropped the girls off."

Hmm. What damn time was it? Jimmy's daddy looked at his watch. It was only nine. Lacey would still be up.

"Oh yeah? And the skating party goes on all night?"

"Yes sir," Jimmy said. He had it on CMT, but they were showing a Shania Twain video where she was dressed like a leopard.

Then where in the hell was she going to be for the rest of the night? Jimmy's daddy wondered. A movie only took two hours. Maybe two and a half if you got there real early and got you some popcorn and a big fountain Coke and then watched all the credits at the end of it and kept sitting there until they turned the lights on.

"What time was she going to the movie?"

"I don't know, Daddy."

"You know what she was gonna see?"

"No sir. She didn't say."

"I got you."

He sat there and drank some more beer and told Jimmy to just watch whatever he wanted to, and Jimmy told him thanks and switched it over to *Wild on E!* and they watched that for a while. It was mostly about a bunch of young people getting drunk down in Mexico from people pouring liquor down their throats at some beach resort and girls grinding and dancing in skimpy swimming suits. Then they ran a commercial for *Girls Gone Wild*. Jimmy's daddy kind of perked up when that came on. He sat there next to Jimmy and watched college girls with their chests censored out flashing their boobs at various locations around the country. It showed a couple of them kissing each other. Some naked and squealing in a shower.

"Gross," Jimmy said, and changed the channel. Jimmy's daddy started to tell him to turn it back but thought better of it. He sipped his beer and lit a cigarette. He was about to get in another hunting funk from not having killed anything again. He'd imagined a nice dove fry at home tonight, plucking the birds he'd shot from the sky in the gravel behind the trailer, pulling off their heads, cutting off their feet, heating some oil in a skillet and washing the birds at the kitchen sink and then rolling them in some flour and frying them up. Nice and crisp. Jimmy could have had a few. But he hadn't killed a goddamn one. And had only gotten to shoot his gun seven times. Seaborn and Rusty had shot over four boxes of shells apiece. The doves had started flying pretty steadily later on in the evening, and he'd swapped places with Seaborn and Rusty, at his suggestion, and then all the birds had started flying directly over them, in the place where he *had* been sitting, and should have stayed, and Rusty and Seaborn had wound up with fifty-three birds between them, and they'd offered Jimmy's daddy some of them, and he'd thought about taking them and telling Jimmy that he'd killed four or five of them, but by then, just at dark, standing in the field, almost out of beer, he'd decided he didn't want to mess with cleaning a bunch of damn dead birds and would just make a sandwich probably. And had asked them to just run him to town so he could get some more beer before he ran out. Which they had. And then dropped him off at home. Where he was now. Sitting in the goddamn living room watching TV with Jimmy. Big night. Hell of a lot of fun. Barrel of laughs.

"What we got to eat?" he asked Jimmy.

"Hot dogs," Jimmy said. He was surfing the channels.

Hot dogs. Fucking hot dogs. He was sick of hot dogs. Could she not buy anything else to eat? How about some sliced ham and salami? What about some cheese around this place once in a while? Had she ever heard of that? Of cheese? You couldn't find a bag of potato chips around here that hadn't been already opened and about half of them eaten and then the rest of the bag just rolled up instead of having a Chip-Clip put on it, and there were plenty of Chip-Clips right there in a drawer. He didn't know why these damn kids couldn't use them and help keep the rest of the potato chips halfway fresh for the next person who might want some potato chips with a sandwich if you could find anything around here to make one out of.

"We ain't got any frozen pizza?" Jimmy's daddy said.

"I think the girls ate all it."

Jimmy's daddy leaned forward and pulled the ashtray closer to him and thumped some ashes in it. Well fuck. Would it be worth going out there and jacking up the car and changing the flat by flashlight to be able to ride up to Oxford and maybe get something to eat from the Sonic? But then he wouldn't have a spare. What he needed was two spares. He had room back there in the trunk. He could keep an extra one that way and not have to worry about it. If he put the good tire on the ground tonight and rode up toward town and then had another flat he'd be fucked. He'd be stuck on the side of the road is what he'd be. There wasn't much that Jimmy's daddy hated more than being stuck on the side of the road. Especially at night. Nobody was going to stop and help you. You'd have to walk to somebody's house and hope they didn't have a biting dog and knock on the door and get somebody to come to the door and ask them if you could use their phone. And if he did change it, and did head toward town, and did have another flat, and had to walk to somebody's house to call somebody, who in the hell would he call? Jimmy? Here? What good could he do? Rusty? Hell no. He was going out to Applebee's to eat. Hell, if he went to town, Jimmy'd probably want to go with him if he went to the Sonic. Shit. He'd bet Jimmy could jack that car up, if he told him how to do it. He'd had it in the back of his mind all day to try and sneak off and ride down to Water Valley tonight to talk to Lacey and see how she was doing, but in another way that he didn't deny, he didn't want to have to deal with it. He was *going* to have to deal with it, no fucking doubt, just when was the question.

"What'd you eat?" he said.

"Hot dogs," Jimmy said.

[. . .]

"We ain't got nothing to make a sandwich out of?" he said.

"I think Mama eat all that," Jimmy said.

"I wonder what she expects us to eat," Jimmy's daddy said.

"Hot dogs, I guess," Jimmy said.

Fat bitch. No damn telling where she was. Or what she was doing. If her daughter was sucking off boys on the school bus, her daughter might be sucking some off at the skating rink. She ought not to go to a damn movie and just leave her kids in there like that. Oh, he knew they had grown people working there who were supposed to watch them, sure, but how did they know what went on in the bathrooms? Kids were sneaky. You had to watch them all the time. And he damn sure didn't want to tell Johnette about what Jimmy had told him, but he couldn't see how he could ignore it either. The next thing would be fucking. If she wasn't already. Hell. If her daddy was a Corvette thief. What kind of genes was that?

[. . .] He heated some water in a pan on the stove. He dropped a couple of hot dogs in there and stuck some of his beer in the icebox. And then he remembered that he had a can of that stuff you use to inflate a flat tire in the shed. What? Stop Leak? Something.

After he ate, he got Jimmy to help him with the flat. It didn't take long, the two of them. He iced down some beer and told Jimmy he'd be back later. And then he left him standing there watching him leave.

And then he stopped and backed up and told him to get in.

46

Jimmy's daddy told Jimmy where they were going and then drove him through the night, up an old dirt road that Jimmy dimly remembered, down close to Potlockney. It wound through the woods, and the gravel on the road jumped up and hit the bottom of the car, and there were tall pines along the road. Not many houses. There were deer that ran into the woods. They saw a fox and two coons. They saw a possum eating an armadillo. There were gates here and there with POSTED signs hung on them and Jimmy asked his daddy what those places were. His daddy told him they were private hunting clubs. You paid a membership to join. One sign said NUB's CLUB and Jimmy wondered who Nub was. Jimmy asked his daddy why didn't he join a private hunting club and Jimmy's daddy said he couldn't afford it. So Jimmy wondered how much that cost. His tooth was starting to hurt a little worse, but he didn't want to say anything about it because he was afraid they'd send him straight to the dentist for a root canal. Might even take him out of school for it.

The road went around curves and it climbed hills and sometimes they'd pass a place where all the trees had been cut and there was a vast wide-open darkness out there beyond the edge of the road. In these spots there could be seen a tall tower way off in the distance where three red lights blinked. Jimmy didn't ask what it was. He was consciously trying to avoid asking too many questions because he knew that got on his daddy's nerves and he didn't want to do that. Not tonight since it was just the two of them, going somewhere again. He hated the last trip had turned out the way it had. It had actually been kind of fun going to jail, though.

Once they met some people on four-wheelers, a string of them with small headlights set close together, and Jimmy's daddy moved the car over to the side of the road and slowed down as he met them. There was a cloud of dust following the line of four-wheelers and Jimmy's daddy rolled his window up as he met them. When the four-wheelers had gone past he rolled the window back down. Jimmy wondered how much a four-wheeler cost. One of those would probably be a lot better than a go-kart. He'd bet the chain wouldn't come off a four-wheeler.

They kept driving. There were brown birds that sat in the road and waited until the car was almost on top of them before they flew up and flared away. Jimmy asked his daddy what those birds were and his daddy said they were whippoorwills. He said when they called at night they said, *Chip off the white oak.* So that's what those were behind the trailer. [. . .]

They drove for a long time without seeing a house. There was nothing but the black woods around them, and more gates with the signs on them. Once they met a big jacked-up pickup with lights and chrome all over it and Jimmy's daddy said something about little bastards running up and down the road. Jimmy could see the stars out the window, little dots sprinkled across the black sky. He didn't tell his daddy this, but he couldn't wait to get a big jacked-up pickup and run up and down the road. He had already made up his mind that when he got grown and out of school he was going to work in the stove factory where his daddy worked, save his money, and buy a big jacked-up pickup. He had it all planned. He could ride with his daddy to work while he was saving his money, and then after he got his pickup he could give his daddy a ride to work and back home. Swap off every other week or something. He'd get some Merle CDs for his daddy to listen to. Keep him some cold beer in a cooler in the back.

They rode and rode. The can of Stop Leak was riding on the seat between them. The '55's dash rattled some on the gravel road, but Jimmy's daddy compensated for that by turning up the volume on the radio. They listened to solid country gold for a while and then the station ran some more commercials. One of the commercials was a guy selling mobile homes. Jimmy's daddy turned the volume down.

"You hear that guy?" he said.

"Yes sir," Jimmy said.

"Hear him trying to sell people trailers?"

"Sounds like they got that easy payment plan," Jimmy said.

"I guarantee you that guy don't live in no trailer," Jimmy's daddy said. He took a drink of his beer and lit a cigarette.

"He don't?" Jimmy said.

"Why, hell naw," Jimmy's daddy said. "The son of a bitch probably lives in a brick house from all the money he's made selling trailers."

"Oh," Jimmy said. His daddy turned the radio back up since the commercial was off. Then they played some more solid country gold.

After a while, Jimmy's daddy flipped his cigarette out the window and turned off where a rusty mailbox was sitting on a post and onto a side road where there were some light poles planted with wires running overhead. This road didn't have gravel on it. It was kind of spooky looking and dark and bumpy and covered with dead leaves and sticks, narrow in places. They squeezed between banks of eroded red clay and once Jimmy's daddy had to stop the car and get out and move a big limb out of the way. Then they drove until they came to a clearing in the woods where an old camper trailer sat almost engulfed by piles of aluminum cans.

There was just one little light burning inside it when they pulled up and stopped. Jimmy's daddy killed the headlights and shut off the car and turned his head to Jimmy, who was sitting kind of close to the door.

"Old fart may not even be up," he said. He sipped from his beer.

Jimmy just sat there. He had run back inside for a moment to grab a T-shirt and his house shoes, too, since it was starting to get a little cooler at night. [. . .]

"Why don't you go knock on the door?" Jimmy said.

"He knows we out here," Jimmy's daddy said.

"How's he know who it is, though?" Jimmy said.

"He knows who it is," Jimmy's daddy said.

That seemed kind of mysterious, so Jimmy just sat there, looking at the place where supposedly his grandfather lived. Unlike the trailer Jimmy lived in, this one still had the wheels on it. It was a faded blue with a striped awning hanging over the front door, and there was a tank of something hooked to it. Jimmy guessed that was cooking gas. There were some electric lines hooked to it, too, coming off a pole that sat beside it. Some old furniture was lying around in front of it. Some fishing poles were leaned up against it. Jimmy hadn't known that his grandfather fished, but he hadn't met his grandfather very many times. He thought he'd only met him about twice. And about all he remembered about him was that he smelled bad and cussed a lot and sometimes got to coughing so hard from all the cigarettes he smoked that he'd bend over and get to going *Bleah heah heah heah heah!* with his red and fuzzy tongue hanging out about six inches. Then he'd light another one and cuss.

They sat there some more. Crickets were chirping all around them. Some of them had gotten inside the car. There was some kind of flickering light going on inside the trailer. Jimmy figured that was the television. He looked at his daddy. His daddy was just sitting there sipping his beer. Jimmy looked back at the trailer. It had rusted holes in it and there was an old-timey TV antenna sticking up from the roof.

Jimmy wondered if now would be a good time to tell his daddy about talking to the man who was driving the big red truck that had TOMMY'S BIG RED FISH TRUCK painted on the doors that day. Getting picked up by the cops had messed it up the time before, when he'd been thinking about telling him. There was one thing for sure he didn't want to tell him and that was about using his binoculars over the last few days to try and see if the mean old man had put some catfish in his pond. Jimmy had found the binoculars while crawling around under his mother and daddy's bed one afternoon before either one of them was home, looking for some change. He knew that whenever his mother moved a bed to clean, there was always money under it. And he'd thought that maybe if he could scrape up a little change here and there, and save it, and maybe get a little more, here and there, then maybe he could eventually buy a new chain for his go-kart. He didn't know how much one cost. He just knew he needed one. And while he was crawling and looking for some change, he found his daddy's binoculars. In a nice leather-looking case with the word BUSHNELL printed on it. With a long black strap you could hang around your neck. Even Jimmy could tell that they cost more money than a bunch of old rusty tools in an old rusty toolbox. That meant they were probably more hazardous to mess with than his daddy's tools. Which had turned out to be pretty hazardous. So he had been wary about opening the case and looking through the binoculars at something. But it wasn't like he could really stop himself either.

He looked at his daddy. His daddy was still drinking beer.

"Too damn good to come out and speak," Jimmy's daddy said.

Jimmy didn't say anything, still sticking to his not-asking-Daddy-too-many-questions plan. He'd taken the binoculars that afternoon and looked through the window at some trees and bushes, and it was amazing how close the glasses brought them up. They made everything bigger and clearer. It was a risk, true, but Jimmy remembered his daddy asking his mother one morning when he came back from hunting if she'd seen his binoculars, and they'd probably been lying under their bed the whole time. And if they had, that probably meant that Jimmy's daddy still didn't know where they were. It was a risk, yeah, messing with something that belonged to his daddy, but Jimmy took the binoculars outside just before it got dark and went up the road and got off into the woods and walked there, instead of out in the road, up toward the mean old man's place, which wasn't any trouble, because the woods were filled with big tall trees and there weren't many bushes growing in between them, and the walking was pretty good. He stopped when he got in front of the pond. He took the binoculars from the case and glassed the pond. There wasn't anybody there. He swung the glasses left and looked down toward the old man's house, but it was hard to see it for all the trees. He could see part of the driveway. He could see the barn. He could see some of the pasture, but it was getting darker fast.

"Unsociable old fart," Jimmy's daddy said.

"I wish I had a Coke," Jimmy said.

"Why didn't you bring one from home?" Jimmy's daddy said.

"I didn't think about it," Jimmy said.

"Well, see, you need to plan ahead," Jimmy's daddy said. "That's what I try to do. Plan ahead. I knew I'd want some beer so I brought some. How about handing me another one out of that new cooler I bought back there?"

Jimmy moved the blanket off the cooler and got the beer for him and Jimmy's daddy tossed the empty one out toward the tiny trailer. It bounced off the front door onto a pile of cans. Jimmy thought for sure that would bring his grandfather out if he was really in there, but it didn't.

"Probably passed out," Jimmy's daddy said. "We gonna set here ten more minutes and if he don't come out, we leaving."

"Where we going then?" Jimmy said.

"You going back home," Jimmy's daddy said.

It took some guts for Jimmy to ask his daddy the next question, but he did anyway:

"Where *you* going?"

"Don't you worry none about where I'm going," Jimmy's daddy said. "I'm going to town to get this flat fixed. So I'll have a spare. I got to have a spare before I go back to work Monday."

"Oh," Jimmy said. He waited a few moments.

"Can I go?"

Jimmy's daddy turned his head to look at him. He had slumped back in the seat and he had his beer can sitting on his belly.

"What you want to go for?" he said.

Jimmy spoke the truth.

"Just to be with you," he said.

Jimmy's daddy didn't answer at first. But he turned his face back toward the windshield. Jimmy could tell that his daddy was getting drunk. He'd seen this transformation before. His daddy slowed down. He talked slower, he moved slower, he thought longer before he spoke. He was doing that now, thinking long. He thought so long that Jimmy thought he wasn't going to answer him. And then he did. In a low, husky voice. A very quiet voice that came deep from somewhere inside him and didn't sound like him at all.

"Look," he said. "A man's got stuff he's got to do. I mean, I might want to go up to a bar and have a beer or something. And I can't take you in there cause you ain't old enough. You'd have to just set in the car and wait on me."

"I wouldn't care," Jimmy said.

"But *I* would," Jimmy's daddy said. "*I* would."

Jimmy just nodded. He decided he wouldn't tell his daddy right now about the man who'd been driving the big red fish truck. Or of how he'd sat there in the darkening woods for a while the day he'd found the binoculars, motionless, hidden behind green leaves, watching across the road through the binoculars, not moving very much, even when the mosquitoes whined close to him. He even let some of them bite him. He figured that's what you had to do when you were hunting and were supposed to be still. So he was still. He kept the glasses close to his eyes and swept the length of the pond with them, examining the dark still water, and then something making ripples along one of the banks. He couldn't tell what it was. Frog? Snake? Snapping turtle? Whatever it was didn't ripple long. The water stilled. Jimmy kept watching the spot and didn't move the glasses. Then he saw another ripple. And then he heard something coming and swung the glasses to the left and saw a very big headlight moving toward him and took the glasses down long enough to take a look and see the mean old man coming up his driveway. Jimmy almost got up and ran, but then he remembered how still the hunters in his daddy's hunting videos stayed when they were up in a tree and not talking to the cameraman, so he just stayed still. He wasn't on the old man's land anyway. He was on some land across the road. And his daddy had already told him that somebody in Memphis owned that piece of land. So Jimmy just stayed where he was. He sat very still with his heart pounding as the old man stopped at the end of his driveway, and then pulled out, headed toward where Jimmy was sitting. The truck passed on the dirt road, screened by the green leaves in the woods. Then it turned down onto the new road that Jimmy had already noticed riding by it on the school bus. He put the glasses back up to his eyes and everything was blurry, even though he could tell he was looking at the pickup's tailgate. He focused the glasses with his thumb and then he read the license plate. At the bottom it said MISSISSIPPI. Jimmy adjusted the glasses as the truck pulled down into the woods, and he saw the old man get out and slam the door of the truck about a second before he heard it. Jimmy kept the glasses on him as he walked over to a tree and took the lid off a steel garbage can. The glasses were so good that he could see the old man scooping up with a quart fruit jar something that looked kind of like dog food, only smaller. And then he walked over to the edge of the pond and started throwing it out over the water. Turning the jar up and pouring it into his hand and then flinging it. It flew out into the air and sprinkled on top of the water like raindrops. Then the old man sat on the ground. Nothing happened for a long time and Jimmy sat there in the woods and watched the old man. He just kept the glasses on him and looked at him. The old man's face was turned to one side as if he were listening for something. Jimmy felt some sort of strange feeling from watching him and knowing the old man didn't know it.

What was that stuff in the garbage can and what was he doing with it? And why was he just sitting there? Was he sick? Jimmy's mama had told him that the old man's wife had died a while back. And the day she'd told him, they'd driven by the cemetery, and had seen a blue tent set up, and Jimmy had asked his mama what that tent was for, and she'd said it was for Mr. Sharp's wife. Jimmy knew he was looking at Mr. Sharp. And that Mr. Sharp was probably pretty sad, missing his dead wife. He didn't look that mean from here, where you could take your time and get a good look at him. He was big. He had gray hair, but he had a lot of it. His hands looked strong. The main thing Jimmy remembered was him yelling *Get the hell off my place!* at him. It was almost too dark to see.

Jimmy glanced at his daddy. He was just sitting there, looking at the trailer. Jimmy didn't know why he didn't want to go knock on the door. And he didn't know why his daddy didn't go see his daddy a little more often. Jimmy's daddy's daddy had never been over to their trailer. And Jimmy's daddy rarely mentioned his daddy. So that caused Jimmy to wonder what was going on between the two of them. And why his daddy's daddy lived off in the woods like this by himself. There was no vehicle parked here. How did he get in and out when he needed some groceries? What if he needed some kind of health care? He bet Jehovah's Witnesses never came up in here knocking on the door. Shoot. What did he do about Christmas? And how much were all these aluminum cans worth?

They kept sitting there. Once Jimmy thought he saw something move inside the trailer, just a shadow on the shade for a moment, but nobody pulled the shade aside and looked out. Jimmy wondered if ten minutes had passed yet. It felt like it had. Then he heard a gentle snoring and looked over at his daddy, who was asleep.

"Daddy?" Jimmy said. Jimmy's daddy didn't say anything. He just kept snoring. His cap was down over his eyes. His beer was almost tilting in his hand and Jimmy reached over and took it out of his hand before he spilled it in his sleep. He held the beer on his lap.

"Daddy?" he said again. There was no answer. And he didn't know if he should wake his daddy or not. Maybe he was tired from working so hard at the stove factory. Maybe he needed some rest.

Jimmy looked at the black woods around them. They were pretty black. He leaned his face out the window and looked up at the stars. They seemed to be fading. He pulled his face back in and looked at his daddy, who had slumped against the door now and was starting to cut some pretty good Zs. Jimmy set the beer in the floor between his feet. The air coming in his window was kind of cool, so he rolled up the window and sat there. The wind coming in through his daddy's window was kind of cool, too, but Jimmy couldn't do anything about that since his daddy was slumped against the door where the window crank was located. So he reached over the front seat and pulled the blanket off the cooler and put it over him, being careful not to turn over his daddy's beer. Then he reached down and picked it up and set it on the dash in front of his daddy. Then he stretched out on the seat with his feet up against his daddy's leg and lay there. He pushed the can of Stop Leak aside with his foot. He wasn't very sleepy, but he didn't want to sit there and look at the trailer anymore. He thought he'd just close his eyes and stay warm under the blanket and let his daddy sleep. Let him get some rest. He worked so hard for them.

When Jimmy woke up again, he was in his bed and it was Sunday morning and he had no idea how he'd gotten there. The last thing he remembered was stretching out on the seat beside his daddy and closing his eyes. So he closed his eyes again. He could hear Velma saying something and his mama saying something back to her. Then the TV came on and he didn't hear anybody else talking. He wished they had some Aunt Jemima syrup and some pancake mix so he could have some when he got up. Like in the restaurant that day his daddy tried to take him to First Monday. He hated they didn't get to see everything his daddy had told him about. His daddy had promised him he'd take him again. And Jimmy sure hoped that would turn out to be true. And maybe one day they could go fishing, too. Maybe that would turn out better than the swimming trip and the First Monday trip. He hoped so.

His tooth was hurting but he wasn't going to say anything about it. He wondered how much the dentist cost. Probably more than a chain for a go-kart.

47

It was hard to see the fish come up for their feed at night, but Cortez was trying to be patient. He remembered the fish man telling him that it took two weeks to train them to come up to eat, and it hadn't even been a week yet. But he was enjoying feeding them. He was looking forward to the time when he could see all three thousand of them trying to eat at the same time. No telling what that was going to look like. They'd probably churn the water all to hell. He hoped so.

[. . .] He was getting ready to put the Bush Hog on the 4020 and go up there and mow down that grass that had sprouted up around the pond. He didn't think it was too muddy. There was one slope on the side that was kind of steep, but he didn't think it would be any problem. He'd put his safety belt on. He always did. [. . .] It was still pretty hot out there even though it was September, and he knew if he'd wait until a little later on in the afternoon, it would be cooler. So he took his brogans off and turned the TV off and lay down on the daybed and got a pillow and put it under his head and closed his eyes and sighed. Lots of times when he took naps he thought about Queen. He ran images through his head that he'd retained in his brain. They were kind of like movies in that the same things happened over and over. The same words were said. The same things happened. She said this, he said that. They fought, they made up. They rode to town in the snow and they picked peas in the June heat. They screwed in the barn. [. . .]

He rolled over onto his side and faced the window. He wasn't very sleepy. But maybe if he stayed here a while he could drift off. So he kept thinking about Queen. He thought about her when she was fourteen and he thought about her when she was twenty-four. He thought about the first time he'd seen her naked and he thought about the last time he'd seen her, after he'd poisoned her. She wasn't naked then. But she was dead. All the light gone from her eyes, and her hands cold and stiff. It had taken him eight hours to dig the grave. In the dark. His wife thinking he was out whoring again, no doubt. He'd come in at daylight after putting the rest of the dirt over her and smoothing it out so that it hadn't looked any different from the rest of the plowed ground. He'd come in and he'd fixed himself a cup of coffee and sat there at the same kitchen table and drank it, with his hands shaking, and then he'd gone to bed. He'd gotten into bed with his wife and she'd been just waking, and she could probably smell the dirt on him because she'd asked him where he'd been all night, had told him that she'd woken at two and he wasn't in the bed. He told her he'd been up all night with a sick heifer, and then he'd rolled over and closed his eyes and listened to the bed creak as she'd gotten up and pulled her robe from the closet, and gone out and closed the bedroom door. And he'd never laid a hand on her again. And she'd never asked him to again. He'd told her that Queen had gone back to South Carolina on the train to take care of her aunt and that she wouldn't be back. His wife had said that she'd miss her corn bread. And that had been the end of it. For his wife, anyway.

Shit. He wasn't sleepy. [. . .] He wondered if that little boy had told his daddy about the big red fish truck. He probably had. He'd probably told all his friends at school, too. It probably wasn't a thing he'd have to worry very much about over the winter, people going down to his pond, but next spring, when the dogwoods bloomed and the days started warming, he'd have to keep an eye on it. But he'd have a gate up by then. That would stop anybody from driving down to it, but it wouldn't stop anybody from just walking in off the road. Maybe he needed to build a fence. But he didn't really want to. He'd already built so many fences that he didn't get too excited about the idea of building another one, although he still had to fix that section down by the pea patch sometime. Maybe next month when it cooled off some. It was too hot to mess with a fence right now.

He rolled over the other way. He wasn't going to be able to go to sleep. He didn't think. But he kept lying there anyway. He'd been thinking about calling Lucinda, but he hadn't. He'd been thinking about getting a phone with caller ID, but he hadn't done that either. Nobody ever called him anyway. Except Toby once in a while. All the old women who used to call his wife never called over here anymore because they didn't want to talk to him. Bunch of old biddies. He never had been able to understand how his wife and her old biddy friends had found so much to talk about over the telephone. Cortez never had used the phone like that, to just call somebody up and talk. But women were different. They could talk for hours. Queen was the only woman he'd ever been with who was content to just be silent sometimes. And more than sometimes. He'd known sometimes that she felt guilty for doing what they had for so long, right under his wife's nose. In the barn. Just up the driveway. And then Queen would have to come to the house and do something like help his wife peel and can tomatoes. Put up corn. Blanch peas and pick out the bad ones and bag them up for the freezer. Even eat with them sometimes. Cortez sometimes wished he was already dead along with his wife so that he wouldn't have to keep on thinking about things. He was tired of thinking about them. He was tired of asking himself if he'd done the right thing or the wrong thing. All he knew was that he missed her so bad. He missed the taste of her mouth. And the weight of her naked breasts in his hands. And if she'd lived he'd have a little half-black bastard running around somewhere. Not little. Thirty-seven years old almost. And you couldn't have that. Maybe some people could but not him. It would have been too embarrassing to stay here on his farm. He would have had to leave.

And telling his wife that she'd up and packed her clothes and gone back to South Carolina in a taxi cab to the station. He had burned her clothes, her shoes, all the things he found that belonged to her in the old house, and he'd almost burned it, too, just so he wouldn't have to keep looking at it. The only thing he'd kept was the locket. And he shouldn't have kept it. But he couldn't stand to part with the only picture of her he had. That's why it was hidden in the barn. Maybe one day, after he was dead, somebody would go through all his stuff, even the stuff in the old tack room in the barn, and find everything. The locket. The machine gun. The Klan robe and hood. He just hoped that person wouldn't be Lucinda. [. . .]

He heard one of the cows bawl up in the pasture. He wasn't going to start feeding his hay until he had to. There was still plenty of grass out there if they'd move around and find it instead of standing there bawling for him to come feed them.

When he woke up it was past three. He hadn't meant to sleep that long. He sat up and reached for his brogans and put them on and tied them and got up and went out the door. The sun was bright and he walked across the backyard to the equipment shed and climbed up on the 4020 and took the cap off the fuel tank and peered in. It was halfway full. More than enough to do that little dab of mowing.

He sat down on the seat and made sure it was in neutral and turned the key over to light the ignition lamp in the control panel. He pushed the fuel control in and turned the key on over and the motor kicked over a few times and then chugged as it came to life. Black smoke rattled the rain top upright on the exhaust pipe and he pulled it down into second and eased out on the clutch and drove it out of the equipment shed. The Bush Hog was in the next stall and he moved the tractor in front of it, stopped, and then turned his head and started backing it up. When he got to within two feet of it he pulled up on the little black knob that operated the three-point hitch and then carefully backed it closer. It took him a few minutes to get down off the tractor and hook up the Bush Hog, and then he had to connect the shaft on it to the PTO on the tractor. Then he climbed back up, raised the three-point hitch, and pulled back out of the equipment shed. He started to go back to the house and fix a jug of ice water, but then he decided that it wasn't going to take him that long to cut that little patch of grass. So he went on up the driveway and turned left and went down the road to the new road and turned in.

The Bush Hog wasn't over two years old and was still in very good shape. The one he'd used up before this one had lasted almost nine years, and that was a long time for a Bush Hog. He pulled down by the pond and looked at the place he was going to mow and tried to see how wet it was. It didn't look wet at all. He started to get down and walk over it, just to make sure, but he didn't. He just lowered the Bush Hog and pushed in the clutch and engaged the lever for the PTO and started mowing. Then he remembered and stopped and put his safety belt on. The tractor had a roll cage built onto it and it was designed to protect the driver in a rollover. Cortez had known a lot of people who'd been killed on tractors, and a lot of them were farmers who'd been using tractors all their lives. But they made one little mistake, or they got old and forgot something, and they had an accident you couldn't live through. Cortez had had some close calls himself. [. . .]

He made the first pass on level ground. The grass was about three feet high and the Bush Hog sheared it off smoothly, about four inches high. Some of the ground was still a little rough from the dozer dude's work, and some of it had washed out a little from the recent rain. Shit. He guessed he needed to get the section harrow and bring it up and run over it a couple of times after he got it mowed and smooth it out a little. He'd noticed it back in the summer, but he never had gotten around to doing it. He could do it today if he wanted to. The days were getting shorter, but they hadn't set the time back yet. He didn't think they did that until October. Not far off.

He mowed on fairly level ground for a while and clipped off all the grass that surrounded the pond. He ran over some of it a couple of times to get the tufts that were sticking up here and there. Then he mowed alongside both sides of the new road, staying close to the clay gravel. After he got through with that he pulled up beside the pond and eased the tractor off onto the slope near the shallow end. He started mowing and it was a little steeper than he liked, but he made the first pass with no trouble and then pulled back out and turned around to make another, lower pass.

It didn't happen fast. He went a little deeper down the slope and the ground broke away from one of the back tires and then the other one, too, and the tractor started sliding back end first down the slope at an angle, tearing the thinly rooted grass loose. He hit the brake and saw that he'd run over a wide patch of clay that was still wet and there was nothing he could do to stop the slide of the heavy tractor down toward the water. He was going to slide right into the pond and be crushed and drown both if it rolled over on top of him, and it was probably going to. These things flashed through his mind and it was nothing but the years of experience that sent his foot quick to the clutch and his hand darting to the PTO lever, which took the Bush Hog out of gear but didn't do anything to stop the big tires from sliding on the slick clay. When he hit the bottom of the bank the waterlogged dirt crumbled away and the tractor tipped right over into the pond on its side. The exhaust pipe hissed as it went under. He took a breath just before his face slammed into the water and his arm hit something very hard and the Bush Hog with its still-whirling blade went into the water and threw up a shower that doused him before it came to a stop. The motor started missing and it ran for a few more seconds before it stopped. Oil started coming up and pooling and spreading out over the water in rainbow-colored hues. He'd played hell now.

His face was splashing water and his hand was trying to unlatch the safety belt, but he couldn't find it. It had always been a little hard to latch and unlatch and he was holding his breath, knowing if he couldn't get it undone just pretty quick, then he was done. He raised his face and could just barely get his mouth and nose out of the water, but it was enough. The tractor had stopped moving. He thought. He drew a careful breath. He breathed a couple of times. He had to force himself to calm down. Was it going to slide some more? He didn't know. He was twisted in the seat and it was hurting his back and he thought maybe he'd broken his right arm. It didn't feel right. It didn't feel the way it had felt all his life.

He felt ridiculous, sitting on his tractor seat with just his face sticking out of the water. His body was putting so much pressure on the safety belt that his hand couldn't get it unlatched. He kept pushing on the button, but he couldn't feel it move. And his leg was bent under the steel plate where the brake was mounted near the right side of the transmission. He didn't know how that had happened, but he was stuck. Stuck tight. Lord God. In his own damn pond.

He took a deep breath and lowered his nose and mouth back into the water. That took some of the strain off his back, and he sat there, with the sun-heated water waving in his hair, holding his breath and fumbling with the latch on the safety belt, just his eyes sticking up above the water. Of all the stupid-ass things to do.

He had to do something quick. He wondered if he could get to his knife and cut the safety belt. It was made from a piece of nylon strapping about two or three inches wide, and his knife was sharp, but the belt was tight across his left front pocket where the knife was, and he couldn't get his hand underneath it easily. He was scared to move too much, afraid the tractor would slide on down in the soft mud in the bottom of the pond. He believed he could feel it creeping that way just a bit at a time, because it was getting harder to hold his head out of the water. He tried again to get his hand in his pocket, but it wouldn't go. And the belt wouldn't unlatch. He knew what he was going to have to do.

He was going to have to get hold of the rim of the seat with his broken right arm and try to push himself down in the seat enough to take the pressure off the safety belt, and that was going to hurt. But he'd been hurt before. He'd fallen fifteen feet off the roof of his house one time, putting some tar around the flashing on his chimney, and broken his ankle. Took him three months to get over that. He'd been slammed into the side of the barn by a bad bull one day and had broken five ribs. Took him a month to get over that, lying in a bed hurting and taking aspirins. A brindle cow had knocked two of his jaw teeth out with a horn one day. He shot her with something like pleasure even though she was worth about five hundred dollars. A strand of barbed wire he'd been stretching across some posts had snapped once and cut him up something terrible. Blood all over him when he went back to the house, like to scared his wife to death. Took eighty-seven stitches for old Doctor Little uptown to sew him up from that one. But he was going to die right now today if he didn't get that safety belt unlatched. So he lifted his broken arm and made his hand go to the rim of the seat and he pushed on it. And cried out when he did. He could feel the broken bone ends rubbing together. He could hear them. It hurt about as bad as anything he'd ever had hurt, maybe worse than when he'd passed some kidney stones ten years back and pissed blood, too.

"Lord *God!*" he said aloud, and hot tears squeezed from his eyes. But his left hand found the button on the safety belt and he felt it release. He grabbed the steering wheel and slid off the seat deeper into the water, but his foot was still hung. His right arm was screaming with fire inside. He was kind of squatting on the right side of the tractor, trying to get his foot loose, but it wouldn't come. And if the tractor slid any deeper into the water it was going to pull him down with it. He didn't know why his foot wouldn't come loose. He couldn't understand why it was hung. He guessed the jolt had slid him sideways in the seat, even with the belt on, and he was still twisted around, and his face kept going down in the water.

And then he thought to himself, with some kind of detached peace that came upon him without warning: *What the hell you struggling so hard for? You had seventy-two years. Which is more than lots of people get. Had children. Had women. Raised cows and cotton. You done what you wanted to all this time. And you known all this time one day you'd have to answer for all that other stuff. For her. For her baby. Everybody dies so what's wrong with today? It's a pretty day. Let go, old man.*

But he couldn't let go. He wanted to see Lucinda again. And he wanted to see these fish grow. So he struggled back up out of the water and tried to gain his strength back. He thought the tractor had stopped moving. But his foot was hung and he'd have to stick his whole head underwater to try and get a better angle for pulling it loose. And that was going to be impossible to do with one broken arm. He figured that his foot was between the side of the transmission and the mud. He could feel pressure bearing down on it, but it didn't hurt. Maybe that meant it was hurt bad. Or maybe the blood was cut off.

And then he realized again that he was surely going to die. He was on the side of the pond that couldn't be seen from the road, and nobody was going to come along and see him down here. Somebody would have to walk right down here to be able to see him. So that meant nobody was going to come. Or not until it was too late. He couldn't just lie here in this water for days. He'd finally get so tired he'd have to put his head down and that would be it. He'd strangle to death on water. His own water. The water he had hoped and wished and almost prayed for.

No, nobody was going to come along. He was going to stay right here for a couple of miserable days and then he was going to drown. Hell. They might not even find him until the buzzards started circling. Which they would. They'd spot a dead cow within an hour if she was out in the open. They'd find him soon enough. He remembered again the hordes of them walking the backs of the dead fish in the river all those years ago.

And then that little boy who lived down the road in that trailer, the one with the go-kart, the one he'd yelled at to get the hell off his place, was wading out in the water toward him with a piece of rubber hose in his hand. He had a scared face and what looked like a pair of binoculars around his neck. But he kept on coming.

"Get back!" Cortez said. Then he said: "You know how to swim?"

"No sir," the little boy said. He'd stopped, standing in almost waist-deep water. Holding that piece of rubber hose. And where had he seen that before? Now he knew. He'd seen two pieces of it. Lying there at the bank on the shallow end, just on the other side of the tractor. He'd thought maybe the dozer guy had broken a hydraulic line on his dozer and had fixed it out there, but then he remembered that he hadn't seen the pieces of hose until after the fish man had come and gone.

"You can breathe through this," the little boy said. "I saw it on a movie."

Cortez was getting tired and he couldn't help letting some water get into his mouth, and he kept spitting it out. Some went down his throat and he coughed a couple of times.

"I'm gonna climb up on the wheel," the little boy said.

"Be careful," Cortez said, and it was all he could think of to say.

The little boy waded on out, almost up to his chest, and then he caught hold of the big black cleats on the huge back tire that was sticking out of the water and he started pulling himself up on it.

"Hold on," the little boy said. "I'm coming."

And he was. Like a monkey or a trained acrobat. He clambered up on the side of the wheel and he knelt there with water dripping from his clothes and tried to reach for Cortez's hand. Cortez put his hand up and he felt the little boy's fingers, small, soft. Raif's had felt like that. He held on to them. Deep shame flooded his whole face. The way he'd yelled at him.

"Here," the little boy said, and handed him the piece of rubber hose. Cortez knew exactly what he meant. Put it in his mouth and breathe through it underwater. But he didn't think he could do it. Not with one arm broken. He handed it back and held on to the steering wheel again. His arm was killing him.

"I can't use that. You got to go call for help," Cortez said.

"Yes sir, I already did," the little boy said. "I run home and done that soon as I seen you tump over."

"You did?" Cortez said.

"Yes sir." Looking down at him from the tractor tire. Not that far away. A few feet. He had freckles and a crew cut. His teeth were real bad. That was a damn shame, to let a kid's teeth get into that kind of shape. Why in the hell didn't his daddy take him to the dentist? Or his mama?

"Who'd you call?" Cortez said.

"Nine one one," the little boy said. "Lafayette County Fire Department. They on the way right now."

Cortez lay there in the water and looked at him. It was kind of hard to look at him. The little boy even smiled at him.

"What's your name?" Cortez said.

"Jimmy," the little boy said.

Cortez nodded at him, water dripping from his nose. He could feel some of it drying from the sun, which was hot on his face.

"I'm sorry about hollering at you," he said.

"That's all right," the little boy said. "You Mister Sharp, ain't you?"

"Yeah I am," Cortez said. "You can just call me Mister Cortez if you want to."

"They'll be here fore long, Mister Cortez," the little boy said. "I'm gonna stay right here with you," he added.

Cortez nodded, and it was hard for him to swallow, but he did.

"I thank you," he said.

[. . .]

48

It was quiet in the hospital room now, finally, at last. It was late and the nurses had turned the lights down in his room. The TV up on a high shelf in front of Cortez's bed was flickering dim bursts of color over the sheet that covered his legs. He had the volume turned down and he'd already found out that the hospital TV didn't have nearly as many channels as the system he had at home. They didn't even have the Western Channel up here. His foot was sore but okay.

His arm didn't feel too bad now. It was throbbing a little was all, and they'd given him something for pain. It had a cast on it and he was ready to go on home, but they wouldn't let him yet. They were keeping him overnight for observation. They said. Shit. They were just trying to squeeze some more money out of his insurance company. He hated having to wear the little hospital gown. He'd been admitted too late for supper, but one of the nurses had gone down to the kitchen and had brought him up a banana and some pudding and some cereal with milk. He was still kind of hungry, but he didn't guess you could get anything else around here to eat at this time of night. He'd have to wait for breakfast. But the nurses had said that it came early. Maybe they'd let him go home after he ate breakfast. He sure hoped so. Being up in here made you think about dying.

And he didn't like this bed. He was used to his own bed and he didn't think he was going to be able to sleep in this damn thing. It was hard. And it wasn't big enough for him. And he wasn't a damn bit sleepy anyway. He'd called Toby and told him where he was, and Toby had come down to see him, and they'd talked some in his room. Toby had tried to talk him into calling Lucinda and letting her know what had happened, but he wouldn't do it. He was afraid she'd come over and bring that retard with her and he didn't think he could handle that right now. He told Toby he'd call her later, after he got back home. If they let him out tomorrow, Toby was going to come get him and take him home. Cortez had made the ambulance crew take him down to his house so he could get his keys from his truck and lock the house and water the heifers before they took him to the hospital. They'd acted like they didn't want to do it at first until he'd started coming off the cot and going for the door, and then they'd changed their minds. He wasn't about to leave his house unlocked all night long. Too many thieves running around these days. And if they thought he was going to go off without watering his stock, they were nutty as a fruitcake.

He'd been lying there thinking about that little boy. Jimmy. Couldn't swim but stayed there in the water with him the whole time. He was going to do something for that boy. He didn't know what yet. But he was going to do something nice for him. He knew one thing already he was going to do for him. As soon as he got out of the hospital and got back home, he was going to drive over to that trailer and knock on the door and ask whoever answered the door if the little boy was home, and if he was, he was going to tell him how much he appreciated what he'd done, and then he was going to tell him he could go fishing in the pond any time he wanted to. That was about the least he could do for him. And the fish weren't big now, for sure, but by next year, they'd be ready. Especially if he fed them until the water turned cold. That ought to be at least another month. What he wished he could do was buy something for that boy. He didn't know what. A fishing pole maybe? What about a nice rod and reel? But he probably already had a rod and reel. He probably went fishing with his daddy. Cortez had seen some fishing poles sticking out the back window of that '56 a few times. That boy's daddy had probably already bought a rod and reel for him. But it didn't matter. He could always get him another one. It wouldn't hurt anything for a little boy to have two fishing poles. Maybe one for Sundays.

He was worried as hell about his tractor, too. Somebody from the fire department had called down to the hospital earlier and told him the wrecker had gotten it out okay, and that it didn't look like anything was damaged on it, and that they'd left it sitting at the side of the pond, but Cortez was afraid water had gotten into the motor, or the fuel lines, or the fuel tank, and he knew he was going to have to call the John Deere dealer, probably the one down at Batesville, and tell them what had happened and get them to bring their big trailer up here and load it and take it back to their shop and do whatever they'd have to do to get it back running. He couldn't do without his tractor. Not with winter coming in a few more months and him having to move hay bales for his cows. And he still needed to put in those fence posts down by the creek. Shit. Maybe he ought to just buy a new one. One with a glassed-in cab. He'd seen those boys who were raising cotton down on DeLay Road on their big tractors and they all had glassed-in cabs. Air-conditioned. And they had heaters you could turn on in the winter. It sure would make it nice, hauling that hay around in February when everything was so muddy and cold. But he still needed to get the 4020 fixed and not let it just sit there with water inside the motor. If he bought a new one he'd need it in good shape for the trade-in.

He heard a knock on the door and the door opened and another nurse came in. She was older than the other nurses, and gray haired, and she'd been in before, and Cortez had noticed that she had a nice big butt on her, just like he liked, and that she wasn't wearing a wedding ring. He pulled the sheet up over him a little higher and she walked over to the bed. Her name was Carol.

"You awake?" she said.

"Yeah," he said. "This bed ain't big enough for me to stretch out good."

"They all the same size up here," she said. "I got to take your temperature again." [. . .]

"How's your arm feel?" she said, country as hell.

"It's all right."

"It ain't hurting?"

"Not too bad."

"Want me to get you something for pain?"

"Naw, I'm fine."

He sat there. He was wanting to maybe flirt with her a little bit, but it had been so long he'd about forgotten how. He looked up at her. She didn't seem to be in any hurry to get out of here. She was still pretty.

"I wish I had something else to eat," he said.

She moved closer and moved his pillow a little and adjusted it for him some. Brushing him with her hands. A soft breast nudged the side of his head. Accidentally? Hell no. They always let you know. By look or touch.

"What you want, honey?" she said.

Honey, huh? He wondered if she'd go out with him. But if they went out, where in the hell would they go? He didn't know any place to take a woman. But the whole town seemed to be full of restaurants now. He guessed he could take her to one of them.

"What they got?" he said.

"The kitchen's closed," she said. "But they's a machine down on the first floor has food in it."

"Like what?"

She slipped the thermometer into a pocket of her uniform and put her hands on the rail of his bed. Her hands didn't have nearly as many liver spots as his. And she was still a well-built woman.

"They've got hamburgers and hot dogs," she said. "I think they keep some pie in there."

"What kind?" he said.

"I don't know. Probably chess or pecan. You want me to go down and look and get you a piece if they have some?"

"You don't mind?" he said.

She patted him on the shoulder.

"I don't mind a bit," she said. She stood there and looked down on him. "We don't have many patients on the floor tonight. You lucky you didn't get killed."

He wondered what she'd been before becoming what she was now. Did she have kids? Had she been a homemaker? Was she a grandmother?

"I know it," he said. "I been driving a tractor fifty years and I never thought I'd roll one of mine."

"Maybe it's time for you to stop driving it," she said.

"I can't," he said. "I got to feed my cows this winter."

"Or maybe just sell them cows," she said. "Most people your age have done retired."

"Yeah," he said. "I know. And most of em's right down the hill there at the old folks home in wheelchairs, hoping somebody'll come see em."

Cortez liked her. He started to ask her how old she was, but he didn't want to do that since it seemed nosy. Instead he said, "You got a boyfriend?"

And she laughed. He liked her laugh, too.

"I ain't had one of them in a long time," she said. "Last one I went out with was nothing but a drunk. And I'd already put up with one of them for thirty years. My husband."

"You ain't married to him no more?" Cortez said.

"He died," she said. "Cirrhosis of the liver. It took him a long time to kill his self but he finally did it."

"I'm a widow, too," Cortez said.

"I'm sorry," she said, but she didn't look that sorry to him.

"That's all right," Cortez said. "All she did was gripe and holler at me through this damn police bullhorn she had when I was out on my tractor trying to work."

"Well," the nurse said, and tried to hide a smile. She was just standing there, but her hand came out and touched him on the shoulder again. He knew he had a date then.

They let him out the next morning about ten o'clock and Toby was there waiting in his room while Cortez changed back into his overalls. They had some stupid rule in the hospital where anybody who got discharged had to ride a wheelchair down in the elevator and then get picked up out front. He started to argue at first and then realized that the quicker he got into the wheelchair, the quicker he could get the hell out of here. So he got into it and Toby went out the back way to get his minivan. [. . .]

The automatic doors opened and the nurse pushed him out onto a concrete apron and then stopped the chair just short of the drive. [. . .] He saw Toby's minivan pulling around at the far end of the parking lot and he started getting up.

"There's my ride," he said, and the nurse helped him, not that he needed it. Just because you were old, people thought you were feeble. He didn't need anybody helping him stand up.

Toby pulled his minivan to a stop right in front of Cortez, and he started to get out and come around, but the nurse opened the door for him and Cortez sat down in it.

[. . .]

"You got all your stuff?" Toby said.

"I didn't have nothing," Cortez said.

"Okay, then," Toby said, and he took his foot off the brake and they started rolling in a tight circle to get out of the entrance. "You need to go anywhere before you go home?"

"Yeah," Cortez said. "If you don't care. I need to run out to Wal-Mart for a minute. I want to see about a good rod and reel."

"You in the market for a new one?" Toby said.

"Yes sir," Cortez said. "I am today."

When they got out on the bypass, some old guy was out in the ditch with a garbage bag, picking up cans.

49

Jimmy woke up that same morning and his tooth was hurting really bad. Worse than bad. It was the worst thing he'd ever felt. It had been hurting pretty bad when he'd gone to bed the night before, but he hadn't wanted to tell anybody because he still didn't want to have to go see the dentist, so he'd just slipped a couple of aspirin out of the medicine cabinet and taken them with a glass of water, and then gotten into bed. It was Thursday. A school day. But the pain had caused Jimmy to wake up early, and now he was standing in the dark hall with his hand pressed against the side of his mouth, with bolts of pain shooting through his whole head. His mama and daddy were both still asleep. His daddy didn't usually get up until six, and sometimes his mama got up and fixed breakfast for Jimmy and Evelyn and Velma, but it was often only cereal, which of course beat nothing. Bacon and eggs would have been a lot better, maybe with some pancakes, but Jimmy didn't get that too much on school mornings. His mama had been staying up later and later, even during the week, and sometimes it caused her to sleep past the time for Jimmy and his half sisters to get outside and wait for the school bus. But Jimmy didn't know how he could get on the school bus today. He was afraid he was going to have to go to the dentist. And he was going to have to wake his mama and his daddy up. He didn't want to, because he knew he wasn't supposed to go into his parents' room if the door was closed, but he had to. His tooth was hurting so bad that tears were squeezing from his eyes.

He put it off for a long time. He walked up and down the hall, putting it off. He went into the living room and sat down for a while, putting it off. But finally he couldn't wait any longer. He opened the door quietly and walked in there.

It was still dark in there, too. His mama and daddy were lying in the bed, his mama on her side facing the outer edge of the bed, and his daddy rolled toward his edge of the bed. Jimmy walked over to him and stood there, holding his hand against the side of his mouth.

"Daddy," he said. His daddy mumbled something in his sleep that sounded like "Put that sumbitch over the top of Mister Richard's Coke machine," and then he snored lightly.

Jimmy was afraid he'd be in a bad mood again. He'd been in a bunch of bad moods lately. Jimmy didn't know why and his mama didn't either. There'd been some kind of fuss with Evelyn and now she would hardly talk to him. He was afraid that his daddy had told his mama what Jimmy had told him about Evelyn and the boys on the school bus, and he was afraid that Evelyn had figured out who'd told on her. Which was him. Evelyn had been punished, he knew that. She'd been grounded and she hadn't been able to talk on the phone for a few weeks. She'd been staying mostly in her room, but she'd pushed Jimmy hard a few times without saying anything, and once when nobody was around, she'd leaned over to him and whispered viciously, "You little pussy redneck, I'm gonna get you."

So that was something else to worry about. He'd also seen Evelyn talking to one of the big boys on the school bus and pointing toward him. And that was something else to worry about. But right now he could hardly think of anything but the pain in his mouth. It was getting worse all the time. The tooth had started throbbing inside his head and he didn't know what he was going to do. He wasn't worried about going to the dentist anymore if the dentist could just make it stop hurting. He thought it might help his case if he was crying when he woke his daddy up, so he started again. It didn't take much. He was already over the brink. The pain was [. . .] pounding a big drum to the beat of his rushing blood. *Shawoom. Shawoom. Shawoom.*

"Daddy," he said again, voice kind of shaky this time, and this time he reached out and touched his daddy's shoulder. "Daddy, wake up."

Jimmy's daddy didn't wake with a jolt. He just opened his eyes, lying on his side, and saw Jimmy standing there. And he smiled at him. Until he saw that Jimmy was crying. And then he did something he rarely did. He sat up under the covers and swung his feet to the floor and reached out and hugged Jimmy. Put his big warm arms around him.

"What's wrong, Sport?" he said softly. His breath was awful.

"My tooth," Jimmy said, and let his daddy fold him in to his arms and hold him for a few seconds. "It's hurting really bad, Daddy." And he cried some more. It was easy to cry some more, with his daddy holding him.

"Okay," his daddy said, and he got up and reached for his pants, which were lying on the floor. He pulled them on and fastened them shut and zipped them and buckled his belt. "Let's go in here and look at it."

Jimmy followed his daddy down the hall to the bathroom. A small light was burning in there but Jimmy's daddy flipped on the overhead light and put the lid down on the toilet and sat on it.

"Let me look at it," he said. "Which one is it? Open your mouth."

Jimmy walked up next to him and opened his mouth.

"Lean your head back."

Jimmy leaned his head back. He felt his daddy stick his finger into his mouth and he pointed to where it was hurting.

"Ish . . . ova hah," he said.

His daddy was looking. Probing with his finger. Gently.

"Damn," he said. "Shit. You got more'n one. I can't believe your teeth have got in this bad a shape. How long's it been since you've been to the dentist?"

"I ain't never been," Jimmy said. His daddy took his finger out of his mouth and Jimmy closed it.

"Well, you're gonna have to go today," his daddy said. "How bad's it hurt?"

"Pretty bad, Daddy. It hurts awful bad."

"Let me wake your mama up," his daddy said, and Jimmy followed him back to the bedroom and watched. Jimmy's daddy leaned over Jimmy's mama and shook her shoulder. He saw her raise up, and then Jimmy's daddy said something to her. She raised up higher and rubbed one hand over her face and then she got up in her nightgown and came over to him. She bent down to him.

"What's the matter, babe?" she said.

"My tooth hurts," Jimmy said.

"He's got a big cavity in there," Jimmy's daddy said. "I guess I might as well go ahead and get dressed."

"Let me go get some Orajel," his mama said, and she went out the hall. Jimmy heard her footsteps going toward the bathroom.

"What's the dentist gonna do to me, Daddy?" Jimmy said.

Jimmy's daddy had turned on the light in the closet and he was pulling a work shirt off a hanger and putting it on.

"I don't know," he said.

"Is he gonna hurt me?" Jimmy said, while more tears came down his cheeks. [. . .]

"I doubt it," Jimmy's daddy said. "I think they've got a lot better dentists now than what they had when I was a kid. They was one up here at Oxford, that son of a bitch ought to be killed today for what he done to me when I was a kid."

Jimmy didn't ask what. He didn't want to know. He wondered what Orajel was. Maybe they could use that and he could go on to school and forget about going to the dentist today. Or maybe just take a whole bottle of aspirin with him.

His daddy got some socks from a drawer and sat down on the bed and started putting them on. Looked like his toenails needed cutting pretty bad.

"She'll have to take you," he said. "They won't let me off from work for nothing like that."

Jimmy stood there. He had told his daddy and his mama the whole story of Mister Sharp and his tractor turnover and how he had stayed in the water with him. [. . .] He still hadn't told his daddy about the big red fish truck, or about Mister Sharp throwing something out into the water, or of how he had been watching him through the binoculars when he'd turned the tractor over. He'd put the binoculars back where he'd found them after carefully wiping them clean with some Windex he found in a kitchen cabinet and some Kleenex. They'd gotten a little wet in the pond. He hoped they were okay.

His mama walked back in the room with a small tube and stopped in front of him. She knelt.

"Let me put some of this on it, honey," she said. "Show me which one."

Jimmy opened his mouth, leaned his head back, pointed, said, "Ang ish ung."

She squeezed some reddish jelly-looking substance onto the tip of her finger and then put her finger inside his mouth and rubbed it over the tooth. Then she took her finger out and squeezed another dab from the tube and by the time she got her finger back inside his mouth, Jimmy could feel his gum getting numb. Oh yeah. A numb gum. She rubbed some more. An even number gum. The pain started getting smaller. It didn't go completely away, but it got better.

She had been watching him intently. Jimmy looked at her and thought she was the most beautiful woman in the world with her brown hair and brown eyes. Nobody could be prettier than his mother. Why didn't his daddy like her more than what he did?

"Is that better?" she said.

Jimmy nodded. "It's not as bad," he said.

"You still got to go to the dentist today," she said. "I should have already sent you up there for a checkup. It's my own fault." And then she muttered something about money.

"You gonna take him?" Jimmy's daddy said from the bed, where he was pulling his boots on.

"I guess I'll have to," she said. "I'll have to call Mister Carpenter and tell him I'll be late. Unless I can get Jimmy in before nine. But I'll have to go back and pick him up. And get him home somehow. "

"Have I got to go back to school after I get back from the dentist?" Jimmy said, hoping like heck he wouldn't have to.

"I don't know," his mama said, and she reached into the closet and pulled out a bathrobe and put it on. Jimmy looked at his daddy. He was buttoning his shirt. Then he bent over and picked up his cap from the floor and put it on his head.

"Hell, just let him skip the rest of the day," he said. "One day ain't gonna make no difference."

Suddenly everything was looking a lot better to Jimmy. The tooth wasn't hurting nearly as bad and it was starting to look like he might get a whole day off from school. He wished his go-kart's chain was fixed. He could ride it when he got back from the dentist. If there was any gas.

"Let me go find the phone book and see when they open up," his mama said, and went out of the room, up the hall toward the living room. Jimmy's daddy stood up and started putting his shirttail in.

"I think I got time to make me some coffee," he said, and he went on out the door, too.

Jimmy sat down on their bed. It felt lumpy. The girls weren't even up yet. His gum was getting number and number. Orajel was a good thing. His mama came back in, looking at an opened phone book. She sat down beside Jimmy and turned on the lamp beside the bed and kissed him on top of the head. Jimmy hugged her and turned her loose.

"Okay, let's see," she said. She had her finger on the page, looking at it. "Here's a family dentist. I bet they don't open till at least eight, though." She looked up at Jimmy. "I can't call for an appointment for two more hours. You may have to go to work with me for a while if I can't get you in before nine. How's it feel now?"

"It's a lot better," he said.

"You feel like eating something?" she said.

"Yes'm," Jimmy said.

Couple of hours later, Jimmy's in the dentist's chair. He didn't know what to expect, but so far everybody had been kind. A nice girl named Margie had brought him back here and put him in the chair and had clipped around his neck some kind of napkin that hung down on his chest. She had taken some X-rays of his teeth after putting a heavy vest across his chest. He was looking out the window at some boy mowing some grass. It felt strange not to be in school on a weekday. All his classmates were in class, listening to the teacher, waiting for lunch. What good was school anyway? It sucked. [. . .]

There was a TV he could watch, up on the wall, but the sound was turned down and it was some kind of a news show anyway. Jimmy never watched the news because they were always showing something about the war and there were always burned-out cars and tanks on fire and people lying bloody and shot dead in the streets. Smoke rising from buildings, helicopters flying overhead. He already knew he didn't want to be a soldier. He kept sitting there. He could hear people talking in some other rooms. Somebody was laughing and talking about Hank Williams Jr. And then a young clean-cut man wearing a tie came into the room and held up his hand and smacked hands with Jimmy. He sat down on a stool.

"Hi, Jimmy," he said. "I'm Tony. You can just call me Doctor Tony if you want to. I hear you've got a toothache."

"Yes sir," Jimmy said.

"Well, let's take a look at it," the dentist said, and he pushed a button on the chair that started raising Jimmy higher. He turned on a bright light above Jimmy and told him to open his mouth. Jimmy did.

The dentist spent some time looking around inside Jimmy's mouth. He poked some with a small hooked instrument. He didn't say anything and Jimmy didn't know if that was a good sign or a bad one. Finally he pulled back and looked at Jimmy.

"How often you brush your teeth, Jimmy?" he said.

"I'm supposed to brush em every night," Jimmy said.

"You really need to brush them after every meal, Jimmy," the dentist said. "You've got five cavities and they all need fixing, but I'm just going to fix the one that's hurting today and one more, okay? But then you need to come back and get the other ones taken care of before they start hurting. Okay?"

"Okay," Jimmy said.

The dentist looked at the wall for a moment and then he looked back at Jimmy. There was a picture of a little baby on the wall behind him.

"How do I get ahold of your mama?" he said.

"She works at the bank," Jimmy said.

"Which one?"

"The one up on the square."

Doctor Tony smiled and laughed.

"There's about four of them up on the square, Jimmy. Do you know the name of the one where she works?"

"No sir," Jimmy said.

Doctor Tony sat there some more. Then he got up.

"I'll be back," he said, and he patted Jimmy on the shoulder before he left. It was kind of reassuring. He was hoping desperately that they weren't going to hurt him. But he was afraid they were.

Doctor Tony stayed gone a few minutes. Jimmy heard him laughing and talking about going to a steak house that had some good single-malt scotch. Then he came back and sat down again. Another girl in a smock walked in and she smiled at Jimmy. She had big white teeth. No cavities there. Jimmy thought maybe he'd better start brushing his teeth.

"Good morning, Jimmy," she said.

"How'd you know my name?" Jimmy said.

"A little birdy told me," she said. She had something in her hand. "Now open wide."

Jimmy could feel his palms sweating, but he opened wide. He was about as scared as he'd ever been. But on the other hand, it wasn't as scary as your daddy almost drowning you.

He was back home before lunch. His mouth was still kind of numb from where Doctor Tony had filled his two front teeth, and they'd told him not to eat anything until the feeling came back, because if he ate something then he might start chewing on his cheek and not know he was chewing on it and maybe chew a hole in it. But his mama had stopped at the Sonic and bought him a chocolate milkshake, which he'd sucked through a straw. He'd looked at his new teeth in the makeup mirror on the way home.

She pulled up in front of the trailer and stopped. She looked kind of upset. Jimmy had watched her write a check to the dentist's office and she'd seemed to be kind of worried, but she didn't seem that way now. Jimmy worried about his mama a lot. She didn't seem to be happy. Not most times anyway. She could be reading a magazine and she'd just sigh. But if you looked at her, she'd look up and smile.

"I've got to go back to work," she said. "I'm running late. I hate to leave you here by yourself, but I don't know what else to do."

"I'll be all right," he said.

She reached over and touched his hair. Then she bent toward him and kissed him on the cheek. Gave him one last lingering touch with her hand.

"I know you will. Just watch some TV or something," she said. "The girls'll be in at three thirty."

"Okay," Jimmy said. He already knew that. And that meant he'd be alone with Evelyn and Velma until his daddy came in. He hoped his daddy would come in before Evelyn could do something nasty to him.

"You can fix you a sandwich or something when the feeling comes back. Not before, okay?"

"Okay," Jimmy said, and got out.

"Bye, babe," she said, and Jimmy said bye and closed the door. He watched her back out of the driveway and then she turned her car toward the county road and took off. Jimmy watched the dust roll out behind her and he waved to her. She waved back and then was gone.

The little dogs were all gone somewhere. Sometimes they did that, just left. Jimmy figured they were probably out hunting rabbits. He didn't know why his daddy didn't take them hunting with him.

He went on inside the trailer and it was absolutely quiet. It was different. It wasn't like being alone in it at night, as he sometimes was. It was daytime now, and the quietness made it feel like a strange place. [. . .] He wondered if it would be okay for him to have a Coke. Surely he wouldn't chew a hole in his cheek with a Coke. So he got one from the icebox, and then he set it down and got a glass and filled it with ice cubes and poured some of the Coke over it, then took it into the living room and set it down and grabbed the remote and turned the TV on.

He was still pretty numb, and the Coke tasted kind of funny when he took a sip from it. But the toothache part was over. He was fixed. And he knew he had to go back, but he wasn't scared anymore, just because the dentist had been so kind. And also because the dentist had stuck a small mask over his face and let him breathe through it for about ten minutes before he gave him the first shot in his gum to deaden his tooth. By then, from breathing whatever it was through the mask, Jimmy wouldn't have cared if the dentist had pulled out an old deer horn to work on him. He'd had all kinds of pleasant daydreams about arrowheads and Indians while the drill turned inside his mouth and tooth dust flew out. It was like every bone in his body had turned to Jell-O. He had actually almost enjoyed it. So much for being scared of a dentist. Jimmy thought Doctor Tony was probably the kindest man in town.

[. . .]

Jimmy thought he'd sit here and watch a little TV, sip his Coke, and he knew he had some M&M's somewhere. He'd sit here and let the feeling come back into his mouth and then he'd fix himself a nice sandwich and get some potato chips and some dip and just lounge around until the girls came home from school. And then he thought he'd walk up the road and look across at the pond and see if he could see Mister Cortez anywhere. He knew he'd gone to the hospital, because he'd still been down at the pond when the ambulance came for him, and had watched them take him away. So he was wondering if he was still in the hospital.

Jimmy had changed his mind about Mister Cortez. He'd decided that he wasn't a mean old man after all. Jimmy knew he shouldn't have been on his land.

It was hard to find much good on the TV in the daytime. They had all those daytime shows and none of it was very interesting, just people sitting around talking. He watched part of a western and then he flipped it around and found a show about bank robbers and watched that. Bonnie and Clyde. John Dillinger. Baby Face Nelson. He sipped his Coke. He could tell that the feeling was slowly coming back. And he was getting a little hungry.

He got up and went over to the icebox and opened the door to see what was in there. His mama had gone to the grocery store yesterday, so he was hoping there was something good to eat in there. But it looked like the girls had already been in there because the pickings were pretty slim. Hot dogs. Some old dried-up pizza still in the box from Pizza Hut. He opened it and looked at it anyway. Old nasty curled-up pepperoni and dry-looking cheese. It didn't look like anything you'd want to eat, although Velma seemed to prefer cold pizza for breakfast over everything else. He closed the box and stuck it back in there. She could have it. He opened one of the bins and looked in there. There was some baloney, but it was old and curled up, turning color. [. . .] So he looked in the cabinets to see what was in there. Spaghetti noodles. Flour and meal. Soup. Did he want soup? There was tomato and chicken noodle. Be hard to chew a hole in your cheek with soup. Nah. He didn't want soup. There were a few cans of tuna fish, but he didn't know how to make tuna salad. There were plenty of vegetables in cans, but he didn't want vegetables for lunch. He needed some meat. There were several cans of pork and beans. Some cake mix in boxes. More noodles. And then he saw some Vienna sausages and got down a can of them. He found some crackers. He got a plate. And then he happened to think to look in the freezer section of the refrigerator to see what was in there, and he found a brand-new unopened half gallon of Rocky Road. He put the plate back and found a bowl instead. And a spoon.

* * *

He was lying on the couch watching *The Real World* with his empty bowl on the coffee table and eating M&M's when he heard some gravel crunching out in front of the trailer. He put his candy down and turned the TV down and heard a door slam, so he went to the trailer door and opened it. He was kind of surprised to see Mister Cortez walking toward him. He had his arm in a cast, but his fingers were sticking out the end.

"Hey," Jimmy said, holding the door wide open.

"Hey there yourself," Mister Cortez said. "What you doing home from school today? You playing hooky?"

"Naw sir. I had to go to the dentist," Jimmy said. "I got my teeth fixed. See?" He opened his mouth so that Mister Cortez could look in there. Mister Cortez stood at the bottom of the steps trying to see up inside Jimmy's mouth which was mostly full of melted M&M's.

"I see," he said. "That looks pretty good."

"You all right?" Jimmy said.

"Aw yeah. I'm fine," Mister Cortez said. He held up his cast. "I just got to wear this thing for a while."

He stood there and looked around.

"Where's all them little dogs at?" he said.

"They took off," Jimmy said. "They'll be back later. I think they go out and run rabbits. But they don't never bring none home. You want to come in? I'm watching TV, but they ain't nothing much good on."

"I was wanting to speak to your mama or your daddy, one," Mister Cortez said. "Is one of them home?"

"No sir," Jimmy said. "They both at work."

"I see," Mister Cortez said, and nodded. "Well. I just wanted to ask em something. I can come back some other time. What time they get in?"

"Mama don't never get in till after five but Daddy gets in sometimes at four. But sometimes he don't come in till later." Jimmy didn't want to tell Mister Cortez that lots of times it was dark when Daddy came home.

And then Mister Cortez looked over there by the pine tree and saw Jimmy's go-kart. He nodded at it.

"What's wrong with your go-kart?" he said. "I ain't seen you on it in a while."

"Chain won't stay on," Jimmy said. "It's done got too loose."

"Will it run?"

"Oh, yes sir," Jimmy said, and came on down the steps. He walked over to the go-kart and flipped the toggle switch marked Off/On and choked it, then pulled the starter cord a few times, and it sputtered to life. He mashed the gas pedal with his fingers and revved it up, then pushed the choke off. It sat there running smoothly and the clutch was turning, but the chain was draped over the driving gear like a loose necklace. He shut it off.

Mister Cortez squatted down next to the go-kart and looked at it. He looked up at Jimmy.

"Can your daddy not fix it?" he said.

"I don't reckon so," Jimmy said.

Mister Cortez was looking closely at the chain by then. He slipped it off the driving gear and looked at the gear. Then he looked at the mounting plate beneath the motor. He looked back up.

"That's all that's wrong with it?" he said.

"Far as I know," Jimmy said. "Daddy tightened it one time and then he said the chain had got stretched and he didn't know how to fix it."

"It just needs a link took out of it," Mister Cortez said. He held it up. It was greasy and it was getting black grease on his fingers, but he didn't seem to care. Maybe he'd been around greasy things before.

"How you do that?" Jimmy said.

"I'll show you," Mister Cortez said, and he got up and walked over to his truck and lifted what looked like a pretty heavy metal box from the back end with his good arm. He brought it over and set it on the ground, and when he opened it, Jimmy saw more tools than he'd ever seen in one place at a time. Mister Cortez had a lot more tools than Jimmy's daddy, and his weren't rusty, they were shiny and clean. He had wrenches, screwdrivers, sockets, all kinds of stuff. He picked up a pair of pliers that had long slim tips. He looked up again.

"Will your daddy care for me fixing it for you?"

"I don't guess," Jimmy said, and then he started to get excited. Oh *boy!* If Mister Cortez could fix it, he could start back *driving* it all the time, as long as he had some gas. He could drive it at night, with his flashlight headlight. He wondered if Mister Cortez had ever seen the dead black lady who walked the road crying. But he didn't ask him. He just sat down in the gravel next to Mister Cortez and watched him as he started fixing the go-kart.

"See this little thing right here?" Mister Cortez said, holding up the chain. Jimmy saw a tiny plate in the links.

"Yes sir?"

"That comes off. It's just like a chain on a hay baler. All we got to do is take it off and cut one link out, then put it back together, and it'll be good as new. Then we'll take them bolts off underneath the motor and put the chain on and add some washers to them bolts, raise that motor until it's tight. I got some washers. Won't take long."

"Boy," Jimmy said. It was all he could think of to say.

"You ain't got a brick around here nowhere, do you?" Mister Cortez said.

"Yes sir, I sure do," Jimmy told him, and walked around behind the trailer and found a couple and brought them back.

"Here's two," he said, and Mister Cortez took one of them and set it down in front of him. He was being careful with his bad arm.

"One may be enough," he said.

Jimmy squatted close to Mister Cortez and watched him closely. He laid the chain on its side on top of the brick and then he rummaged around in his tool box and came up with a small hammer with a rounded head on one side and a flat side on the other. And he found a small punch. He put the punch on top of the link in the chain and tapped it gently with the hammer. Then he stopped.

"Let me see that other brick," he said, and Jimmy handed it to him. He set the second brick down so that there was a gap of about an inch between them, and he put the link in the chain over that empty space. Then he set the punch carefully on top of the tiny plate, and tapped it with the hammer. The tiny plate popped off and fell to the ground. Mister Cortez picked it up and handed it to Jimmy.

"Don't lose that," he said.

Jimmy took it and looked at it. It was just a little piece of metal that resembled a figure eight, with two small holes in it. Then Mister Cortez put his tools down and worked the chain apart, and he came up with another little piece of metal like the first one, only this one had two pins in it. Mister Cortez handed it to him.

"Don't lose that neither," he said. "That's your master link."

Jimmy looked at it. *Master link?* Mister Cortez was rummaging around in his tool box again and he came out with what looked like a brand-new file in a plastic sleeve. He pulled the file from the sleeve and laid the sleeve aside.

"If I had this in my vise I could do it quicker," he said. "But this'll work. It may take me a little bit. You know how to check your oil?"

Not even an hour later Jimmy was running up and down the road. He was power sliding, cutting donuts, pressing the gas as hard as he could, and the chain didn't come off. He roared down the road and roared back up it, and Mister Cortez stood in front of the trailer and watched him as he put his tools away. Jimmy knew he didn't have much gas, because he'd already pulled the cap off the gas tank and looked inside. And there wasn't any way to get any more until his daddy came home, and even then he might not get any, if his daddy didn't want to go to the store. So he pulled back in front of the trailer and shut it off. Mister Cortez was leaning on the fender of his truck.

"Running pretty good, ain't it?" he said.

Jimmy got off his go-kart and looked down at it, then up at Mister Cortez.

"It sure is," he said. "I sure thank you for fixing it for me."

"You welcome," Mister Cortez said. He stood there looking at Jimmy for a few moments. "I been wanting to ask you something," he said.

"Okay," Jimmy said. He already knew what he was going to ask him.

"How come you to see me when I rolled my tractor over?" he said. "Did you just happen to be walking by?"

"Well," Jimmy said, and looked down. He hated to tell him that he'd been watching him through the binoculars, but he hated to lie, too, even though he had to lie sometimes merely for self-preservation purposes. Like if Evelyn wanted to know what little fucker ate all the Twinkies, he'd say, Not me. He looked back up. "I was watching you," he said.

"How come?"

"Well," Jimmy said. "That man come by here other day, and his truck said 'Tommy's Big Red Fish Truck,' and I was wondering if you put some fish in your pond."

Mister Cortez was smiling just a little.

"So you was kind of spying on me, huh?" he said.

"Yes sir," Jimmy said. "I guess I was."

Mister Cortez nodded.

"I'm glad you was," he said. "Nobody would have found me till I was dead."

"Can I ask you something?" Jimmy said.

"Sure."

"What's that stuff you throwing out in the water?"

"It's catfish feed," Mister Cortez said. "I got three thousand of em in there. I feed em at night."

"Golly," Jimmy said. "How big are they?"

"Oh, they're just little bitty things right now," Mister Sharp said. "But I'm gonna keep feeding em and by next year they'll be big enough to eat. You like to fish?"

"I never have been," Jimmy said. "My daddy keeps saying he's gonna take me, but he ain't never took me yet."

Mister Cortrez looked like he was really surprised by that.

"How old are you?" he said.

"Almost ten," Jimmy said.

"You almost ten and you ain't never been fishing?"

"Yes sir."

"Does your daddy fish?"

"Yes sir. He goes with Mister Rusty and Mister Seaborn."

"He just don't never take you?"

"No sir. He don't never have time to, I don't reckon."

"Hmm," Mister Cortez said, and he turned toward his truck. He reached over into the bed and brought out a beautiful red reel on a shiny black rod, and the rod had SHAKESPEARE written on it. The reel was already strung with line that stretched out through the ferrules and the rod had a little yellow rubber practice-casting plug on the end of it. He handed the rod and reel to Jimmy. And then he reached back into the truck for a new Plano tackle box and handed that to him as well. When Jimmy set the rod down long enough to open the tackle box and look in, he saw that it was loaded with fishing gear: crappie hooks, bream hooks, bass hooks, catfish hooks, red-and-white plastic bobbers, supersensitive porcupine-quill bobbers, lures and jigs, packets of lead weights, some nylon stringers, a fish scale, a fish scaler, a Fiskars fillet knife in a leather holster, even a hook disgorger for getting hooks out of fish that had swallowed hooks deep. "Well, now you've got something to fish with whenever he takes you," Mister Cortez said. "And you can fish in my pond any time you want to. Long as it's okay with your daddy and your mama. I was gonna wait and ask them if it was okay for me to give you this stuff, but if it ain't, they can let me know."

Jimmy looked at the fishing pole. It was the most awesome thing he had ever seen, including his go-kart when it was new. It was sleek. It looked expensive. And somehow, it was his. Along with what looked like everything a boy would need to fish. He looked up at Mister Cortez. The world had suddenly changed on him again. And for once, not in some chickenshit way.

"What does catfish eat?" Jimmy said.

"Your fingers if you stick em in their mouth," Mister Cortez said. "Get you some red worms and try them. Or night crawlers."

Then he bent over toward Jimmy and lowered his voice a little.

"Just don't tell nobody about the catfish, okay?"

"Okay," Jimmy said immediately, and then wondered immediately if it would be okay to tell his daddy about the catfish. But he didn't ask. Everything was going way too good that day to mess it up with a bunch of stupid questions.

50

Seretha cried for three days when she found out Montrel was gone and then she left. Packed up one night while Cleve was asleep, was gone the next morning along with her hair curlers. Some clothes and shoes. A small FM radio. Montrel's car was still sitting beside the house, spotted with tree sap, old dog piss showing yellow on the whitewall tires.

Cleve sat out on the porch with Peter Rabbit sleeping in his lap and figured on what to do with the car. He knew she wouldn't go against him if it came to the law. Best thing would be to just get rid of it. He didn't have the title, so he couldn't sell it. It probably wasn't paid for anyway.

He sat there, rocking. She'd know for sure now, but she probably already did anyway, so he got up and went inside and found the keys on her dresser. He got three Budweiser tallboys from the ancient icebox and shut Peter Rabbit up in his bedroom so that he couldn't follow him.

He slipped on a pair of Playtex Living Gloves that Seretha used to wash dishes and went out and slipped behind the wheel of Montrel's ragged-out '79 deuce and a quarter. It fired right up. Then he got out and found a couple of bricks and put them in the floorboards. He opened the first beer when he pulled it down in Drive.

He stopped out at the mailbox to see if the mail had run. It hadn't, or maybe the mail girl just hadn't brought him anything today. Most of the time it was circulars and stuff from Home Depot anyway. He got back in the car and turned left out of his drive and headed up the dirt road toward Old Dallas. There weren't many people who lived back in there anymore. Most of them were in the graveyard now, under the old cedars.

He kind of wished he had Peter Rabbit with him, but he didn't want to make him walk that far since he was just a puppy. There would be plenty of long walks soon enough. He'd get him a squirrel skin before long. Maybe within the next day or two.

It was as pretty a morning as he'd seen, driving the big Buick, dust rolling out behind him. It needed some shocks bad. And that damn

perfume. He'd be glad when he got out of this son of a bitch. But there
was stuff to look at. Some of the leaves were starting to turn and they
stood out in little yellow and orange specks in the green walls of trees
around him. People didn't fish around here much in the winter. If he
was lucky nobody would find him until spring. If he was real lucky nobody would ever find him at all.

He drove slowly, and he didn't meet anybody, but the hot light in the
dash came on and flickered and then went back out. That bad head gasket. He didn't care. He'd leave the son of a bitch on the side of the road
if he had to.

But it kept on going. Once in a while the hot light would flicker, and
then go back off. He finished the first beer and opened the second one.
It wasn't nearly as cold as the first one had been, and the third one would
surely be worse. It didn't matter. He had some more at home. He lit one
of his Swishers and drove to a place high in the hills and stopped the
car to see if he could smell it yet. And there it was, unmistakable, just
like it was every year, in this one spot, at this time of year: the almost
overpowering scent of a vast field of marijuana somewhere out there in
the wooded hills beyond the ditch. He figured they had it under a tent.
He sat there and breathed it in. It smelled like some good shit. And he
sure would have liked to have some of it. But not enough to walk out
there in the woods trying to find where it was growing. Oh no. A man
could get killed like that.

He turned in on a road where a crazy old white man lived in a trailer,
somebody who walked up and down the roads all day picking up aluminum cans. But he didn't go down that far. On a flat piece of land at the
top of a hill he left the road and bulldozed the Buick over young pines
and oaks that snapped upright again behind him and he stopped the car
at the edge of a draw that overlooked a couple of thousand acres of pines.
He put it in Park and got out. Sage grass was turning brown around him
and he took a piss beside the open door, listening to the motor running.
He looked up and saw a couple of red-tailed hawks soaring. He took the
last puff off the Swisher and then stomped it into the ground.

She'd get over it. Might take her a while. She'd just have to understand
that Pappy knows best.

He finished the second beer and reached in for the third one and set it in the sage grass behind his feet. He reached into the car and set one of the bricks on top of the gas pedal and the motor revved up. He set the second brick on top of the first one and the motor noise rose to a mild howl. He could tell that it was missing a little.

He'd always been quick and nimble in the same way that small fighters are always the fastest. He reached in for the gearshift and pulled it down into Drive and snatched his arm back. The Buick left with a lurch and careened down the hill, bouncing over fallen logs and smashing sweet gum saplings down, dust rising from the dusty ground. He saw the whole thing rise two feet into the air, and then it launched itself out into open space, and for one brief moment he saw the foam dice hanging from the rearview mirror swaying. Then the car went out of sight, and there was just the sound of the motor racing, until it landed down there somewhere with a thunderous crash, and a plume of dust rose up, and a lone tall pine shook so hard that some of its needles fell.

He turned around and picked up the beer. The hawks were still sailing like ships. He took off the gloves and stuck them into his back pocket, then cut a small tree and went back up to where the tire tracks were, and started brushing them out. He'd seen that in a movie one time.

He took his rifle from behind the door the next morning before daybreak, and shut Peter Rabbit up in the house again. He sprayed some Off! on his arms and face and slipped some cartridges from a box on his dresser into his pants pocket. He went out the back door and told the other dogs to go back when they tried to follow him. They returned to their beds under the house.

He knew the land so well he didn't have to see. The only thing he was worried about was maybe stepping on a snake in the darkness. They were still crawling in these last warm days. He made his way down the hill to the pasture fence where a couple of scrubby orange cows stood with Y-shaped yokes around their necks. The yokes were made from small trees he'd cut and they were the only way to keep them from jumping the fence. All their ribs were showing beneath their ragged hides. Riddled with worms. Not worth eating. Not worth anything. They were almost good enough to be the kind they made potted meat from.

He went around the fence down to the corner and slipped through the wire and across the rocky pasture and out the other side. The timber out there was big and old, beeches, white oaks and red oaks, the scaly-barked hickories already standing among the hulled fragments of their nuts. He started to stop under one of them, but he knew an even better place and headed on to it. Dawn was almost ready to break, and in the distance he saw the paling light against the trees to the east. He loaded the gun and put the safety on. It was just a single shot, a gun from Sears, Roebuck & Company forty years ago. He'd paid twelve dollars for it new. He had a rubber baby nipple with an X cut into it in his pocket and he slipped the nipple over the muzzle of the rifle, just in front of the sight.

The creek had dropped to a trickle and he crossed it quietly, stepping softly on the shattered little stones. He eased up the hill and treaded on the soft moss that lined the banks like carpet, and he settled to rest against a giant beech that held holes in its massive trunk. Squirrel houses full of squirrels.

Already some of them were walking about on their limbs, shaking droplets of dew to the leaves around him. But it wasn't light enough to shoot. He held his head still and watched them jump and climb. He heard one on the ground. Then another. Others were barking in the distance.

He sat perfectly still and watched one come headfirst down a tree, its tail arched over its back. It barked at him, dim thing in the woods walking on two legs sitting so still now. He never moved.

The mosquitoes flew close to him but he didn't flinch. He hated their whining noise. Lying in the black bunks down on the prison farm he'd hated them then, too. Radios playing in the darkness. Men screaming for God knew why. Out there beyond the fields where thousands of acres of corn and peas and cotton were growing, the twelve-foot fences stood topped with razor wire, and he'd never thought of trying to run. He'd just decided not to get caught again. But it had taken him two trips down there to learn his lesson. Some things were like that. Some things you had to do twice to understand that they wouldn't work. He knew now what did: stay away from the white man unless he had something you needed.

They were starting to move everywhere now. The branches were moving and the woods were filled with nests and they were barking at each other in the growing light. He slipped the safety off and raised the rifle a little in his arms, waiting for the shot he knew would eventually come. He only wanted one for now, mostly for the skin. But he'd eat it, too. He wouldn't waste it. He didn't waste much of anything.

He saw a couple of them walking a grapevine that ran up into an old post oak and he raised the rifle and sighted on them. But they were too far away. And moving too fast. He heard one up in the tree above him, and then he heard it jump, and by looking up without moving his head much he saw it run out on a limb and stop. It wasn't over twenty feet above him, and the light was still not good, but he raised the rifle and sighted along the barrel. He lined up the little notch in the rear with the thin brass-beaded post on the front and held it on the squirrel's head. It ran forward three feet and stopped. Then it jumped to the off side of the tree and ran up it. He saw its tail in a glimpse here and there. Then it was gone.

Off in the distance he could hear a car or truck coming down the road. He wanted a smoke but knew he had to wait. The light was getting stronger all the time and he wondered how long she'd stay gone. And where would she go? Far as he knew she didn't have any place to go. No place but back home.

He kept sitting there and waiting for the right shot. Two climbed into the tree he was sitting under, but he didn't turn his head to see where they went. Most of them were heading to a big hickory just down the hill and he began to wish he'd sat down closer to it. Or that he'd brought his shotgun. He just hated to shoot it down here since it was so loud. They were pretty tame and he wanted to keep them that way. If you could bring a .22 and kill one or two or three or four and pick them up quietly and then leave quietly, you could come back the next morning and do the same thing. They got wild when you made too much noise and hunted them too hard.

The sun was still twenty minutes away from rising above the woods beyond him when one stuck its head around the side of a white oak in front of him and sat there. He fastened the sights on its head and held his breath and pulled the trigger slowly. The rifle made a faint *spat* no louder than a small stick snapping and the squirrel dropped and fell.

For a moment there was silence. A branch swished and drops of dew fell. He sat there for a few more minutes, until they got to jumping and barking again, and then he got up slowly and walked very quietly over to the base of the white oak and bent over and picked it up. In his black and corded hand he nestled its warm and furry little body. Pink brains drooped in a cluster from one ear. On a fat teat low on its belly a single drop of milk stood beaded like a pearl.

51

She didn't answer the door on the first knock this time. She didn't rush up the hall wearing a sexy red negligee either. Jimmy's daddy wasn't surprised. Jimmy's daddy had to stand out there and wait. The porch light was off and it was already dark. The days were so much shorter now. Football games on all the time. Pretty soon they'd set the time back and then it would be dark by five o'clock. He had a beer in his hand and he didn't know what the hell he was doing down here again. It wasn't going to help anything. But he just felt like he needed to come see her. He felt like it was the least he could do. And it was so hard to talk to her at the plant. All those people watching. Probably whispering behind their backs.

He'd been working on his '55 earlier in the afternoon, and it was cool enough that he'd worn a long-sleeved flannel shirt. He had on a clean one now. Her car was sitting beside the house, so he guessed she was home. He knocked again. He'd had to put a new belt on his generator and they'd had a hard time finding the proper one at AutoZone, and Rusty had taken off this afternoon, they said, so Jimmy's daddy had walked up and down the aisles and looked at spark plugs and oil filters and floor mats while he was waiting for them to find the belt. And that wasn't a bad thing to have to do. It was good to keep up with all the new products you wished you could afford. He wished he had enough money to buy whatever he wanted, to take one of those yellow plastic baskets at the front door and walk all over the whole store and load it up with Armor All, and GOJO, and STP, and that stuff you used to get bugs and road tar off the bumper, and socket sets, and Turtle Wax, and new windshield wiper blades, and anything else you needed. It didn't look like he was going to be able to afford those Keystone mags from Gateway now. Johnette had been forced to take out another personal loan with her bank to pay for Jimmy's teeth since he was going to need more dental work. And she was talking about maybe taking a part-time job, maybe calling down to Taylor Grocery to see if they needed anybody else to wait tables on the weekends. He hated for her to have to do that. But it might be for the best. Hell. Health insurance kept going up. Groceries. Everything kept going up except his paycheck.

A car came slowly up the street and Jimmy's daddy hid his beer in front of him in case it was a cop. He was almost broke from having to pay the fine for having beer in a dry county over at New Albany. He'd even been wondering if maybe he needed to sell the '55 and get something else. It always had something going wrong with it and he spent about half his off time working on it. And half his money buying parts for it. They loved seeing him come in up at AutoZone. He'd fixed no telling how many things on it already. It was hard on water pumps for some reason, and the brushes kept wearing out in the generator. And it took a couple of hours to take it off and disassemble it and put new brushes in, and then put it back on, hook the belts back up. It had some kind of electrical problem in it somewhere that caused it to blow fuses pretty often, and sometimes he didn't know what to do to it and could waste a whole afternoon out there in the gravel in front of the trailer messing with it. But he had to have a ride to work every morning. He had to have something he could depend on. He'd noticed that Johnette's little Toyota never gave her a minute's trouble. But he didn't like driving something that came from Japan. It didn't seem American.

He knocked again and he heard something, he couldn't tell what it was. He guessed he needed to get on home after he talked to Lacey for a while. He wanted to see how she was doing. And find out what she was going to do. He'd been thinking about it every day, at work and when he was riding around, and he couldn't see any way around her getting an abortion. It was the only thing that made any sense. It was the only thing that would undo what had been done. Get rid of it. People did it all the time. It wasn't like it was anything new.

Through the curtain he saw her coming down the hall. He lifted his beer and took another sip. He didn't really know what to say to her. He guessed he'd wait and see how it went. He hoped it would go okay, but he was afraid it wouldn't. He was afraid she'd start crying again.

He saw her wipe at her eyes before she opened the door. She swung it back and pushed open the screen door and stood there in a short kimono he'd seen her wear before. It was made from black silk and it had red dragons on it and he liked the feel of it. There was no doubt that she'd already been crying. Her eyes were red. He stood there waiting.

"Hey," she said. Sniffled.

"Hey," Jimmy's daddy said. "How you doing?"

"I'm doing all right," she said real softly. And: "Come on in."

"You want a beer?" he said.

"They's still some here," she said. He caught the screen door with his hand and went on in, and she stood there and waited and then shut the other door behind him. He thought maybe she'd kiss him, but she didn't. She just turned and started back down the hall. Her house was old and huge and she'd told him once that it was almost paid for. He followed her back to the kitchen, watching her sturdy legs. She opened the refrigerator door and turned to him.

"You need anything?" she said.

"I'm good," he said. He lifted his beer. He started to walk over there and kiss her, but he didn't know if she wanted that or not. It was hard to tell what kind of mood she was in. She reached in for a bottle of orange juice and set it on the table.

"Just let me get me some juice," she said. "Then we can go in my bedroom and talk. You sure you don't want me to fix you something? I got some good bourbon."

"Aw yeah?" Jimmy's daddy said. "You got any Coke?"

"I got plenty of Coke," she said. And then she walked to him with her lower lip quivering and she put her arms around him. He had to set his beer on the table so that he could put his arms around her. He could feel her breasts shaking against him and it caused him to start getting hard. This, too, had been in the back of his mind all the time. For days. At work. Riding the roads. Lying in his bed at night next to Johnette. Twisting on a greasy bolt with his head up under a Towmotor and thinking about John Wayne Payne. [. . .]

"I didn't think you'd come," she said, and Jimmy's daddy stood there holding her and rubbing her back. She turned her mouth up and kissed him and slipped his cap off. He heard it hit the floor. And then his hands went to her breasts and she started breathing harder and touching him. [. . .] And in just a few minutes they were back in her bedroom with their clothes off fucking their brains out and she was telling him to come, that it wouldn't hurt anything now, that she wanted to feel him come inside her, that she needed it. Needed *him*. And at that moment, he needed her, too. Or at least he needed whatever she wanted to give him. Maybe for the last time. Much later she put her kimono back on and he put his pants and T-shirt back on and she mixed him a drink in the kitchen. It was a little after ten. Probably time for him to get on. Where was he going to say he'd been this time? It got old, having to think up lies. It was almost more trouble than it was worth. It didn't seem that way before. But it always did after.

From a chair at the kitchen table he watched her tip the bourbon over the ice cubes in the glass. She had those old-timey ice trays made from aluminum, with a handle built in to break the ice loose. She reached for a Coke from the refrigerator, which looked like a pretty new one. She had lots of nice things in her house. She had nice furniture and a nice stereo, and her freezer and refrigerator were always full of good things to eat. She'd made him some spaghetti once, the best he'd ever had. With buttered garlic bread. He'd wanted to ask her if she knew how to make chili but had held off. He'd told her once about his mama and his daddy cooking chitterlings in the kitchen and she said she'd always liked hers fried.

She'd made the drink in a tall water glass and now she brought it to him and set it down beside him. She pushed an ashtray close to him.

"Thanks," he said, and took a sip from the drink. It was good, too. Just right.

"You want to set in here or go up to the living room?" she said.

"It don't matter to me," Jimmy's daddy said. He pulled his cigarettes out and lit one. She'd already told him that she hadn't had a drink or a smoke since she'd found out she was pregnant. He didn't know how she could do that, just turn it off. Hell. Didn't she *want* a beer and a smoke? How could she just quit both of them that easy?

He sat there and sipped his drink. He didn't want to go home. He knew what that would be like. But he couldn't just sit here all night long and drink whisky. He had to get himself back to the trailer. Tomorrow was Sunday. One more day and then back to work.

She pulled out a chair and sat down at the table. She had tied her hair back with a blue ribbon and she looked like she was over her crying spell.

"You hungry?" she said. "You want me to fix you something to eat?"

"I ain't hungry," he said. "I just come down to see how you were. You know. How you're feeling."

"I'm feeling pretty good," she said. "I went to the doctor and got my due date."

Jimmy's daddy sipped the drink. Maybe he'd have time for one or two more. It was comfortable here in the kitchen, just him and her. She had flowers in vases. She had a clean and shiny floor. She didn't have dirty clothes lying around all over the place.

She reached out and touched his hand for a moment. Then she pulled it back like maybe she'd done the wrong thing.

"Oh yeah?" Jimmy's daddy said. "When is it?"

"April thirtieth," she said. She smiled briefly. Then she didn't say anything else. She just looked down at the table.

Now what in the hell was he supposed to say? He had only one question, and she already knew what it was probably.

"What we gonna do?" he said.

He could tell right away that maybe that wasn't the right question. She got up and went to the refrigerator and took out a glass jar of sliced peaches and twisted off the top. She got a spoon and sat back down at the table.

"What you want me to do?" she said. She dipped up one of the peaches and ate it. Then she got up and went to a cookie jar and grabbed a handful of Oreos and a paper towel and came back with them.

"I don't know," Jimmy's daddy said. He took another drink. He tipped the ashes off his cigarette. "I guess I was kind of wondering what you was gonna do with it."

"It?" she said.

"I mean the baby," he said. "I mean . . ."

"Are you asking me if I'm gonna have it?" She had a look on her face that he hadn't seen before. It wasn't hostile yet, but she looked like she was bracing up for something. He took another drag on his cigarette.

"Well . . . yeah, I guess so."

"Did you have some other idea?" she said.

"Holy shit," he said. "I'm just asking what you're gonna do."

"I'm not gonna get rid of it if that's what you're asking. Is that what you're asking?" She was still eating the peaches and the Oreos. But she looked like she was getting mad. Her face was getting a little red, and she was crunching the Oreos kind of fast. Jimmy's daddy sipped his drink.

"I guess so," he said.

She ate one more of the peaches and then got up and put the lid back on the jar and stuck it back in the refrigerator. Then she turned around to him without closing the refrigerator door.

"I wish I could have a beer," she said. "You ain't got no idea how bad I'd like to have a beer. And a fucking cigarette too."

"Well. Shit. Have one," he said.

"I can't," she said. "I can't have one cause of the baby. I can't have one for the same reason I can't go have no abortion in Memphis or some goddamnwhere, cause I don't believe in it, okay?"

"Okay," Jimmy's daddy said quickly. Shit, she was touchy.

"Just get rid of your problem, right?" she said. "I guess that's how some folks handles it. Just kill it."

"I didn't say that," Jimmy's daddy said. But he almost had.

"I wasn't raised that way," she said.

"Okay," Jimmy's daddy said.

"Is that what you want me to do?" she said. Her voice had choked up and her face was getting red again.

"Do what?" Jimmy's daddy said.

"Get rid of it. Have a abortion."

"Hell naw, I ain't said that," Jimmy's daddy said.

"Well, what are you gonna do?" she said.

"Do?" he said. "What the hell you mean, do? What the hell *can* I do?"

This wasn't going at all the way he'd wanted it to. He thought maybe he'd better just get out of here. And then what? See her at work and try to talk there? In front of everybody? It wasn't going to be long before she'd start showing. And then everybody would know. He'd been hoping that maybe she'd quit before then.

"Are you gonna tell your wife about us?" she said.

And that just flat out stunned him. Was she fucking crazy? Tell his wife? Tell her what? That he was fixing to have a kid with another woman? Somebody he met at work?

"Well, are you?" she said.

"I don't much think that's the thing to do," he said. "I'd have to get divorced if I did that."

"Are you in love with her?" she said.

He didn't even have to think about that.

"No," he said. "I ain't no more. I told you about us."

"Yeah you did," she said. "And I don't understand why you stay with her if you're so damn unhappy."

"I told you that, too," he said.

"Oh yeah," she said. "You did. You don't want to leave cause of Jimmy." She turned her back on him and looked inside the refrigerator, he guessed for something else to eat. He guessed she was getting cravings for food already. He wondered if she'd had any morning sickness. He remembered that Johnette had stayed sick as a dog with Jimmy. And not just in the mornings. Where had those years gone to?

She bent over and opened a bin and pulled out a hunk of cheese and closed the refrigerator door and then she went over to a drawer and got a knife. She found some crackers in a cabinet and brought everything over and set it on the table, then sat down again. She took the cheese from its wrapper and sliced off a small piece. She opened the crackers and put the cheese on one and stuck it into her mouth and chewed. Jimmy's daddy saw one cracker crumb fall from her mouth. Then she cut off another piece of cheese.

He sipped his drink. This shit was going from bad to worse. He put out his cigarette and scratched the side of his neck. He sat there, listening to her eat, watching her slice each piece of cheese, wondering if she was wanting to maybe stick that knife in him.

"Look," he said. She looked up.

"Look what?" she said.

"I'm just trying to talk to you," he said. "I can't talk to you at work."

"Why can't you talk to me at work? You talk to ever body else at work. You talk to people all over the plant. I see you. But you can't stop by Porcelain and talk to me, can you?"

"You're always busy," he said, feebly.

"That's horseshit," she said. And it was. There were plenty of times when she was just standing there waiting for her line to start up. Plenty of times when he'd walked by and known she was standing there looking at him walk by.

"Are you ashamed of me?" she said.

"Naw, I ain't ashamed of you," he said, and took another sip from his drink. He wondered if she'd let him have another one.

"I think you are," she said. "I know I'm fat. I know I ain't pretty. But I guess I'm good enough to fuck on the weekends, ain't I?"

Jimmy's daddy didn't answer. There was no need to.

"Ain't I?"

"I just don't want people talking about us," he said.

She laughed and cut off one more enormous piece of cheese and ate it, then put the rest of it back in the wrapper, her cheeks stuffed, chewing.

"What you think's gonna happen in about two more months when my belly's stickin out further'n my tits? You think they ain't gonna talk then? Them tongues are gonna wag all over that plant."

"You gonna keep working?" he said. He sipped at the drink again.

"I got to," she said. She glanced up at the ceiling. "I'm helping my little brother through college and I got a house to pay for. I got to have a place to raise it. What? Did you think I was gonna quit?"

"Well, I didn't know," Jimmy's daddy said. "I thought maybe so."

She looked at him like he was the stupidest thing she'd ever seen.

"I got to pay my health insurance. Unless you're planning on paying for all the doctor visits and the hospital and everything yourself. Was you planning on that?"

She wasn't just mad now. Now she was getting mean. And that was making him kind of mad, but he didn't want to *get* mad. He didn't feel like he could afford to. He felt like he was going to have to sit here and take whatever she dished out. If he pissed her off she might call Johnette.

"I can't afford that," he said. "I barely pay my bills as it is."

"You drink plenty of beer, though," she said.

"I got a right to drink a beer on the weekends," he said.

She got up and went back to the refrigerator and pulled out a bag of white grapes and closed the refrigerator and sat down at the table with the grapes and started pulling one at a time from the bunch and eating them.

"Yeah you do," she said around some of the grapes. "You also got the responsibility of a child that'll be here fore next summer."

She sat there eating the grapes and calmly chewing them. He didn't like the way she was fluctuating. He had never seen her fluctuate before. Maybe it had something to do with her being pregnant. Hell. Some guy at the plant had told him one time that when his wife got pregnant, *he* got the morning sickness.

"Are you gonna keep it?" he said. "Are you gonna raise it?"

And that was really the wrong thing to say. She did some thing with her mouth, and she kind of resembled a mad pig in the way she narrowed her eyes at him. She lowered her voice when she leaned toward him, chewing on a grape.

"Well, who in the hell you *think's* gonna raise it? Did you think I was gonna give it up for adoption or something? After I done carried it in me nine months and give it birth? You think I'm gonna give my baby to some stranger?"

"Well, I — ," Jimmy's daddy said.

And then he just shut up.

"Are you gonna help me with it?"

"Help you how?" Jimmy's daddy said. "You mean give you some money?"

And then she didn't look mad anymore. She looked like she pitied him. She shook her head just a little as she studied him. Like he was a piece of shit. He imagined she was thinking that: *You piece a shit.*

"Is that all it's about to you? About money?"

She was starting to cry again now and she was getting really mad, too, looked like he might not be having another drink here if things didn't improve quickly.

"I don't know what you want me to say," he said.

"You don't give a shit about me or the baby neither one," she said. "Do you?"

"I do care about you," he said. Which he knew was a total lie. And she probably knew it, too. And he saw that he couldn't sit here anymore, like this, talking. Since she wasn't going to listen to reason.

"I think maybe I better go," he said.

"I think that's a fucking good idea right about now," she said. "Why don't you just get in your junky-ass fifty-five and get on back up to Lafayette County where you belong?"

So there wasn't anything for him to do but get up. He had to go back to her bedroom for his boots and socks and his other shirt and then he had to find his cap. She found it for him. He didn't even get to finish his drink since she was holding the front door open for him. Slammed it behind him. And he heard it lock. But he still had some beer in the car.

On the way home he drove under a moonlit sky that showed the cotton standing white and open in the rows, ready to be picked. The moon wore a glow around it and it had risen high in the sky. Jimmy's daddy was sipping a beer and he had his window rolled down, even though the night air was cool. It wasn't midnight yet, but it would be before long.

He saw some coon hunters loading their dogs at the edge of a cornfield where a picker had already swept the rows, nothing but broken stalks standing there now. He didn't want to go home. And he didn't care anything about riding around anymore tonight. All he wanted was for this mess to get straightened out somehow, but he didn't have a clue on how to do that.

He crossed Highway 7 without running through any roadblocks, something he feared greatly now. He had realized that you could run up on one of them without warning, and if you were drinking, you might be in trouble. And he couldn't afford any more of that. So he really didn't understand why he was driving down the road with a cold beer between his legs.

He turned off onto Old 7 and followed it up the hill and turned onto Fudgetown Road, and the transmission made a horrible sound when he tried to downshift from fourth to second. He had to keep the clutch in and let it roll a little, trying to mesh the gears, and he had to settle for dropping it into fourth after revving it up pretty high. It lugged and bucked, but it went on. He should have already had it fixed. But it was always the same damn thing: money. And this car was almost fifty years old. It was no wonder that nearly everything on it was worn out. He felt sure that he'd be worn out by the time he got to fifty. If he made it to fifty. His mama didn't.

He passed some more fields and the moon showed houses sitting dark in their yards. There were cotton pickers parked at the edges of fields and a module builder sat in one. They didn't haul it out in trailers anymore. Now they had this new thing with a hydraulic ram that packed the raw cotton into a long tall box and then slid it out all compressed. Then they covered it with a tight-fitting tarp to keep the rain and dew off it until they could back a special truck up to it and slide the whole thing on for the trip to the gin. He thought that might be a good life, being a farmer. At least you'd be working for yourself, out in the fresh air. Instead of standing on concrete all your life and taking orders from some asshole like Collums. He'd thought about quitting. He'd thought about trying to find something else. But when you were stuck in the same place all day long from Monday until Friday, it made it hard to go out during business hours and look for a job. It was easier to just stay where you were.

He picked up the beer from between his legs and sipped on it. He lit a cigarette and coughed. He had plenty of gas. And tomorrow was Sunday. He guessed he could ride down Old Union Road before he went home. Have a few more beers. Maybe see if he could see a few wild hogs.

That sure was a nice rod and reel that old man had given Jimmy. Jimmy's daddy wished he had one that nice. He'd shown Jimmy how to use it, standing out in the gravel in front of the trailer. It threw that casting plug way out there. And Jimmy was getting pretty good with it now. He'd put an old tire out in front of the trailer and had been practicing throwing the casting plug at it, and most times he could drop it into the tire. He was learning how to feather his touch on the reel button, to slow down the plug while it was in flight. And all the good shit he had in that tackle box. That old man had fixed him up. Jimmy's daddy's tackle box didn't have nearly that much good shit in it. Most of it was a snarled mess of old fishing line wrapped around rusty lures and steak knives, and he didn't have a decent collection of corks or hooks, and he'd lost all his stringers. Seaborn was bad about making off with them whenever they caught some fish together. Never would give them back. Butthole.

He had to come to a complete stop at the end of Fudgetown Road, at

Old 6, and he pulled it down into first and looked both ways before he pulled out. He shifted it up into second and wound the hell out of it going toward the curve, and then dropped it down into fourth. It made another horrible grinding sound for a moment, and then it went on. Holy shit. He hoped this son of a bitch wasn't fixing to quit on him.

The New Albany cops had taken his old cooler and hadn't given it back to him, so he'd had to go out to Sky-Mart and buy one of those little cheapo foam models. It wasn't worth a shit. It would keep beer cold, but that was about it. You couldn't bang it around much or you'd knock a hole in the side of it. It was sitting in his front floorboard now on the passenger side, and he tossed out the one he'd just finished and fished another one from it. Most of his ice was melted, so that the beer was just sloshing around in cool water with a few chunks of ice floating in it. He'd have to go to the store and get some more ice tomorrow. Or either raid the ice maker in the trailer's refrigerator. And Johnette raised holy hell whenever he did that, whenever he took all the ice and left none for them. It was always something. Work your ass off and for what? Somebody just bitching at you.

He opened the fresh beer and cruised past Pumpkin Road. It was getting close to time to start going out in the woods and looking for deer sign. He thought he was going to hunt with Rusty and Seaborn over in Old Dallas this year. Rusty had joined a hunting club and he was allowed to bring guests on certain weekends. He said it was mostly cutover but that it still had some deer on it. Jimmy's daddy had thought of going up on the national forest and hunting there, but the only thing about it was that there were already so many people hunting on it. He'd hunted on it a few times and saw more people in orange than deer. Froze his ass off. Saw a glimpse of a deer one time, but couldn't tell what it was. He hoped this place Rusty had was better. [. . .]

He went by a tin-roofed shop where some eighteen-wheelers and partially disassembled bulldozers were parked. A light on a pole shone over them. He went by more houses and trailers and yards. He passed a pasture full of cows, lying on their bellies. The sky was pale and faintly lit.

He sipped his beer and went on down the road toward Yocona. He met a car once but it wasn't a cop. Usually on Saturday nights the roads were full of kids running up and down the roads in big jacked-up pickups. He drove by another big cornfield where some trucks were parked.

He was going to have a child. It seemed scary and not wonderful. What was he supposed to do? Time would pass. One day it would be ten years old. And then twenty. What if it was a boy? That would be Jimmy's half brother. And would Jimmy ever get to know him? Or even know about him? Was he going to tell him some day?

After a few more miles he started slowing down. He was going to try and turn in on DeLay Road without going to a lower gear, and he thought he could do it if he kept his momentum going. There was a restaurant in Yocona and he often saw well-dressed people standing out beside it, drinking wine, waiting their turns to go inside, but he never had been in there. He knew he wouldn't be able to afford it. It was a place for rich people who came out from town to eat and drink wine in the country. It was dark and closed down when he went by it.

He turned in on DeLay Road and didn't downshift, and the transmission didn't protest. [. . .] He crossed over the river bridge and looked out there into the open space beside it. It was dark, the tall banks covered with tall grass. There hadn't been a frost yet, but it probably wouldn't be long. Already you could feel the nip in the air in the mornings. The leaves were starting to turn. Bow season was opening next weekend. He wished he had a bow. He'd seen in some magazine where Fred Bear had once killed an elephant with a bow.

He started pulling the Hartsfield hill and he had to stomp on the gas to make the '55 take it. But he'd waited a little too long. It lugged. He didn't want to have to downshift on this hill but it looked like he didn't have any choice. The transmission made a terrible grinding sound when he pulled it down into second, and then he had to just keep it in second and get up the hill, and it went on and on, onto another hill, and then another hill, and he was only doing about 20 mph by then, but there wasn't any choice. When he finally crested the very top and looked left down into the river bottom, he could see the white cows that lived on that farm sitting like white dots among the grass, and he dropped it down into fourth. There were bulls in a pasture. There was a bobcat that walked across the road in front of him. [. . .]

Two days later he was standing in front of the Coke machine in the break room when the big-tittied heifer walked up. He was putting some money into the machine and he glanced at her.

A Miracle of Catfish 361

"Hey," he said. "How you?"

"You piece a shit," she said in a very low voice.

"You talking to me?" Jimmy's daddy said.

And then she was up in his face. Leaning over him. He hadn't realized she was so tall.

"I don't see anybody else standing here," she said.

And then he saw Lacey sitting at a table in the back with some other women. They were all looking at him and he figured they had been talking about him. That made him feel kind of small.

"You know what I'm talking about," she said quietly.

"I don't know what the hell you talking about," Jimmy's daddy said, speaking quietly, too, and pushed the button for a Coke. Nothing happened. Piece of shit! He almost slammed it with his fist.

"I'm talking about Lacey," she said. "And how you're treating her."

He looked over at Lacey. She was eating her lunch and she wasn't looking at him now. And now that he was up close to the big-tittied heifer, he could see that she wasn't as young as he'd thought. Originally he'd thought that she was in her early twenties, but now that he was up close to her, he could see that she was no spring chicken after all. She had some wrinkles around her eyes. She even looked a little used. She wasn't a college student unless she was an older college student.

"I don't see how that's any of your business, lady," he said, and flipped the lever on the coin return. Nothing happened. No money came down. No Coke appeared. His chili was getting cold again.

"I've met men like you before," she said. "You just want to have your fun and you don't care who you hurt."

Jimmy's daddy flipped the coin return lever again. He looked over at her. She was still standing there and over her shoulder Jimmy's daddy could see people looking at them. Enjoying the show?

"Why don't you just get out of my damn face?" he said.

"Because Lacey's a friend of mine, that's why," she said. "Are you not going to take any responsibility at all?"

Jimmy's daddy was about to get pissed. He considered slapping the piss out of her. But they'd probably fire him if he did that. On the other hand, would it be a disaster if they did? The sons of bitches didn't pay him nothing. He'd had only a fifteen-cent raise in the last year. What did that translate to? A dollar and twenty cents a day? Six dollars a week? And the income tax got most of that anyway. Bastards.

"Look," he said.

"No, you look," she said, still speaking quietly, and she leaned closer. "Lacey's in love with you. Do you know that?"

"Naw, I don't know that," he said. He glanced over at Seaborn sitting with the Tool-and-Die guys and he saw that Seaborn was watching them. He was chewing slowly on what looked like an egg salad sandwich.

"Well, she is," the big-tittied heifer said. "I don't know why she is, but she is, and she's going to have your baby. I think you ought to be a man about it."

Now what the fuck did that mean? Be a man about it? Be a man about it how?

"You don't know a goddamn thing about me," he said.

"Oh yes I do," she said. "I know what kind of man you are."

"You don't know shit about me," Jimmy's daddy said. He hit the coin return lever again, but nothing happened. He just wanted her to get away from him. Leave him alone. Let him eat his chili and have a few cigarettes before he had to get back to work. The goddamn toilet in the ladies' bathroom was stopped up again and he was going to have to go up there and unplug that son of a bitch again.

"And what kind of man am I?" Jimmy's daddy said.

She didn't even bother to answer that.

"I wouldn't let my dog piss on you if you's on fire," she said, and walked away. She went back to the table with Lacey and the other women and she sat down and then leaned over and said something to Lacey. And Lacey laughed! He was afraid she was going to tell them about him shitting in his britches.

52

Now that the go-kart was running again, Velma and Evelyn were being a lot nicer to Jimmy in order to secure go-kart rides up and down the dirt road. He took turns with them, and even carried one or the other one of them up to the pond sometimes, which he figured was okay since Mister Cortez had told him that he could fish in there any time he wanted to. He'd been kind of nervous about actually going fishing, because he didn't really know how, and had spent a lot of time just practicing with his casting plug, usually in the afternoons after school. He'd gotten good enough that he could drop it into the tire in the driveway four out of five times, from roughly fifty feet. But now he was in a dilemma. He was ready to fish. He had a good place to fish. He had all the gear. But how could he get his daddy to show him *how* to fish? He didn't want to have to wait around for three or four years until his daddy got in the mood. And what if Jimmy went fishing in Mister Cortez's pond, and caught a bunch of fish? How could he bring them back home to get his daddy to dress them without telling his daddy where he'd caught them? He guessed he could lie, and say he'd caught them out of the creek down the road, but he hated to lie to his daddy. On the other hand, Mister Cortez had asked Jimmy not to tell anybody about the fish. Jimmy wished now that he'd gone ahead and asked Mister Cortez if it was all right for him to tell his daddy about the fish, but he'd known that wouldn't be a good idea, because he'd also sort of known that the only reason Mister Cortez had told him *he* could fish was because of what Jimmy had done for him down at the pond that afternoon. He hadn't seen Mister Cortez since the day he'd given him the rod and reel, and the tackle box with all the good stuff in it, and he'd stopped watching him with the binoculars since he'd told his daddy that he'd looked under his daddy's bed and had seen the binoculars under there. His daddy had gotten the binoculars and put them somewhere. But he didn't need to watch Mister Cortez anymore anyway. What he needed was some red worms. Or some night crawlers. And he didn't have any idea where to find any. But he thought he'd try. He'd figured all this stuff out at school when he was supposed to be listening to the teacher talking about personal hygiene. He went out to the shed one afternoon after school while Evelyn was talking on the phone and Velma was watching TV, and he found a shovel and an empty paint bucket. Armed with these, he headed down into the woods behind the trailer and walked through the carpets of brown leaves. The leaves on the trees were still green. There were logs lying here and there and he rolled some of them over. Fat worms that lay beneath the rotted wood squirmed in abundance and he didn't even have to dig. He didn't know they were night crawlers. He thought they were red worms. He grabbed them and started putting them in the bucket. He turned over five logs and by then he had over thirty worms. More than enough, he figured. But how did you fish? That was the thing. Maybe he needed to go ask Mister Cortez. Surely he knew how to fish.

When he got back up to the trailer, he put the shovel back in the shed in the same exact place he'd found it. When he got through fishing, he would put the paint bucket back, too. [. . .]

His mama had done something nice for him. And stuff like that was why he loved his mama so much. She'd gone somewhere uptown on her lunch break one day and had bought Jimmy a red three-gallon fuel container, and she'd gone down to the store on the other side of Yocona, had taken Jimmy with her, and she'd bought him three gallons of gas just for his go-kart. Jimmy didn't get to go to the store much, so he'd gone inside and looked around while his mama was pumping his gas into the fuel container that was sitting in the trunk of her Toyota. He didn't know they made pizzas at the store. He watched a girl making a pizza. Some young men who weren't wearing shirts came in and ordered some pizzas and started standing around waiting for them. Some more people came in and stood around, waiting for the girl to finish making those other pizzas so she could take off her gloves and wait on them. Some baby was screaming in a playpen back behind the counter. There were some old men sitting around a table in the back sipping coffee and playing dominoes and smoking cigarettes. They had lots of ice cream in an ice-cream box. The girl who was making the pizzas and waiting on the customers at the counter had tears running down her cheeks. His mama bought him an ice cream on a stick when she came in to pay for the gas, but they had to stand around and wait for a pretty long while before they could pay. They had to wait about ten minutes because some guy came in with a whole stalk of bananas on his back and the girl who was making the pizzas and taking the gloves off and putting them back on and rushing between the counter and ringing things up for people and then going back and putting the gloves back on and making more pizzas had to stop everything she was doing and pay the man for the bananas. But Jimmy was sure glad his mama had bought him some gas. And he still had about two gallons left.

He gassed up his go-kart carefully, not spilling any since it was so precious. It would run for a couple of hours on a tankful. When he had it almost full he took the spout out and put the cap back on the tank. Then he checked his oil. It was okay. Then he went in the trailer and went back to his room and got his rod and reel and his tackle box. The girls didn't pay him any attention when he went back through the living room. He didn't tell them he was leaving because he didn't want them to ask him where he was going. He had his go-kart back. He was a free bird.

He cranked up the go-kart and put his tackle box on the seat beside him. It was a good thing it was a two-seater. Then he stuck the rod upright in the seat beside him. He could steer with one hand and hold the rod and reel with the other. Then he sat down in the seat and mashed the gas and rolled out of the driveway, up the road. Then he stopped and got off and went back for his paint bucket full of worms. He set them on the seat, too.

The nights were getting cooler now. It was a lot cooler in the mornings when Evelyn and Jimmy and Velma were standing out by the road waiting on the school bus. Jimmy had heard his daddy talking about going deer hunting, and once he'd seen him sharpening his hunting knife. He always did that before deer season, sharpened his knife. Went out and sighted in his rifle. Put his hunting clothes in a bag and hung them outside for a couple of days. Went out in the woods and looked for deer sign. Put up tree stands. Watched lots of deer-hunting videos. Maybe he'd be able to kill something this year. Maybe that would put him in a better mood. Jimmy hoped so.

He went on up the road to Mister Cortez's driveway and drove past it to the new pond road and there he stopped. He'd thought maybe Mister

Cortez's pickup would be parked there, but he didn't see it anywhere. He turned down the road and when he got halfway down it he could see Mister Cortez's house and his pickup parked beside it. But he drove on down to the pond and stopped beside it, the go-kart idling smoothly, the chain still nice and tight. He looked out across the water. He could still see the gouge marks the tires had made in the bank from when Mister Cortez had turned it over. That Bush Hog thing was sitting on the bank.

He looked down the hill, across the pasture where some of Mister Cortez's cows were grazing, and looked at the house. He never had been down there before, and he didn't know if he should go down there or not, but surely it wouldn't hurt anything. Shoot. Maybe he'd better not. He might be taking a nap or something.

So he just got off the go-kart and cut it off. Dang it, he wished he'd thought to bring a cold Coke out of the refrigerator with him. A cold Coke would be good while he was fishing. But he could always run back down there later if he wanted one. The go-kart made life easier.

Okay now, where did you fish? [. . .]

He thought he could figure it out, so he sat down next to the go-kart and picked up his rod and reel. He pressed the thumb button on the reel and threw the casting plug out there about ten feet, and then he turned the crank handle to make the thumb button pop back out and lock the line. Then he opened his tackle box. What was he going to use to cut the line? Ah. The new fillet knife. It was packaged in some stiff plastic, and it would have been handy if he'd had another knife to cut the plastic from around the first knife, but he just had to gnaw a hole in it and then rip it open. The fillet knife fell out on the ground, and Jimmy put the ripped plastic on the seat of the go-kart to take back home with him when he was done. He wasn't about to trash up Mister Cortez's pond bank after he'd been nice enough to let him fish.

Okay now. He knew you needed a bobber, a weight, and a hook because he'd looked at his daddy's rods and reels before and that was what they all had on them. What size hook? What size bobber? What size weight? It looked like he had a little of everything, so he tore open a package of the red-and-white bobbers. He picked out one the size of a Ping-Pong ball. It had a little button on top and a little button on the bottom. Jimmy squeezed the button on top, and saw that a little brass hook sticking out on the bottom was what you used to hook the line to it. Okay. So far so good. He picked up the rod and swung the practice plug back to him, and then he took the fillet knife from its leather holster and cut off the practice plug. He put it back in the tackle box so that he could practice cast some more this winter if he wanted to, just to keep his hand in. Then he looked at hooks for a minute. He had small ones with long shanks, big ones with short shanks, and everything in between. He found some he thought would work, and he opened the hook package and took one out. Then he picked up the lead weights. They were all different sizes, too, in a round plastic box with a lid that rotated to allow you to get out whatever size you wanted. He got one. Then he got another one. They were small [. . .]. They had little jaws on them that you squeezed onto the line, pretty self-explanatory.

It took him a few minutes to tie a hook on, snap on the bobber, and put the lead on. Okay. He looked at it. He swung it in the air in a practice move. He thought he was ready. He knew you had to put the worm on the hook. That was just common sense.

Wait a minute, though. Shouldn't he throw it out there to make sure he didn't have too much lead on it, first? He thought he probably should. He made a good cast out into the water and the bobber immediately sank. He didn't think that was going to work. If you had a bobber, it had to bob, right? So he reeled it back in and looked at it. It looked okay. But he was pretty sure he had too much lead on it, so he took one of the weights off. Then he threw it out into the water again. The bobber floated perfectly. So he reeled it back in. He was now ready for bait, and finally, at long last, actual fishing. Jimmy didn't know how he'd managed to get so lucky. He started humming "Mama Tried."

He got the paint bucket of worms from the go-kart and reached into the rotted leaf mold he'd added to the worm bucket to give them something natural to crawl around on instead of just dried-up paint, and he came up with one squirming. He took a good look at it. It was about four or five inches long and thicker than the pencils he used for homework. And which end did the hook go in? Did it matter? He didn't figure it did, so he stuck the hook into the worm and threaded the worm on. That caused some slimy stuff to get on his fingers. But after he got the hook completely filled up with worm, he still had about three or four inches of worm hanging off. *Just let it hang,* he thought, and he stood up to make his first baited cast. It went out there about fifty feet and landed with a splash. Some small ripples went out from the bobber and then the bobber sat there. Only for a moment. In the next moment it dove beneath the water and went out of sight. Oh shit! He had a fish! His first fish! Jimmy started reeling. And something reeled back. The line got tight and it was tugging and Jimmy instinctively held the tip up and kept turning the crank, his tongue sticking out the corner of his mouth. The fish was pulling, but Jimmy didn't think it was a very big one. That was okay. He didn't mind catching some small ones at first. Mister Cortez had said they would grow.

He worked the fish closer and worked himself closer to the edge of the bank, and then he saw it. It was a little catfish about eight inches long, swimming back and forth. It had part of the worm hanging out of its mouth. Was it big enough to eat? It looked big enough to Jimmy to eat. He kept turning the handle and working the fish closer, and just when he thought he could raise the rod tip and swing it onto the bank, something happened. He didn't know what it was. Just something big that grabbed the little catfish, which caused the bobber to go back out of sight, and when Jimmy tried to turn the handle, it wouldn't turn. It wouldn't turn at all. It was like it was locked. But it wasn't locked. Something was pulling really really *really* hard and Jimmy didn't know what to do. He didn't know anything about setting the drag. He hadn't read his owner's manual. He didn't know that there was a small thumb wheel right there on the reel that would allow line to be pulled off without breaking if a big fish got on. So he just stood there tugging on the rod, trying to raise it, but whatever had taken his little catfish was going deeper and deeper and deeper and pulling the rod tip down and down and down and the line sliced across the water with drops of water leaping from it until Jimmy was forced to hold it straight out and he knew that he couldn't hold it because it was pulling too hard and he almost cried out for some help and then the line went *zing!* and broke. Jimmy had been leaning backward against the pull of whatever it was and he had to take a step back to keep his balance.

Jimmy stood there, stunned, his line lying limp in the water. He reeled it in and looked at it. Everything was gone, bobber, sinker, hook. He caught the end of the line and looked at it. It was pretty thick line. Then he looked back out at the water, which had gone all black and still now that all the commotion had died down. And it had happened so fast.

Something mighty funny going on here, Jimmy thought. *Mm hmm.* But he didn't want to take a chance on messing up his new rod and reel, accidentally breaking it or something, so he loaded up all his stuff and went back down the road toward the trailer. He looked down toward Mister Cortez's house when he passed his driveway, but he didn't see him. He was probably still sad over losing his wife, so maybe he'd better not go see him right now. He thought he'd ride around a little before supper since he still had plenty of gas. So he did.

Jimmy's daddy was home earlier than usual that evening, and he seemed to be in a pretty good mood. He was already in when Jimmy got in from fishing and riding around. Jimmy's daddy wasn't drinking, and he helped Velma with some of her homework, and he cooked some french fries in the kitchen while Jimmy's mama was cooking minute steaks and gravy, and the two of them were talking in there and sometimes even laughing. They all sat down and ate supper together, and Jimmy's mama had made a salad with tomatoes and lettuce and croutons and Bac'n Pieces and slices of cucumber, but Jimmy didn't like cucumber, so he slid his to the side of his plate. The girls talked about school and Kid Rock and Jimmy's mama talked about the new girl they had working at the bank and Jimmy's daddy said he might go out and look for some deer sign this weekend. Jimmy's daddy helped Jimmy's mama clean up the kitchen and wash the dishes and Jimmy heard his mama tell his daddy that she sure appreciated him helping her cook and clean up, that it was a whole lot easier when you had two people doing it, and he said he was glad to and was going to try and do it more often.

After supper, Jimmy went outside and opened his tackle box and looked around in the bottom until he found a little booklet he'd seen in there before but never had read. It had a picture of Jimmy's reel on the front of it, so Jimmy took it inside and opened it up and started reading it. That's when he found out about the drag on his reel. He raised his head and looked over at his daddy, who instead of being back in his bedroom by himself watching hunting videos and drinking beer, was sitting in the living room on the couch watching *Law and Order* with Jimmy's mama. The girls were in the bathroom, fussing quietly. Running the hair dryer and playing the radio.

"Daddy?" Jimmy said.

"Yeah, Sport?" Jimmy's daddy said.

"You know how to set the drag on my reel?"

"I imagine so," Jimmy's daddy said. "Bring it in here in the kitchen and we'll look at it."

Jimmy got up and went back to his bedroom and brought it out. He wasn't trying to *hide* his new rod and reel from his daddy, but at the same time he didn't want his daddy messing with it without his knowledge. His daddy was already up, standing in the kitchen putting some ice cubes into a glass, pouring some straight Coke in. His daddy sat down at the kitchen table and lit a cigarette and then laid it in an ashtray. Jimmy put the rod and reel on the table and sat down. Jimmy's daddy sipped his Coke and picked up the rod and reel and looked at it. He did something with a little wheel next to the thumb button. Then he tugged on the line. It didn't move. He did something else to the wheel and tugged on the line again. It didn't move. Then he did something else to the wheel and this time when he tugged on the line, it made a peculiar sound almost like a cricket chirping as it peeled off the reel and out through the ferrules.

"C'mere, Jimmy," Jimmy's daddy said. Jimmy got up and went to stand next to his daddy. He almost put his arm around him. His daddy turned the reel toward him.

"See this little wheel right here?" he said.

"Yes sir?" Jimmy said.

"That's your drag, Hot Rod. You can adjust it for tight or loose. That way if you hang a big fish, he can pull the line off and give you a chance to wear him down and land him. If it's set too tight, and you hang a big one, he's liable to break your line. You always got to set your drag before you go fishing."

"I didn't know that," Jimmy said. He wished he had known it. He wished to *hell* he'd known it! He might have caught that big thing what-ever it was.

"Oh yeah," Jimmy's daddy said.

"Can I try it?" Jimmy said.

"Sure," his daddy said, and handed him the rod and reel and picked up his cigarette and sipped his Coke. Jimmy's mama walked into the kitchen and walked behind Jimmy's daddy's chair and put her hands on Jimmy's daddy's shoulders. She looked happy for a change and Jimmy was glad to see that.

"What y'all doing?" she said.

"Showing Jimmy how to use his drag," Jimmy's daddy said. "We gonna go fishing one of these days."

"I wish you would take him," she said. "It sure was nice of Mister Sharp to give him that rod and reel. You can tell he spent some money on it."

"Oh hell yeah," Jimmy's daddy said. "I know that rod cost at least fifty bucks and the reel probably eighty. He's got thirty or forty bucks' worth of fishing gear. New tackle box. I wish I had stuff that good."

Jimmy wasn't listening that closely to what they were saying since he was busy pulling on the line and turning the wheel and then it dawned on him how it worked. It was simple. If you tightened the wheel all the way, the line wouldn't slip off. If you loosened it, it would. But then he had a question. What would it take to break the line if the drag was tight-ened all the way down? He'd figured out by then that the drag had been tightened all the way down this afternoon. And he'd also figured out that some huge turtle had already gotten into Mister Cortez's pond, and that that was probably what had grabbed his little catfish and eaten it.

Jimmy's mama bent over and kissed Jimmy's daddy on top of his bald head since he had his cap off. Then she got out the ice cream from the top of the refrigerator. Jimmy's daddy was sitting there smoking and sipping his Coke.

"How strong's this line?" Jimmy said.

"I don't know," his daddy said. "Was that your little booklet that come with the reel you's looking at while ago?"

"Yes sir."

"Bring it over here for me, how about it?"

Jimmy got it from the coffee table and brought it back over, still carrying his rod and reel. Jimmy's daddy opened it up and looked at it for a minute, reading in it. Then he pointed to it with his finger.

"Right here. 'This reel is prewound at the factory with twenty-pound test DuPont monofilament.' There you go. Twenty-pound test." He handed the booklet back to Jimmy.

Jimmy said, "Does that mean it takes something that weighs twenty pounds to break it?"

Jimmy's daddy picked up his Coke and his cigarette again. Jimmy's mama was scooping Rocky Road into a bowl. She also had a big pile of Famous Amos chocolate chip cookies. Like ham and cheese Hot Pockets, Famous Amos chocolate chip cookies didn't last long around there either.

"Well . . . yeah," Jimmy's daddy said. "Basically. But if your drag's set right, it would probably take something that weighed more than twenty pounds to break it. Cause it'll just keep coming off if the drag's set right, I mean if you don't run out of line. I mean if you ain't out in the middle of the ocean or something."

Jimmy stood there thinking about that. *More* than twenty pounds? *More* than *twenty pounds?*

He almost told his daddy. He almost almost almost almost *almost* told him. Almost told him everything, almost spilled all the beans. Almost told him about the big red fish truck, and the man with white hair, almost told him about the three thousand little catfish, almost told him he'd hung something in Mister Cortez's pond this afternoon that had broken his line. But when his daddy asked him where his casting plug was, Jimmy just told him that he'd taken it off. Which was no lie.

53

Jimmy's daddy went to bed by ten that night. The kids were already in their beds since it was a school night. Johnette said she thought she might watch a little TV and Jimmy's daddy told her he thought he'd try to get a good night's sleep for a change. She told him she'd be in later and told him again that she appreciated him helping her with supper and cleaning up afterward and he said she was welcome. Jimmy's daddy kissed her and she kissed him back and rubbed his back some while she was doing it, but he left it at that. Was she losing weight? Maybe they needed to go back to Seafood Junction at Algoma sometime. Maybe they wouldn't run into the preacher and his stupid dog stories. Maybe he needed to fuck her.

He didn't take a shower. Jimmy's daddy didn't take many showers because showers were a lot of trouble. You had to take your clothes off and get wet and then get dry and then get more clothes on. They took too long. He didn't stink anyway. At least he couldn't smell himself. He went back to their bedroom and got undressed and standing there in his shorts and gray fuzzy socks he stuck a hunting video into the VCR and picked up the remote and pulled the covers back and got himself an ashtray and plumped up a few pillows and piled them against the headrest and got into bed and pulled the covers up over him and pushed Play. Then he turned off the bedside lamp so that it was nice and dark except for the TV screen, kind of like being in a movie theater, all he needed was some popcorn. But it seemed like every time he ate popcorn, he wound up getting a hull or two between some of his teeth and would sometimes have to dig at it with his tongue for two or three days, almost drove him apeshit.

He'd seen this one before, but only five or six times. It was a hog-hunting video, too, except this one had been shot in some mountains with snow all over them up in Tennessee somewhere. It was pretty hairy. The hunters were out in the snow, wearing white clothes and tramping around in hog country with Ruger .44 Magnum rifles, and every single

374

time they saw a hog, the hog charged. These were not feral pigs like the ones down in the river bottom on Old Union Road. These were genuine badass Russian boars somebody had imported to Tennessee. They shot about four or five of them. Talk about some big tuskers. One of them ran the cameraman up a tree. Shit. He didn't want to watch that crap again. He got out of bed and ejected that one and put it on the dresser and got one that showed guys in black wet suits like the one Burt Reynolds had worn in *Deliverance* wrestling big monster catfish out of logs in some reservoir and shoved it in. [. . .]

He got back into bed and lit a cigarette and pushed Play again and the video started up. Jimmy's daddy lay there and thought about watching Jimmy through the binoculars this afternoon. When he'd come in from work, Jimmy was gone, and the girls had told him that Jimmy had left on his go-kart, and Jimmy's daddy had just driven up from the county road, and hadn't met Jimmy anywhere, which meant that if he was on his go-kart and in the road, he was off in the other direction. So he got his binoculars from where he'd stashed them on the top shelf of the closet in his bedroom and he walked up the road toward the old man's place. He kind of had an idea that Jimmy might be up there. Since the old man had been so nice to Jimmy, and had given him that nice new rod and reel, and a tackle box, and all that gear, Jimmy's daddy thought that maybe the old man had told Jimmy that it would be all right for him to go up to the pond.

It only took him a few minutes to walk up there. When he got close to the old man's barn, he stepped into the woods along the other side and got off the road and when he got up even with the new clay gravel road that he'd already seen, he stopped beside a tree and raised the binoculars and looked through them at the pond. That's when he saw Jimmy. He was sitting on the ground beside his go-kart doing something, and when Jimmy's daddy focused the glasses on Jimmy's hands, he could see that he was rigging up a line. Then he saw him get something from a paint bucket that looked like one that had been in the shed. Worms probably. Maybe some night crawlers. Then Jimmy threw his line out there. Jimmy's daddy stood there leaning against the tree watching Jimmy fish. It kind of made him feel funny to watch him like that without Jimmy knowing it. He wondered what the fuck he was going to do about

Lacey. What if Johnette found out about it somehow and he had to get divorced? He'd lose Jimmy. And he didn't want to lose Jimmy. And he wasn't ever going to whip him again as hard as he'd whipped him over the tools. That had been wrong. And standing there watching him and thinking about all that made Jimmy's daddy feel bad in his heart. But in about two seconds Jimmy's daddy stopped thinking about all that because by then Jimmy had one hooked. But what had he hooked? Had the old man already put some fish in his pond? Hell, it wasn't even full of water yet. But he'd hooked something. And he was reeling it in. Doing a pretty good job of it, too. That was when the rod bowed almost double and then suddenly Jimmy was fighting hard with something big. Jimmy's daddy watched it, his heart kicking a little faster, and he could see how hard Jimmy was trying to fight the fish, and it was easy to see when the line snapped because Jimmy took a step back to regain his balance. And then he just stood there. Damn. What the hell *was* that?

The guys in the boats on the TV screen were talking to somebody in another boat while they were going out over the water. Then it cut to a scene where the boats were stopped and the men were getting out of them into chest-deep muddy water. But Jimmy's daddy wasn't listening to what they were saying. He was wondering what that old man had in that pond.

There was one thing about it. He was damn sure going to find out. He didn't like it that the old man had fixed Jimmy's go-kart. It kind of made him feel a little embarrassed that he hadn't known how to fix it and/or hadn't taken much time to *try* and fix it. It wasn't any of the old man's business, what went on down here. The way he looked at it, the old man was poking his nose into Jimmy's daddy's business. Aw, he knew the old man was grateful to Jimmy for calling the fire department when he was under his tractor in his pond and all that shit. But still. Jimmy was his boy, not the old man's. In his mind, it gave him a good reason to go on up there sometime and see if he could hook what Jimmy had. Revenge or something like that. At night. In the dark. Maybe with a flashlight.

But how did a fish that big get in there that quick?

Unless somebody had *put* it in? Nah. *Shit.* Go your ass to bed.

54

Cortez's 4020 was in the tractor shop at Batesville after the John Deere people drove their low boy over and loaded it up with a winch and took it away. He hated to see it gone from the stall where it always sat in the equipment shed. He felt useless without it. It was the first time there hadn't been a tractor sitting on the place in all this time. He couldn't even move his Bush Hog from where they'd unhitched it and left it sitting beside the pond. If it rained it was going to get rained on. He didn't want it to get rained on.

He kept feeding his fish at night, wondering why he couldn't feed them in the daytime. Wouldn't they eat in the daytime? He didn't see what difference it made, but that's what the fish man had said, and if he'd been in the business for all those years, he ought to know. So Cortez would wait until dark, and then get into his pickup and go up the driveway and turn down the road to the new road and drive down to the pond and park there. He'd get some feed from the steel garbage can, and he'd throw it out there, and it wouldn't be over twenty seconds before a whole lot of little splashes would be forming across the top of the pond. He hated that cold weather was coming so soon, because it meant they'd stop eating over the winter. He wondered if they'd grow any over the winter, without being fed. If so, by next spring, plenty of them would be big enough to eat. He stood there a lot of nights, listening to them feed. He'd thought about taking a flashlight and looking out there with it, but he was afraid that would scare them off and they'd quit eating.

One night he heard something that was splashing out there in the dark, and it was making so much racket that he couldn't figure out what it was, so he drove back down to the house and got his flashlight and drove back up there and turned it on. All the feed was gone. The water was black and smooth. He got some more fish feed from the garbage can and threw it out into the pond. When the splashing started up again, he looked again with the flashlight. Hundreds of little eyes were out there, showing red in the flashlight's beam. There were so many of them that they were making a hell of a splash. So that's what it was. Just so many of them. He nodded to himself. Next year the splashes would be much bigger. And with the winter rains, the pond would probably be totally full of water by Christmas. He was really looking forward to seeing that. Jimmy could fish all he wanted to next spring and summer. Shoot. Maybe they could fish together once in a while. That would be nice. That would be almost like it had been with Raif. Just as he got into the truck he heard another big splash.

Lucinda called him one night and talked for about twenty minutes, but he failed to tell her that he'd rolled the 4020 off into the pond. And had broken his arm. And had to be rescued by the fire department. And had been admitted to the hospital overnight. He did tell her that he'd met this little boy down the road named Jimmy. He didn't tell her that the little boy had saved his life or that he'd bought him a nice rod and reel. He thought he'd keep all that to himself for now. She said they might be there for Thanksgiving. He told her to come on and asked her if she knew how to cook a turkey and she said no, because her mama always did it. He didn't tell her that Queen used to cook all theirs. When she was still around.

He rode down to Batesville one day to see how they were coming with his tractor and to do a few other things, too. It took him about twenty-five minutes to get over there from his house. His arm wasn't hurting anymore, and one reason he hadn't told Lucinda about rolling his tractor off into the pond was because he didn't want her to start telling him how he needed to stop driving his tractor. He'd only made one little mistake in about fifty years of tractor driving. Two mistakes if you counted when he tried to pull that post that was set in concrete.

Tri-County Marine was on the way, just a few miles out of Batesville, so he pulled in there to see if they had any boats. He was thinking that maybe he needed one. He'd gone out to the barn that morning and grabbed about two thousand dollars from one of his many hidey holes and stuck it in his pocket in case he found just what he wanted. He was also wondering how much it would cost to build a boat dock. Hell. He didn't even know anybody who knew *how* to build a boat dock.

A salesman came out to meet him as soon as Cortez got out of his truck. They had lots of boats. Lots of them looked like ski boats, but they had some big fiberglass fishing rigs, too. Cortez saw exactly what he wanted almost right away, actually a whole stack of them: olive drab twelve-foot aluminum boats with handles on each end. ALUMACRAFT was written down their sides.

The salesman came over and shook hands and introduced himself and Cortez asked him how much they were getting for those twelve-foot boats. The salesman said he could let have him a real good deal today since fall was here and they wouldn't keep as much stock over the winter. Cortez asked him if he had any paddles and he said he did and in not over ten minutes Cortez was out of there with a new boat tied in the back end of his pickup. From there he drove on down to the John Deere dealership just on the other side of the bridge in town and turned in.

He parked in front but no salesman came out to meet him. He looked at a couple of big glassed-in-cab John Deere tractors with their pretty green-and-yellow paint, but none of them had price tags hanging on them. They never did. The John Deere salesmen didn't want you to be able to walk up to a new one in the parking lot and see how much it was because that might scare you off the parking lot right away. You might figure you'd just keep on using your old one. Or maybe buy a Kubota. Or a Belarus. Or a Kioti. And the John Deere salesmen didn't want you to do that. They wanted you to buy a new John Deere from them because they wanted that sales commission. But Cortez wasn't ready to talk to a salesman until he found out something about his 4020, specifically whether it was ever going to be worth a shit again after being rolled off into a pond, so he walked on back to the shop and let himself in. They had his 4020 out in the middle of the big concrete floor and they had the hood off it and some parts were lying around. He didn't see anybody in the shop.

"Anybody home?" Cortez hollered. He looked around but he still didn't see anybody. So he walked on over to the 4020. He could tell they'd put some new fuel lines on it. A new linkage rod for the throttle. Must have bent it. A new exhaust pipe and muffler. He'd needed a new muffler anyway, loud son of a bitch. There was a drain pan sitting under it full of black oil and his old blue Chevron filter. He'd bet anything the motor had gotten some water in it. It probably wasn't going to be worth a shit. He was probably going to have to trade. Shit. He *wanted* to trade. But there was no need in letting these money-grubbing sons of bitches know how eager he was for one of those new ones out front. He could imagine himself Bush Hogging on hot August days in air-conditioned comfort.

"Can I help you?" he heard somebody say behind him. Cortez turned to see a tall young man in tan Carhartt coveralls walking toward him with a sandwich in his hand. The young man was chewing and he had a quart of buttermilk in his other hand.

"That's my tractor," Cortez told him. "I was wondering how y'all was coming along with it."

The young man walked over and took another bite of his sandwich. He chewed for a bit and then swallowed. Then he lifted the box of buttermilk and turned a long draft down his throat. Cortez almost cringed watching him. One of the worst things he'd ever had to do his whole life was watch his wife eat corn bread and drink buttermilk. He didn't know how anybody could drink that shit, but she could. And here this young fellow was the same way. The young man took the box of buttermilk down and took another bite of his sandwich.

"This the one that went in the pond?" he said, spewing bits of Cortez didn't know what. Looked like pieces of lettuce maybe.

"That's right," Cortez said. "Reckon how long it's gonna take y'all to get done with it?"

"I don't think it's gonna take too much longer," the young man said. He took another big long drink of that buttermilk and Cortez turned his head toward the tractor. His mama had tried to make him drink buttermilk when he was a kid and after he almost vomited a few times she stopped trying to make him. He just couldn't swallow it. It tasted like it was ruined. All clabbered up with all those chunks in it? He didn't want any buttermilk.

"Was they any water in that motor?" Cortez said.

"It's hard to tell," the young man said. "We gone start her up this afternoon, Joe said, and let her run a few minutes and then drain her again and put some more new oil in her and Joe said he thought she'd be okay. We can't see no water on the dipstick. How come her to roll off in a pond?"

Nosy son of a bitch, too. Cortez didn't want to tell him. It wasn't any of his business. People wanted to know everything, though.

"Don't you worry none about why it went off in there," Cortez said. "I can promise you it won't go off in there no more. Now what's the price on them new tractors out front?"

The young man looked like he'd been slightly offended. He lifted his shoulders briefly and scratched at his nose with the open spout on the box of buttermilk. Then he took another big drink of it.

"You'd have to talk to Joe, mister," the young man said, and took another bite of his sandwich. It had some tomatoes in it too and it was dripping onto the floor. "Sixteen something I think for that littlest one."

"Reckon what my old one's worth?" Cortez said.

"I don't know," the young man said. "I ain't really the one to talk to about that. I just work on em. I don't sell em. You'd have to talk to Joe."

"Ever body gone to lunch?" Cortez said.

"Yes sir. I'm just catching the phone while I eat."

He kept eating. Cortez kept standing there. He wanted to get some idea of how they'd trade with him, but he didn't want to have to wait around for somebody to get back. That might make him look eager.

"What'd you do to your dang arm?" the young man said.

"Broke it," Cortez said.

The young man chewed some more and then he looked at the tractor sitting there.

"What would you take for that old forty twenty?" he said.

"You interested in it?" Cortez said.

"My daddy might be," the young man said. "His old one's about wore out."

"I can't sell it till I get another one," Cortez said. "You think y'all'll be through with it in another week?"

"I think we'll be through with it by tomorrow," the young man said. "How could I get ahold of you if my daddy wants to talk to you about that forty twenty?"

"I'm in the phone book," Cortez said. "My name's Cortez Sharp. I live over close to Oxford."

"Okay," the young man said. "I bet Joe's got your number already. We'll call you before we bring it home. You ain't got no idea what you'd have to have for it?"

Cortez thought for a moment. It had a lot of hours on it. The seat was ripped. The tires on the front weren't that good. And he really wanted one of those new ones out front with a cab on it so that he could stay warm in the winter and air-conditioned in the summer.

"Just tell your daddy to call me sometime," he said, and he walked out and left the young man standing there, nodding and chewing.

That night Cortez saw lights up at the pond. He was just about to go to bed and he stepped out the front door to take a leak off the edge of the porch and the porch light wasn't on, so a bobbing yellow light was easy to see up on the hill. It was Friday night and he was going over to Moore's at Pontotoc in the morning to get some salt blocks and some minerals for his cows. Unless that was Jimmy up there with a flashlight, somebody was trespassing on him. He stood there in the dark and watched the light. Then it went off. Who would it be if it wasn't Jimmy?

He started to go up there. Just to see. But he figured it was Jimmy. Maybe he was up there tightlining. If he knew how to tightline. He couldn't believe his daddy never had taken him fishing.

He kept standing there. He didn't see the light anymore. And he didn't really want to have to go put his shoes back on and get the keys and start the truck and drive all the way up there when it was probably just Jimmy anyway. So he didn't go investigate. He just went back inside and went to bed.

Later, just at the point when he was almost asleep, he heard the sound of a vehicle up on the road. And then it went down the road and out of hearing. Or else somebody killed it. But he just rolled over. He'd be glad when he could get that cast off his arm. Son of a bitch was heavy. And it itched where you couldn't scratch it.

55

Peter Rabbit woke from his afternoon nap and came out the back door with his nose to the boards and vacuumed the scent up his nostrils as he followed it over to the end of the porch and around the old wringer washing machine and then back to the steps and down them. He snuffled and snorted and blew bits of grass and dust and dead bugs up with short explosions from his nose and then headed out across the yard. He was actively snorting and snuffling some kind of enthusiastic nose language as he followed it around one of the catalpa trees and then out past one of the leaning sheds and then back around the old pickup and then over to the side of the house and then back across the yard where he crossed the scent again and was puzzled and then began to go in circles until he crossed out on the other side of it and followed it over to where Montrel's car used to sit and then back across the yard under the clothesline that was propped up with a few rotted planks and that held only Cleve's underwear and a few T-shirts. He stopped and snorted. He wagged his tail. He didn't bark. He started moving again and he followed it around the chicken house and back by a pile of old rotting wooden Coke cases and down beside the edge of the yard. He stopped again. He backtracked. He backtracked again and picked it back up where he had turned around and followed it along the wall of tall grass beside the hog pen and then he stopped at the other catalpa tree and looked up it. He sat down, looking up it. Then he stood up on his hind legs and put one paw on the trunk. And then he barked. Once. Then he barked again. By then he could see the squirrel skin that was hanging in the tree by a rope and he put both feet on the trunk and started barking steadily. He barked and barked and barked and barked and Cleve, hidden behind the door of the corncrib where he could watch him and see how he did with just a skin, sat there looking through the cracks in the boards with something like a shy smile, a pint of whisky in his hand, nodding, sipping.

56

The weather turned overnight [. . .]. Jimmy watched the leaves on the trees from the windows of the school bus each morning and each afternoon and saw how they went from green to yellow and orange. His daddy had been out in the woods looking for deer sign, but he hadn't said if he'd found any signs of deer or not.

One afternoon Jimmy came in from school and changed clothes while the girls were getting snacks. He got his rod and reel and took a raw hot dog from the icebox and cut it up into chunks and put it in a sandwich bag and got his tackle box and got on his go-kart and went up to Mister Cortez's pond. He fished for a while and caught four little catfish about six inches long, but he didn't keep any of them. He just turned them loose and then he sat there. The pond was pretty. He looked down the hill at Mister Cortez's house. His truck wasn't home, but there was a big new-looking green-and-yellow tractor sitting beside the house. It had a nice glassed-in cab. Jimmy guessed his old one had gotten messed up from being in the pond.

He sat there a little longer and then he put another piece of hot dog on his hook and threw it out there. His daddy had been staying out late again, and the peaceful happiness that he'd begun to feel and hope might last for a long time was gone again and he wondered why. He heard them arguing about money some nights. His daddy was talking about selling his '55. Even Jimmy thought that was probably a good idea. It always had something wrong with it and he'd gotten used to hearing his daddy cuss about it. He was hoping that if his daddy bought something else, it would be a big jacked-up pickup.

Jimmy wished he could see Mister Cortez. He could see a bunch of big round bales of hay stacked neatly beside each other next to Mister Cortez's yard. He could see some of his cows. And then it was on. The rod was almost pulled out of his hands and he looked out there to see nothing but a tight line whipping deep beneath the water. Was his drag set? The reel went *screeeeee* and *scree*, and then the reel was talking to him by going *Screeeeeeeeeeeeeeeeeeeeeeeeeeeeeeeeeeeeeeeeeeeeeeee!* and Jimmy knew he was doing no good at reeling, but he had the crank going as fast as he could turn it. The line kept peeling off and peeling off and peeling off and then it stopped peeling off and he tried to lift the rod. And that just made more line peel off, so he stopped. He turned the hand crank some but didn't gain any line back. He was watching the line closely. It moved in the other direction, tight as could be, and Jimmy kept trying to reel, but that didn't do any good. Something sluggish and heavy was on the other end. Something that was down close to the bottom. He'd never had this much line off his reel before.

He could feel his heart beating pretty hard, but he was trying to stay calm and not lose it. If it wasn't a turtle, what was it? It had to be a turtle. But could a turtle move that fast? If it was a fish, what kind of fish was it? Not a catfish. There couldn't be one that big in here. There wasn't even any water in here back in the summer. A fish couldn't grow that fast. So what was it? And if he lost it again, was he going to tell his daddy this time? What would it hurt to tell his daddy?

The line made a great surge again and it went in a curve around the pond, the line cutting the water in a sweep. Jimmy started working his way toward the shallow end, figuring it might be easier to get it in if he could get it over there. The line stopped again and it moved his way and he was quick to turn his reel handle. This time a little line went back in. That meant he was getting him closer. But then it peeled back off a lot more than he had gained, until it went to the far end of the pond, and then it stopped again. Jimmy was almost over to the clay gravel parking lot where the fire truck had rolled in. The water at the edge was only a few inches deep at this end. Jimmy kept reeling and he got some more line back. But still he couldn't raise whatever it was. It was deep in the water, and Jimmy remembered how the pond had looked when it was dry. That end was the deepest. He kept reeling and he got a little more back because the line moved back his way. But then it stopped again and then it went right and came around the edge of the bank, closer. He kept reeling and got some more line back. And then he saw just a flash of his bobber and his heart leaped again. His bobber was only two feet above the hook. So maybe in a few minutes, if he could ever raise it, he might be able to see what it was. If his arms held out. He hadn't noticed it at first, in all the excitement, how much strain it was on his arms to keep the tension on the fish. And he knew by now it was a fish. It couldn't be anything else. Unless it was a beaver. It couldn't be a beaver, could it? Nah. Beavers didn't eat hot dogs. They ate bark. But his arms were almost starting to shake, and the worst strain was in the muscles of his forearms, and they were standing up in little ridges. He kept turning the crank, and then he stopped and just concentrated on holding the rod steady as the line moved right and then left and then circled and came back to where it had been, and he couldn't reel in any more line. And his bobber went back out of sight.

He wished Mister Cortez would come in. He wished he'd drive home from wherever he was and see Jimmy up here and come up to say hi and then see that he was in trouble and come over and help him and then maybe both of them could get it in. He didn't think he was going to be able to get it in. He didn't think his arms were going to hold out. He turned the hand crank again and took back a little more line, not much. He wondered if his drag was too loose. Twenty-pound test. How much would it take to break it if it was tightened down a little more? What if it caused him to lose the fish? He'd already lost it one time. But he thought he'd try it anyway. He wasn't doing any good this way because he couldn't force it closer. He looked down at the reel for a moment and checked to see which way the arrows were pointing for more or less and turned the wheel toward more with his thumb. That cranked up the tension a little. The line was still coming off when the fish pulled, but not as easily. He cranked a little more in. The fish was closer to the shallow end now. Didn't that mean that he was getting closer to catching it? Boy. If it weighed maybe five pounds or something maybe he could get his mama to take a picture of it and he could take that to school for Show and Tell. He cranked a little more in and he thought he saw another flash of his bobber. He was tempted to tighten the drag a little more, but it was better now and he didn't want to take the chance on having his line broken again, and losing the fish again, so he left it alone. But his arms were killing him. They were definitely shaking now, and they were hurting. Even his back was hurting. It was in a strain, too, a constant one he couldn't get away from. He'd never thought fighting a fish would have been this hard.

He tried something. He tried pressing his thumb down on the line where it rode above the rod, just out in front of the reel, and he found out that he could pull on the line that way. But whatever it was out there was so heavy he couldn't move it. *It* was moving, but he couldn't make it go where he wanted to, which was closer to the bank. So he just kept standing there with his arms getting worse and worse, and shaking more and more, and wishing he had some help.

But that didn't do any good. He wondered how long he could stand here and just hold it. Could he stand here until dark? Could he stand here until past dark, until his daddy missed him and came looking for him? He didn't think he could. And then he didn't have to try and decide anymore. The fish made a great surge and even though the line slipped off the reel, and the drag screamed, the line went limp. And Jimmy's heart sank. Dang it! Dang it dang it dang it dang it dang it!

He went ahead and reeled it in and looked at it. The hook was draped with little rags of flesh, little hunks of . . . what? Catfish mouth?

Tore the hook out!

[. . .]

57

The fish in the pond stopped eating toward the end of October when the nights turned colder. Three cool and windy evenings in a row Cortez went up to the pond and threw the feed out and three evenings it lay there floating on the surface of the water untouched. It was kind of a letdown, but he'd been knowing it was coming, and there wasn't anything he could do about it, so he took a black rubber bungee cord and ran it through the handle on the lid of the steel garbage can and hooked it through the handles on each side to keep the coons out of it over the winter. And then he went back up to Sneed's and got a length of chain and a padlock and ran the chain through the handles and locked the can around the big white oak so that the deer couldn't turn it over. He'd already made up his mind that next year he was going to feed the fish in the daytime, screw what the fish man said.

The leaves were starting to fall from the trees everywhere and the road he lived on was littered with them, maple and oak and sweet gum and hickory, curled in yellow and brown and orange, rustling dryly across the gravel, crackling lightly under his tires whenever he drove out of the driveway. He didn't drive out much. The grass had gone to seed and he was using the new tractor to put out the big bales of hay for his cows, backing the long iron hay spear into the center of a bale carefully, then lifting it and taking off with it. The new John Deere was a farmer's joy. It was smooth and quiet with a comfortable seat, and riding inside the glassed-in cab was like being insulated from the world. He had a heater if he needed it, an air conditioner if he needed it. It had power steering and four-wheel drive and a digital clock. The salesman had tried to get him to have a radio installed, but Cortez told him he didn't need a radio. The main thing about it was that he could stay warm in the winter and cool in the summer.

He drove it up to the pond one day and hooked the Bush Hog to it and mowed the rest of the grass and he didn't worry about what was growing on the slopes. As soon as a few frosts hit it would be dead anyway. When he finished mowing he drove it back down to the house and backed the Bush Hog into the equipment shed and unhooked it. Then he found his grease gun hanging on a nail and put a new cartridge in it and greased the gear box and all the zerk fittings in the driveshaft.

Now the days were shorter and the stars in the black sky seemed to be clearer at night whenever he stepped out after supper to sit for a little while on the front porch in the darkness, kind of watching to see if there were any more lights up at the pond. He'd gone up there the morning after he'd seen them the first time, looking for evidence of some sort, maybe some beer cans or something, but he hadn't found anything. No tracks that he could see. And it might have been Jimmy anyway. He wished he could see him, but he didn't want to go down there to his trailer just to see him. He didn't know his folks, didn't know what kind of people they were. The nights kept getting colder and he didn't sit out long. He'd thought about calling that Carol, but so far he hadn't. He was afraid he wouldn't know what to say to her. It had been so long since he had courted his wife. Another life he once had. He'd had several already. One with her. One with Queen and her. Now this one without either one of them. Cortez asked himself out there one night: *Why did you kill the one you loved to stay with the one you didn't?*

His arm still itched under the cast and it was awkward washing his hands with it on. Awkward cooking, awkward doing anything that used your fingers and thumb.

It seemed lonesome around the house now with the weather colder, the skies grayer. He didn't care anything about sitting in the house and watching television in the daytime. So he got out and found things around the place to do. He'd turned all his heifers out into the main pasture with the rest of the cows now that the heifers were all bred, which meant he was feeding hay to thirty-four head instead of just twenty. But he had plenty of hay. More than enough to get him through to the first week of April. And then about a month after that he could start looking for at least some of his heifers to get in trouble. That's when he'd have to be up at night a lot, driving up in the pasture, checking on them, seeing if they were in labor, walking around with his flashlight and wading the damp grass in his rubber boots to find them wherever they'd hidden themselves to have their babies. But he was looking forward to that, too.

Early summer was his favorite time with his cows, when they'd had their babies and the babies were walking around with them, nursing, or picking up a hind foot to scratch delicately between their eyes at whatever was itching them. The grass would be green again then, and the sun would be bright, and the sky would be blue. White clouds floating. Rebirth. Nature having its way in the world. When was that spring coming that he wouldn't get to see? He guessed he ought to put some flowers on his wife's grave sometime. There was something else he'd been thinking about doing, too. But it was probably a foolish thing to be thinking. Especially after all this time.

He patched some fences that needed patching and he cleaned a couple of truckloads of crap out of the barn and hauled it off and he took his little cane pole tepee apart and stored the canes in the barn so that he wouldn't have to cut fresh ones next year. He put the tarp away. He put some paint on the front porch. He cleaned his machine gun. And then one day he got up early and cranked the new John Deere and backed it up to the chinaberry tree and started putting on his PTO post-hole digger. He wanted to replace that bad section of fence before it started raining all the time. It was a little harder to get it on with the cast, so it took him almost thirty minutes to get the pins in it and hook the driveshaft to it. But once he had it mounted, he climbed back up into the cab and looked over his shoulder and raised the three-point hitch and engaged the PTO lever with his hand. The auger started turning and he let it run for a minute, making sure everything was working okay, and then he disengaged it and pulled the tractor around by the side of the house and shut it off.

He wished he had somebody to help him. He wished he had Jimmy to help him. But there wasn't anybody to help him, not now, so he got into the truck and started it, and then pulled up the driveway, the bed loaded with creosote posts and tools and rolls of barbed wire. He had some new Red Brand that he'd gotten over at Moore's in Pontotoc. It would only be a ten-minute walk back for the tractor.

He pulled out of his driveway and turned right and then right again at the intersection where the Cutoff road ran into CR 434. It looked like there was nobody home at Jimmy's trailer, no cars. The kids in school. His mama and daddy at work, he guessed. He didn't see any of the little dogs.

He drove on down the road toward Queen's old house and stopped at the wire gap and opened it and drove on through and stopped the truck and got out and closed the gap. Then he drove down into the lower end of his pasture and pulled the truck up close to where the old posts stood leaning, the rusty wire sagging. He shut off the truck and got out and left the door open and headed back up toward his house through the pasture. The cows were eating from a big round bale of hay with a steel hay ring around it. He'd once owned a Hereford bull that got his horns stuck in an empty one, and the crazy damn thing had dragged the hay ring around in the pasture for half a day until Cortez could get a rope around his head and tie him to the pickup and get a hacksaw and cut the thing off him.

He wasn't going to take the old fence down. No need to. He was just going to build the new one three or four feet inside it and tie it into the section that ran out to the road.

He took his time walking up through the pasture. He saw that it wouldn't hurt anything, once he got through with the fence, to take the post-hole digger off and put the Bush Hog back on, and clip all this down before the first frost hit. Make it look neater. Not that anybody was going to see it. Give him something else to do. All the stuff in the garden was gone and he hadn't pulled his tomato stakes up yet. He'd thought about planting some turnip greens but he hadn't gotten around to it. He wasn't that crazy about greens anyway. But his wife had liked them, so he'd always raised some for her. He guessed he wouldn't need a very big garden next year. But he was going to plant his peas and corn early. And probably cut back on his tomatoes. He didn't need very many now.

He fixed a jug of ice water when he got to the house, mostly out of habit, just in case he worked up a sweat, and set it up in the floor of the glassed-in cab. Then he started the tractor and took it down the road and drove by Jimmy's trailer again. Now there was a little car there, looked like one of those Japanese models. There was a pickup sitting beside it, and he'd seen it and the car sitting there before in the middle of the day, but he didn't know who drove the pickup or who it belonged to. He'd seen the woman he figured was Jimmy's mama driving the little Japanese car. There was nobody outside. He went on down the road and stopped at the gap and opened it and pulled through and got back down and closed it. He needed to put a cattle gap down here, too. Stop having to open and close that gap. That might be a good thing to do in the spring. When he started feeding the fish in the daytime. He hoped Jimmy would come over and fish pretty often. He hoped the winter would go by pretty fast. Maybe he needed to call up that Carol. She sure had a nice big butt, kind of like Jimmy's mama.

He stopped the tractor behind his truck and left it running when he got down. The stakes and the twine were in the back end of the truck and he found his hammer and drove one stake at each end of the section he was going to replace, about three feet off the old fence line. Then he got the twine and unwound some of it and tied one end to the first stake, then stretched the twine tight and tied it off on the other stake. Just something to let him make a straight line. He got back on the tractor and backed the auger around and stopped it just short of the twine. He put the transmission in neutral and engaged the PTO lever, and the auger started turning. [. . .]

By noon he had all the posts in and tamped tightly with dirt and he drove the truck back up to the house for lunch. He took his shoes off and fixed himself a ham sandwich and ate it in front of the TV, washed it down with a glass of milk. The news was showing a bunch of stuff that had happened in Memphis. Some people had been shot. Some kids had been orphaned. He didn't care anything about seeing any of that so he turned it over to the Western Channel to see if there was a good movie on, and there was, an old black-and-white one about John Brown, and he'd only missed about fifteen minutes of it. He sat there and watched about an hour of it and then he put his shoes back on and drove back down to the place where he was working. Both the vehicles were gone from the trailer by then.

He spent half the afternoon building braces and stretching barbed wire and nailing it to the posts with fence staples, almost hitting his thumb once. He'd knocked his thumbnail off completely with a hammer twice in his life and he didn't want to do that anymore. He was putting up five strands of wire. Most people put up four but he'd always liked five. Small calves could slip through four. He'd seen them do it. And a deer would crawl under it rather than jump it unless it was in a hurry.

It clouded up a little after he got the fifth strand on and he was surprised to see that he was almost finished. [. . .] He thought about stopping two hours before dark, but then he decided he wanted to get his tractor and his truck both back to the house tonight in case it rained, so he went ahead and tied everything together and cut all his ends off and wrapped them around the posts and tacked them down with the staples and then he was done. He stepped back and looked at it. Seventy feet of new fence and it looked pretty good. He stepped forward and caught a strand with his fingers and tugged on it. It didn't move much. That was fine.

[. . .]

When he drove the pickup slowly past Jimmy's trailer, the old '55 or '56 or whatever it was was sitting out there with the hood up and he guessed that was Jimmy's daddy with his head under it. Cortez was going to wave at him but he didn't take his head out from under the hood. Cortez lifted his hand anyway and went on. He looked behind the trailer and saw the go-kart sitting out there by their little shed. He was surprised Jimmy wasn't riding it this afternoon. Probably had homework.

When he got the truck back to his house, he headed down through the pasture again, and the wind had come up a little. It looked like it was going to rain. And that was fine with him. Let it rain. Let it rain all night. All winter if it wanted to. He wanted to see what the pond would look like when it was full. He was yearning already for spring.

58

After listening to a bunch of whining and begging and pleading for about a week, Jimmy's mama and daddy reluctantly agreed to let Jimmy spend the night with Herschel Horowitz, who had asked him over for a Friday night a few weeks before Thanksgiving. The plan was to cook hot dogs in the backyard, and then camp out back there in a green Coleman tent Herschel had, and then hang around Herschel's house all day Saturday, mess around with some metal detectors Herschel's daddy owned, go out to eat uptown, maybe some place like Applebee's or Chili's, or Captain D's or the Rib Cage (they'd expanded from Tupelo), and then Herschel's mama and daddy and Herschel would bring Jimmy home and deposit him safely at his trailer.

So Jimmy took some extra clothes to school with him that Friday morning in a backpack he borrowed from Velma. His mama gave him two dollars in case he needed any money. His daddy didn't seem to be interested in hearing about all the interesting arrowheads Herschel probably had. His daddy hadn't been in very many good moods lately and he'd snapped at Jimmy a few times, once for leaving his tennis shoes in the floor by the couch, and once for leaving a kitchen cabinet door just slightly open.

Jimmy tried to leave all that behind him, riding the kind-of-bumpy school bus home through the fall sunshine with Herschel that afternoon. Herschel lived out by Harmontown, on the other side of Sardis Lake, which meant the school bus route took an hour and fifteen minutes every morning and every afternoon. But Jimmy didn't mind the ride since he got to see some new things. He got to look at the big muddy Tallahatchie River and the two trestle bridges that spanned it, one for trucks and cars, one for trains, and he got to look at the turnoff to Abbeville, and he got to look at Starnes Catfish Place. There was a sign with a large catfish out front. The catfish had a chef's hat on his head. The school bus kept rolling. The driver had the wheel in both hands and he was singing "Queen of My Double Wide Trailer," doing a pretty good rendition of Sammy Kershaw for a bus driver without a band.

"Is that a good place to eat?" Jimmy asked Herschel, sitting next to him on the bus seat. Jimmy had the window. There weren't a whole lot of kids on this bus, just the ones who lived in Harmontown, about eight of them.

"Oh yeah," Herschel said. "They got that all-you-can-eat catfish buffet in there. They got alligator and everything else in there."

"I got a good catfish pond I can fish in," Jimmy said.

"Oh yeah?" Herschel said. "Can you take me sometime?"

"I don't know," Jimmy said. "It ain't mine."

"Whose is it?"

"This old guy lives up the road."

Jimmy hadn't told his daddy about the big fish he'd hooked in Mister Cortez's pond. It hadn't been easy keeping it to himself, and he'd thought about telling his mama, but he hadn't told her either, once he'd figured that she probably wouldn't be as interested in hearing about a big fish as his daddy, and he couldn't tell his daddy because he figured his daddy would try to sneak in up there, and he didn't know, maybe Mister Cortez would catch him or something, something might happen, he didn't know what, but he figured it was just better to leave his daddy out of it. What his daddy didn't know wasn't going to hurt him. But the main thing was that Mister Cortez had asked him not to tell anybody. So far he hadn't.

"How big's the biggest fish you ever caught?" Herschel said.

"Aw. I don't know. Not too big," Jimmy said, thinking of the little eight-inch catfish he'd caught. Just babies, really. He wondered if Herschel knew how to set a drag.

"I caught a nine-pound striper out of the spillway last summer," Herschel said. "What kind of rod and reel you got?"

"I got a Shakespeare rod and a Abu Garcia reel."

"Naw you don't," Herschel said.

"Yes I do," Jimmy said.

"You sure it's a Abu Garcia?" Herschel said.

"I know it is," Jimmy said. "It's got Abu Garcia wrote on it."

"Dang," Herschel said. He was obviously impressed.

"What kinda rod and reel you got?" Jimmy said.

"I got a Zebco thirty-three and my daddy give me his old Eagle Claw rod," Herschel said. "It's a good rig."

A Miracle of Catfish 395

"That *is* a good rig," Jimmy said, feeling good about being able to be so magnanimous to Herschel about his inferior tackle.

The school bus turned off the main highway and went up a blacktop road for a while and then stopped and let off the first kid. It pulled into a driveway and turned around and then it went back down the blacktop road and turned off onto a dirt road.

"This is where I live," Herschel said.

Jimmy nodded. It was the first time he had ever spent the night away from home. Herschel had told him that his daddy had a whole bunch of old *Playboy* magazines stashed in his closet and that they were going to sneak a few of them out of there and take them out to the tent and look at them after they got finished with their hot dogs because one of them had Anna Nicole Smith in it and she was butt naked and they could beat off. Jimmy didn't know what beating off was, but he said okay anyway. Herschel's daddy was supposed to come out and tell them some ghost stories around the campfire. Jimmy was really looking forward to everything. Things were always so bad around the trailer that he didn't much like staying there most of the time, and he'd been using that as an excuse to get out on the go-kart with his flashlight headlight after dark, in the little bit of time he had when he wasn't doing homework. Which wasn't much.

The road turned to hard-packed sand and it led between walls of pines planted closely together. A sign on a tree said TREE FARM.

"My granddaddy planted all these pine trees for me," Herschel said.

"He did?" Jimmy said.

"Yep. They're for my college education. He planted them eight years ago and in ten more years they'll be ready to cut for pulpwood. You know how much an acre of pine trees is worth?"

"Naw," Jimmy said. "How much?"

"About six hundred thousand dollars," Herschel said. "Enough for me to get me a car and go to Duke."

"What's Duke?" Jimmy said.

"It's up in North Carolina," Herschel said. "That's where the Blue Devils are."

The bus pulled to a stop in a clearing in the middle of the trees and the doors opened. Jimmy saw a wood-sided house set back from the driveway, and he got up with his books and his backpack when Herschel did and went down the aisle and stepped down the steps behind Herschel and they got off and the doors closed. The driver waved and the bus pulled off, back down the driveway.

"Come on in," Herschel said. "We'll get us something to eat."

Herschel's house was really nice. It had green shingles and brown wood on the walls and there was a rock chimney coming out the roof. The front porch was made of broken tile laid in mortar and there were big posts that looked like trees holding up the porch roof. A huge pair of deer horns were hanging on the front wall and there were rockers out there. Jimmy followed Herschel inside and there were paintings of ducks on the walls. Some stuffed flying turkeys were on shelves and there was a stone fireplace and leather couches and rugs. It was the nicest house Jimmy had ever been in and he wondered what Herschel's daddy did for a living. Maybe he was some kind of a rocket scientist or something.

"Come on and you can put your stuff in my room," Herschel said, so Jimmy followed him down the hall. It was unbelievable how big Herschel's room was and how much stuff he had in there. He had a personal computer and a stereo and a big-screen TV and a DVD player and a ham radio and an ant farm and racks of CDs and posters of KISS and *The Dukes of Hazzard* on the walls. He also had a gun rack with several guns, and a fishing rod rack with several fishing rods. Jimmy checked out the Zebco 33 with the Eagle Claw rod. Herschel had a Heddon's Tiny Lucky 13 hung on the end of it.

"You sure got a lot of neat stuff," Jimmy said. Herschel's room made his look pitiful. He saw right away that he was going to have to get some more stuff for his room, because he was hoping that maybe Herschel could come home and spend the night with him sometime. Ride the go-kart. Take him up there and show him the pond.

Herschel sat down on his bed and started taking off his school shoes. He pulled some tennis shoes from under his bed and started putting them on.

"Yeah," he said. "That's cause I'm a only child. I can get about anything I want."

"You can?" Jimmy said.

"Just about," Herschel said. "They won't let me have a high-powered rifle yet. I have to wait till I'm twelve. And they won't let me have a four-wheeler because this kid we knew got killed on one last year. Just put your stuff on the desk if you want to."

Then Herschel took Jimmy back to the kitchen, which had two stoves and several tall stools arranged around a counter. There were shiny copper pots hanging from a thing in the ceiling. Herschel swung the refrigerator door open and asked Jimmy what he wanted to eat. Jimmy took a look in there and saw that it was loaded with food. Good food. Sliced turkey and sliced ham and sliced roast beef and salami and bologna and Jell-O pudding in little plastic packs and fruit cocktail and french onion dip and Cokes and Sprite and orange juice and milk and corn dogs and hot dogs and cold dill pickles, and then Herschel opened the freezer section of the refrigerator and told Jimmy to look in there and he saw that it was loaded with ham and cheese Hot Pockets and half gallons of ice cream and Eskimo Pies and Fudge Bars and Nutty Buddies.

"Can I have a Nutty Buddy?" Jimmy said.

Herschel got one and handed it to him.

"You can have anything you want," Herschel said. "You're my guest. How about a sandwich, too?"

"Sure," Jimmy said, and started unwrapping the Nutty Buddy. He pulled back one of the tall stools and sat on it and started contentedly nibbling the cold hard chocolate and chopped nuts off the top of the Nutty Buddy while Herschel hauled out stuff from the refrigerator and got down some plates and a bag of fresh hoagie buns and started making them some sandwiches with salami and bologna and cheese and mayonnaise and sliced tomatoes and lettuce and sliced banana peppers. He put salt and pepper on them and he opened a big bag of Lay's potato chips and then got the french onion dip and a spoon and put a big dollop of dip on each plate.

"What you want to drink?" Herschel said.

"Milk," Jimmy said, and Herschel poured him a tall glass and got himself a cold Sprite in a green bottle. [. . .]

"Let's go out and eat on the patio," Herschel said. He went over and opened the door and they carried their plates and drinks outside to the patio, where there was an oval-shaped pool and a table with an umbrella over it. A dog barked and Jimmy looked out there and saw a German shepherd on a long chain. The dog was sitting on his hindquarters with his tongue hanging out. He'd killed most of the grass around him with the chain.

"Is that your dog?" Jimmy said. He set his milk and his plate on the table and pulled back a chair. The woods were thick behind the house.

"Yeah, that's Rex," Herschel said, and sat down beside Jimmy. They sat there eating and Jimmy wished he could eat like this all the time. Herschel really knew how to make a sandwich. It was so big that it was hard to get it in your mouth, but *boy*, it was good, all cold and wet and spicy.

"I'll show you all my arrowheads after we get through eating," Herschel said, after they'd eaten for a while. "Did you ever get your spear point back?"

"Naw," Jimmy said. "I think maybe my daddy lost it."

"That's too bad," Herschel said. "A good spear point is hard to find."

Jimmy nodded and kept chewing. He was looking at the German shepherd, who had unsheathed an inch or two of his penis and was watching Jimmy with his head at a slight angle.

"How come you got him on a chain?" Jimmy said.

"He killed some chickens that belonged to one of our neighbors," Herschel said. "And he got some other dog pregnant."

"Oh," Jimmy said. Herschel had put so many potato chips on Jimmy's plate that Jimmy didn't know if he could eat them all.

"We can have some cookies after this if you want some," Herschel said.

"I'm pretty full," Jimmy said.

When they got through eating, they carried their plates back inside and left them in the sink after Herschel ran some water over them. Then he took Jimmy into the living room and showed him all the arrowheads his daddy had put in glass display cases. He had hundreds of them and they were arranged in circles with the tips pointing outward. [. . .]

When they got through looking at the arrowheads, they went out into the carport and Herschel picked up the duffel bag that held the tent and all the stakes and the poles. He got a hammer from the utility room and they took the tent out into the backyard and started setting it up.

Jimmy didn't know anything about setting up a tent, but Herschel knew it all. He showed Jimmy how to lay the floor of the tent out flat and then drive the stakes into the corner loops and the side loops. Then he put together the aluminum poles and ran them through the loops on the walls and top of the tent, and together they raised it. It didn't take over ten minutes.

"Dang, that's neat," Jimmy said, once the tent was standing.

"Come on in," Herschel said, and unzipped the door. "We need to sweep it out before we get our blankets and stuff in there."

The tent smelled like pine needles on the inside. Herschel had already raised the side flaps that covered the screens, so Jimmy could see outside once he got in. The dog was looking at him and wagging his tail.

"I got some air mattresses we'll inflate after a while," Herschel said. "And we got to get some wood up for the fire."

"Where we gonna get that?" Jimmy said.

"We'll go down in the woods behind the house," Herschel said. "There's plenty of wood down there."

"This is really cool," Jimmy said. He wondered how much a tent cost. If he had a tent, he could camp out in his own backyard. If he'd had a backyard. It might not be too comfortable setting a tent up on gravel. But then, if you had an air mattress, it would probably be all right.

They went down into the woods and picked up some wood and made three trips altogether, their arms piled high with broken branches and pine knots. Herschel had some rocks at the side of the house and he made a fire ring in the yard with them, not too close to the tent. Then they piled the wood up in the middle of the fire ring and saved some for later. Herschel's mama had already put some coat hangers on a little table for them and Herschel got a pair of pliers from a kitchen drawer and they straightened out four of the coat hangers, two extra just in case Herschel's mama and daddy wanted some hot dogs. By then it was almost dark, but it looked like everything was ready. Jimmy had already seen the hot dogs sitting in the refrigerator, and he'd noticed a pack of fresh buns on the counter.

"Now all we got to do is get some blankets and pillows and the air mattresses," Herschel said. "Then we got to get them *Playboy* magazines out of Daddy's closet fore he gets home." Then Herschel said, "Oh crap!"

"What is it?" Jimmy said.

"I gotta go to the bathroom," Herschel said, already moving rapidly toward the house.

"Okay," Jimmy said.

"You can play with Rex while I'm in there," Herschel said, and hurried toward the house and went inside. The door slammed behind him.

Jimmy looked at the dog. It was sitting there watching him, and it held up one paw, obviously inviting him to come over and shake hands. Jimmy went over, bent down on one knee, and reached for the paw.

"Hey, Rex," he said. The German shepherd was a big dog, a heavy dog, and he knocked Jimmy over and somehow turned him around and then started hunching enthusiastically against his butt and groaning. Jimmy was on all fours and horrified and he tried to pull away, but the dog growled in his ear and then locked his front legs around Jimmy's neck, pounding at him. And making this terrible groaning. And scratching the hell out of Jimmy's neck with his claws. Jimmy tried to pull away again, and the dog let loose a ferocious growl against Jimmy's ear, and Jimmy was too scared to move. But he didn't really want to stay where he was either, so he started trying to crawl away very slowly. The dog went with him, steadily humping against Jimmy's butt. Jimmy wondered if he should scream for help. But who was there to hear him? Herschel was in there sitting on the commode. Jimmy didn't have any idea what was going on, but he thought he might be getting pregnant. Would it make him have puppies? It might. He thought about hitting the dog, but he was afraid the dog would bite him if he did that or maybe even tear his throat out. He kept trying to get away and the dog kept humping him and they went across the yard like that, until Jimmy got to the end of the chain, and then he made a big jerk and pulled away from Rex. Finally. His neck felt scratched.

He got up and dusted his hands off and looked at the dog. His red rubber rod was way out. *Oh my God,* Jimmy thought. *I'm pregnant.* He tried to look around and see the seat of his pants, but he couldn't see anything. He didn't know if anything had gone up inside him or not. It kind of felt like maybe something had.

* * *

[. . .] Herschel's daddy, Herman, came home before Herschel could get out of the bathroom, and Herman came out in the backyard and introduced himself to Jimmy and petted Rex, and then Herschel came back out and they lit the fire with some old newspapers. They didn't get to get the *Playboy* magazines from the closet. It wasn't actually cold enough for a fire, [. . .] and the smoke kept shifting and getting in their faces, and then Jimmy kept burning his hot dogs because the coat hangers kept drooping down way too low over the fire, so that they were burned totally black on one end, and raw on the other end [. . .].

And then the ghost stories that Herschel's daddy told after dark around the campfire weren't very scary, and Jimmy had a pretty good suspicion that Herschel's daddy was just making them up as he went along, because he kept pausing to think of what came next, and even when he finished one it wasn't very good. They went into the house for some ice cream and cookies at one point, and Rex kept whining on his chain, and later Jimmy could hear him through the thin walls of the tent while they were trying to get to sleep. Probably wanting another go at him. Sometime during the night he saw dimly Herschel doing something to himself, down there, with his hand, and figured he was probably beating off. Whatever that was.

The next day they got up and messed around with Herschel's daddy's metal detectors, but one of them had a low battery, and the other one was according to Herschel a real piece of shit and would go off for something like an old ink pen, so they spent most of the day messing around the foundation of a bait shop up the road that had been torn down about ten years ago, just some cinder blocks sitting in the weeds, and they didn't find anything but bottle caps and a key and a few rusty nails and a hair barrette and nuts and bolts.

[. . .]

They went out to eat that night at Applebee's, but it was pretty crowded, and they had to wait in line for about forty-five minutes until they even got to put their name on the waiting list, because Ole Miss had played football with Alabama that day and had lost, so all the Alabama people were still in town and gloating over the win and wanting to eat and drink and gloat some more before they went home, so it took a while to get inside. And after they got seated, the manager had some kind of screaming shouting match with one of the waitresses and fired her, right in front of a bunch of people, and Jimmy sat in a padded booth and watched all that and wondered if he was pregnant with a bunch of puppies. And if he was, where would they come out? Would they come out his butthole? And how long did it take? Because he was pretty sure something had gone up inside him. Sitting there looking at the menu, trying to decide between chicken fried steak and fried chicken, he wondered about it. He wondered what beating off was. Had he missed anything by not joining Herschel in beating off? Was he going to have some puppies? He sure hoped not. Wouldn't they drown in the toilet bowl water when they came out?

59

Jimmy's daddy was freezing his ass off. His feet were so cold that he couldn't feel them anymore, and the sun wasn't even up yet. He was perched shivering on a metal deer stand that he and Rusty had hauled into the cutover in Old Dallas a few weeks back, and raised up and chained to a pine tree. Jimmy's daddy didn't much like sitting in a pine tree. It didn't seem natural. He would have preferred to be sitting in some thick woods in something like a big white oak, but there weren't any of those left anywhere close around him, since cutover was just what it sounded like. All the big trees were gone except for some dead snags still standing here and there, nothing but roosts for buzzards. And there was nothing out there in front of Jimmy's daddy but hundreds of acres of small pines about four or five feet tall, and he knew already that he wasn't going to see anything mainly because it was a shitty place to hunt. He wasn't in a very good mood, and part of that was still because of Lacey. She wouldn't even look at him at work now, like she'd already written him off completely, and she was starting to show. She also seemed to be pretty happy. Whenever he saw her in the break room, she was laughing and joking with her friends. The big-tittied heifer had quit, but since he wasn't on speaking terms with Lacey anymore, he couldn't ask her where the big-tittied heifer had gone. He didn't care anyway. She wasn't nothing but a bitch. Sticking her damn nose in places where it didn't belong.

Jimmy's daddy had been sitting here since before daylight, and there was a hard white frost on, and he could see it everywhere on the grass in front of him. The temperature had gone way down last night, close to twenty, and he was shaking inside his clothes. His breath was fogging in front of his face. His nose was running. He wished he had better hunting clothes. He wished he had some Gore-Tex long underwear, and maybe some heated hunting socks with batteries that strapped around your ankle to keep your feet warm. They used two AA batteries. He'd seen some in a Cabela's catalog. About fifty bucks. Same price as a nice spear point. He hadn't smoked a cigarette yet, but he was sure wanting one. He knew he wasn't supposed to smoke while he was hunting, because the deer could smell the cigarette smoke, but he didn't know if he could wait much longer or not.

He tried to be still, but it was hard when it was this cold. His ass had already gone to sleep and his rifle was cold in his hands because he'd forgotten to get some gloves. That was another thing he needed: gloves. Maybe he could drop a hint to Johnette and get some for Christmas. Which was right around the corner. No telling how much Christmas was going to cost. He didn't have any idea what to get anybody. He'd probably have to go shopping with Johnette and he hated having to do that almost worse than anything else. And he wished he had a sleeping bag. That's what Rusty hunted from, a sleeping bag. Rusty hauled his rolled-up sleeping bag up into the tree stand with him, and unrolled it, and he took off his boots, and slipped down inside the sleeping bag and pushed the top down so that he could see over it, and then he sat down in his chair that he had bolted up there and picked up his rifle. He said his feet never got cold in the sleeping bag. He said you could be out there on the coldest morning there was, and if you had that sleeping bag pulled up around you, you didn't even have to wear a coat. But Jimmy's daddy wasn't sitting inside a sleeping bag, and he was cold. He thought he was colder than he'd ever been in his life, and that included a coon-hunting trip with his daddy a long time ago when he was just a boy. They'd been down in a river bottom somewhere, with a bunch of blue-ticks and redbones and treeing walkers, with ice crackling underfoot everywhere, and they'd gotten lost and had been forced to wade a couple of sloughs to find their way back to the truck, breaking ice as they went, and the water had gone up past his thighs, and then he'd had to keep walking in his slowly freezing wet pants for almost an hour. And it had been unbearable. When he'd started to cry from the cold and the pain, his daddy had called him a sissy and told him he'd never take him hunting again. And he had kept his word. *Old hardass son of a bitch. Sit your ass over there in the damn woods by yourself if you want to. See if I care.*

[. . .]

Jimmy's daddy began to wish that he'd brought a Thermos of hot coffee with him. He knew he had a Thermos somewhere because Johnette had given him one for Christmas a few years ago. How good would that be right now? A steaming cup, the vapors drifting up to his nose, in the middle of all this cold. Why didn't he ever plan for stuff like that? Why didn't he start looking for a good place to hunt about six months before hunting season instead of depending on Rusty to find him a place and then being disappointed? It was always like this. He was always sitting in the wrong place, whether it was a dove field or a deer stand.

He heard a rifle fire somewhere far off, a faint *pow,* he couldn't even tell in which direction. Just one shot. It wasn't close enough to be Rusty because Rusty was only a few ridges over, out of sight of Jimmy's daddy.

Jimmy's daddy sat there, thinking about lighting a cigarette. He hadn't had one now in over thirty minutes, because he hadn't wanted to smoke walking in to the stand. Right now he thought maybe a cigarette might make him warmer somehow. But he held off. You never knew. There might be a big buck out there just about to step from behind one of those pine trees. You had to remain alert. You had to be still. You didn't need to smoke. Scratch your ass. Sneeze. Cough. He'd never seen anybody smoking in any of his hunting videos. That didn't mean that they didn't do it off-camera. Jimmy's daddy knew they could edit stuff out. The videos didn't show them eating meals or going to the bathroom or blowing their noses either, but he knew they did.

He kept sitting there and thinking about it. What was one cigarette going to hurt? Hell, he was almost twenty feet off the ground. That smoke was going to drift off. And if a deer never had smelled cigarette smoke, how did it know to be scared of it? He didn't think it would hurt anything to smoke just one. Since he wasn't going to see anything any-way. But he held off a while longer. It was important to remain strong as long as you could.

He took one hand off his rifle and stuck it just inside the zipper of his coat to try and warm it up a little because it was so stiff from the cold. That was the hand that held his trigger finger. Hell, he *had* to keep it warm. That big monster buck might be right out there in front of him, only hidden.

He kept sitting there. Sitting there and sitting there and sitting there. Nothing was moving. Not even a bird. Then he saw one bird. A cardinal.

The sun still wasn't up. It was kind of cloudy, so maybe it wasn't going to come up. When his hand warmed up a little, he took it out of his coat and stuck the other one in. If a big buck jumped up he'd have to switch hands. But no big buck jumped up. He kept sitting there. He tried to wriggle his toes but they were so dead to him that he couldn't feel them wriggling. And then he saw a deer. Two deer. A doe and her baby. Just stepping from the edge of the pines. Not over a hundred feet away.

Jimmy's daddy immediately started shaking from excitement. It was just a doe and her baby, true, but they were deer. If there were two deer here, there might be more. There might be a big buck following them, wanting to breed the doe. The rut might have already started. The baby had already lost its spots, but it wasn't very big. It might have weighed thirty pounds. Jimmy's daddy knew that it wasn't a legal deer. But the doe was. You could take a doe. Rusty might cut his shirttail off if he shot a doe, but hey, it was still fresh deer meat. But what about this? If he shot the doe, what would happen to the baby? Would it starve? Nah. It wouldn't starve. Hell. It lived in the woods. It could find something to eat. All it had to do was walk over there into the edge of those hardwoods and start picking up some acorns. So Jimmy's daddy started positioning himself for a shot. Very slowly. Moving in little increments of movement. He had to get his trigger-finger hand around the grip and start raising the rifle, which he'd already sighted in about three months ago. He had bumped the scope getting out of the truck with Rusty this morning, in the dark, but Rusty had said that it probably hadn't hurt anything. And Jimmy's daddy sure hoped that it hadn't.

The doe lowered her head and nibbled at something on the ground. The fawn flicked its tail and walked forward and stuck its head between its mother's back legs and started nursing. Aw shit. It wasn't even weaned yet. Jimmy's daddy had been in the process of raising the rifle, but now he stopped. Maybe it wasn't big enough to eat acorns. Maybe it would starve. And then, as he sometimes did, like when he first kissed Lacey, he had a revelation. Maybe he ought to shoot both of them and gut them and then come back tonight and sneak them out of the woods. If you got caught with two and one of them was illegal, no telling what the fine would be. Much more than for having wet beer in a dry county probably.

He kept watching them and watching them caused him to forget about the cold. What if he went home and got the '55 and drove it over here and parked off the road somewhere and dragged them out and put them both in the trunk? The only way he'd get caught would be if a game warden personally stopped him and searched his car. But what if he went home and got rid of all his hunting clothes, got rid of his orange vest, got rid of his hunting boots, got rid of his rifle, got rid of his orange hat, [. . .] and put on some more clothes, maybe some blue jeans, and maybe his Tony Lama ostrich-skin boots, the ones Lacey liked so much, and came back over here and parked the '55 out on the road, and then got Rusty to listen for traffic for him, and loaded them into the trunk and took them home and unloaded them behind the trailer and hung them up in the shed to skin them by flashlight? He wouldn't get caught that way, would he? Look how much meat he'd have. Two whole deer. But where was he going to put it? They didn't have a deep freeze. Hell, Carol had one. He could get them dressed and cut them up and slice them up and wrap up all the meat in some freezer paper and tape it up good and mark it with a Magic Marker, put STEAKS or ROAST or whatever it was on it and haul it down to Carol's house at Bruce and leave it down there in *her* deep freeze. He could tell her she could have some of it if she wanted it. He didn't know if she liked deer meat or not. He wondered if she was fucking anybody. She still looked pretty good for an old chick.

He kept sitting there trying to decide what to do. The doe and the fawn were slowly working their way past him. And at any moment they might step back into the sheltering pine saplings and be hidden again. He needed to shoot was what he needed to do. Shoot something. While it was standing right in front of him. So he raised the rifle on up, very slowly. They didn't know he was there. They hadn't seen him. It was a real good thing he hadn't lit that cigarette. It was good to be strong. It paid off.

He slowly fitted the scope to his eye and swung the 30.30 to cover the doe. He was still shaking a little from the excitement, but he tried to hold the gun steady. He wished he had a rest. Rusty had gun rests on all his stands that he used. This one was just an extra one that had been lying in Rusty's backyard gathering rust. It didn't have a gun rest.

The doe was nibbling at something on the ground and Jimmy's daddy had the crosshairs of the scope centered on her chest. The fawn walked forward and suddenly blocked the doe's chest with its hindquarters. Jimmy's daddy waited. He was surprised that they couldn't see the breath fogging from his mouth. And he didn't care if Rusty did cut his shirttail off. He was going home today with some fresh deer meat. That he'd killed all by himself. For the first time. He couldn't wait to show the deer to Jimmy whenever he got it or them home.

He swung the rifle left suddenly, onto the fawn. Why not just shoot that little son of a bitch? Kind of leave the doe for seed? Naw, shit, it was too small. Look how tender it would be, though. You could probably cut that meat with a fork. Once you got it cooked.

The deer kept working their way past him while he sat there trying to decide what to do. He couldn't shoot both of them. No way. As soon as he shot the first one, the other one was going to run. There was more meat on the doe. That was what tipped the scales. The little one would just have to make it on its own. It would just have to learn that it was a cold cruel world out there. So Jimmy's daddy swung the crosshairs back onto the doe's chest, pulled the hammer all the way back to full cock, and fired. The rifle slammed him a sharp jolt in the shoulder and the deep boom from the muzzle rolled out across the frosted stillness. The fawn dropped and the doe froze for a moment, tail clamped tight against her hindquarters, and Jimmy's daddy said out loud, "Fuck!" The doe looked up, saw him, ran, two hops and she was gone. The fawn was kicking on the ground and Jimmy's daddy levered another shell into the chamber, the spent one flipping out of the way in a brass blur. He was shaking worse now. Did he need to shoot it again? And how the hell did he shoot four feet to the left of where he was aiming? The fawn was still kicking and Jimmy's daddy was afraid it was going to run off, so he shot at it again. And nothing happened except the jolt to his shoulder and the echo of the second report rolling out across the pine trees. Rusty was going to hear him. He thought he'd missed it completely that time. Should he shoot again? Was he shooting four feet to the left? Should he hold four feet to the right and shoot again? Jesus. It was still kicking, and now it started making this throat-clogged blatting noise, like a strangling goat. Oh my God. He had to put the little son of a bitch out of its misery. Shoot again? Or get down and cut its throat? None of the hunting videos had ever showed any of this shit. He levered the spent shell out and a fresh one in and held four feet to the right of the fawn and fired. He saw a puff of hair from a hindquarter. But it still wasn't dead. Of course it wasn't dead. No way it was dead. You weren't going to kill anything shooting it in the damn ass. He levered another shell in and sat there. He was going to have to get down and cut its throat. That's all there was to it. So he stood up and turned around and started down the ladder that Rusty had welded to the deer stand. He made it fine about three steps and then he accidentally bumped the rifle pretty hard against the ladder and it went off almost beside his ear, *boom!*, which scared him so badly that he dropped it, and grabbed the ladder with both hands just in time to keep from falling off. Oh my God! He'd damn near shot himself! He heard his beloved Marlin Glenfield hit the ground, and that *hurt* him, and he had to stop for a moment, seventeen feet off the ground, and compose himself. His heart was racing incredibly fast. Son of a bitch hit the ground! From twenty feet up! Holy shit! The little deer was still blatting, and it was an awful sound. But he knew his hunting knife was right there on his belt. What was he going to do, stab it or cut its throat?

He hung there, swaying on the ladder, his breath still fogging out in front of his face. His legs were shaking and he didn't trust his feet to lower him safely yet. So he had to stand there and listen to the little deer and the noises it was making. He wished it would shut up, and he wondered if Rusty could hear it. He was definitely going to cut his shirt-tail off now. He guessed that bump in the dark this morning must have been harder than he'd thought.

Finally he started lowering himself. He took it slow and made sure he didn't miss a rung. His hands were cold against the cold metal, and he wished he'd eaten some breakfast. And now it felt like he might be going to have a little diarrhea on top of everything else. But he had put part of a roll of toilet paper in his coat pocket, just in case he needed to go to the bathroom while he was out hunting. So he *had* thought of one thing to bring.

At last he was on the ground, but he couldn't see the little deer now. He bent over and picked up his rifle. Oo. Oo-oo. The end of the barrel was full of dirt, must have landed muzzle down. He couldn't shoot it without getting that shit out of there. It would blow up in his face. And one of the mounting brackets on the back of the scope was bent. It must have fallen over against the tree after it hit the ground. So he just set it back down, sick as a damn dog. Then he started to draw his hunting knife from its scabbard on his belt, but instead he lit a cigarette. It didn't make any difference now. His quarry was down. And lying somewhere just on the other side of that clump of honeysuckle that had been killed by the frost. He took a few puffs, and then he drew his knife. [. . .]

The little deer wasn't hard to find, blatting like that. Jimmy's daddy went forward, cigarette in one hand, knife in the other. He parted the pine saplings with his body and there it was, lying on its side and trying to raise its head, front legs trembling. There was some blood but not much. Jimmy's daddy eased up to it and stood there looking at it. He'd never been this close to a live one before. He could see the bloody hole in its hind leg, but that wasn't the shot that knocked it down, he didn't think. Unless he'd hit it in the same spot twice. He tried not to listen to it, but it was hard not to. It was so loud that he thought anybody around could hear it. And there were other people around. They'd driven past some parked pickups this morning in the dark, a couple of them sitting not too far from where they'd turned off and opened a gate that Rusty had a key to. So he needed to go ahead and shut it up.

But he walked around to the other side, still trying to see where the first shot had hit. And then he saw it. There was a short groove cut right across its back. He'd shot it through the backbone, and he guessed that was why its back legs weren't moving. What the hell was he going to do, stab it or cut its throat? Somehow he couldn't stand the idea of cutting its throat, and he knew he had to do something quick, so he stuck the cigarette in his mouth and bent over and pulled its head up by one ear, and stabbed it in the throat. The knife didn't go in very deep, so he had to stab it harder, again. And again. And again and again and again! The little deer blatted and blood dripped from its tongue and spattered on the frozen ground and Jimmy's daddy thought he might be going to throw up. But it didn't last long. The little deer relaxed and Jimmy's daddy turned loose of its ear and watched its head slump to the ground, and while he watched, the dark eye fixed and glazed over like paint healing over in a bucket, only lots faster.

Jimmy's daddy took the cigarette from his mouth and stood there, panting a little, looking down on it. It didn't look like much. It looked about like a thirty-pound deer. It looked illegal as hell. Son of a bitch. What the hell? Four feet to the damn left? He wondered if Rusty had any coffee in the pickup. He looked at his knife. It had some blood on it, so he bent and wiped each side of the blade in the frosted grass, then put the knife back into the scabbard on his belt. Then he looked around, still smoking. He was cold again now that all the excitement was over. Maybe he ought to drag it toward Rusty's pickup and hide it somewhere, and then if he wanted to he could go ahead and get in the pickup. Rusty had put the key on top of the right front tire. There was a cooler in the back and knowing Rusty it had some beer in it. He'd probably warm up dragging the deer. But what if he ran into somebody? What if he ran into some law-abiding son of a bitch who'd run right out to his truck and get on his CB radio and call a game warden? Maybe he needed to hide it here, get his rifle, get the dirt out of the barrel with a little stick if he could find one, go back to the truck, get the key, crank it up, get the heater going and get warm, look in the cooler and get a good cold beer, and then just sit in the truck and drink beer and wait on Rusty to come out of his stand. Take his boots off and rub his cold feet. Let his toes warm up. So that's what he did.

That night Jimmy's daddy placed thick-sliced steaks of a pale color over an almost perfect bed of coals, red showing within the gray-ashed briquets, small yellow flames lapping among them, Jimmy sitting quietly on the trailer steps watching him as he sprinkled the steaks with salt and pepper and Worcestershire sauce, and then poked them gently with a fork. He knew not to cook them too long, to keep them naturally tender. He'd read a few deer-cooking recipes here and there. He sipped his beer, glad now that Jimmy hadn't seen the dead baby deer, just the parts of it that he'd brought home, one hindquarter and one shoulder, since the bullet had ruined the other hindquarter and Rusty had reluctantly accepted the other shoulder as a gift from Jimmy's daddy, sort of a hunter-sharing-the-spoils thing, saying that it was barely big enough to make a sandwich. They'd skinned it in the woods and chopped it apart with a little sharp hatchet Rusty kept in the truck, Rusty cussing the whole time, and walked out with the three pieces under their coats. Took all the ice and beer out of the cooler and put the meat in the bottom and the ice and beer back on top of it, all the way to the top. Didn't see a game warden. Didn't even see a green truck. Didn't see a soul. Drove right on out with it.

Jimmy's daddy stood there and poked at the meat. There was very little grease dropping from the grill onto the charcoal. It just kind of sat there and sizzled dryly. But it was going to be good. It was also free.

The Marlin was broken. He hadn't noticed it when he'd first picked it up, but the lever had been at a halfway position, and now it wouldn't move at all and Rusty thought a part inside it must have gotten broken in the fall. But Rusty also knew a gunsmith who worked at Nationwide Gun Store in town and he thought this guy could probably fix it, he'd fixed one for Rusty once. So that was more money if he wanted to deer hunt anymore this year. Or shoot at some hogs.

Jimmy was sitting there on the porch steps holding a plate and watching his daddy cook. His daddy had told him to hold the plate until the meat got ready.

"How you doing there, Hot Rod?" Jimmy's daddy said.

"I'm doing good," Jimmy said. "That sure smells good, Daddy."

"Shoot," Jimmy's daddy said. "It *is* gonna be good. Why don't you get me another beer, Sport?"

"Okay," Jimmy said. He put the plate down on the step and walked over to the cooler and reached in and got his daddy a fresh cold one. He handed it to him and his daddy handed him the empty. His daddy opened the fresh one while Jimmy went back to his seat and picked up the plate again and tossed the beer can into a garbage can.

"You think them taters is ready?" Jimmy's daddy said.

"I stuck a fork all the way through em," Jimmy said. "I believe they done."

"Good," Jimmy's daddy said. "It won't be long now."

He stood there poking at the steaks a little more, and sipping his beer. "Johnette and them girls don't know what they missed, eating uptown," Jimmy's daddy said.

"They got some good fried chicken at Applebee's," Jimmy said.

"Is that where they went?" Jimmy's daddy said.

"I don't think so," Jimmy said.

"Well, where'd they go then?" Jimmy's daddy said, and took another sip from his beer. If he was going to go hog hunting, he was going to have to get that rifle fixed. Or get another one. He was sure wanting to go hog hunting. Rusty had told him on the way home that he knew a guy over at Dogtown who had some hog dogs and had actually hog hunted and killed hogs down there in the river bottom at the end of Old Union Road and he'd told Rusty that Rusty and a few of his buddies could go with him sometime if they wanted to. Said the whole damn bottom was crawling with them. Said this guy said there were so many of them back in the summer that they had wide trails in the woods like highways where there was nothing but thousands of hoof prints churned into the black mud, and that they'd evidently eaten every snake in the river bottom, because the guy said you just didn't see snakes down there anymore, and that was saying something. That was eating a lot of snakes. So Jimmy's daddy was kind of excited about that, but he was worried about how he was going to pay for having his gun fixed.

"I think the girls went to the movies while Mama went somewhere else," Jimmy said.

"Somewhere else like where?" Jimmy's daddy said.

"I don't know," Jimmy said.

"What was the girls gonna eat?" Jimmy's daddy said.

"I think she was gonna take them by the Sonic first," Jimmy said.

"How come you didn't go with em?"

"Didn't want to."

"How come?"

"I don't know."

Jimmy's daddy looked at his son. He'd noticed that Jimmy had been acting a little worried lately, but he hadn't asked him if anything was wrong with him. What could he have wrong with him? Shit, he had it made. He had some of his teeth fixed. He had his go-kart going and his fishing rod going although pretty soon it was going to be too cold to fish or ride the go-kart either one. All he had to do was go to school. Do his homework.

"Daddy, can I ask you something?" Jimmy said.

"Sure," Jimmy's daddy said, wondering what it was going to be. Jimmy was pretty good about not asking a lot of questions now that he'd learned that his daddy didn't like a lot of questions, so occasionally Jimmy's daddy didn't mind a question. And it was a nice night. He had a cold beer in his hand and he had some fresh deer meat on the grill that he'd brought down himself and he had his son with him. Screw all that shit with Lacey for now. If she wouldn't speak to him, he couldn't help her. Maybe later on he could talk to her. Or what? Maybe go up to the hospital when it was born and look at it? In April? And then what? Send some flowers? Buy a few pacifiers? Go to Big Star and get some formula?

"How long does it take to have puppies?"

"Sixty-four days," Jimmy's daddy said. "That's what my daddy always told me. Cow's nine months. Same as a woman. Takes a elephant twenty-two."

Jimmy nodded but he didn't say anything. He just looked off into the black woods that surrounded the trailer like he was listening to something.

[. . .]

60

Somewhere about thirty-three thousand feet over Montgomery, in her tight designer jeans and her dark blue velour pullover, with Albert sleeping in the seat beside her, and the window cover pulled down, and her empty Budweiser can on the tray in front of her, Lucinda made up her mind. She had been thinking about it for a long time and she had asked herself many questions, and she still didn't know all the answers, but she decided that she had waited long enough. She knew some things. She knew her mother was dead and that her father was getting older and that she was the only child they had left. Everything her daddy owned would go to her. Cows, land, house, vehicles, tractor and equipment, catfish pond, catfish, however much money he had in the bank. Or the barn. And she had a good bit of money saved up. She'd gotten what she'd wanted from Atlanta and didn't have to keep staying there and modeling large ladies' lingerie, even though it was a job she liked. She was forty-three years old and if she didn't have a baby soon, she would never have one. And it would be risky enough at forty-three. But things were different now. You heard about older women having babies more now. Just because she never had had a baby didn't mean she couldn't have one now. Curtis Sliwa's sister had one at fifty-six.

She turned her head and looked at Albert. Nothing had set him off today, and his manners had been immaculate. He had been so pleasant and self-assured and polite and humorous with all the airline people they had dealt with today. She knew something about him, too. She knew she loved him and that he was the man she was going to stay with for the rest of her life. And that he was a kind and generous man. Who just had a little something wrong with him. And even though he had said over and over and over and over and over and over and over that he didn't want a baby, because he didn't want it to turn out like him, Lucinda knew that she wouldn't care if it turned out exactly like him. Hoped, in fact, that it *would* turn out exactly like him. That was when she knew what to do, when she leaned across sleeping Albert and pushed the window cover up, to look out and see the sun going down ahead of them, so that it felt like they were chasing it at thirty-three thousand feet. They were above the clouds and starting to sink back down into them and rags of white vapor were streaking past the wings. She'd find some pins at Daddy's house tonight and poke some holes in all of Albert's rubbers. Then wait for Daddy to go to sleep. Then ask Albert if he was ready to get to bed. And once he saw what she was wearing, he would be. She had packed some new lingerie that Albert hadn't seen yet, little bennies from her job. [. . .] They would come home and find a place to live somewhere nearby. She would raise her child where she had been raised. She would make her daddy happy before he died. She would conceive where she was conceived.

It was past dark when they rolled in in the rental car, and Lucinda saw that the front porch light was on. Her daddy was standing out there in his overalls. She stopped the car near the porch and saw right away that he had a cast on his arm. Albert was in the process of getting out and she was glad they hadn't seen a rabbit coming down the road. He'd been fine all day and was still fine. So she walked on over to the front steps and went up them and hugged her daddy hard. She felt him brush her back with the cast, and then he pulled back from her, the way he always did. Almost always had. She could remember a time when he wasn't the way he was now. A warmer daddy.

"What in the world?" she said, looking at the thing. It looked pretty nasty. It had a lot of dirt and grease on it.

"Aw, I had a little accident," he said.

"A little accident when?" she said.

"While back," he said. He looked out toward the car, where Albert was standing, opening the back door to reach in for some luggage. He got two bags and walked up on the porch and set them down. He shook hands with her daddy.

"Nice to see you again, Mister Sharp," he said. "I hear we're gonna cook a turkey."

"Well, I'm gonna *try* to cook a turkey," Lucinda said. And then she smiled. She was so glad to be back home for Thanksgiving. It wouldn't be the same without her mama, but it would still be Thanksgiving at home.

"I figure between the three of us we can get it cooked," her daddy said. He looked pretty good despite the cast on his arm.

"Let me get the rest of our stuff from the car," Albert said, and he went back down the steps.

"Well what happened?" Lucinda said. "How did you get that thing so *dirty*? My God."

"It's a long story," her daddy said. "Y'all come on in and I'll tell you about it. I'm cooking some pork chops I saw on sale when I went and got the turkey."

Albert was raising the trunk of the rental car. Lucinda looked at him for a moment and knew that everything was going to be all right. Then she followed her daddy the way she used to.

By the time they finished supper, Lucinda knew all about Jimmy and his go-kart and what the fire department had done [. . .] and how the hospital uptown didn't have any decent beds. Her daddy was all excited about his catfish and he'd been telling her about feeding them. Albert had gone out to look at the new tractor, which she hadn't seen when they'd first driven up because it was parked out by the equipment shed. Lucinda had bought some beer when they'd come through Oxford, had turned in on University Avenue and had run into Kroger for a twelve-pack of Bud and some ice cream for Daddy and some Cokes and Hershey bars for Albert. She was sipping one of the cold Buds at the kitchen table now and her daddy had already washed the dishes and put them away, not letting her help him, saying that he'd gotten pretty used to having to do everything with a cast on. He'd gone out to check on a cow about something.

Supper had been good and she was pleasantly full. He'd fried the pork chops the way her mama used to and had cooked some peas from the garden with some okra he'd put up and he had some corn he said he'd gotten from the Amish people over close to Pontotoc for ten cents an ear. It was some of the best she'd had in a long time. He'd even wrapped three big fat sweet potatoes in foil and stuck them into the oven about an hour before suppertime and they had melted huge hunks of butter inside them. Albert had cleaned his plate. And her daddy had been talking to him. That was a good sign. It gave her some hope.

She got up and opened the refrigerator door and reached inside for another beer and looked again at the turkey. Daddy had set it inside this morning, he said, and she pushed her finger against the bag it was wrapped in, and her finger sank in a little, not much. She wondered if she ought to leave it in the sink tonight just to make sure it got thawed in time. She got the beer and opened the kitchen door and stepped down onto the screened-in back porch just as the tractor started up. She wondered where he was going this time of night. She'd left her cigarettes out there on the table and she sat down in one of the old metal chairs and lit up. She took a sip of her beer and then set it on the table. His old army cot had been folded and pushed against the wall. She couldn't believe he still had it because she remembered him taking naps on it when she was a kid. She saw the headlights come on, the twin powerful beams shining between the big pecans in the back, and then the tractor was moving toward the house. She sat there watching it, and it rolled down the pea gravel until it lit the figure of Albert, standing there waiting for it. What were they doing? The tractor stopped and a light came on inside the cab and she could see her daddy sitting up there with his hand on the wheel. And then the cab door was opening and Albert was climbing up into the cab with him. She didn't know how both of them were going to fit in there. But when the cab door closed and the tractor started moving again, she understood that her father and her lover were going for a ride. Which was nice timing. She finished her cigarette after she heard the tractor go down the driveway and went back to the bedroom and unzipped her small overnight bag. She'd already found a straight pin in a pincushion of her mother's and had stashed it on the dresser. [. . .]

Out on the back porch again, she lit another cigarette and picked up her beer. She couldn't hear the tractor anymore. They must have gone down the road. It was the first time the two of them had ever done anything together, and she was holding her breath almost that it would be all right. Maybe they wouldn't see a rabbit. Maybe they would. It didn't matter. Daddy would get to know him better if they moved back home. Maybe they could go fishing.

She sat there, enjoying her beer and her cigarette, knowing that if she got pregnant, she'd have to give both of them up for nine months. But she could do it. She knew she could. She still missed her mama. Saw her in her memory in so many places in the house just tonight. They were going to be here for four days, and she was going to town one day and get some fresh flowers to take over there and put on her grave. She knew Daddy had ordered the stone after the funeral, but he said it hadn't arrived yet. She guessed it took time to make those things. They probably had a waiting list, like Harley-Davidson.

She leaned back and put her feet up on the table, feeling the chill in the air out here on the back porch. But it was nearly December. It was time for it to be getting cold. She guessed people were out deer hunting now. Coming down DeLay Road, she'd seen some pickups hauling trailers with four-wheelers on them. People in orange hats and vests driving the pickups. Daddy never had done that. He never had hunted deer. He'd hunted squirrels. She seemed to remember him and Cleve going some when she was little. Cleve. She still wished she could see him. Just to see him. Just to see how he was doing. She knew his wife had left him, gone off, taken the boys, years ago. But Daddy said last time she was here that his girl had come back home. Lucinda didn't know her. Tyrone and Woodrow used to ride Lucinda's school bus when she was a senior or a junior, she couldn't remember which. And they were just little bitty boys. So the girl must have been just a baby then. It had to be a hard thing, to lose your children like that. To have them just move away. But she was glad the girl had come back. She was glad for Cleve. And she still wished she could see him. Just to say hi. Just to let him know that she still remembered him. Daddy always said he was mean. And maybe that was true. But he never had been mean to her.

And then she heard the tractor coming back up the road, and she went inside to get her toothbrush out and turn back the covers.

[. . .]

61

They had been running through the woods in the river bottom and they were still running, dodging past the trees and past the big hanging wild grapevines and over the dead leaves with their guns and following the sounds of the dogs and the squealing of the hog as he turned occasionally and stopped to fight. Jimmy's daddy was almost out of breath and he hadn't known it was going to be like this. The snow was still falling and everything was dusted in this surprising December white.

Daniels, the hog guy, stopped again and put up his hand, and Jimmy's daddy and Rusty stopped, too. They were in the deep woods, and the oaks and beeches were tall and stripped now of their leaves. Christmas was only two weeks away, and Jimmy's daddy was supposed to be Christmas shopping today with Johnette. She'd raised some hell about not getting to go, too. Right in front of Rusty and Seaborn in front of the trailer when they came to pick him up this morning. Embarrassed the hell out of him. He was still pissed off about that. Should have slapped the shit out of her. Didn't know why he didn't.

"Let's listen a minute," Daniels said, and Jimmy's daddy could hear him heaving. "Son of a bitch," he said. "I could use a drink of water."

Jimmy's daddy nodded, but he didn't say anything. He was saving his breath. He wondered if they were going to stop long enough for him to have a cigarette since it was hard to smoke while you were running. Rusty squatted beside a leaning cypress in his camo coveralls and rested his back against the trunk, holding the short-barreled .44 Ruger across his knees. They were seeing more cypresses now, as they got closer to the river. Rusty was listening, too, and Jimmy's daddy could hear the dogs faintly, up ahead somewhere, just a vague clamor of voices that faded again back into the timber in hollow echoes.

"He's running again," Daniels said. "Let's head that way."

He took off at a fast walk, cutting back toward the east, and Rusty got up and turned after him. Jimmy's daddy followed him, stepping between the trees and past sunken places that held cypress knees sometimes two feet high and black water, his wet feet squishing in the black muck. He'd already seen the hog highways. They were unbelievable. What was unbelievable was that all this wilderness was right under his nose and he hadn't known about it. They'd seen some huge buck rubs. Daniels had said there were some giant deer in this river bottom, but it was posted, all seven hundred acres of it. Daniels knew the old man who owned the land and the old man was glad to see some of the hogs killed because they'd raised hell with his corn crop this year so badly that a guy had come out from the *Oxford Eagle* to take some pictures of the devastation, and they had run the picture on the front page in color. And Jimmy's daddy remembered seeing it in a rack down at the store one day, the old man standing in the middle of his wrecked field, with stalks of corn torn down all around him, and the ground torn up from their ravages. Daniels thought there were hundreds of them down here. Maybe thousands. Nobody really knew. The river bottom was vast and they could go wherever they wanted. Jimmy's daddy had seen so many fresh hog wallows that he'd stopped counting them.

Daniels kept trotting along, the chrome leash chains he had fastened around his waist clicking against each other as he went. They'd brought six Plott hounds and one had suffered a deep cut the first time the hog stopped to fight, and Daniels always carried a first-aid kit and had put a dressing and some Neosporin on it, and had tied him to a tree until he could get back and help him out to the road where the trucks were parked. He'd already called the vet on his cell phone and the vet had said to bring him in whatever time it was and he'd sew him up. Another dog had gotten separated from them somehow and now there were only four to hold the hog until they could get there with their guns, but so far it hadn't happened. Daniels was afraid it was a big one. He had already shot a black one this year that weighed 324 pounds at the deer-processing place on Bell River Road. He'd said its tusks were seven inches long and he was getting it mounted right now. He was carrying a Remington 12-gauge Magnum Express pump, loaded with three-and-a-half-inch Brenneke rifled slugs, and there was a revolver in a holster on his belt. Jimmy's daddy had only gotten his Marlin back from the gunsmith yesterday and he hadn't had time to shoot it. But the gunsmith had taken the scope off, saying the mounts were ruined anyway, and possibly the scope, too, but Jimmy's daddy figured the factory iron sights were okay. He just hoped he got the chance to use it.

Daniels stopped again and turned to Jimmy's daddy.

"I wish your friend would catch on back up with us so we'd know where he is. We get in there and have to shoot, and don't know where he is . . ." He didn't finish his sentence. He was listening for the dogs.

Seaborn hadn't caught up with them yet. He'd had to stop and take a shit about ten minutes back, of all times. Right in the middle of the race. He'd been lagging behind, almost out of sight, out of wind, sweating even with the snow falling. Jimmy's daddy didn't know where he was now.

"He'll catch up with us," he said, not sure if that was true or not. Hell, maybe he'd gone back to the truck.

"I hope so," Daniels said. "I believe they've turned again. If they could ever get him hemmed up against the river, we might have a chance to get in there and get a shot."

There was that faint clamoring in the distance again, and it seemed to be getting louder. And then there was the sound of something running.

"Holy fucking shit!" Rusty said, and raised his rifle about the same time Daniels raised his shotgun. Jimmy's daddy heard the shotgun roar and Daniels's shoulder rocked back, and Rusty stepped up beside him and leveled the .44 and it boomed twice. That was when Jimmy's daddy saw it, black and huge, covered with mud, slobber coming from its mouth, tearing through the trees and vines out there about a hundred feet and moving a lot faster than Jimmy's daddy would have thought a hog could run. They both missed it. And then it was gone.

"Son of a bitch," Daniels said. He ejected his empty and shucked another one into the chamber and put his safety on and looked over at Rusty. "I think I hit a damn tree," he said.

"I know I did," Rusty said. Then he looked at Jimmy's daddy. "Why didn't you shoot?"

"Hell. Time I seen him he was done gone."

"They gonna have to catch him and let us get a shot," Daniels said. "Well, come on. We got to try and stay close."

"Is he as big as that one you shot?" Jimmy's daddy said.

"He looks bigger," Daniels said.

The dogs were getting closer and then Jimmy's daddy could see them, black-and-brindle shapes loping toward them, and when they drew nearer he could see that some of them were bloody on their faces and legs and sides. But they didn't stop. They swept past, their voices ringing in the woods and making the woods echo with their passing and sending a chill running down Jimmy's daddy's backbone. Jimmy's daddy started running again.

It was getting harder now. He was slowing down, and he could see Rusty and Daniels pulling away from him. They kept glancing back at him, but all he could do was wave for them to keep going. The ground was getting muckier, and sometimes there were holes where you could go up to your knee. Daniels had learned some way to navigate through this and keep going, and Rusty was right behind him, but Jimmy's daddy was out of breath again and was afraid he was going to have to stop and rest. And finally he did. He stopped and bent over, holding his rifle, and he saw Daniels and Rusty stop and look back at him.

"I'm coming!" he shouted, and he started moving toward them. Daniels said something to Rusty and they went on. Jimmy's daddy stopped again. Holy shit. He hadn't run this hard since tenth grade in football. Jesus. He was afraid he was going to have a heart attack. All them damn cigarettes. He bent over and heaved. If it hadn't been so wet he would have sat down. And then he saw what looked like a fairly solid log and he walked over to it and did sit down. Damn. Shit. He pulled his rifle upright and rested the stock on the ground and leaned his head against the lower part of the barrel while he got his breath. He couldn't even hear the dogs now.

God. His legs were shaking. And he wanted to be there when it happened. He didn't want to miss out. He wanted to stop here for a few minutes and maybe have a cigarette, but instead he pushed himself up and went the way they'd gone. He heard one of them say something up ahead of him somewhere, but there were thousands of trees and the sound seemed almost directionless, and he wasn't sure which way to go. He kept walking and he couldn't hear anything but his own feet squishing in the black mud. And hog tracks everywhere. More wallows. Jimmy's daddy thought he could even smell them.

And then he heard it: the hysterical squealing up ahead and the snarl of hounds. And he heard somebody yell. But the two sounds didn't sound like they were coming from the same place. So he headed toward the sound of the dogs. There were vines and briars and he had to climb down in a ditch and up the other side, grabbing at the mud to pull himself up, trying to keep his rifle's muzzle out of the mud, and when he got up on the other side he saw something that froze him. It was one of the Plotts, and he was crawling, and ten feet of his intestines were bloody on the ground with bits of leaves sticking to him and he was dragging them behind him.

"Aw shit," Jimmy's daddy said. "Aw *shit.*"

What would Daniels do? Take it back to the truck? Shoot it? How the hell was he going to get it back to the truck before it bled to death? And then the dog stopped moving and his eyes glazed over the same way the baby deer's had done. So Jimmy's daddy went on. His blood was racing and then he heard them fighting again. He ripped his way through the hanging vines and tried to bat away the clinging thorny vines and felt one of them rip his cheek. He dabbed the back of one hand against his face and it came away slick with blood. Fuck it. And then he saw them. And it was something he would never forget. The hog had backed himself against the trunk of an enormous cypress and he was cutting at the dogs that had encircled him, dogs that were almost unrecognizable because of the mud on their hides, and they were dashing in and out and nipping at the hog. The lost dog had somehow found them so that there were four of them in a ring around the beast, who was enraged and snapping his jowls at the dogs, the hair raised on their backs, their fangs long and white and exposed. The hog had sunk to his hocks in the soft ground and he was struggling to keep his footing and still make a fight and it was still snowing. Every time he turned his head to cut at a dog, the other three rushed in and slashed at him with their teeth, and the hog was dripping blood from his face, and Jimmy's daddy was scared of it just standing there looking at it. And it took him a moment to realize that he had a shot. He could hear Rusty and Daniels yelling, drawing closer, and with shaking hands he raised the rifle and cocked the hammer and sighted down the barrel and held the front sight on the hog's chest, waiting for the dogs to move out of the way, and then in one brief flash the hog broke loose and was coming straight for him like the Russian boars in the video, squealing that high-pitched infuriated squeal Jimmy's daddy had heard when his daddy castrated the little ones on their place so many years ago. So Jimmy's daddy accidentally shot one of the dogs. He knew it the instant he pulled the trigger, because the dog screamed and flopped over like a broken doll and blood started spurting from his muddy coat. Gut shot. Steam rising from his shot guts into the cold air. He lay there and howled and the hog fought his way past the other dogs and turned and crashed through the undergrowth, dragging vines with him, only two of them chasing him now, one of them quitting and whining and licking at his torn leg, and then walking back to stand looking at the dog that was shot, cowering, his tail between his trembling legs. A dog in shock. A dog looking his own death in the eye. Jimmy's daddy stood there and looked at what he'd done and realized that he was nothing but a fuckup, would never be anything but a fuckup, and never had been anything but that. And then Daniels and Rusty and Seaborn walked up.

At first, Daniels just stopped and stood there looking down at his mortally wounded dog. Then he looked up at Jimmy's daddy. Daniels had turned white and he was shaking and he looked like he had murder on his mind. He handed his gun to Rusty. Seaborn just stood there.

Daniels knelt next to the dog and put his hand around his muzzle, Jimmy's daddy guessed to keep from being bitten.

"What are you doing?" Rusty said to him. Daniels was unbuckling from the dog's neck a band of wide brown leather, embossed with pointed chrome studs. A brass plate held Daniels's name and phone number.

"Getting my collar," Daniels said. When he had it undone he pulled the strap from the buckle and none of them really saw him do it, but the revolver that had been on his belt was suddenly in his hand and he put the muzzle of it against the dog's ear and the gun fired and it was incredibly loud there in the woods that had gone silent, and then the Plott's brains were lying on the forest floor and he wasn't howling anymore. Daniels stood up. He looked at Jimmy's daddy and he looked down at his holster and he opened the cylinder of the handgun and rotated the cylinder around to the ejector rod and pushed the rod down and ejected the spent round and then carefully revolved an empty chamber in the cylinder back up to align with the barrel and closed the cylinder and put the gun in the holster and took his Remington pump back from Rusty. It was Jimmy's daddy he looked at, but it was Rusty he spoke to.

"You get that son of a bitch out of here before I kill him," he said.

Jimmy's daddy didn't know what in the hell to say. So he didn't say anything. Daniels turned away from them, and within a minute he had disappeared into the woods. Jimmy's daddy wished he could disappear somewhere himself. A deep hole in the ground would have been perfect.

62

Cleve took the small ax from the shed and they went out in the woods in their coats looking for a nice tree. Peter Rabbit was trailing along behind them. Seretha had been back for a while now and her belly was getting out there, but she had on a pair of Cleve's rubber boots with her jeans and she seemed to enjoy tramping around in the snow from the way she was giggling and laughing. She'd tried to make a snowball to throw at him, but there wasn't enough snow on the ground yet. And she'd been singing. He knew a woman's homones went crazy when she was pregnant. He knew women had homones. He was glad men didn't. They hadn't talked about Montrel. He hoped they wouldn't.

They walked over to the pipeline through the naked winter woods and crossed through the light tan sage grass that was standing dead on it and climbed up one oak-covered ridge that was dusted with snow and he stood there looking down into a patch of cutover and saw some small cedars down there.

"They's some nice ones down yonder," he said. He pointed toward them.

"Let me go look at em," she said. "You may not get the right one."

"Why, I will, too," he said. "What, you the tree expert?"

"I'm the tree expert," she said, and went ahead of him, pushing some limbs aside, slipping and sliding on the snow. He grinned at her back. She'd already picked up some pinecones and stuffed them into the big pockets of her coat. She had a red bandanna tied around her head. She wanted some mistletoe if they could find it, too, but he wasn't going to tease her about her not having anybody to kiss under it the way he used to when she was sixteen. She was past all that now. So he followed her down the hill, calling back to Peter Rabbit to come on. Peter Rabbit was more interested in trying to find some squirrels, but it was midafternoon and most of them were in their nests and dens, their trails as cold as the ground. So he came on.

Cleve told her to be careful. He didn't want her slipping in the snow and falling. He was already worrying about the baby, if it would be all right and everything. And he'd been worried about her, too, for a long time. She'd been vague about where she'd been. He thought maybe she'd been to see her mother in Flint, but she wouldn't say. And he wasn't going to push. He was too glad to have her back home. And he didn't want her to leave again. In truth he'd thought he'd lost her the same way he'd lost Tyrone and Woodrow. When she didn't let him hear from her for so long. Almost two months. Not a letter or nothing. But now she was back and it looked like maybe everything would be okay. They'd already gone and bought some baby clothes at Wal-Mart. He let her drive because she had a license. And could run him by the liquor store with no problem from city cops.

He went carefully down the hill, holding the ax by the shaft just below the head, so that he could throw it safely away from himself if he slipped. But he didn't. And neither did she. She used to climb every tree in the yard and had broken her arm falling out of one when she was a kid. That arm still looked a little crooked when she turned it a certain way. He wondered if it would be a boy or a girl. It didn't matter to him. Either one would be fine. A boy was fine, a girl was fine.

She pointed to a tree and he followed her as she went toward it. It was a nicely shaped cedar but he thought it was too tall to fit under the ceiling, since the ceiling was so low in his homemade house. They stood there looking at it. Seretha walked around it, pulling at the limbs, fluffing it. Then putting her hands on her hips and standing there to look at him.

"That's a nice one," she said.

"Look how big it is, though."

"I ain't about to have no shrimp tree in my house," she said.

"Long way to drag it."

"Go get the truck, Ebenezer," she said.

He stood there looking at it. He knew it was too tall. But he also knew he'd chop down whichever one she wanted.

"I guess maybe get it back to the house we could cut the bottom off of it," he said. He looked up to see a hawk wheeling in the winter sky.

Just floating. He looked at the tree again. With a little trimming it might fit.

"What you gonna put on it?" he said.

"I'm gonna paint these pinecones white and hang on it. And hang some popcorn on it. And run back up to Wal-Mart and get some of them silver icicles. I saw some other day. Go on and cut it. I'll hold them bottom limbs out of the way for you."

She did. Knelt and held the limbs back and allowed him to bend in, chop lightly at the tree, but the little ax was very sharp and it didn't take long to bring it down. He had a rope in his pocket and he tied that to it. Then they both got a grip on the rope and started dragging it back up the hill. It was snowing again. Little sparrows were hopping around on the ground. And the wind had turned cold. But he had done this with his own father when he was a little boy. It had been snowing then, too. So there was again sweetness in his life.

That night he sat in the dim kitchen with the warm stove out there in front of his sock feet. She'd made chicken and dumplings and he was cooking the corn bread that they would crumble up and put in a bowl. They had fresh milk to pour over it, a big white onion he'd soon slice, and she'd made some tea. You couldn't ask for anything better than that. And you couldn't ask for anything better than spending Christmas with some of your family. He'd bought her a watch that he'd already wrapped and hidden. She'd always wanted a watch. The tip of the tree was brushing the ceiling, but he'd made it fit, had sawed and hammered together a stand with a big nail in it that went into the center of the tree's trunk on the bottom. She had already painted the pinecones white with some spray paint she'd bought uptown and now she had her sewing needle and her string of popcorn laid out on the kitchen table, working at it. Peter Rabbit was sleeping on his rug. They had the radio on a Memphis station and the man on the air said it looked like a pretty good chance for a white Christmas. Cleve hoped that was so. They had plenty of food and he had some whisky and beer and some cigarillos. He could stand a white Christmas.

He lifted his bottle and took a sip. He thought he might play a while later. Before he went to bed. He needed to get some wood cut tomorrow.

And then he guessed they needed to figure out what they were going to cook for Christmas. He'd always liked turkey, and she'd always liked ham. He was thinking maybe they could buy a small one of each. Put the rest of it in the icebox. Make sandwiches out of it.

He bent forward and checked the corn bread. It had risen in the black iron skillet, but it hadn't cracked open and turned brown yet. Maybe a few more minutes. He closed the oven door and took another sip of whisky. He'd noticed that she hadn't had a drink around him since she'd been home. He'd even offered her a beer one day just to see what she'd say, but she'd turned it down. He kept turning it over in his mind: Boy or girl? Girl or boy?

"You thought up any names yet?" he said.

She had her tortoiseshell glasses perched on the end of her nose and she was intent upon her popcorn stringing. She didn't look up.

"Yes sir," she said. "A few."

"What you thought of?" he said.

She'd already fixed herself a glass of tea and now she put down her needle and thread and lifted her glass and took a drink. He was eating a lot better again now that she was back. Once a week she got in the truck and went to town with the money he'd given her and brought back pork chops and sliced picnic and cracklings and strawberry preserves to put on their biscuits in the mornings, and sometimes she whipped up some of the eggs that she gathered regularly from the chicken nests outside and made a really good thing he'd never had before that she called an omelet. Filled with chopped-up ham and bits of cheese melted inside it. She didn't turn her nose up at fresh deer meat. And she could do some wonderful things with the black iron skillet and a couple of young squirrels.

"I thought of KuShonda if it's a girl and Leroy if it's a boy. After that 'Bad, Bad Leroy Brown' song."

"Mm hmm," he said, nodding. He liked both those.

"Mm hmm what?" she said. "You thought of any?"

"Ain't my place to think of none," he said. "I'm just the grandpappy."

They sat there a little longer. He checked the corn bread again and it was done. He got a pot holder and took the skillet out and set it on top of the stove and with a dull knife broke the crust away from the sides of the skillet. She brought him a plate and he held the plate over the corn bread and turned it and the skillet over, and the pone slid out, solid brown and crusty, steaming. He set it on the table. He was so happy about the baby coming that he didn't know what to do. Didn't matter if it was a boy or a girl, he was buying it a fishing pole. A girl could fish as well as a boy.

"Let's eat," he said. [. . .]

63

Christmas vacation seemed to last a long time after Christmas was over. Jimmy had to spend quite a few of those days inside, kind of trapped in the trailer with the girls while his mama and daddy were at work, because it started raining and kept on. Days on end, rain falling from the sky off and on, the sun not coming out, the days all alike and gray and cloudy. Too muddy and cold to ride the go-kart. He tried it once, but since it didn't have any fenders, it threw mud all over him, so he didn't try again. He walked up to the pond a couple of times to see how much water it had in it, and it had come up a good bit and was a lot bigger than what it used to be. A green boat was tied to the bank. He wondered if that big fish was still in there. He looked down toward the house when he was up there, but he didn't see Mister Cortez anywhere. He wondered if he had the cast off his arm yet. He almost went down to the house to knock on the door but then didn't. Something kept him back, but he didn't know what it was.

And he worried about delivering some puppies out his butthole. He counted off the days on the calendar and whenever he went to the bathroom he made sure the door was locked and always checked to see what had come out of him. Nothing ever looked any different. But he kept an eye on things just the same.

Evelyn asked him one day if he wanted to make five dollars and Jimmy said yes. He asked her what he had to do to make the five dollars and she said all he had to do was keep his mouth shut and he said okay and she handed him five dollars. Jimmy didn't know where she'd gotten five dollars. Probably from their mama. In about fifteen minutes one of the big boys off the school bus opened the door of the trailer and walked in without even wiping his really muddy feet off like he owned the damn place. He looked at Jimmy, but he didn't say anything to Jimmy. He walked across the living room carpet tracking red mud and into the kitchen where Evelyn was and kissed her and she kind of swooned and then Velma came walking by with what looked like five dollars in her hand. Jimmy hadn't heard any car pull up outside. Usually you heard some tires crunching in the gravel at least. He went to the front door and opened it and looked out there and there wasn't any car out there. He wondered how the big boy had gotten there, but he didn't figure he should say anything since he'd agreed to keep his mouth shut. Evelyn took the big boy back to the bedroom she shared with Velma and locked Velma out, and Velma and Jimmy sat on the couch in the living room and watched TV with the volume up pretty good while the big boy stayed back in the bedroom with Evelyn for about thirty minutes, and then there were some steady regular bumping noises that lasted for about two minutes, and then about a minute after that the big boy came out and left in a hell of a hurry, tracking more red mud across the carpet as he went. Jimmy hoped his daddy wouldn't see all that mud on the carpet. And about two minutes later Jimmy's daddy walked in. He had a beer in his hand. He plopped down on the couch next to Jimmy. Velma was in the kitchen making herself a mayonnaise sandwich since she was still crazy about mayonnaise sandwiches.

"Hey, Daddy," Jimmy said.

"Hey, Hot Rod," Jimmy's daddy said, and tilted his head back while he took a long drink of beer. He twisted his head around. "Hey, Velma."

"Hey," she said, slathering about a half inch of mayonnaise on her bread, both pieces.

"Where's Evelyn?" Jimmy's daddy said.

Jimmy didn't say anything. Velma didn't say anything. Jimmy's daddy sat there for a few moments and then took a long look at both of them.

"I said where's Evelyn?" Jimmy's daddy said.

Velma didn't say anything, so it had to fall on Jimmy to take up the slack.

"I think she's back there in the bedroom," Jimmy said, concentrating like hell on changing channels with the remote.

Jimmy's daddy turned his head to look down the hall at the closed door to that bedroom. Then he turned back around and took another drink of his beer.

"What's she doing in the bedroom at this time of day?" he said. "Hell, it ain't but four thirty. She sick?"

Jimmy thought he'd let Velma catch this one, but she was evidently a tough little cookie with plans for her five dollars. She kept her mouth shut, so Jimmy had to answer again.

"I don't know," he said.

"Why hell," Jimmy's daddy said, and stood up. He turned to Velma, still standing in the kitchen, trying to put the bread away. "Velma."

She looked up.

"Yes sir?"

"Is your sister sick?"

Velma shook her head, her long black hair shaking for a moment, dark eyes enormous, lovely, and scared.

"Can you not talk?" Jimmy's daddy said, and took another drink of his beer. Jimmy started getting a little nervous. There were clumps of red mud on the carpet. Some of them had pine needles stuck in them. And *gravel*. It was only a matter of time until his daddy saw them.

"Yes sir," she said. "I can talk."

"Well answer me then when I ask you a question. You hear?"

"Yes sir," she said. "I hear."

"All right, then, goddamn it," Jimmy's daddy said. "Is Evelyn sick?"

"I don't know," she whispered.

"Well, how long's she been in the bedroom?" Jimmy's daddy said.

"She's been back there about thirty minutes," Jimmy said, just to kind of keep the ball rolling.

"Well, is she sick?" Jimmy's daddy said.

"I don't know," Jimmy said.

"Y'all don't know very damn much," Jimmy's daddy said, and took another drink of his beer. Then he went back to his bedroom and stayed in there for about five seconds and came back out with a coat. He stopped in front of Jimmy.

"Tell your mama if I ain't here when she gets in that I've gone to look at a transmission a guy's got that's sposed to fit my car. All right?"

"Yes sir," Jimmy said.

"Yes sir," Velma said.

Jimmy's daddy started out the door and then he stopped. He looked down. He stepped back. His voice rose in outrage.

"What in the . . . who in the *hell* tracked all this mud in the house?"

He turned around and looked at Jimmy and Velma. This was real trouble, and a no-win situation that Jimmy could already see coming. And he'd been so close to just walking on out the door. There was no way Jimmy was going to claim the mud as his just to protect the big boy and keep the five dollars. Oh no. His daddy might whip him for that. And five dollars wasn't worth that. But if he didn't lie and say it *was* his mud, and if Velma said it wasn't her mud, then what was going to happen? Who were they going to blame it on? He might whip *both* of them just for general principles.

"How many times have I told y'all to wipe your feet off fore you come in the damn house?"

Jimmy didn't say anything. He looked over at Velma and she didn't look like she was going to say anything. She looked like she was wanting to get her mouth around that mayonnaise sandwich.

"Looks like a dog took a shit in here," Jimmy's daddy said. Then he bent over a little bit, looking at the mud. "Damn," he said. "This one's got some pine needles in it. And this one's got some gravel in it."

"I didn't do it," Jimmy said, self-preservation leaping in.

"Well, whoever did it, clean the shit up fore your mama gets home. Bye."

Jimmy's daddy put the coat on and went out the door as relief welled in. It had been a close call. Jimmy heard the '55 crank up, and then it backed out of the driveway and went down toward the cotton fields and the wooden bridge and the old rotted house until it went out of hearing. Jimmy hadn't heard the dead black lady crying in a while. He thought maybe she'd gone on vacation. And then Evelyn stuck just her head out the door and called softly for Velma. Velma was in the process of trying to start eating her sandwich, but she stopped what she was doing and went back there. Evelyn let her in and then the door shut. Then Jimmy heard it lock. Then silence. He turned the TV down. He could hear them talking, but he couldn't tell what they were saying. So he got up and walked very softly across the carpet to the door of the girls' bedroom and put his ear against the door and listened. It sounded like Evelyn was crying. She *was* crying. Then he heard the door start to open and went quick and soft back across the carpet and was in the process of sitting down when the door opened and Velma came out and the door closed and locked again. Jimmy looked at her, but she didn't look at him. She went back to the utility room down the hall and it sounded like she either opened the lid on the washing machine or opened the door on the dryer. Something was going on. He started to get up and go back there to see what she was doing, but instead he waited. His mama would be home in about another hour. And somebody was going to have to clean that mud up before she got in. Jimmy was naturally in favor of Evelyn doing it since she was the one who caused it to be there.

But Velma came out of the utility room and stopped in the bathroom and came out with a towel and went back to the bedroom door and knocked on it. The door opened and Velma went in, then the door closed and locked again. Something had happened and Jimmy knew it had something to do with the big boy from the school bus who had just barely made it out of here before Jimmy's daddy came home. And that was another close call. There was no telling what Jimmy's daddy would have done if he'd come home and found some boy off the school bus in the bedroom with Evelyn. Jimmy knew that somebody would have gotten their ass kicked, and it wouldn't have been Jimmy's daddy. He kind of hated that the big boy had made it out on time. He would have really enjoyed seeing his daddy kick the big boy's ass, because Jimmy thought he was the same one who used to hit him on the ears with those wadded-up pieces of paper.

He sat there and listened. After a few minutes, the door to the bedroom opened and Velma came out, carrying a wadded-up bunch of bedsheets. She went down the hall with them and Jimmy got up softly and followed her. When she went back into the utility room, she closed the door behind her. But it didn't have a lock on it, and Jimmy waited about five seconds and then opened it. Velma looked up. She was stuffing the sheets into the washing machine and the sheets had blood on them. Oh my God! It looked like Evelyn was having a baby!

"What's that?" Jimmy said. It was only then that he saw Velma crying. She stopped what she was doing and fell to her knees, and Jimmy knelt next to her and put his arm around her shoulder. She leaned into him with her hands up against her face, and then she started sobbing. He just stayed there and held her. She wasn't really his sister. But in another way she was. She was older than him but it didn't matter. He just held her. But she didn't cry long. She wiped her sniffles and got back up.

"We got to get these sheets clean and dry and back on the bed before Mama gets home," she said. "If we don't, Evelyn's gonna be in a whole lot of trouble." And she turned around and again started stuffing the sheets into the washing machine. Jimmy helped her. He found the scoop and scooped up some washing powders and dumped them in and Velma set the timer for the shortest cycle on the machine and closed the lid and started it. Jimmy heard the water running into it.

"Did she hurt herself?" he said. Velma shook her head.

"Did she have a baby?" Jimmy said.

"No, she didn't have no baby! Are you crazy?"

"Well, where'd all that blood come from, then?" Jimmy said.

"I can't tell you," Velma said. "But please don't say nothing to Mama. Please? Please, Jimmy."

From the way she was looking at him, Jimmy knew this was something pretty bad. So he just nodded.

"Help me fold these clothes and put em away," Velma said, so Jimmy did. They folded towels and bath cloths and some underwear and put it all away and then Velma said she had to go back in there with Evelyn, so she did. This time she stayed for about ten minutes, except for coming out one time and going back to the bathroom and running the water and then coming out with a wadded-up wet bath cloth. She went back into the bedroom with it and the door locked again. Jimmy went back to watching television. It was about to get dark outside and Jimmy wondered if they were going to make it on time. He could hear the washing machine still going on the sheets, and the dryer was really slow about drying things. Something was wrong with it. An element or something was burned out. His mama cussed about it pretty often. And what if the washing machine didn't take the blood out of the sheets? Wasn't blood supposed to be hard to get out of something? And where had the blood come from anyway if Evelyn hadn't hurt herself or had a baby?

He kept sitting there, trying to listen to the TV and still hear what was going on in the bedroom. After a while the washing machine stopped. Velma must have been listening, too, because she came out right away and went back there. It sounded like she was taking the sheets out of the washing machine and putting them in the dryer. Then Evelyn came out of the bedroom. She was wearing only a bra that even Jimmy could see was way too small for her, and a towel was wrapped around her bottom half. She was holding on to the wall as she walked down the hall toward the bathroom, taking baby steps. She looked over at Jimmy for a moment, tears coming down her cheeks, and she gave him a grim smile, as if she suffered willingly. Velma came out of the utility room and helped her into the bathroom. Then that door closed and locked. Then silence. Then there was nothing to hear but the dryer running. Running and running and running.

Jimmy kept sitting there watching TV. It was getting closer and closer to time for his mama to get home. But sometimes she stopped in town and bought groceries. Sometimes she'd call on her cell phone and say she was going to be late, but sometimes she wouldn't.

After a while, Velma and Evelyn came out of the bathroom. Evelyn had put on a pair of shorts and a T-shirt and she walked slowly over to the couch and stood there. Jimmy looked up at her. She looked a lot better than she had when she'd first come down the hall.

"Can I sit down?" she said.

"Sure," Jimmy said. "I can move if you want to lay down."

"That's okay," Evelyn said. He saw that she was trying to bend down carefully and he got up and helped her ease onto the couch.

"Whew," she said, when she'd leaned back against the cushions. "That's better. Thanks."

Velma came in and sat down nearby [. . .] with her sandwich and took a bite of it. She chewed, her small mouth working, one dab of mayonnaise on the corner of her lips. She licked it off with the tip of her tongue.

Evelyn did something that surprised Jimmy. She leaned up and reached beneath the couch cushion and pulled out a pack of Marlboro Lights and a lighter and opened the cigarettes and took one out and lit up. There was an ashtray on the coffee table and she slid it closer. Jimmy was almost shocked.

"When'd you start smoking?" he said.

"A few weeks ago," Evelyn said. "Herbert got me started."

"Who's Herbert?" Jimmy said.

"That was Herbert in here a while ago."

She took a drag and leaned back again and crossed one leg over the other very slowly, like somebody in slow motion. Jimmy could tell that she didn't really know how to smoke yet, that she was just practicing. Plus she coughed a few times.

"Now we've got to talk, Jimmy," she said. And she looked at him. All serious. He never had seen her like this before. A different Evelyn. Maybe she was fixing to run off and get married to Herbert.

"What you want to talk about?" Jimmy said. "The weather?" She was making him nervous, acting this way and sitting all close to him like this. She smelled kind of good. She smelled the same way his mama smelled sometimes.

"You know how easy your daddy gets upset. Right?"

"Right," Jimmy said.

Evelyn leaned forward and thumped the ashes off the end of her cigarette, then pulled the ashtray over in her lap and leaned back.

"Then let me ask you a question," Evelyn said. Velma kept sitting there taking small bites from her sandwich, her nubby ears poking through the long strands of her black hair.

"Okay," Jimmy said.

"Would you or would you not agree that things go a lot smoother around here when your daddy's not upset about something?"

Jimmy thought it over.

"I would agree," he said.

"That's what I thought," Evelyn said. "Now Jimmy . . ." Here she paused to stroke her chin, and to painfully shift one of her legs. The dryer binged and Velma jumped up, leaving her sandwich on the coffee table while she rushed back to the utility room.

"What did Herbert do to you?" Jimmy said.

"You're too little to understand," Evelyn said.

"Try me," Jimmy said.

He could tell that Evelyn was starting to get a little pissed off. Her face had this little sour expression it could make when she was starting to get pissed off. It was starting to make it now.

"Just let me talk, okay, Jimmy?"

"Okay," Jimmy said, and started flipping through the channels again with the remote. CMT. MTV. CNN. ESPN2. TBS. PBS. CBS.

"Can you put that down and let me talk to you for a minute?" Evelyn said. "Goddamn it?"

"Ain't no need to cuss about it," Jimmy said, and left it on CMT and dropped the remote on the couch between them. She picked it up and lowered the volume on it, then dropped it back on the couch.

"It's just that you need to understand how important it is for you not to say anything about Herbert being over here today," she said. "Can I trust you not to?"

"That's what you paid me the five bucks for, wasn't it?" Jimmy said.

Evelyn smiled then. And she did something she'd never done before. She leaned over and put her arm around Jimmy's shoulder. He thought maybe she was fixing to kiss him, but she didn't.

"Look, Jimmy," she said. "I like you. I may not always show it, but I do like you. And I want us to be better brothers and sisters to each other. Is that okay with you?"

"What's in it for me?" Jimmy said.

"Well, I'll tell you, Jimmy," she said. "There might be a lot for you in it one of these old days."

"Like what?" Jimmy said.

That flustered Evelyn. She kept smoking her cigarette, taking quick little fake puffs off it. That seemed to keep her from coughing.

"Well, for one thing," she said. "I'll be getting my license before long and when I get a car you might want to go places."

"You ain't got no car," Jimmy said.

"I know that. Mama's gonna buy me one."

"Shit," Jimmy said. "Daddy ain't gonna let Mama buy you no car. You know how much a car costs? About six hundred thousand dollars."

"I know how much a car costs, Jimmy," she said.

"I thought your daddy was gonna buy you a Corvette," Jimmy said.

"My daddy's still incarcerated," Evelyn said.

Jimmy didn't know what the hell that was so he didn't even ask. He already had it figured out. Evelyn was wanting him to keep his mouth shut about the blood on the sheets and she was willing to bribe him to do it. So he put a quick end to it, just so he could get back to CMT and see if they had any Merle videos on.

"I'll keep my mouth shut if you give me twenty bucks," Jimmy said. And the only reason he said twenty bucks was because he'd never had twenty bucks before and had always wanted twenty.

"I don't have twenty bucks right now," Evelyn said.

"Tell Herbert to cough it up," Jimmy said. "Or I'll tell. And if you send him over here to beat the crap out of me, it'll leave bruises, and when I show em to Daddy he'll kill Herbert. Then you won't have a boyfriend. Plus, you got to clean up all that mud he left before Mama gets home."

Evelyn thought it over. Velma came down the hall carrying the dried sheets and Evelyn turned her head to speak to her.

"Did it come out?"

"Yeah," Velma said, and carried the sheets into their bedroom. Evelyn got up and put her cigarette out and shuffled into the bedroom to help Velma make up the bed. Jimmy turned the volume back up on CMT. And there was Kenny Chesney, singing on a stage with Peyton Manning. Jimmy turned the volume up. Maybe they'd put Merle on next.

A First Monday weekend rolled around just before school started back, so Jimmy's daddy got him up early on Saturday again and they dressed while the girls and Jimmy's mama slept on. This time they went through Oxford and hit the Sonic for a steaming-hot pair of sausage-egg-cheese toasters and coffee and orange juice. A girl brought it to them on a tray and handed Jimmy's daddy his change, which he kept. It wasn't much. Thirteen cents. Jimmy's daddy dosed up his coffee while they were still sitting in the parking slot and unwrapped enough of his toaster to get his mouth around a mouthful of it, and with Jimmy eating his breakfast on his lap they went back down University Avenue through sparse traffic and hit the bypass just below Kroger's, headed north toward Highway 30. They turned off on it just south of the power company.

It was cold and it had been raining. Jimmy was ready to go back to school just because going back to school meant that some more time was passing and that in a few more months, the winter would be over and the spring would be coming. And when it got spring, he was going to start fishing in the pond again. He hadn't tried them in a long time now, especially since he'd heard his daddy say one day over the winter that catfish didn't bite too good in the winter. Jimmy still hadn't said a word to anybody about the big red fish truck, or the big something he'd hung in the pond, and now he was glad he'd kept quiet about all that. It was okay to have secrets. It was okay to know things that nobody much else knew. And it was nice to be trusted with a secret. That's what Mister Cortez had done: he had entrusted Jimmy with a secret. And Jimmy had been worthy of that trust. He would be repaid endless times over for that trust when the wind turned warm and the green things began to grow. And the catfish began to bite. Oh the golden days he'd have, go-kart parked beside him in the shade, cool drink and rod and reel in hand. Nights of ripping up and down the gravel road, guided by the bright yellow beam of the flashlight headlight.

By the time they got to Ripley, a drizzling rain had set in. They could see the flea market grounds from the wet highway, and the parking lots were not full of cars. It looked like a good many of the vendor tents had already closed. But they could also see a few people out there walking around. Some in rain suits. Some with umbrellas. People loading soggy-looking couches onto trucks.

"Well, shit," Jimmy's daddy said. "We already here. We might as well get out for a while."

Jimmy's daddy turned into the parking lot and stopped at a red-painted plywood booth where a man with a blue parka sat sipping from a foam cup. A big sign said PARKING $2.

"Hey," Jimmy's daddy said, hauling out his wallet.

"Hey," the man said. "That's two dollars."

"Yes sir," Jimmy's daddy said, handing the money out the open window. They rolled on into the pea gravel parking lot. Some campers were set up and Jimmy could see people cooking under awnings where smoke rose from charcoal fires.

"I guess this is good as any," Jimmy's daddy said. Jimmy had noticed that his daddy hadn't brought any beer with him inside the car. He didn't know what was in the trunk. But he hadn't opened any beer this morning. Jimmy guessed his daddy was worried about the cops over here now.

They got out and Jimmy zipped up his jacket. The cold wind hit his legs through his jeans and his daddy walked around in front of the car and motioned for Jimmy to follow him.

"Let's go down this way and see what we can see," he said, and Jimmy followed him through the drizzle down a muddy lane between the tents. There was mud everywhere and there were puddles you had to step around. Jimmy couldn't smell any food cooking. The whole thing looked like it was about to shut down. He saw some bundled-up older women sitting in steel chairs in an open tent, and they were holding umbrellas over their heads. It looked like they were selling vases. Jimmy knew he didn't want any vases, even though the women looked hopefully at them as they walked past.

Jimmy's daddy stopped at a booth that was still open. There were five or six tables with gray wool blankets spread over them and the tables held piece-of-shit knives and military insignia and fake plastic guns and white ceramic pigs with baby pacifiers in their mouths. Jimmy didn't see anything he wanted. He hadn't gotten a whole lot of good stuff for Christmas, just a few lures to go with his rod and reel and a remote-controlled battery-operated car that Velma had already broken and a bow and arrow set like maybe a first-grader would want and a train set and a pair of socks and some clothes and a pair of gloves and some cowboy boots. And he'd already given up on ever seeing Tupelo Buffalo Park. Or Kenny in concert.

[. . .]

There was an intersection where a closed hamburger stand was sitting and they walked past it and looked down the lane. Most of the tents down there were closing. Somebody had backed a trailer up to one of the tents and people were loading it with bolts of cloth and guns.

"Well shit," Jimmy's daddy said. "Let's go this way."

[. . .]

On down the lane there was a cattle trailer backed into the lane where another old man was sitting inside it with some crates full of chickens and guineas. He was smoking a homemade cigarette and he nodded to Jimmy and his daddy as they passed. Jimmy thought his face looked like it was made out of leather, so brown and wrinkled it was. He'd wondered a few times what his daddy's daddy had done for Christmas, but there hadn't been any mention of him around the trailer, and Jimmy hadn't asked. Evelyn had talked to her daddy on the telephone after he'd called her from prison, and Velma had cried when her daddy hadn't called her at all. Jimmy had seen their mama rocking her and holding her and cussing Velma's daddy. It seemed strange to Jimmy sometimes that his mama had been married to people he didn't even know.

[. . .] They walked on down to the end of the lane and stood there looking suddenly at the ponies. They were standing in the rain and they were wearing saddles and bridles and their tails were wet and drooping. There were four of them, small, some brown, some black-and-white spotted, and their bridles were chained to some kind of a circular rusty metal apparatus with arms that could revolve.

"Hey, you want to ride a pony?" Jimmy's daddy said.

Jimmy never had ridden a pony so he looked at the ponies. They were standing with their heads down, or as low as they could put their heads, since the chains were pretty short.

"I bet them saddles are wet," Jimmy said.

"I got a towel," said a man in a poncho who'd been sitting in a lawn chair on the other side of the ponies, a man who got up and went to his pickup nearby and opened the door and pulled a towel out.

"How much is a ride?" Jimmy's daddy said.

The man took the towel over to one of the ponies and started wiping down the saddle. He looked up at them, smiling through gapped yellow teeth.

"Two dollars for two minutes," he said. "But I'll let you go longer than that. You can ride five minutes if you want to. We ain't just real busy today."

He finished wiping the saddle dry and Jimmy's daddy pulled two dollars from his billfold and handed it to the man, who folded it and stuck it in his pocket.

"Hop up," he said. He motioned to the stirrup.

Jimmy walked over to the pony and stood there looking at it.

The pony didn't turn his head to look at him. He couldn't.

"Hop up, Hot Rod," Jimmy's daddy said. He was grinning.

Jimmy didn't much want to, but he did anyway. He put his foot in the stirrup and pulled himself up with that thing sticking out on the top front of the saddle and swung his leg over and sat there. The saddle creaked under him. He picked up the reins even though he could see there was no need to. The man had moved back to the rear of the thing the ponies were hooked to and he had his hand near a switch.

"You ready?" he said, and Jimmy nodded. The man hit the switch and the thing the ponies were hooked to started turning very slowly. The pony Jimmy was riding started walking very slowly, just like the other three ponies that didn't have riders. The circle they made was about eight feet in diameter. They walked within that circle and the machine hummed and the ponies' hooves sucked loudly in the mud as they walked. Jimmy just sat there. His daddy started talking to the man. Jimmy didn't listen. He was wishing he could buy one of the ponies. If he had one of the ponies, he could ask Mister Cortez if he could keep it at his place since it looked like he had plenty of hay down there. The pony went round and round. Jimmy went round and round. Very slowly. Jimmy reached out and patted the pony on the neck, but the pony shook his head as if Jimmy's touch was irritating to him, so Jimmy didn't do it again even though he wanted to.

What if the puppies came without warning? What if he had puppies in his pants? What if he was on the school bus? Or right in the middle of the cafeteria in front of all the other kids? What would he do then? They might have to call the school nurse. Or he might have to go to the hospital. There were all kinds of possibilities. Look what happened to Evelyn. She evidently just started bleeding. And he knew that women bled sometimes, but he didn't know why. He'd seen bloody things in the bathroom garbage at the trailer and he'd picked up tidbits of things here and there, but so far he hadn't been able to put the whole thing together. He could have asked Herschel Horowitz to give him the lowdown on everything, but he didn't want to look dumb. He figured he'd find out everything he needed to know one of these days, just by listening, but it seemed to be taking a long time. Just like this puppy thing. And you couldn't ask grown-ups about it because something might happen and it might backfire and get you in trouble somehow.

The pony kept walking in a circle and between his knees Jimmy could feel the little animal shivering. He could feel himself shivering in his wet clothes. And if you were a pony you couldn't take a towel and dry off. He wondered if the man would take a towel and dry the ponies off before he loaded them back into the rusty horse trailer sitting there hooked to the man's pickup. The man and Jimmy's daddy were still talking and the pony kept walking. [. . .] On and on. Shivering. It went on for so long that it was all Jimmy could do to keep from asking somebody to please make it stop.

✳ ✳ ✳

But that wasn't the worst. On the way home, through rain that was pouring now, Jimmy's daddy turned down the solid country gold on the radio and told Jimmy that he had to talk to him. He told him he had some bad news for him, and tried to beef him up for it at first, telling him it was something he didn't want to have to do and wouldn't do at all no way shape or fashion unless he just absolutely had to, but he felt like he absolutely had to. And instead of beefing Jimmy up, it probably scared him worse than it would have if his daddy hadn't tried to beef him up. What Jimmy figured was that somehow his daddy had found out about Herbert coming over and knew about the blood on Evelyn's bedsheets, and also knew that Jimmy'd been keeping his mouth shut about it for twenty dollars he hadn't even gotten yet, and was maybe going to whip him. Jimmy's daddy hadn't whipped Jimmy since the time he *really* whipped him over the getting-into-his-tools fiasco, and a big reason for that was because Jimmy had been taking pains ever since then to not do *anything* that would make his daddy want to whip him. It was part of the not-asking-a-whole-bunch-of-questions thing. He had that down to perfection almost. He'd gotten to where about 80 percent of the time he could accurately judge his daddy's moods. Or maybe he'd just learned the *times* not to ask him some questions. You absolutely did not want to *ever* ask him a question if he was working on the '55. That might get you screamed at, unless he was whistling. If he was whistling, all bets were off. It was safe to ask him a question then no matter what he was doing unless he was sitting on the commode and you were trying to ask him questions through the door. He didn't go for questions then. He was usually reading if he was sitting on the commode and he kept a fairly current selection of hunting and fishing magazines like *Outdoor Life* and *Field & Stream* in there in a wicker basket just for that purpose. And it was useless to ask him a question if he was reading. If he was reading, he wouldn't get mad or anything, he just wouldn't answer you. You didn't want to ask him questions in the morning because he was getting ready to go to work and he might be in a bad mood since he was frequently in a bad mood before he went to work. If he came in in the afternoon with a beer in his hand, and plopped down beside you on the couch, it was probably safe to ask him a question. He was always in a better mood when he was off from work than he was when he was *going* to work. Weekends were sometimes good times to ask him questions. If he was sharpening his hunting knife in the kitchen, it was okay to ask him questions. You could ask him questions for hours if he was sharpening his hunting knife. Usually, if he was watching TV, it was okay to ask him a question. There were other variables, like weather and temperature and whether or not his daddy had been fussing with his mama, and Jimmy had learned how to operate pretty safely around his daddy, but he didn't know what was coming now. Maybe it was something about the little dogs. They'd all left and they never had come back, just like it had been when they first arrived, which had been about seven or eight months ago. They had come up in a herd out of the woods behind the trailer and Jimmy's mama and the girls thought they were so cute that they'd decided to keep them all, since they were so small, and they had talked Jimmy's daddy into building a dog house that he shoved up under the trailer. But now they were all gone again and nobody knew where. Or maybe he'd found out somehow that it was Herbert who had put the mud on the carpet and was going to question Jimmy about what he knew. If that was what it was, Jimmy was going to tell the truth. After all, he still didn't have the twenty dollars. How did he know that Herbert could even come up with twenty dollars?

"We may have to sell your go-kart," Jimmy's daddy said.

Sell it? What did he mean? Was he kidding? Surely he was kidding, wasn't he?

"Just temporarily," Jimmy's daddy said.

"Temporarily?" Jimmy said. That sounded like bullshit.

Jimmy's daddy let out a sigh. He had a beer in his hand. He'd sneaked it out of the hidden cooler in the trunk just before they left Ripley and had poured it into a red plastic cup so that he could drink it going down the road, undetected. Actually he'd sneaked out three. The other two were lying wrapped in an Ole Miss Rebels towel between Jimmy and his daddy on the seat.

"I need the money to fix my car," Jimmy's daddy said. "I wouldn't do it at all if I didn't have to."

Well, he'd already said that, so he was just repeating himself. It was like some kind of real bad dream coming true. Jimmy wanted to cry, but he didn't. He was trying to be a big boy. That's what his mama always told him to do, be a big boy about this or that. But it was going to be pretty hard to be a big boy about losing his go-kart. Especially now that it was running so good since Mister Cortez had fixed it. The chain hadn't come off a single time since he'd fixed it. And Jimmy had been planning on taking the five dollars he'd gotten from Evelyn and buying some red spray paint to give it a new paint job and restore it to its former glory. Cover up all those rock pecks. What about his plans? What about going fishing in Mister Cortez's pond on it and running up and down the road at night with his flashlight headlight? What did he mean sell it? Sell it to who?

"Who you gonna sell it to?" Jimmy said, as if asking might somehow make it untrue. He felt like he had the right to ask that. At least that.

"I know a guy at work who wants it," Jimmy's daddy said. "He made me an offer on it unseen. I told him how good it was running."

Jimmy nodded, even though he felt unspeakable bitterness. So his daddy had already been talking to somebody about it, without even asking Jimmy about it. That wasn't fair worth a shit. It was his go-kart. His daddy had given it to him. Didn't that make it his? And what had happened to his spear point anyway? Had his daddy sold it? To somebody at work?

"I don't want you to sell my go-kart, Daddy," Jimmy said, surprising even himself. But this was life and death. "Please don't sell my go-kart!"

"You want me to walk to work?" Jimmy's daddy said sharply. "The transmission is gonna fall out of the son of a bitch one morning on the way to work unless me and Rusty put another one in it."

Jimmy's daddy looked like he was starting to get a little mad. Jimmy's daddy lifted his cup and sipped from it. He licked beer from his upper lip and reached into his pocket for a smoke. He shook one from the pack and nabbed it with his lips, then restashed the pack and pushed the cigarette lighter in on the dash. He'd gotten it working. He held his finger on it until it popped out, then brought the glowing red coil to the tip of his smoke and lit it. He shoved the lighter back into the hole in the dash.

"Like I said, it would just be temporary," Jimmy's daddy said. "I found that transmission I told you about and the guy wants three hundred dollars and if you try to order one out of AutoZone, I mean one like I need, a four-speed, it's over five hundred bucks. Even with Rusty's discount."

"I don't want to sell my go-kart."

"Hell, you can't drive it in the winter."

"Sometimes it's warm enough to drive it in the winter. Like in February? Sometimes it's warm then."

"Yeah, but most times it ain't. I'll buy you another one by next spring when it warms up. I promise."

"I don't want another one, Daddy," Jimmy said. "I want mine."

They rode for a while in silence. Jimmy knew this was a losing situation, because when it came down to it, his daddy could do whatever he wanted. But Jimmy had a burning question: *why?* He thought about asking him if he wanted his rod and reel, too. Nah. He'd get slapped for that. But he had to keep talking. He had to *know* something. There had to be some scrap of reason to hang to.

"Is it cause of my teeth costing so much to get fixed?" Jimmy said.

"No, it ain't that."

"Is it cause of the high cost of living?"

Jimmy's daddy turned his head and looked at him.

"Now what in the shit would you know about the high cost of living?"

"I just know it's high," Jimmy said.

"Well. It's a lot of things," Jimmy's daddy said. "It's insurance and groceries and the light bill and the gas bill and the phone bill and the goddamn water bill and the damn satellite dish bill and the trailer payment and the whole shitting shooting match. Drives me up the goddamn wall."

Jimmy's daddy was getting a little worked up now and was sipping his beer hard and Jimmy didn't say anything else. He hadn't meant to get him stirred up and he didn't want to get him stirred up but it wasn't fair and he didn't want to get rid of his go-kart and he wondered if his mama could do any good for him. Could he whine his side of it into her ear?

"Have you and Mama talked about it?" Jimmy said.

"I mentioned it to her."

"What'd she say?" Jimmy said.

"She said she could borrow some more money from the bank and I told her we'd done borrowed enough from them already. Now they ain't no need in us talking about it no more, you just gonna have to get used to the idea. And like I said, I'll buy you another one in the spring."

It was over and lost and Jimmy felt the hot wetness of tears starting up anyway in the corners of his eyes, but he blinked them back. As bad as things had been sometimes, they'd never been this bad. The world hadn't crumbled in this particular way until just now. He wasn't going to cry, no matter how much he felt like crying. It was already a done deal. And he didn't have any say.

"Spring'll be here fore you know it," Jimmy's daddy said.

[. . .]

And as unbelievable as it was, the man came for the go-kart that afternoon, just before dark, which was coming pretty early now. Jimmy's daddy made a phone call from the kitchen and Jimmy's mama came into the living room and it was easy to tell that she'd been crying and she sat down beside Jimmy and put her arm around him and held him. She even said something to Jimmy's daddy, in front of Jimmy. She said it wasn't right and Jimmy's daddy got mad and slammed the trailer door open and then slammed it shut and went outside and stayed out there until about twenty minutes later when they heard somebody pull up in front of the trailer. Jimmy got up to go to the window.

"Don't, Jimmy," his mama said.

"I want to see who it is," Jimmy said. "I want to see who's getting my go-kart."

"What good's that gonna do, honey?" she said.

Jimmy pushed the curtains aside and peeked out, and his daddy was standing there talking to some man in blue jeans and a jean jacket with shiny brown boots who was counting some money into Jimmy's daddy's hands. There was a shiny pickup parked behind the man, and he had backed it into their driveway. Jimmy watched his daddy put the money in his pocket and then both of them walked out of sight, and Jimmy could hear them going around the corner of the trailer where his go-kart always stayed parked. Then he heard his go-kart crank up. Then it shot out in front of the trailer, with the man driving it. It went down the dirt road out of sight, and Jimmy knew the man was going to get mud all over him. He hoped he did. He hoped he ruined his clothes. Got his eye knocked out by a flying piece of gravel. Ran off the bridge, flipped, and broke his neck. Was run over by a car or truck. Was run over by a big green tractor.

After a while it came back, and the man had some mud spattered on him, but he didn't seem to be upset about it. He pulled the go-kart up close to his truck and then he shut it off. He got off the go-kart and was laughing and telling Jimmy's daddy something. Jimmy pulled back from the curtain and let it fall back in front of the window. He didn't want to watch them load it up. He didn't think he could take that.

64

Cortez paddled out in his boat one day and paddled around for a while. The sun was out and it was warm for February. There was even some green grass here and there in patches.

The water was calm and dark and the winter rains had finally raised the pond to the level of the spillway, which proved to work just fine. Another good thing Newell knew how to build. Cortez wondered what he was doing these days. He wondered if he knew anybody who could build a boat dock. He'd decided already that he definitely needed one of those, because he'd envisioned himself sitting in a comfortable lawn chair and tossing the feed to the fish from some kind of platform that would get him closer to the fish. Shoot. Maybe later he'd get some bream. The fish man had said something about that. Jimmy might like to catch some of those. The only thing was that the fish man wouldn't be coming back. But there were other fish men. The Co-op would have to find somebody else to sell fish from their parking lot.

But he wasn't fishing today. He was just paddling around on his pond on a warm February afternoon. He'd been working in his barn, with wood and saws and nails and a rasp and a block plane. Making something. He didn't know how it would look. It was hard making the letters backward, and he wasn't done yet. Maybe he never would be. Maybe it wasn't the right thing to do. But who was going to see it? Who would know anything if they *did* see it?

He wondered how big the fish were now. Surely some of those eight-inch ones had grown big enough to eat. In about three more months he'd find out. He was hoping Jimmy would come up pretty often and fish. It would be kind of nice to have a kid to talk to sometimes. Kids were pretty easygoing. And they had big imaginations. And they didn't need a whole lot to keep them happy. He remembered his. He remembered that time his wife had been hanging out clothes and had turned her back on Raif for just a few moments, long enough for him to crawl under the bottom board of the hog pen and into the pen with that big red sow and how he saw her going for him and got over the top board and in between them, just barely scooping him up in time before she got to him. Lord God. That still scared him to think about even though the boy was dead. Just what all can happen to you. To the ones close to you. Take that retard. Hell, he wasn't so bad. He just didn't like rabbits because they brought on those spells he had. When he wasn't having a spell he was a right smart young fellow with a pretty good sense of humor. Lucinda was sure crazy about him. He wished she'd move back home. Or somewhere at least close to home. Hell, she could bring him with her. Young people these days didn't think nothing about living together. Times changed and the way people acted changed with them. Look how much change you saw in a lifetime.

The sun was warm on Cortez's hands and on his neck. The paddle splashed gently in the water. He wished now that he'd brought his fishing rod, and had turned a few logs over and found some night crawlers. You could find them in this warm weather. Even if it was February. Cortez thought the weather in the world was changing. It didn't seem to get as cold as it used to. He remembered how cold the winters were when he was a boy. Or maybe it was just because they lived in houses with cracks in the plank walls and didn't have any insulation and nothing but an old woodstove to keep them warm.

LARRY BROWN'S NOTES FOR THE FINAL CHAPTERS OF
A Miracle of Catfish

Feb. Cortez chapters, maybe a sex scene with Carol combined with him making a mold for a concrete stone that would say Queen

March Trouble at the pond somehow

April I'm Her Brother, You Redneck Mother

May Seretha's baby born and baptized in the Rock Hill M. B. Church

June Jimmy and Cortez fishing on the river, find Montrel's bones. At roadblock that evening, cops get Jimmy's daddy. That needs to be the end of the action.

And finish, somehow, epilogue with Tommy and Lucinda seven years down the road with little boy with Tourette's cussing and spitting, silent man painting in backyard under shade of pecans, she'll tell Tommy that her daddy passed away a few years ago. But do I have a scene where she finds the locket in the barn? I think I need that.